"I WON YO⬛⬛⬛⬛⬛⬛"

Rod paused for ⬛⬛⬛⬛⬛⬛⬛⬛⬛ not disappointed.

"A young man na⬛⬛⬛⬛⬛⬛⬛⬛⬛ your way to San Francisco. He and I met in a poker game several weeks ago. O'Brien lost heavily and in the end wagered the only thing he had left of value...you. His hand was good. But not good enough."

"You were the man Kevin O'Brien lost to," Julie whispered. "Did you cheat the poor man out of his possessions?"

Rod exploded in a whirlwind of anger. "I do not cheat at cards! Kevin O'Brien was a young fool who wagered a fortune on a turn of a card. As it turned out, you were the one to come out the winner. O'Brien was not the man for you."

"And I suppose you are?"

Rod turned thoughtfully, suddenly certain that he was exactly the right man for the little hellion. She needed someone to match her fire, a man capable of taming the wild streak in her. He was convinced their coming together would be more like an explosion than an act of love, and his tense body yearned to be the first to elicit those cries of ecstasy from her full red lips....

For Honor's Sake

CONNIE MASON

LOVE SPELL BOOKS   NEW YORK CITY

To Jerry—because he deserves it.

LOVE SPELL®

May 1998

Published by

Dorchester Publishing Co., Inc.
276 Fifth Avenue
New York, NY 10001

ISBN 0-505-52262-4

The name "Love Spell" and its logo are trademarks of Dorchester Publishing Co., Inc.

Printed in the United States of America.

PROLOGUE

San Francisco—September 1851

The noise in Casey's Pleasure Palace was deafening. Though the evening was still young, the crowd pressing around the gaming tables and cheering at the scantily clad dancing girls as they high-stepped about the stage could barely be contained within the four walls of the huge, gaudily decorated saloon. Yet the five men seated around a circular table in a far corner of the room seemed oblivious to the revelry erupting all about them.

In San Francisco in 1851 a man's fortune could be made or lost in a poker game. A lucky turn of a card meant a stake to another backbreaking year in the gold fields. An unlucky draw could send a man back from whence he came, penniless, broken, all his hopes and dreams of elusive riches shattered.

It mattered little that the average yield of gold was one-half ounce per day per man, for before each prospective miner dangled the lure of the big vein, the mother lode just waiting for the right man to stumble upon it.

Don Rodrigo Delgado fanned his cards out, holding them close to his body. His darkly handsome features were expressionless; not even a blink of a thickly lashed eyelid gave a hint of his thoughts. On his left, Brute Kelly, so named because of his size and ugly features, gave a noncommittal grunt and eyed Rod narrowly. To his right, Digger Walker, one of the first prospectors to reach California, spat contemptuously into a spitoon, wiped the brown stain dribbling down his chin with the back of a grimy sleeve and slapped his cards face down on the scarred table.

The young man across from Rod chewed his bottom lip nervously, his bright blue eyes intent upon the cards in his hand. His expressive face registered first disbelief and then joy, as if he couldn't believe what he saw. A shock of rusty hair blocked his view and he swiped at it impatiently as his eyes darted around the table and then dropped to his cards once more. Kevin O'Brien's future hung on the outcome of this hand. Down to his last grain of gold dust, Kevin could not disguise his optimism as beads of sweat gathered on his brow and trickled down his freckled face. The outcome of this hand was his last chance to win the stake he so desperately needed to see him through the winter, and it appeared his fervent prayers were about to become reality. Hoping his eyes hadn't played tricks on him, Kevin fanned out the three queens and two tens, suppressing a sigh of relief when he saw he hadn't been mistaken.

Beside Kevin, Bud Morley quietly folded his hand and sat back, his eyes shifting to each of the other four players. "I'm folding," Bud announced morosely as he silently contemplated the huge pot building up in the center of the table.

All eyes turned to Kevin. Fearing that his voice would give him away, Kevin pushed his last remaining grains of gold forward and then looked expectantly toward Digger. Digger spat again, this time missing the spitoon by a good foot and said, "Damned if I can find a reason to stay. Count me out."

A hint of a smile touched Rod's black eyes and just as quickly disappeared. It was obvious by the pile of nuggets and dust in front of him that he had no cause for complaining about his night's work. "I'll call and raise," Rod announced calmly, noting the crestfallen look speading over young O'Brien's face.

Brute Kelly cursed loudly, slamming a ham-like fist on the table and rattling the clutch of nuggets. "Damn you, Delgado! How in the hell you do it is beyond me! If I didn't know better, I'd say you were—"

"Careful, *amigo*," warned Rod ominously, his voice soft yet deadly. "To finish your sentence might prove fatal."

"Aw, come on, Delgado, he didn't mean nothin' by it," soothed Digger. "Everyone here knows you ain't a cheater. What do you do, Kelly?" he nudged, "are you in or out?"

"Shit!" exploded Kelly. "I'm out!" His mutterings were ignored as Rod turned his attention to O'Brien.

"Looks like it's between you and me, O'Brien," Rod said, smiling affably. "Are you going to see my raise?"

His face a vivid shade of red, O'Brien made a frantic search of his pockets but came up empty. "You cleaned me out, Delgado, I ain't got a speck of dust left," he moaned, disheartened.

"Well, then, I guess the pot's mine," Rod shrugged as he reached out to rake in his winnings.

"Wait!" cried O'Brien, staying his hands.

Rod looked up, frowning as a piece of white paper fluttered from O'Brien's hand to rest atop the glittering pile in the center of the table. "What's this?" Rod asked, picking the folded sheet of paper up gingerly.

"It's all I have left of value," O'Brien offered apologetically.

Rod opened the folded sheet, his straight black brows knitted together as a number written in bold letters and bearing an official stamp leaped before his eyes. "What in the hell good is this worthless piece of paper?" Rod asked, willing to give the youth the benefit of the doubt.

"It's not worthless," O'Brien insisted hotly. "I . . . I was one of the lucky men to draw a numer in the lottery.

I've been offered a lot of money for this piece of paper.''

It was obvious Rod still had no idea what O'Brien was talking about. "Lottery? What kind of lottery?"

"You mean you ain't heard?" amazed O'Brien. "Why, a boatload of women are arriving next week. The woman holding number thirty, the number matching mine, is to be my wife."

Rod was incredulous. "What kind of fool do you take me for?" he scoffed, openly skeptical.

"He's tellin' the truth, Delgado," Digger assured him. "The drawing was held months ago. Hundreds of men vied for the chance to draw for a wife. Looks like our young friend here was one of the fortunate few to win a bride. Each man who drew a number paid for the woman's passage to California. Were he to sell his right to a wife he could get ten, hell, twenty times what he paid for her passage."

"Bah!" spoke up Morley who already had a wife and children back east. "Who wants a whore for a wife."

"These women ain't whores," spoke up O'Brien indignantly. "They're good women recruited by reputable people."

"Well, I ain't vouchsafing their reputation," chuckled Digger, "but any woman brave enough to venture to California, where I hear tell only eight percent of the population is female, is okay in my books."

"Why are you so willing to part with your woman?" questioned Rod, his dark eyes fixed on O'Brien's reddening features.

"If I lose, it ain't gonna do me no good anyway. There ain't no way I could support a wife. Guess I'd have to head back home. It won't be difficult, what with the sailors jumping ship when they reach California, to find a berth back east. My family was against me coming out west in the first place."

"And if you win?" Rod asked quietly.

"I aim to win," bragged O'Brien, tapping his cards confidently. "Then I'll collect my winnings and my bride and have enough to stake me until I strike it rich."

Rod almost felt sorry for the green youth, ill-equipped to deal with the harsh realities of life in the west, especially since gold was discovered in 1848 at Sutter's Mill on the American River. Rod had little use for a bride since his own *novia*, his fiancée, Elena Rodriguez y Montoya, a fiery woman whose Castillian blood was as pure as his own, awaited him at his father's *rancho*.

But something within him compelled Rod to give the boy a chance. If O'Brien won, then so be it. But if the youth lost, Rod would go home much the richer. "All right, O'Brien," Rod finally said, tossing the paper he had been holding back onto the pile of nuggets and dust. "Your bet stands. Show your hand."

One by one O'Brien turned up his cards, his eyes searching Rod's face for some sort of reaction. "Very good," allowed Rod, his expression unreadable. Jubilant, O'Brien's hands moved shakily toward the pot, a broad grin splitting his features. "But not good enough." Rod's last words startled O'Brien and he watched with stricken eyes as one by one Rod revealed his own cards.

A collective gasp arose from the men seated around the table as well as from onlookers who had gravitated toward the action. "I'll be damned," said Digger, scratching his shaggy head.

"Four kings," acknowledged Bud Morley reverently as he sneaked a glance at O'Brien, whose face had turned pasty.

"Son-of-a-bitch!" exclaimed Brute Kelly bitterly. "Leave it to a damn greaser to have all the luck, if that's what you want to call it," he insinuated nastily.

In the time it took to exhale, Rod had his gun unsheathed and aimed at Brute's midsection. Brute drew in his breath sharply, paling beneath his deep tan. "What were you saying against my race, *amigo*?" Rod asked with quiet menace.

Several people nearby began drifting toward the table, always ready to witness a good gunfight, even one so obviously one-sided. "Aw, hell, Delgado," began Kelly, gesturing wildly, "I ain't got nothin' against your race. Why, you Spanish dons own half of California. Can't you take a little joke?"

Before Rod could answer, O'Brien, finally over the shock of losing, cut in. "Mr. Delgado won fair and square, Kelly, I got no call to fight with him and neither have you."

"Don't aim to fight," grumbled Kelly, squirming uncomfortably as he stared down the barrel of Rod's gun.

"Get out of here, Kelly," Rod warned, waving the gun toward the door, "before I forget I'm a man of honor."

Relaxing visibly, Kelly turned without another word and strolled off toward the bar, silently vowing to one day get even with Rodrigo Delgado for the affront to his pride. The crowd that ringed the table, disappointed by the peaceful settlement of the argument, melted away in search of livelier entertainment.

Rod turned his full attention back to his winnings. Drawing a leather pouch from his pocket he quickly scooped the nuggets and dust inside, knotting the strings securely. At first, Rod considered returning to O'Brien the money he had lost. He soon discarded the idea, aware that the youth was ill-prepared to deal with the harsh realities of western civilization, especially since the gold discovery had brought every type of scoundrel and criminal to California in search of wealth and fame. He would be doing O'Brien a favor, Rod decided, by allowing him to return east to his doting family who no doubt would welcome him with open arms. Who knows, he might even be saving the young man's life.

"What will you do now?" Rod asked the drooping youth.

"I aim to be on the Flying Sally when she sails out of San Francisco Bay tomorrow morning," O'Brien said grimly. "Maybe it's for the better. What . . . what are you going to do about the young lady who expects to find a bridegroom waiting for her?"

The question startled Rod. Until that moment he had given little thought to the woman represented by the folded slip of paper now in his possession. "Her ship is the Westwind out of New York, due next week. It's your problem now, Mr. Delgado," O'Brien shrugged carelessly. "Mine is getting myself back to Boston." Abruptly the youth whirled on his heel, leaving Rod more than a little disgruntled by the turn of events fate had dealt him.

Sliding the slip of paper into his vest pocket Rod headed through the crowded room toward the door. He had had enough of Casey's Pleasure Palace for one night. A voice at his elbow stopped him in his tracks.

"How much do you want for it, Delgado?"

"What are you talking about, Kelly?" Rod asked, turning to face a leering Brute Kelly.

"The woman. The idea of a wife pleases me. There ain't nearly enough whores to go around and the thought of a woman around when I needed her suits me. What are you asking for the kid's lottery number? You probably have one of your own kind somewheres so I'd be willing to take this eastern woman off your hands."

Rod realized that now was his chance to rid himself of an unwanted responsibility as well as collect a tidy sum. But, strangely, his code of ethics prevented him from allowing an innocent woman to fall victim to an abusive, mean-tempered man like Brute Kelly.

"Sorry, Kelly," Rod said nastily, "I wouldn't entrust

a dog to your keeping, let alone a helpless woman.''

"Why you son-of-a—'' Brute never got to finish his sentence as Rod, catching the man off guard, slammed a well-aimed fist into his midsection. Brute doubled over in pain, gasping for breath.

"I warned you about calling me names, *amigo*,'' Rod said contemptuously. Kelly was in no condition to reply as Rod calmly turned on his heel and disappeared through the swinging doors.

ONE
DUTY BOUND

1

New York City—March 1851

Errant rays of early spring sunshine stole through the windows, falling upon the enticing form and beautiful features of Juliet Darcy. But Juliet, called Julie by her family and friends, was oblivious of her appearance as she wandered about the quiet house touching objects that once belonged to her Aunt Lavinia.

Since Aunt Lavinia, Julie's father's only sister, had died two weeks ago, life hadn't been very pleasant for the lovely young woman left into the care of her Uncle Hugo, Aunt Lavinia's ne'er-do-well husband. Julie cared little for the way Uncle Hugo looked at her through those light-colored eyes of his that seem to grow bolder and bolder with each passing day.

If only papa hadn't left her nearly two years ago in the care of Lavinia and Hugo while he went off to California to fulfill his dreams of riches, Julie silently lamented. She was so happy living with her father in their tiny apartment over his tobacco shop where she learned to love the many exotic fragrances of aged tobacco. Since her mother died five years ago, Julie and her father, Carl Darcy, had lived a comfortable existence in the rooms above the store. But much to Julie's everlasting sorrow, her father sold his shop and joined the hordes of fortune seekers streaming west when gold had been discovered at Sutter's Mill. Julie had been left behind in the care of Lavinia and Hugo until her father made his fortune in the gold fields. Carl

Darcy had written one letter to his daughter from San Francisco just before he left to work his claim, and then nothing more.

For months now Lavinia and Hugo had accepted the fact that Carl was probably dead, but Julie continued to resist the possibility that her father had died either while working his claim or was killed by claim jumpers or outlaws so prevalent in the lawless west.

And now, even Lavinia was gone, felled by pneumonia after a heavy cold that refused to be quelled. While Aunt Lavinia was alive Uncle Hugo dared not touch her, but now, she could not trust him. Julie began locking her bedroom door each night and staying as far away from Hugo as possible. But even that was difficult for she was obliged to prepare their meals and sit at the same table with the despicable man.

As if on cue, Hugo Kiley appeared from behind a closed door, scratching his shaggy head and yawning hugely. He was not an ugly man. Certainly a gentle creature like Aunt Lavinia had seen some redeeming features in the huge frame and florid good looks of the bluff Irishman raised in New York's shantytown. But with Aunt Lavinia's death Hugo's true character, until now tempered by his wife's innate gentleness, manifested itself in ways that truly frightened Julie.

"Have ye a little breakfast for yer uncle, lass?" Hugo asked, his colorless eyes fixed on the generous curve of Julie's breasts.

"It's on the back of the stove, uncle," Julie was quick to reply. "I'll set it out for you."

As she hurried past her uncle, one long arm snaked out and wrapped itself about her tiny waist. "Ah, yer a toothsome morsel, me girl," Hugo exclaimed as he pulled her roughly against his barrel-like chest. "The lads at the firehouse envy me. That they do," he beamed.

Hugo Kiley was a fireman. A job he proudly held for many years, boasting of his strength and agility despite his advancing years. He was well known around the neighborhood and thought to be an upstanding citizen, even though his drinking was fast becoming a problem.

"Please, Uncle Hugo, let me go," cried Julie, twisting from his cruel grip. "What would Aunt Lavinia say if she saw you behaving toward me in such a shameful manner?"

For a moment Hugo looked uncomfortable. Then his face split in a wide grin. "Yer aunt is dead, me girl, God rest her soul, but me, I'm alive. And so are ye. But go on with ye," he said, giving her a shove toward the kitchen, "fix me breakfast. I'll have ye yet, lass. Yer cherry belongs to me." Her cheeks reddened by her uncle's vulgar words and implication, Julie fled into the kitchen, certain it was no longer safe to remain under her uncle's roof and living off his charity.

Hugo Kiley chewed his food in thoughtful silence as Julie went about her chores. He thought the girl more beautiful and provocative than any woman he had ever known. Two years ago she had been placed in his charge by her fanciful father whose dreams of gold were likely his undoing. At sixteen Juliet Darcy had just begun to exhibit the beginnings of a great beauty she would one day possess. During the next two years Hugo watched her closely as her slim contours filled and molded into womanly proportions, her lush breasts and flaring hips swelling sensuously beneath her dress.

But to Hugo, Julie's face was the most arresting with her small pointed chin, delicate nose and full lips, red as ripe cherries. Long wavy hair the color of warm honey fell to her waist in a tangled mass of wayward curls. Dark brows arched above eyes the color of a clear blue sky thickly lashed with feathery spirals that some considered too long to be decent. Any man would be proud to call such a woman his. And Hugo intended to have her. He considered Lavinia's unexpected death providential, proving that he was meant to have the lass.

Even Father O'Neil had given his grudging blessing to Hugo's plans. Now it was time for Julie to learn of them . . . and accept them.

"Set ye down, lass, I would talk with ye," Hugo smiled graciously, gesturing toward a chair.

"Talk, Uncle Hugo? Whatever about?"

"Yer future, lass, that's what. With yer aunt gone and yer father probably dead, I'm yer legal guardian." Julie remained silent, eyeing Hugo warily. "Have ye ever thought of marriage?" he asked her.

"Marriage! Why, no," Julie said truthfully. "How could I think of marriage when I know no men? No, uncle, I have no desire to marry. At least not until papa returns."

"Bah! How many times must I tell ye yer father is long dead by now. Not one word have ye heard from the man in two years."

"He's not dead!" Julie insisted stubbornly. "I'd know if he were."

"Be that as it may, me girl, the fact still remains that I'm yer guardian. And it's come to me ears that people are beginning to talk about us living alone here in this house, what with our not being blood kin and all. Even the good Father O'Neil spoke to me of it just yesterday."

"Father O'Neil?" questioned Julie dumbly. "I can't believe a Godly man like him would think—"

"It's not him, lass," interrupted Hugo impatiently, "tis others who are doing the talking. Father O'Neil just brought it to my attention. He suggested I do the right thing by ye."

"The right thing?" A finger of dread snaked its way up Julie's spine as Hugo's words took on sinister meaning.

"I'm thinking the only way to stop the gossips is for us to get married," announced Hugo grandly. "What do ye say to that, me girl?"

"You're crazy!" Julie gasped, shocked. "The idea is preposterous! My father would never allow such a thing. Why, Aunt Lavinia would turn in her grave if she knew what you have in mind."

"Father O'Neil will marry us tomorrow in the church," continued Hugo blithely, completely ignoring Julie's protests. "He agrees with me that in our case we are justified in not observing a full year of mourning. Yer reputation must be protected at all costs."

"Protected by whom, you?" spat Julie, her face flushed with anger. "No, uncle, I'll not marry you. I'd rather leave this house."

Undaunted by Julie's outburst, Hugo smiled indulgently. "Where will ye go, lass?"

"Anywhere," declared Julie hotly. "I'll get a job as a governess, or a maid, anything."

"I think not," Hugh smiled slyly. "Ye need me permission to leave this house. If ye are determined to run away I'll find ye. The law is on my side. I'll have the police out searching for ye and ye'll not get far."

Julie stared at her uncle, mouth agape. As unjust as it seemed, the police would indeed be on his side. As a young woman of eighteen she had no rights whatsoever. As her guardian her uncle could do whatever he pleased with her short of murder. But Julie, always resourceful and spirited, would never allow herself to be used in such a vile manner. She would throw herself on Father O'Neil's mercy and beg him to place her with a family in return for her services.

As if reading her thoughts Hugo grasped Julie's wrists, dragging her from her chair. "I'm thinking ye might be trying to run away, me darlin'," he smiled nastily. "I'm also thinking I'm knowing of a way to make sure me bride-to-be don't fly from me lovin' arms."

Before Julie could react to his words Hugo slammed

his mouth down on hers, forcing his tongue between her tight lips. Julie gagged, growing faint from the unexpected attack. A hard object protruded into her stomach as Hugo's huge hands roamed freely over breasts and buttocks, pulling her tightly against his stabbing flesh.

Whimpering softly, Julie struggled, her arms reaching out frantically for something, anything. "I'll not wait. I'll have ye now, me darlin'," Hugo panted, lifting her slight form in his burly arms and striding purposefully into the bedroom, depositing her none too gently in the center of the bed. "Father O'Neil won't fault me for having me bride a day early. I've waited two long years for this moment. I've watched ye grow from a gangling lass into a rare beauty, yer woman's body begging for the attention of a man."

The moment Hugo's hands left her to remove his clothes Julie was up and running. But not fast enough as Hugo caught her before she reached the door. "Uncle, please, don't do this. At least wait until we are married," she pleaded, hedging. "I . . . I want to go to my wedding a virgin. Surely you won't begrudge me that."

Hugo looked confused. "Are ye telling me ye won't fight this marriage?"

"I'll . . . I'll marry you, uncle, willingly, if you agree to my wishes," Julie lied, willing to agree to almost anything to save herself.

At first Hugo was openly skeptical, refusing to believe that his strong-willed niece would suddenly acquiesce to his wishes. "Ye swear? Ye swear on yer aunt's dead body that ye won't change yer mind?"

"I swear on Aunt Lavinia's dead body," Julie said solemnly, "that my mind is made up and I won't change it."

"Ye won't regret it, lass," Hugo grinned toothily. "I'll be good to ye. Once yer broke in proper-like ye'll learn to love what I can do for ye in bed. Yer Aunt Lavinia had no complaints.''

Julie shuddered. It was true that she swore she wouldn't change her mind, and she meant it. But what Uncle Hugo couldn't know was that Julie had already made up her mind to escape. The moment the despicable man left the house she was gone . . . for good.

"Well," Hugo finally decided, "I'm thinking I've not the time now to finish what I started so it suits me purposes to grant yer wish. It's pure ye'll be when I take ye to wife but pure ye won't remain for no longer than it takes me to remove yer clothes. It's off to work I am now, lass. Give yer bridegroom a kiss to keep him going the rest of the day.''

Vastly relieved, Julie concealed her revulsion the best she could and dutifully gave Hugo a peck on the cheek. Chuckling, Hugo pulled her protesting body into his burly arms. "That's not what I had in mind, lass," he said as his mouth covered her trembling lips, sucking the very breath from her soul. Before he released her he boldly fondled her breasts, rudely inserting his hands down the front of her bodice. Julie squirmed uncomfortably but bravely stood her ground.

The moment Hugo Kiley left the house whistling a spritely tune, Julie literally leaped into action. Dragging a large carpetbag from beneath the bed she stuffed it with her meager articles of clothing, adding to it a comb and brush and several pieces of her mother's jewelry. Though not of extreme value they were nonetheless precious to Julie. On a sudden whim she took her aunt's good wool cape with the velvet collar and lining, leaving her own threadbare garment in its place. Thankfully, she had the presence of mind to confiscate the few coins her uncle kept in the house for emergencies.

Wrapping some bread, cheese and sausage in a napkin and stuffing an apple in her pocket, Julie left the house, not once looking back. She knew exactly what

she was going to do. She was going to California to look
for her father. She had no idea how she would get there
but there was no doubt in her mind that she would one
day reach California and find her father.

Lugging her ungainly burden Julie began walking
with no particular destination in mind, knowing that her
safety depended on putting as much distance as possible
between herself and her uncle. By late afternoon Julie
found herself standing on the docks, tired, hungry and
footsore, watching the longshoremen loading and un-
loading the many ships lining the harbor. Selecting a
sturdy box she seated herself and munched on her apple,
wishing herself aboard one of those stalwart ships on
her way to California.

So engrossed was Julie in her own dilemma that she
failed to notice the small form standing nearby, gazing
at her curiously. "Are you one of the California
wives?"

"What?" Julie was startled to find she was not alone.
"Were you speaking to me? I'm sorry, I wasn't paying
attention."

The girl facing Julie was about her own age with
clouds of dark hair swirling about her slim shoulders
and an impish face sprinkled with pale freckles. Green
eyes laughed at her through thick black lashes. A wide
generous mouth kept her from true beauty but there was
no denying she was vastly attractive. Though slim of
hips, her breasts small but shapely, the girl was
undeniably feminine.

"I merely wondered if you were one of the women
sailing for California aboard the Westwind in two
days," repeated the girl, laughing at Julie's obvious
confusion. "I was hoping we might be shipmates. I'm
Polly Carter, who are you?"

"I'm Juliet Darcy," said Julie, smiling at the friendly
girl. "But I have no idea what you are talking about."

"Oh," said Polly, slightly embarrassed. "I

thought . . . well, never mind, Juliet.''

"No," persisted Julie. "Tell me about it. Are you going to California? And please, call me Julie.''

"Yes, Julie, isn't it exciting? It will be a great adventure. Of course, I'm hoping my husband-to-be is a kind man. And not too old or ugly," she added with a mischievous sparkle in her green eyes.

"You mean to tell me you are going to California to be married?" queried Julie, "to a man you've never met?''

"It's not as bad as it sounds," Polly assured her. "The man who arranged it all, Mr. Goddard, recruited us and has assured us that everything is above board. He is a good and kindly man. Women are desperately needed in California. Not . . . bad women, but decent ones willing to settle in the west and raise families. Mr. Goddard is the instigator in a sort of lottery held in California. After everything was arranged there he returned here to recruit women willing to become wives to the lonely men in California. All our expenses are being paid by the prospective grooms.''

"How did you learn about this, Polly?" Julie was astounded by what Polly had told her.

"In the newspaper. Didn't you see the ad? It ran for weeks.''

"No, Uncle Hugo never wasted coin on a newspaper. He always read the copy passed around the firehouse before he came home. Do your parents approve of what you are doing?''

Polly's pert features crumbled, making Julie almost sorry she brought up the subject. "My father died ten years ago and my . . . my mother, only a month ago. I have no one, neither friend nor relative who cares what I do.''

"I'm sorry, Polly," Julie said softly. "But you and I are much alike in that respect.''

Polly was immediately interested. "Are your parents

also dead?''

"My mother died years ago. But I'm sure my father is alive. He left me in the care of his sister and her husband two years ago when he went off to California to look for gold. I haven't heard from him in nearly two years but I know he is still alive. Now my aunt is dead and my uncle is forcing me to marry him.''

"So you ran away," surmised Polly, spying the carpetbag partially hidden beneath the hem of Julie's cape.

"I had no choice," Julie shrugged. "He tried to . . . to . . . well, needless to say I will not marry that despicable man no matter what he says. I left his house this morning and have no intention of returning.''

"Where will you go? Do you have someone to help you?'' asked Polly, worry over her newfound friend wrinkling her smooth brow.

"I have no one," admitted Julie sadly. "I don't know what I'll do. I only know that I can't return home to Uncle Hugo.''

"Come to California, Julie," Polly urged, excited. "You said your father is there. Think how surprised he'll be when you find him.''

"But, Polly, how do I know I won't be trading one despicable husband for another? Can you guarantee me a man I could love? Or happiness?''

"We are women, Julie. Are we ever given any guarantees in life? How many women do you know who are forced into loveless marriages by conniving fathers without a thought for their daughter's feelings? I'll wager there are too many to count. Love is a luxury not many of us are fortunate enough to experience.''

"I've . . . I've never thought of it that way," admitted Julie, awed by her newfound friend's understanding that far surpassed her years.

"At least I'm placing my future in my own hands. It's my choice to go to California. I have faith that the man chosen to become my husband is a good and kind man. And I'll make him a good wife. What about you, Julie?'' Polly challenged. ''Are you brave enough to take charge of your own future?''

Julie hesitated but a few moments before giving her answer. ''Where will I find your Mr. Goddard?''

Polly hugged Julie exuberantly. ''I'm so glad, Julie. It will work out, you'll see.''

Together Polly and Julie hoisted Julie's carpetbag between them and walked the few blocks to a small storefront office sandwiched between two large buildings. The sign posted on the front window in bold, black letters drew Julie like a magnet as she paused to read the advertisement. ''Young ladies of good reputation wanted,'' the sign proclaimed. ''If you are willing to travel to California, all expenses paid, to embark upon a great adventure, inquire inside. Thirty berths available to the lucky women who will find husbands waiting for them at the end of their journey.''

Taking a deep, steadying breath, Julie pushed open the door and stepped inside, followed closely by Polly. Bolstered by the support of her new friend, Julie walked on quaking limbs to where a middleaged man with thinning hair sat behind a desk. Looking up the man smiled pleasantly as he spied Julie. ''I'm Julius Goddard,'' he said, extending his hand.

Exactly one-half hour later, Julie left the office clutching an official paper bearing the number thirty. She was astounded at the ease with which she decided her future. Mr. Goddard had been all Polly said he was. With skill and patience he had extracted information concerning her background without her actually knowing what he was about. Julie had the presence of mind to say she was alone in the world after the untimely death of her aunt. Julius Goddard was tactful and understanding of the great upheaval facing most of the girls who, for reasons of their own, chose to take up the challenge and journey west to marry complete strangers.

"I had almost given up hope of finding my last girl," lamented Mr. Goddard when he handed Julie the last berth available aboard the Westwind. "You are an answer to my prayer, my dear," the congenial man beamed. "I hated to disappoint any of the young men anxiously awaiting your arrival. I am greatly relieved to have fulfilled the obligation I have undertaken. My wife, Martha, and myself felt it our Christian duty to bring marriage and a home life to young men who otherwise would fall prey to prostitutes and fortune hunters."

In a state bordering on numbness, Julie found herself outside on the sidewalk staring dumbly at the sheet of paper, trying to conjure up the image of the man holding the corresponding number in far off California.

"Come along, Julie," Polly urged, nudging the nearly paralyzed girl forward. "You'd better come home with me. My rent is paid for a few more days and we can't take the chance of your uncle finding you and forcing you to return to him."

At the mention of her uncle Julie finally came alive. Producing one of the coins she had stolen from Hugo the girls hired a carriage to take them to a tiny two room apartment above a saloon that Polly had shared with her mother. After a meager meal consisting of the cheese, bread and sausage Julie had taken from home and hot tea produced by Polly, they retired early. Because the Westwind was sailing on the early morning tide two days hence, the girls would be allowed to board the next afternoon to settle themselves into their cabins and acquaint themselves with their fellow passengers and new home for the next six months.

The only bad moment came when they left Polly's rooms and saw two policemen at the end of the street questioning residents. Thinking her uncle had set the authorities onto her, Julie quickly produced another coin and hailed a hack to carry them and their baggage to the docks. At precisely noon, Julie and Polly boarded the Westwind and were shown to a cabin they would share with three other women.

Julie and Polly were nearly the only ones up the next morning at dawn when the Westwind slipped her moorings and slid from her berth into the gray mists surrounding the harbor. As the shrouded buildings and winding streets disappeared from sight Julie could not help but feel icy fingers of apprehension clutch at her heart. Was she doing the right thing, she wondered? What fate awaited her in far off California? Would she be reunited with her father? Squaring her slim shoulders and lifting her small pointed chin, Julie knew that come what may, she was prepared to meet her destiny.

2

San Francisco—September 1851

Julie stood on the deck of the Westwind as it pulled slowly into San Francisco Bay, maneuvering carefully around the deserted ships that littered the bay. She had been told by Captain Langford that during the year more than eight-hundred of the vessels that had been anchored in the cove were abandoned by their crews who had jumped ship to join the gold rush. It was an eerie sight to see the empty hulks bobbing up and down, waves slapping against their hulls.

From her vantage point on deck, Julie could see a filthy clutter of small, crude buildings sprawled haphazardly along deeply rutted roads. It was not exactly what she had expected. Even Polly, standing next to Julie, appeared dismayed. They had assumed that San Francisco was a thriving city, but from what they could make out it was little more than a sprawling, overgrown slum.

It was several hours later before the thirty young ladies, led by a beaming Julius Goddard and his pleasant wife, disembarked. The group walked sedately through crowded streets to a hostel type hotel where they would be housed until the next day when they met their husbands for the first time. Their trunks were to follow in a horse-drawn wagon.

People of every nationality crowded about the area: Englishmen, Irishmen, Spaniards, Frenchmen, and even

Chinese and Negroes. Raised voices proclaimed loudly in every language imaginable. Never had Julie seen so many Chinese gathered in one place. Their shiny black hair was nearly as long as long as hers, hanging in neat queues down their backs. Their colorful robes nearly hid their yellowish skins and their dark eyes slanted upwards. She almost burst out laughing at the odd little hats perched atop their heads. Many of the Chinese carried passengers in two-wheeled vehicles Mr. Goddard called "rickshaws."

Julie was dismayed by the hordes of grimy, unshaven men filling the streets. It seemed like thousands of would-be miners had come to San Francisco too late to get rich and now roamed about listlessly, their dreams of riches shattered, their money depleted. Julie could not help but wonder if her father was among those broken men camped in tents where no buildings had been erected.

As they passed by, Julie could hear many of these men hawking their supplies along the roadside. Tin pans went for the amazing sum of five dollars or more, shovels for ten or twelve. The entire scene was like something out of a bad dream.

Soon Julie was forced to focus her full attention on keeping her feet on the wooden sidewalk skirting both sides of the street lest she slip and find herself devoured by a sea of mud. Julie and Polly stayed close and managed to get beds next to each other. The rest of the day was spent making themselves presentable for their presentation the next day and selecting their wardrobes for the all important meeting with their bridegrooms.

Julie chose her best dress that really wasn't very new but one she knew flattered her slim-waisted figure and golden coloring. The blue of the full-skirted dress nearly matched her eyes. The tight-fitting bodice with insets of beige lace buttoned demurely to her throat, the cut accentuating the high, upthrust tilt of perfectly proportioned breasts. Long sleeves hugged well-shaped, slender arms ending with a froth of lace at Julie's delicate wrists. Aunt Lavinia's velvet-lined cape added an elegant touch that pleased Julie.

To set off her cloud of black hair Polly chose a pale yellow confection sprigged with green embroidered flowers to match her eyes. A square neckline and high waist outlined and defined her trim figure. Neither girl owned a decent bonnet so they opted to go hatless, letting their hair serve as their crowning glory.

The next day when they nervously approached the large building hastily constructed of raw, untreated wood where they were to meet their future husbands, neither Julie nor Polly were prepared for the huge mass of cheering, shoving men of all types and description that awaited them. Not only was the street outside the building teeming with humanity but inside Julie thought she would suffocate as the jostling crowd made way for the nearly terrified women.

The thirty hapless girls were led to a low platform while Mr. Goddard tried unsuccessfully to quiet the whooping men aroused by the sight of so many attractive women. That only thirty of them were destined to become husbands mattered little. What did matter was that these particular women chose to journey thousands of miles, braving all sorts of dangers, to become wives in a land populated mostly by men. Where these brave women ventured, others were bound to follow. Finally, Mr. Goddard managed to subdue the noisy crowd and the serious business of matching husbands and wives began.

What first attracted Rod to the building was the mob scene being enacted in the immediate vicinity. He had just returned from an exhausting trip to Monterey and wanted nothing more than to relax in a hot bath and sleep the clock around. Luckily, this was his last trip to San Francisco for awhile and then he could return home to Rancho Delgado where Elena awaited him. Their wedding could no longer be put off. His marriage to Elena Montoya, arranged by their respective fathers when they were children, must finally come to pass despite the fact that Rod had managed to postpone the long awaited event for several years. But finally Elena had grown impatient. And when his father, Don Diego, invited Elena to live at his rancho while her father and mother visited Spain, Rod knew the time for procrastination had ended. On his return to San Luis Obispo he and Elena would become man and wife in accordance with his father's wishes.

It was almost with a feeling of destiny fulfilled that Rod approached the building and fought his way inside. The moment he spied the young ladies standing on the platform he knew exactly what was taking place. Stealthily he slid his hand inside the pocket of his leather vest and touched the folded sheet of paper he had completely forgotten about during his trying week of confronting bureaucratic courts, shyster lawyers and judges inclined to overlook the claims of proud Castilian landowners whose land lay mostly along the El Camino Real.

Since the Land Act of 1851 in which Rancheros must prove ownership of family lands and where sizes were reduced in most of the original holdings, Rod and his father had been working tirelessly to obtain the proper documents to define boundries of lands alloted to them long years past. It had taken months to gather accurate documentation of their vast holdings, nearly 70,000 acres surrounding San Louis Obispo, but finally Rod had taken everything to Monterey this past week to present before the courts. Anti-Mexican sentiment ran high, legal fees exorbitant, venal judges on the side of the would-be land grabbers. But Don Diego, with the help of his son, had emerged victorious after great personal cost of both time and money. The Delgado holdings once again belonged exclusively to the Delgado family and they were free to rid themselves of the squatters who had settled like leeches upon their land. It is no wonder that Rod had forgotten about the poker game and the ultimate prize he had won.

Making his way to a relatively deserted corner, Rod leaned his long frame into the wall and coolly surveyed his surroundings. Time and again his penetrating dark eyes were inexplicably drawn to the platform displaying the blushing brides-to-be. The proceedings had already begun and nearly ten young ladies had been matched to their mates and were in an adjoining room waiting their turn before the preacher. Scrupulously honest and concerned for his young charges' welfare, one of Mr. Goddard's stipulations was that the couples would be married immediately, before they even left the premises. Only then would he consider his duty discharged.

One by one the ranks of the young brides were diminished until only five remained. Of the women being triumphantly claimed only two held any interest for Rod. One was a dark-haired girl dressed in yellow and the other a vision of loveliness in blue with a mass of honey-colored hair tumbling down her back in a riot of artless curls. The next number was called and the dark-haired girl gave a squeal, hugged the blond beauty beside her and stepped forward. Rod could not help but note the fear visible in the startling blue eyes of the blond and felt a twinge of pity for her. In his estimation she was far too fine to waste herself on one of the crude miners flocking into San Francisco seeking riches that for most would never materialize.

To Julie the waiting was worse than anything she had ever experienced. Watching the disreputable-looking men surrounding the platform made her wonder what she had gotten herself into and she wished she had not listened to Polly those six long months ago. The one redeeming feature of this whole fiasco was the hope that one day she would find her father. Could he be somewhere in the crowd? she wondered, glancing about the room with renewed interest.

The tall, dark man was so different from the rest of the men in the crowded room that Julie's eyes were drawn to him immediately. He seemed totally out of place, almost bored with the proceedings, which made Julie curious as to his presence here in the first place.

The man was tall and strongly muscled, his lean, sinuous body as lithe as a whipcord. His skin was swarthy; his hair dark as midnight. His eyes were black beneath jet brows, and his full, sensuous mouth set below a long, aquiline nose smiled lazily at no one in particular, white teeth flashing. His cheekbones were high, the planes of his cheeks spare, the set of his jaw arrogant, as though the world was his for the asking. His dark eyes held a deeply cynical, almost insolent look and the full, sensuous mouth had a reckless, faintly derisive twist that only added to his attractiveness.

His powerful shoulders and broad chest tapered to a narrow waist and a firm, flat stomach. His tight leather clothing emphasized the bold thrust of his pelvis and thick, corded thighs. A slightly rumpled white shirt open at the neck with long full sleeves, a leather belt with large silver buckle and a flat-brimmed sombrero completed his impressive appearance. Try as she might Julie could not take her eyes from the handsome man. Although there was a savage quality about him that frightened her even while it attracted her, Julie could not help but wish the man she was to marry would look like him.

Suddenly Julie heard Polly squeal and abruptly came out of her reverie to find her friend embracing her. A wild whoop rent the air as a young man burst through the crowd intent on claiming his bride. The man couldn't have been more than twenty-one and was good-looking in a rough sort of way. He was big and brawny with a shock of blond hair that grew shaggy about the nape of his neck. He was dressed in typical miner's garb which was surprisingly clean. His name was Conner Furley and it was obvious that he was immediately smitten with the young woman about to become his wife. Before Polly departed with her young man she shot an exultant look at Julie as if to say, "I told you so."

Finally Julie found herself standing alone on the platform and she shifted nervously from foot to foot. She started violently when number thirty was called, holding her breath as she scanned the room, inexplicably meeting the fathomless gaze of the man dressed in leather. She stood very still, her eyes held by his, and suddenly a feeling of warmth suffused her body. It was as if something from deep inside him reached out and touched her. Something from the depths of her burst into life as their eyes met and held.

"Who holds number thirty?" repeated Mr. Goddard for the third time. Julie grew uncomfortable as a deathly silence fell in the room.

Rod stared at Julie, unable to believe that in his large hand rested the right to claim the lovely girl standing alone on the platform. Obligation was all that kept him from bounding up and claiming his woman as each of his predecessors had done. Rod could well imagine the scene should he show up at Rancho Delgado with an Anglo bride. Not to mention Elena's rage, which he had no wish to experience.

"What are you waiting for, Delgado?" asked a voice at his elbow. "The woman is yours. Don't you want her?"

Rod whirled, his hand poised above his gun in a purely reflexive action. "Next time you sneak up on a man, Kelly, make damn sure you are prepared to defend yourself," he warned ominously.

"I want that woman, Delgado," said Kelly, licking

his thick lips wetly. "If you ain't got no use for her let me have her. Damn, she's a tasty piece. Name your price. I'm willing to pay almost anything to have her in my bed."

Rod snorted with disgust, turning his back on the huge ruffian as he focused his attention on Mr. Goddard and the girl standing beside him on the platform.

"If no one claims number thirty I wll be obliged to hold a drawing right here and now in order to fulfill my duty to the young lady placed in my charge," Mr. Goddard proclaimed loudly. Immediately a tremendous roar of approval rent the air.

"This is your last chance, Delgado," Kelly persisted. "Do I get the girl or not? Surely it can't matter to you who weds and beds the woman."

Kelly has a point, Rod thought, gazing longingly at Julie's lithe form. It should make little difference to him who eventually won the enticing blond. But strangely it did. It mattered a great deal. He just couldn't allow the girl to go up for grabs. It went against his principle to throw a young innocent girl to the wolves, so to speak. As if in a trance Rod found himself pushing through the crowd, the paper Kelly desperately wanted waving high in the air.

"Well step forward, young man," Mr. Goddard beamed when he saw Rod fighting his way through the hosts of men. "You are tardy but welcome." By the time Rod realized his folly it was too late. He had already been introduced to Juliet Darcy and was instantly lost in the twin pools of azure blue.

Cheering loudly the crowd pushed and shoved the reluctant couple forward until they stood before the preacher. Within minutes Rod found himself married to Juliet Darcy, thereby becoming the first Delgado in generations to break a tradition by marrying someone not of his race.

With the last marriage ceremony performed, the room cleared out rapidly. Julie moved as if in a trance. From the moment she learned the man she had been attracted to was to be her husband she had been beyond speech, merely mumbling the words during the blessedly brief ceremony. Somehow, Julie sensed that everything was not as it should be. This dark, brooding man was not the happy bridegroom she had expected. From the moment they were introduced a permanent scowl darkened his handsome features and his lips were drawn tightly together in a taut line. Except for their brief introduction he had not spoken one word to her.

Julie breathed a sigh of relief when Polly came bounding over with her new husband. "Isn't it exciting?" she said, her green eyes shimmering with happiness. "We're going to spend the night at the best hotel in town and leave tomorrow for Conner's claim. He built a cabin for us while he was waiting for the Westwind to arrive."

Introductions were made all around and when Rod and Conner were engaged in conversation Polly sidled close to Julie and whispered, "Your husband is so handsome, Julie, but I think I'd rather have my Conner. He's much more uncomplicated than your Rodrigo. I'm not sure I could survive the passion of your tall *caballero*."

Julie gasped, shocked by Polly's bold words, although by now she should be accustomed to her friend's habit of openly speaking her mind. But before she could reply, Conner flashed his bride a look of intense longing and made their excuses.

Turning to his own bride, Rod said, "Come along, Juliet."

"Where are we going, Rodrigo?" Julie asked timidly, wondering if they would be staying at the same hotel with Conner and Polly.

"Call me Rod, Juliet, it's less formal," Rod said, still

frowning. "I'm taking you to my room."

"Oh," was all Julie said. "My . . . my friends call me Julie."

"Do you consider me a friend, Julie?" Rod asked, his lip curling in amusement. If she knew what he had planned for her, Rod decided, she would be far from friendly.

Julie bristled at his words. "I had hoped we could be friends. It would make our marriage much more pleasant."

"It is not to be, *querida*," Rod said softly, almost regretfully.

"What . . . what did you say?" Julie asked, not certain she had heard right.

"Never mind, I'll explain later," Rod muttered, shrugging. Somehow he must explain to Julie the circumstances that made their union impossible.

They proceeded to the end of the street where Rod crossed the road, expecting Julie to follow. He was nearly to the middle, mud sucking at his boots, when he became aware that Julie was no longer at his side. Perplexed, he glanced over his shoulder to see her poised on the far edge of a deep puddle holding up her blue skirt, one slim foot and well-turned ankle lifted daintily.

Cursing under his breath, Rod turned back intending to carry Julie to the other side of the road, but he was too late. Scowling fiercely, Rod stood helplessly by while another man scooped Julie into his brawny arms and carried her effortlessly across the street, setting her on her feet with a flourish. Rod quickly caught up with them, recognizing his wife's rescuer immediately.

Brett Casey owned Casey's Pleasure Palace and was a renowned womanizer. He changed mistresses as easily as he changed his shirts. He was the type of man Rod did not wish his wife to associate with. Abruptly Rod faltered, realizing that his thoughts were taking a

dangerous direction. Never could he consider Juliet
Darcy his wife. The title belonged to Elena, one of his
own kind. By the time he reached Julie, Casey had
already taken his leave.

"You should not have been so friendly with that man,
Julie," Rod warned darkly. "He's not the sort for you
to consort with."

"He certainly was polite enough, Rod," Julie
insisted, blushing under his reproof. "It was very
gallant of him to come to my aid."

"Is that a slur upon my character, *querida*?" Rod
sneered lazily.

"Take it any way you want," sniffed Julie,
wondering why she and her husband barely had a civil
word for each other when they hardly knew one
another. It was eerie the way a strange tenseness invaded
her body whenever Rod looked at her with those hooded
dark eyes. A tingle of anticipation raced through her
blood, making her aware of their wedding night and
what would no doubt take place when they were alone.
Would he be a gentle, considerate lover? Julie
wondered, blushing at the direction of her wayward
thoughts. Or was he the kind to take his own pleasure,
caring nothing for her tender feelings.

Julie knew very little about the relationship between
husband and wife until Polly, bless her, imparted all
that she had been told by her mother. Julie knew she
would feel pain the first time Rod took her, but if he
was gentle and understanding she would feel great
pleasure, also. Now, watching the play of emotion upon
Rod's stony features, fingers of fear clutched at her
heart. She doubted that her haughty, arrogant husband
had a shred of tenderness in his tall, well-proportioned
frame.

Before long, Rod stopped before a sprawling two
story house sporting a wide front porch. The sign above
the front door said simply, ROOMS FOR RENT. Rod led

her inside where they were met by a short, round woman of late middleage with whispy graying hair and pleasant features. Her bow-like lips were pursed in disapproval as she eyed the young couple warily, hands on ample hips.

"Don Rodrigo, you know I run a respectable house," the woman bristled, eyeing Julie through slightly myopic eyes. "There will be no hanky-panky going on upstairs. You will have to find another place to entertain your . . . er . . . lady friend."

Julie blushed furiously, knowing full well that the woman thought her to be a woman of loose morals. Rod raised his head and laughed uproariously, the first time Julie had seen him in good humor since their hasty marriage. "Mae, this lady is my wife, Julie," he said, wiping the tears from his eyes. "Julie, meet Mae Parker. She owns this boarding house and thinks she's mother to every homeless young man ever to set foot in San Francisco."

Julie could tell Mae Parker was truly astounded by Rod's declaration. "I'm glad to meet you, Mrs. Parker," Julie said timidly.

"Call me Mae, honey, everyone else does. Is it true? Are you really Rod's wife?"

"Yes," verified Julie. "We were married less than an hour ago."

"Are you one of those girls from the east who came out here to become brides?" Solemnly, Julie nodded. "I don't understand, Rod," Mae said, truly puzzled. "You told me yourself your father expected you to marry—"

"I'll explain later, Mae," Rod cut in quickly before Mae had a chance to finish her sentence. "It's a long story. Right now I'd like to take Julie upstairs. She's had a tiring day and I know she'd like a hot bath."

"How thoughtless of me," Mae apologized. "Take your wife to your room and I'll have Ling Wu heat water for her bath. I'll bet you're both hungry, too. I'll

cook you up a proper wedding feast.'' Before Julie
could offer her thanks the friendly woman bustled out
of the room.

Within a few minutes Julie found herself standing in
the center of a large room whose two long windows
faced the street. Though the room was by no means
lavishly appointed, it was adequate and appeared
scrupulously clean. Julie gazed about thoughtfully,
directing her eyes everywhere but at the large bed
decorating the center of the room.

"I come to San Francisco quite often," Rod said,
startling Julie out of her reverie, "and always stay here
rather than at one of the hotels. Even San Francisco's
finest leaves much to be desired. Mae Parker's is more
to my liking."

"It's very nice," Julie agreed in a stilted voice. Try as
she might, she could not relax. She had no idea what to
expect from the tall, commanding man she had married.

Rod was not unaware of Julie's tenseness and immediately recognized her fear. *Dio mio*, she was lovely,
he thought, with her hair the color of warm honey
tumbling about her shoulders. His eyes fell unbiddingly
to her miniscule waist before focusing on her
magnificent full breasts straining against the lace inserts
of her bodice. She was all woman and Rod found
himself reacting violently to her nearness. His body
began to swell with desire, a desire he refused to
recognize when he first laid eyes on her standing on the
platform looking like a lamb being led to the slaughter.

Julie saw the direction of Rod's gaze and shifted uncomfortably, wondering if he intended to ravish her on
the spot. It was within his right to do whatever he
pleased to her, she knew, but she prayed desperately
that there was some compassion in his soul. She had
heard much about the cruelty of Spaniards. But what
troubled her most was the fact that Rod had felt the
need to acquire an unknown bride from the east. She

had thought the aristocratic Spanish usually married within their own race. Julie suppressed a shudder of dread as Rod's inky eyes boldly raked over her lush curves, visibly undressing her.

Sighing heavily, Rod lifted his eyes to settle finally on Julie's face. No matter how much he wanted the girl, he could not in all conscience take her . . . unless . . .

"Are you a virgin, Julie?" he asked abruptly, his question bringing roses to her cheeks. Completely confused, Julie could only nod dumbly. "*Por Dios*," Rod cursed, disappointment furrowing his brow. "Then you have nothing to fear from me. I will not claim your maidenhead."

To Julie, Rod's staccato-like words could only mean that she did not please him or that she had said or done something to anger him. Only minutes before she had recognized the glimmer of lust in his eyes, but now there was nothing but cold indiference in their fathomless depths.

"I . . . I don't understand," she stammered. "If I've done something to anger you, or—"

"It's nothing you've done, *querida*," Rod said, his voice softening with regret. "Circumstances have ordained that we can never be man and wife, even though I find myself desiring you as a man desires a woman. But I will not ruin you for another."

Suddenly Julie became very angry, her rage transcending any fear she might have felt for her intimidating husband. "Are you telling me we are not truly wed? That the ceremony was merely a sham? I can't believe Mr. Goddard would . . ." She faltered, unable to continue.

Rod smiled indulgently, highly amused by Julie's show of temper. It proved she was no meek miss and he briefly regretted the code of ethics that prevented him from giving in to his desire. "In the eyes of the law we are legally bound," Rod explained patiently, "but it is a marriage my father will never accept. I have been engaged since childhood to the daughter of an old aristocratic family. Even now Elena awaits my return so we can be wed.''

Red dots of rage exploded in Julie's brain, turning her eyes into shards of blue ice. "You bastard!" she charged, shocking him with her unladylike language. "You bigamist! What did you intend? To keep one wife at your ranch and one in San Francisco? How dare you trick me!" Unable to control herself she flew at the unsuspecting man, her bared fingernails gouging deep grooves into both cheeks.

"*Bruja!*" Rod cried out. "Witch!" Catching her arms and whipping her about he forced her body against his until she was immobilized in his punishing embrace. "If you allowed me a moment I would have explained it to you. Do you always act so impulsively?"

Struggling in his arms, Julie gasped, "Let me go!"

"Not until you hear me out," Rod insisted, tightening his grasp about her slim form.

"Why did you pay my way over here if you already had a fiancée?" Julie challenged, kicking backwards in a futile attempt to free herself. Her soft slipper encountered a well-muscled leg encased in leather and Rod chuckled as she uttered a soft cry of pain.

"Are you ready to listen?" Rod asked, shaking her until her teeth rattled.

"Y . . . y . . . yes," Julie ground out.

Dragging her to the bed, Rod sat her down none too gently and settled beside her. "I did not send for you, *querida*," he informed her. Julie's eyes opened wide but she said nothing. "I won you in a poker game." Rod paused for her gasp of outrage and was not disappointed.

"A young man named Kevin O'Brien paid your way to San Francisco. He and I met in a poker game several weeks ago. O'Brien lost heavily and in the end wagered the only thing he had left of value . . . you. His hand was good. But not good enough.''

"You were the man Kevin O'Brien lost to," Julie intoned dryly. "Did you cheat the poor man out of his possessions?''

Rod exploded in a whirlwind of anger. "*Bruja*! I do not cheat at cards! Kevin O'Brien was a young fool who wagered a fortune on a turn of a card. Had he any sense he would never have gotten in over his head in the first place. As it turned out you were the one to come out the winner. O'Brien was not the man for you.''

"And I suppose you are?''

Rod turned thoughtful, suddenly certain that he was exactly the right man for the little hellion. She needed someone to match her fire, a man capable of taming the wild streak in her. He was convinced their coming together would be more like an explosion than an act of love and his tense body yearned to be the first to elicit those cries of ecstasy from her full red lips.

"Whether or not I am the man for you is unimportant," Rod finally said. "Of necessity, our marriage is over before it begins.''

"Why? Why did you marry me? You could have backed out.''

"If it is any consolation to you, I did consider walking out of the room and deserting you to your fate.''

"What changed your mind?''

Rod flushed. What indeed? he wondered dismally. Were his motives purely selfish? That was something he would ask himself the rest of his life. "If I didn't claim you, you would have gone up for grabs. I understand Julius Goddard screened the prospective bridegrooms quite thoroughly and only the best of the lot were allowed to participate in the drawing. Did you get a good look at the men in the room today? They are the dregs of humanity. Scum. Criminals. Had I not appeared you would now be the possession of one of them for they would have held a lottery for you then and there.''

"So you saved me from a fate worse than death,'' snapped Julie sarcastically. "Am I supposed to thank you, Don Rodrigo?''

Her gibe stung. "You little fool. I am giving you back your life. As long as our marriage isn't consummated it will be relatively simple to obtain an annulment. I'll pay your way back east where you can take up your life as if nothing happened. One day you'll find a man of your own choosing.''

"Back east!'' Julie exploded. "I will not be shipped back to New York like so much discarded baggage! I came to California with a purpose and I won't leave until I accomplish what I set out to do.''

"I realize you came here with the intention of being married,'' Rod contended, "but—''

"You're a fool if you think that's what brought me here. I couldn't care less about a husband.''

"Then, why . . .''

"I came to find my father,'' Julie blurted out. "I didn't have the price of passage and Polly persuaded me to join Mr. Goddard's group of girls going west to become brides.''

"Your father! You have a father in California? Why, that simplifies matters. Of course you don't have to return east if you have a father to protect you. Where is he?''

A blush of crimson stained Julie's high cheekbones. "I . . . I don't know.''

"Surely you have some idea where he can be found.''

"He left New York two years ago. I've heard from him only once since then, shortly after he landed in San Francisco.''

"Julie,'' Rod said gently, "did you ever consider the possibility that your father might be dead?''

"No!" Julie cried. "I won't believe that."

"It's something you must face, *querida*. Two years ago, one-hundred thousand new people arrived in California, most of them rough apportunists who thought nothing of killing to get what they wanted. Since 1848 when the war with Mexico terminated and the Treaty of Guadalupe Hidalgo gave all of California to the United States, it has been most difficult to maintain peace. Especially since military rule and Mexican law technically ended. At this time nothing exists but lynch law, popular courts and vigilance committees to enforce order. Perhaps your father was a victim of a foul crime. He could disappear and no one would be the wiser."

"I refuse to believe that," Julie persisted stubbornly. "You're just trying to scare me."

Seeing her distress, Rod's tone softened. "Many of the men who came to California aren't cut out for the life of a miner and quickly succumb to the rigors of hard work and the elements."

"I'll find my father, Rod," Julie insisted doggedly. "Go ahead and get your annulment. Go back and marry your . . . your betrothed. I'll manage on my own. I don't need you or anyone else."

"*Por Dios*!" cursed Rod. "Haven't you been listening? You are an innocent if you think you are capable of surviving in San Francisco on your own. As an unmarried, unprotected woman you will become the target of every unscrupulous man around."

"Mae Parker seems to be doing well enough on her own," contended Julie hotly.

"Mae Parker isn't a young, beautiful virgin. Would you throw yourself in a den of lions? Tomorrow I'll purchase your passage on the first ship available and arrange with Mae for you to remain here until you leave." In Rod's mind it was all settled, but he didn't reckon with Julie's stubbornness or her impulsive nature.

"I'm staying," declared Julie with grim determination. "I refuse to discuss it further. I'll find a job and inquire about my father. Don't worry about me, I'll be fine. You are right in thinking you did me a favor. Now I am free to do as I please."

"*Caramba*, you're stubborn!" Rod exclaimed disgustedly. "Have it your way. Tomorrow morning I'll start the annulment proceedings. My lawyer will inform you the moment we are legally separated." Without another word he stomped from the room.

Later, Julie luxuriated in a hot bath, enjoying her first all over wash since leaving New York. It was heavenly and she lolled lazily in the water until it grew cold. Rod, too, was enjoying the same privilege. Leaving Julie, he visited a barber, had a shave and haircut and then a bath in the back room where customers were able to enjoy all the comforts of home. He returned to his room in better spirits than when he left, hoping to talk some sense into Julie. He opened the door just as Julie dropped the wet towel to the floor and reached for her wrapper. In Rod's absence her bag containing her meager wardrobe had arrived and Mae had it carried to her room.

Rod was stunned. Never was he more aware of a woman than he was of Julie. And Rod was certainly no stranger to women. He was well known to every attractive *señorita* along the El Camino Real. He had spent many pleasurable hours in the arms of beautiful women between San Francisco and San Luis Obispo. And even farther south, should the truth be known. Even his first love, Maria . . . but no, he would not think of Maria now. Not with Julie displayed so enticingly before him.

He stepped quietly into the room, closing the door firmly behind him. "You are exquisite, *querida*. I think you have truly bewitched me."

Startled, Julie turned, blushing furiously when she saw Rod staring at her. "Go away, Rod," she said, holding the wrapper before her. "You have no right."

How tantalizing, Rod thought, mesmerized by the tiny droplets of water glistening on creamy skin as smooth as alabaster. Every instinct urged him to reach out, to touch, caress, to fondle to his heart's content.

"I have every right. We are married," Rod finally said, his voice hoarse with longing.

"But you said . . ." Julie was confused, as well as fearful. The bold look in Rod's dark eyes bode no good for her.

"I know what I said, but that was before I knew what I was denying myself. Come here, *bruja*. You are a witch, you know."

Before Julie could react, Rod was at her side, snatching the robe from her nerveless fingers and tossing it across the room where it landed in a careless heap. She stood before him clothed in nothing but her glorious nudity and Rod felt himself swell with barely suppressed desire. It was a picture that would haunt Rod's dreams for months to come. His eyelids drooped slightly over eyes now filled with passion, dark, smoldering, compelling. A growing sense of dispair overcame Julie when she realized she had not the strength nor the desire to resist him should he try to make love to her. Her eyes met Rod's across the short distance and her own desire kindled, then flamed.

Suddenly she was in Rod's arms as his hands roamed freely over her flesh. Feebly, Julie protested, but when his mouth came down hard over her parted lips she was lost. Nothing Julie had ever known or imagined had prepared her for the violence of Rod's kiss. His tongue traced the outline of her lips, then plunged within to explore the sweetness of her mouth, open with shock, leaving Julie shaken, her knees weak. The force of his passion both thrilled and repelled her.

In view of Rod's words earlier, Julie knew what he was doing was wrong. Weakly, she struggled against his hardening body, feeling herself succumb to the power of his passion. His hand found her breast and sharp circles of delight radiated from her nipple as his rough palms slid caressingly over the pink bud. Suddenly Julie was beyond resistence as she felt herself responding wildly to his nearness. Then his mouth left hers and his moist, hot tongue touched the swollen tip, finally taking it between his lips, nipping gently with strong, white teeth.

Julie groaned. She felt as if she were melting, dissolving right here as she lay in Rob's arms, his throbbing, swollen manhood pressing insistenly against her roiling stomach. Her heart slammed wildly, setting off a trembling in her slender body that triggered a like response in Rod. For a moment he hesitated, his mind battling the tatters of his good sense, but her sweet surrender swept him over the edge into an abyss of swirling, all-consuming passion.

Scooping Julie into his strong arms he carried her the few steps to the bed, murmuring love words in Spanish she didn't understand. *"Mi Cara, mi amor, mi alma."* The words meant nothing to her but his low seductive voice mesmerized her into acquiescence.

Julie was lost in a strange world of sensual pleasure so intense she thought she would die of wanting as Rod's lips discovered her woman's body, devoting his special brand of attention to all the secret places until now she never knew existed. When he started to withdraw, Julie groaned in protest, tightening her arms about his neck, threading her fingers in the curling hairs at the nape of his neck.

"Wait, *querida*," he whispered huskily, fully aware of the need he had aroused in her. "It will take but a moment to remove my clothes." Reluctantly Julie loosened her grip as Rod rose unsteadily to his feet.

It was several seconds before either of them became aware of Mae Parker's voice calling to them from the other side of the door. Cursing roundly in Spanish, Rod hastily pulled the sheet over Julie's flushed body, took several deep breaths to still his raging ardor, and walked to the door on shaking legs. The tide of passion that had been building in him slowly began to ebb, but not before dealing a stab of disappointment.

"I'm sorry, Rod," apologized Mae, smiling at Rod's obvious state of arousal, "but an important message just arrived for you and I promised I'd deliver it immediately." She handed an envelope to Rod who merely nodded his thanks and slammed the door in the bemused woman's face.

Tearing open the letter, Rod scowled darkly as he read the words. "Is . . . is it bad news?" Julie asked, noting Rod's glowering features.

"You could call it that," Rod answered distractedly. "You'd better get dressed," he added abruptly. "You can thank Mae for your escape. I had no business seducing you. Had I succeeded I would have been compelled to do the honorable thing and continue with this farce of a marriage. I must admit you were willing enough once you got over your initial shyness," he added thoughtfully. "I find myself envying the man who eventually has the pleasure of taming you."

Eyes bright with anger, Julie shot bolt upright, clutching the sheet to her breasts. "You arrogant bastard! To think I almost let you . . . let you . . ."

"Make love to you?" Rod supplied.

"Rape me!" Julie retorted, more hurt by his careless words than she cared to admit.

"Have no fear, *querida*," Rod said softly, "you have nothing more to fear from me. I must leave immediately for Monterey. It seems the courts weren't quite satisfied with my documents. That note was from my lawyer."

"Will . . . will you return to San Francisco?"

Rod smiled, displaying a bright line of even, white teeth. "Will you miss me, *querida*?"

"Not likely!" shot back Julie.

"No, Julie, I will not return to San Francisco any time soon," Rod said, almost regretfully. "I must return to Rancho Delgado where Elena . . ."

"Of course," interjected Julie, feigning boredom. "Just make certain you speak to your lawyer about an annulment before you leave."

Slanting her an inscrutable look, Rod nodded his agreement. "I will leave some money with you should you decide to return east."

"Don't bother, I don't want your money," Julie returned hotly. "Goodbye, Don Rodrigo."

"*Adios, querida. Vaya con Dios.*" Then he was gone, leaving Julie with a strange feeling of emptiness.

3

The next day Julie discovered that Rod had left a substantial sum of money for her in Mac Parker's keeping. He also explained the situation between him and Julie to Mae who was sympathetic to Julie's circumstances but echoed Rod's words advising her to leave California and go back to her people.

"I know Don Rodrigo is a handsome devil, honey," Mae told her, "but he is right, you know. You are an Anglo, an American. He is a Californio, a man of proud Spanish stock. He belongs to a different world. Besides, he has been promised to another woman since he was a child."

"I know, Mae, and . . . and I can accept that," Julie contended. "But I will not leave California. Did Rod tell you about my father?"

"He mentioned him, Julie, but I'm afraid your search is destined for failure. Thousands of men disappear in the mountains never to be heard from again. Likely your father is one of those men."

"Not you too!" wailed Julie, disheartened. "Is everyone against me? I will stay! I will find my father!"

"I hope you do, honey. But, frankly, I never heard of him before you came. What is his first name?"

"His name is Carl, Carl Darcy. He's about forty-five, slightly balding, slender, blond like myself."

Mae shrugged. "Could be any one of dozens of men, Julie. I'm sorry, I don't remember him."

"That's all right, Mae. I'll find him."

Judging from the determined tilt to Julie's pointed chin, Mae decided that if Carl Darcy was alive his daughter was sure to find him. "What are your plans, honey?" she asked solicitously.

"A job," determined Julie resolutely. "I need a job. Can you help me?"

"That's easier said than done, Julie," Mae admonished. "I'm not sure there is an honest job for a decent girl in all of San Francisco. The Chinese found themselves ill-equipped to work the mines and more inclined to seek employment in the cities for a fraction of the normal wages. Of course," she paused dramatically, "there is always Casey's Pleasure Palace and a few other gambling halls and saloons that are constantly on the lookout for beautiful women."

"Mae!" chided Julie, highly incensed. "I'd have to be quite desperate to resort to that . . . that kind of work. Think, Mae, you know this town. Is there no one willing to give me a job in all of San Francisco?"

Pursing her lips in deep concentration, Mae wagged her head from side-to-side. "Julie, there just isn't . . . wait . . . of course . . . Marty. Marty Sloan. Many a time Marty said tō me she wished she could find some decent help."

"Who is Marty Sloan?" Julie asked, her curiosity piqued.

"She's a widow just like me. Only her husband died of snake bite back in '48 on their trek up from Texas while mine lost his life defending his claim against claim jumpers. We became friends. I opened a boarding house with what my husband left me and Marty took their savings and bought a huge tent. You might have seen it on your way here yesterday. She provides meals for the hundreds of men passing through the city. There aren't nearly enough restaurants to feed the hoards of men reaching San Francisco daily. I'm sure Marty would give you a job if I asked her."

"Perfect," clapped Julie, excited. "I'm certain one of those men who eat at Marty's will have heard of my father. Perhaps even know where he can be found. Thank you, Mae."

"Don't get your hopes up, Julie," Mae admonished, trying not to sound too discouraging.

"When can I start?"

"I'll take you over there myself after breakfast. But I feel duty bound to warn you."

"Warn me? About what?"

"Well," Mae said thoughtfully, searching for the right words, "Marty isn't exactly a lady like you and me. She's a tough woman forced to resort to violence at times to protect herself. She's a survivor, but don't let her rough exterior and salty speech fool you. Inside, her heart is as big as all outdoors. Just don't cross her and you'll get along fine."

Julie was to remember those words when she met the intimidating Marty Sloan. Nearly as tall as a man, Marty's ample girth was girdled with a belt and holster instead of an apron, the butt of a colt pistol prominently displayed. Though far from fat, Marty's raw-boned frame was well-padded. Her hair, once red and still abundant, was stuffed beneath a man's broad-brimmed hat. Her sharp brown eyes missed nothing when she was introduced to Julie.

"A might scrawny, ain't she, Mae?" Marty asked, eyeing Julie dubiously.

Julie bristled indignantly. "I'm healthy, strong and willing to work," she insisted, drawing herself up to her full five foot-three.

Marty grinned, displaying a mouthful of teeth stained by tobacco. "Cute little thing when she's got her feathers ruffled. What did you say your name was, gal?"

"Julie. Julie . . . Darcy." She had no intention of being known as Julie Delgado.

"Do you think you can wait tables, wash dishes and dodge horny customers trying to get their hands up your skirts?"

"Julie slanted a glance at Mae who raised her eyebrows as if to say, "I warned you."

"I think so," Julie declared with more confidence than she felt.

"Well then, get your tail in the kitchen while me and Mae have a little gab session."

In the kitchen Julie encountered a funny little Chinese man who told her his name was Wong Li. In pidgeon English he informed her that he performed the heavy tasks around the kitchen as well as waited on tables. The man looked so frail that Julie seriously doubted his ability to perform the heavy tasks he detailed.

While Mae and Marty chatted, Julie studied her surroundings. The food tent was monstrous. She was certain it could seat a hundred men at the long tables lined up in neat rows. The floor was dirt but painstakingly cleared of fallen scraps and debris. The large main door faced the street but there was a smaller rear door behind the cooking area. The kitchen itself wasn't a separate room but an open area set aside at the back of the tent sporting one of the few woodburning cookstoves in San Francisco. A good share of the cooking was done outdoors over open firepits behind the tent.

Before long Mae waved goodbye and Julie began what proved to be the most exhausting day of her entire life. Before she had time to breathe, the lunch crowd descended upon her and Julie suffered through the whistles and crude remarks of the rough men, most of whom were startled to find a beautiful young woman in their midst. When one man became overbold and squeezed Julie's breast in passing, causing her to cry out, Marty was immediately at her side, gun in hand.

"Do that one more time, Mel, and you won't have the balls to try it again," Marty threatened. The gun waved menacingly at the man's genitals.

"Shit, Marty, I was just funning," Mel said sheepishly, his eyes glued to the weapon in Marty's hand. "It won't happen again."

"See that it don't. That goes for every one of you misbegotten sons-of-bitches," Marty's gravely voice warned. "I'm mighty fond of this here little gal and don't take kindly to her being mauled by any of you scum. Do I make myself clear?"

There was some grumbling but the shouts of those in agreement soon drowned them out. After that, Julie was not bothered again. In fact, by the end of her first week of work she had gained the respect of nearly every one of Marty's customers. During that week she questioned dozens of men, hoping that at least one of them had heard of her father. But she was met with disappointment at every turn. It was as if her father had disappeared into thin air. But Julie refused to give up.

Not only was Julie under Marty's protective eye while on the job, but that protection extended until she reached the safety of Mae Parker's boarding house in the form of the funny little Chinese man, Wong Li. At first, when Marty insisted Wong Li accompany her home, Julie was openly skeptical of his ability to defend her should the need arise until she saw the man in action, using what Marty called martial arts, an ancient form of self-defense. After that demonstration she gratefully accepted the man's company, knowing herself to be safe from unwanted attention.

Julie learned that Marty knew about her and Rod. Mae had told Marty all about their strange relationship that first day. Several of the men also remembered that she and Rod had been married, had in fact witnessed the ceremony, and if they wondered about her status, they said nothing, fearful no doubt of Marty's wrath. There was one of Marty's customers who Julie came to fear. An ugly giant named Brute Kelly whose beady eyes followed her everywhere. Though he had made no untoward move thus far, Julie steered clear of him. She refrained from telling Marty of her fears, unwilling to cause trouble, especially since Kelly had not so much as spoken to her.

By the end of the second week Julie grew accustomed to the demands of her job. Though she fell into bed exhausted each night, it suited her just fine. It afforded her less time to think about Rod and the way he made her feel when he had kissed her and put his hands upon her body. She remembered distinctly the way her flesh tingled and burned at the touch of his lips and hands which had robbed her of reason and thought. Oh, but it was wicked to feel that way, Julie thought; to be so weak and spineless because of a stranger's touch.

She had met scores of men since Rod but not one of them could compare to him in stature and looks. He had a certain something that made her blood sing through her veins whenever his dark, brooding eyes fell on her. Would any other man affect her in the same way? Somehow she doubted it. But try as she might she was unable to put Rod from her mind. Not even when she imagined him in the arms of his Spanish fiancée.

Julie laughed to herself. It seemed ludicrous to think of Rod's bride-to-be when he already had a wife, although one of short duration. So far she had heard nothing from Rod's lawyer but supposed these matters took time.

One day Brute Kelly broke his silence by speaking to her, his words sending a cold chill down her spine. "Where's your 'greaser' husband, lady? Don't tell me he tired of you already?"

Julie looked around for help and frowned when she saw that most of the men had already left after the evening meal. Marty was outside dousing the fires and Wong Li was helping her. Julie tried desperately to push hcr way around Brute Kelly but he blocked her at every turn.

"What is it you want, Mr. Kelly?" Julie asked, plucking ineffectually at his huge hand as it curled around her upper arm.

"You, honey. I want you. If that damn don wouldn't have been so damned stubborn you'd be mine right now. I'd keep you too busy to work in this hash house, even if it meant spending most of the time on your back."

"If you persist in bothering me I'll make sure my husband learns of it when he returns," Julie bluffed.

"Who are you trying to fool?" Kelly laughed nastily. "It's a well known fact that Delgado has a woman stashed away on his ranch. You're nothing more than a bit of fluff who temporarily caught his eye. He left you, lady. You're up for grabs and I aim to stake my claim here and now."

Brute Kelly reached for Julie, catching her about her waist and slamming her up against his rock-hard body. Her cry of distress brought Marty racing from the kitchen which she had just entered through the back door. "Back off, you bastard," Marty's gravely voice warned, her mean-looking colt already in her hand, "or you'll find yourself with two new holes in your head to match those already there."

"Damn it, Marty, what's eating at you?" Kelly roared. "I ain't hurting the girl none. I just aim to be friendly."

Cocking a shaggy eyebrow, Marty asked, "Do you want Kelly for a friend, Julie."

"No! No, I don't," Julie quickly replied, her look of disgust telling Marty all she needed to know.

"Get out of here, Kelly," Marty ordered, bolstering her words with a wave of her pistol. "And don't come back. From now on you can find your meals elsewhere."

Releasing Julie, Kelly stepped backwards, slowly

inching his way to the door. "I'm going, Marty, no need to get nasty about it. I sure as hell ain't going to risk my neck over a piece of tail." Lowering his voice so only Julie could hear, he warned ominously, "I'll take care of you yet, bitch, when that mother hen ain't riding herd on you." Then he was gone, leaving Julie shaken but vastly relieved.

For the next two days Julie was watchful and on edge. But when Brute Kelly failed to return she breathed a sigh of relief, thinking she'd seen the last of him. Even Marty relaxed her vigilance when no other trouble presented itself in the form of Brute Kelly, though Wong Li still took the precaution of walking Julie home each night after work.

By the end of her second week with Marty, Julie began to feel like an old hand in the food tent. She had made many casual friends among the men hungry for a decent woman's company, but could not help but feel a great disappointment when she failed to uncover a clue to her father's whereabouts. Despite her failure, she refused to harbor thoughts that he might be dead.

Julie was exhausted that night when she and Wong Li left the food tent for home. The scant few blocks to the boarding house seemed like miles. There was a definite chill in the air and Julie pulled her warm cape tightly about her slim shoulders. Beside her, the taciturn Chinaman seemed impervious to the cold in his long colorful Chinese robe. The din coming from inside the dance halls and saloons was ear shattering and Julie was more than thankful that Mae's house was in a quieter section of town. She was equally grateful for Wong Li's protection, for since coming to San Francisco she learned that Rod was not exaggerating when he described the lawless situation existing in California. In 1850, the year that California became a state, more than fifty-thousand unsolved murders occurred, Julie learned.

It surprised Julie how often of late she thought of Rod. She had known him such a short time yet he had made a great impact on her life. She couldn't help but wonder what might have become of them if he wasn't obligated to return to his betrothed. Given the chance, would they ultimately have come to love one another? She realized it wouldn't be difficult to love the tall, handsome *caballero*. There were times even now . . . But she mustn't think of that. It was too late for them. Rodrigo Delgado wasn't for her, as Rod had so carefully pointed out.

Julie came out of her reverie to find that she was nearly home. She and Wong Li were just passing an extremely dark alley whose shadowy depths always made Julie nervous when disaster struck. Not even Wong Li's considerable knowledge of martial arts was able to prevent what happened, for the little man was struck from behind by an unseen assailant wielding a thick club. Without a sound he fell heavily to the ground. Julie opened her mouth to scream, but all except a muted squeak was stifled when a gag was rudely thrust between her open lips. Then she was dragged into the deserted alley and thrown into the bed of a horse-drawn wagon waiting nearby. Before she knew what was happening her hands and feet were tightly bound and a smelly canvas thrown over her body. The suffocating gag drastically cut off her air supply and the stifling canvas added the final insult. Great waves of dizziness surged around her and she sank into a deep void as blackness engulfed her. But not before she recognized the ugly face and leering grin of Brute Kelly!''

4

Don Rodrigo Delgado felt nothing but disgust with himself as he reined his horse before Mae Parker's boarding house. There was absolutely no reason for him to be back in San Francisco now that his mission was completed to his satisfaction. He had spent two grueling weeks in Monterey presenting documents and paying bribes until the courts were finally convinced of the legality of the Delgado claim. He had thought everything was settled before but when he reached Monterey he was told there was still some question concerning a section of land containing water rights.

Of course it was all a ruse to enable the courts to gain control of a valuable section of land so it could be deeded to a high ranking Anglo. But fortunately, Don Ricardo Delgado, the first Delgado who had been deeded the land by Spain two-hundred years ago, managed to hang onto the original papers defining borders and bounderies, which was more than many *rancheros* along El Camino Real were able to do.

It was a well known fact that many proud Castilian land owners died of starvation when they were forced from their lands. *Hidalgos* sometimes were forced to hire out as *vaqueros*, sometimes on the very land stolen from them. Rod's father, Don Diego, was one of the lucky ones inasmuch as his original grant was intact.

Elena's father was not so lucky. Gilberto Rodriguez y Montoya was in Spain right now trying to obtain proof

of his ancient land grant. Don Diego had offered his
home and his protection to Elena in Don Gilberto's
absence and Elena had come to live at *Rancho* Delgado
these past six months.

But now, as Rod stood before Mae's house, Elena
was the furthest thing from his mind. His wayward
thoughts were possessed by a honey-haired vixen with
eyes as blue as the sky over California and a lithe,
supple body with skin like pale satin. Rod had worried
incessantly about Julie during his absence; he knew
Julie was stubborn enough to remain in San Francisco
in spite of his dire warning. He felt obligated to return
to San Francisco and try to talk some sense into her one
last time. If necessary, Rod was prepared to put her
bodily aboard the first ship sailing east. Duty was the
only reason he returned, he told himself, ignoring the
tug at his heart whenever he allowed himself the luxury
of dwelling on those few glorious minutes when Julie
was on the verge of surrendering to him.

Shaking his head to clear it of such dangerous
thoughts Rod entered the house, calling out loudly for
Mae Parker. "Land sakes, Don Rodrigo," Mae chided,
wiping her hands on her apron, "must you bellow so?"
If she was surprised to see Rod she gave no hint of it.

"Where's my wife, Mae?" Rod asked, his eyes
darting impatiently toward the stairs.

Mae raised a shapely eyebrow, missing none of Rod's
proprietory tone regarding Julie or his impatience in
finding her. "She's not here yet, Rod. I'm expecting her
any minute."

"Not here!" stormed Rod. "Don't tell me she's out
roaming the streets at this time of night. How could you
allow such a thing when you know it's not safe?"

"Simmer down, son. Julie is in no danger."

"How do you know that?"

"Julie is working for Marty Sloan," Mae informed
Rod. "Marty's man, Wong Li, escorts her home each

night. And if you know Marty you know she won't let anything happen to that girl. Sit down," she invited, "Julie shouldn't be long."

Disdaining Mae's invitation, Rod said, "I had hoped Julie would be on her way east by now but I can see she chose to ignore my advice. How long has she been working for Marty? Has she gone through the money I left her already?"

"Since you left. And she hasn't touched a cent of that money."

Rod cursed. "*Por Dios*! Is she still bent on finding her missing father?"

"Yes, but so far not one clue has turned up." Mae paused, gazing at Rod thoughtfully. "Why are you here, Rod? You aren't doing Julie any good by complicating her life. What about the annulment?"

"Mae, I don't mean Julie any harm. I'm only thinking of her welfare. I . . . I couldn't return home until I know she is safely on her way back east where she belongs."

"Are you certain that is your only reason returning?" Mae probed relentlessly.

"What other—" Rod was never to finish his sentence.

At that precise moment Wong Li staggered through the door, dazed and bleeding profusely from a gash on his head.

"*Madre de Dios*!" exclaimed Rod. "Who is this man?"

"Wong Li, Marty's hired man," Mae said, rushing forward to help the wounded man. "What happened, Wong Li? Where is Julie?"

"Missy gone!" wailed Wong Li in a sing-song voice. "Missy gone."

"Gone?" sputtered Rod, fear and anguish a hard knot inside his chest. "Gone where?"

"Don't know," moaned the Chinaman. "Don't

know where missy go.''

Rod wanted to grab the little man and shake him until he made sense. Only Mae's restraining hand prevented him from doing so. "That won't help, Rod," she cautioned softly. "Let me try." Dully, Rod nodded.

"Wong Li," Mae began gently, "start from the beginning. Tell us what happened.''

"Missy gone," Wong Li repeated until Rod wanted to scream with frustration. "Wong Li walk missy home like always, only this time not the same. Man hit Wong Li from behind, wake up, find missy gone. Boss lady much angry with Wong Li when she find out. *Aiiee, aiiee*!" he wailed, shaking his head from side to side.

"You did your best Wong Li," Mae consoled. "Do you have any idea who hit you?"

"No see. Wong Li see no one. Wong Li hit from behind.''

"Have you any idea who could have done this?" cut in Rod, unable to hold his tongue a moment longer.

"Everyone love Missy Julie," said Wong Li. "Who wish to do her harm?''

"I don't know," Rod said, gritting his teeth. "But I certainly intend to find out." Mae watched him storm out, suddenly very sorry for the person or persons responsible for the abduction of Julie Darcy Delgado.

The first person Rod questioned was Marty Sloan who was just leaving her messhall. When informed of what had transpired she nearly went wild with rage. "Who would want to harm that sweet little gal?" Marty fumed. "I'll tear the bastard limb from limb when I find him.''

"You'll have to beat me to it, Marty," Rod grimly informed her, "for I intend to be there first. Think, Marty, please. Can't you think of anyone who would abduct Julie or wish her harm?''

"Hell's fire, Rod, there's no one who—'' Suddenly Marty went still, her eyes hard as marbles as an incident that took place days ago flashed before her eyes. "Why that ugly bastard!" she spat, eyes blazing, startling Rod.

"Who, Marty?" Rod demanded to know. "Tell me his name!"

"Brute Kelly, that's who," she bristled. "I chased him out of here a couple of weeks ago when I caught him pestering Julie. I thought I'd seen the last of that son-of-a-bitch."

"Brute Kelly, *Madre de Dios*," said Rod softly. Fear, stark and vivid, glittered in his eyes. Abruptly he wheeled, heading for the door.

"Rodrigo, wait for me!" Marty called out to his departing back.

"I can't wait, Marty. I have to find Julie before it's too late. Go over to Mae's and tell her I won't return until I find my wife." Cursing loudly Marty had no choice but to do as she was told.

Following Julie's route home proved futile. Those Rod questioned either had seen nothing or for reasons of their own preferred to keep what they knew to themselves. He was at his wit's end. He had no idea where Kelly could have taken Julie or what he intended to do with her, although Rod had an inkling of the fate that awaited her at the hands of Brute Kelly. No doubt Kelly meant to rape Julie. That was something, though unpleasant, she could live with. What Rod feared most was that the brute would kill her when he finished with her.

Rod had no idea what caused him to glance into the alley. But he thanked God that he did. On the ground, nearly obscured in the dark, was a small, black slipper that Rod recognized immediately as belonging to Julie. Using the skills he learned as a youth he found fresh tracks made by a horse pulling a four-wheeled vehicle. Rod was elated. Mounting his horse, sharp eyes glued to the ground, he tracked the wagon as it headed south along El Camino Real, offering a prayer of thanks for the brilliant moonlight.

Julie swam through layers of blackness to surface into a nightmare more terrifying than any dream. Brute Kelly, his ugly countenance set with salacious intent, was methodically tearing off her clothes and Julie shivered as the cold air touched her bare flesh. Her eyes flew open, finding it difficult to focus on her assailant.

Kelly sensed her awareness, smiling cruelly at her helplessness. "So you finally decided to join the living," he gibed crudely. "I would have waited, though. I like my women with a little life in them."

Julie began struggling, the gag preventing her from crying out. "Slut!" Kelly said, slapping her sharply across the face. "Hold still or I'll really hurt you. All I want to do is love you a little." Julie moaned as her last piece of clothing was rent in two and cast aside. Sheer, black fright shot through her.

Kelly began massaging Julie's breasts, laughing in triumph when her nipples, reacting to fear as well as to the icy air, drew up into tight buds. Kelly's mouth fastened onto one pink crest, his teeth clamping down cruelly. The scream of pain muffled by her bound mouth never left her throat as Kelly struggled to remove his own restricting clothing, cursing the limited space. Only then did Julie become aware of her surroundings, realizing that she lay on the hard boards of a wagon bed amid boxes and sacks of supplies.

Finally Kelly had his pants off and moved to position himself above Julie's slight form. He cut the ropes binding her legs together with his knife and spread her limbs wide apart. "I'm a lot better than that 'greaser' you married," he bragged. "Once you've had a real man between your legs you'll be begging me for more."

Finding her legs suddenly free, Julie began thrashing about, kicking with all her strength. While attempting to subdue her wild gyrations, Kelly caught the back of his hand on a sharp splinter protruding from a split board on the wagon's rough side. The splinter cut deeply, tearing the skin until a stream of bright blood spurted forth.

"Shit!" exploded Kelly, startled at the sudden pain, "You damn bitch!" He was so incensed by her continued struggles that he dealt her a stunning blow with his uninjured hand, sending her spinning into oblivion.

All resistance gone, Kelly returned to complete the act that was so rudely interrupted only moments before. Once again his hands dipped between Julie's now limp legs and in the process inadvertently smearing fresh blood from his injury along the smooth velvety skin of her inner thighs. His manhood, thick and purple, throbbing eagerly, sought entry at the virgin portals where no man had ventured before.

Brute Kelly never knew what hit him, so engrossed was he in his own pleasure. Without warning he was picked up bodily and thrown from the wagon by a spitting, snarling whirlwind of unleashed violence. When he finally recognized his enraged assailant all he could do was groan out his name, "Delgado, damn you!"

Rod, an expert in tracking his prey, even in the dark, abruptly came upon the wagon parked just off the trail in the chaparral. At first he saw no sign of life, but then the struggles being waged in the wagon bed caught hs attention and he slithered along the ground stealthily until, with a tremendous roar of outrage, he flung himself upon the man laboring above the inert form of the woman beneath him. Intense rage added to Rod's already considerable strength as he lifted Kelly's huge frame and tossed him effortlessly from the wagon, falling upon him with a vengeance. The only thing that saved Kelly's life was a muffled groan coming from the wagon bed. Fearing that Julie might be badly injured, Rod left Kelly lying on the ground more dead than alive and rushed to the aid of his wife.

Julie lay unmoving amidst the tattered remnants of her torn clothing, her bruised body pale in the filtered moonlight. Acting swiftly, Rod retrieved the blanket roll from the back of his saddle and tenderly wrapped it about her chilled flesh, murmuring soothing words meant to console her. When he spied the smeared blood between Julie's outstretched thighs his gentle words turned to loud curses, all evidence pointing to her brutal ravishment by Brute Kelly. A growl of outrage tore through his throat as he turned from his wife, fully intending to finish off the despicable raper of innocent virgins.

But when Rod turned back to where he left Kelly lying on the ground, he was startled to find that the man had roused himself sufficiently to crawl off into the shadows and disappear while Rod had been busy tending Julie. Another moan coming from the wagon bed dissuaded him from giving chase and he hurried back to his wife's side to find her coming out of her swoon, wide-eyed with fright.

Kneeling by her side, he tenderly gathered her shaking form in his arms. "You're safe, *querida*," he crooned softly, rocking her back and forth like a hurt child. "No one will harm you again. I'll take care of you."

Julie's fuzzy brain registered the fact that a man she had never thought to see again was holding her in his arms, whispering words of comfort and love. If she was dreaming she wished never to awaken. "Rod?" she managed to croak. "Is it really you? How . . . ? I don't understand how—"

"I'll answer all your questions later," he quickly assured her. "After I get you back to the boarding house. Will you be all right in the back of the wagon?" Julie nodded, too stunned and bruised to speak.

Rod wasted no time in tying the reins of his own horse to the back of the wagon, pulling himself onto the seat and driving as fast as the darkness and Julie's comfort allowed. It was nearly dawn when finally he carried a sleeping Julie into the house.

Three people immediately rushed up to greet him. "Thank God, you've found her," Mae breathed, heaving a great sigh of relief. "Is . . . is she . . . all right?"

"Did that bastard hurt her?" asked Marty, her lip curled into a snarl. Wong Li stood beside Marty, silent concern etching his worn features.

"Julie is sleeping," Rod said quietly, cradling her inert form in his arms. "I believe she'll be all right once she recovers from the shock. She is strong and will soon forget what that bastard did to her." Though Rod did not put it into words, his meaning was all too clear.

"Oh, no!" uttered Mae softly, the back of her hand muffling the sound. "How could he? How could he hurt a sweet innocent thing like that?"

Marty exploded into a tornado of fury. "I hope you killed that no good skunk," she sputtered loudly, her face flushed with anger. "Did you make him suffer first?"

"He got away, Marty," Rod admitted sourly. "Julie needed immediate attention and Kelly crawled away into the darkness while my back was turned. But I can't concern myself with him now. I must see to my wife."

"I'll help you," Mae offered quickly.

"No!" said Rod, startling her with his vehemence. "I . . . I'll do it myself. You've been up all night and your other boarders will be wanting breakfast soon. Just send up some hot water."

"Well," said Mae skeptically, "if you say so."

"I'll manage," replied Rod grimly, starting up the stairs with his slight burden.

"I'd better get back to work, too," declared Marty, looking around for Wong Li. But the Chinaman had mysteriously departed only moments before, his yellow features set in hard lines.

Julie awoke while Rod was bathing her. "Rod," she whispered weakly, "I wasn't dreaming. It is you. You are here."

"I'm here," Rod said grimly. "But *madre mio*, Julie, I was too late!"

"Too late?" asked Julie, dazed. "If you hadn't arrived when you did, Kelly would have killed me. I'm sure of it."

"Don't think about it, *querida*," Rod soothed gently. "If only I hadn't left you on your own that beast wouldn't have raped you. I should have been more persistent. I should have put you aboard the first ship going east."

"Raped!" repeated Julie, stunned by Rod's words. "He couldn't have! I would know if I had been raped. I'm sure you're wrong, Rod."

Rod wanted to tell her about the blood and all the other signs pointing to her rape by Brute Kelly but was too much of a gentleman to divulge all the hard, cruel facts. "Do you hurt badly?" he asked softly, gently.

"No . . . I . . . I feel nothing. He . . . Kelly, knocked me unconscious. He could have raped me but I'm certain he didn't. Could . . . could you have been mistaken? Surely I am capable of determining if my own body had been violated."

"Perhaps," Rod hedged, refusing to meet her questioning gaze. "Perhaps it is best we forget Kelly and all that happened." If she didn't want to face up to what had happened to her, Rod decided, then that's the way it would be. He realized that rape was a terrible thing for a woman to experience and he was far too honorable to mention it again.

"Relax, *querida*," he urged, his face tender as he laved her bruised flesh. "Kelly won't hurt you again. I'm going to take care of you from now on." He finished his gentle ministrations and sat back, studying

Julie with quiet concern. Her right eye was beginning to swell and turn purple and a reddish bruise covered one cheekbone.

"Take care of me?" Julie repeated dumbly. "What do you mean?"

"*Querida*, I feel a responsibility towards you," Rod explained patiently. "After Kelly ra—, after he hurt you, I can no longer shirk my responsibility. My duty is clear."

"What are you talking about, Rod?" Julie asked, still mystified.

"I'm taking you home with me, Julie. To *Rancho* Delgado. You are my wife and I owe you my protection."

Julie gasped, shocked by his surprising declaration. "What about Elena? What will your father say? What . . ."

"One thing at a time, *querida*. It matters little what anyone thinks. By the time we arrive we will be truly wed."

His words confused Julie. Weren't they already married? Surely it was too soon for the annulment to be granted, wasn't it? She asked him, his answer astounding her.

"I . . . haven't spoken to my lawyer yet concerning our annulment," Rod admitted, flustered. If the truth be known he had plenty of time to speak to his lawyer but somehow he kept putting it off until it was too late and he was already on his way to San Francisco. The reason behind the procrastination escaped him but the way things turned out it was just as well.

"I don't understand," Julie said, more baffled than ever. "You said—"

"Forget what I said," Rod stated more harshly than he meant to. "You are my responsibility. I shouldn't have married you but I did. From now on I'll take care of everything."

Despite her deep fatigue, despite her bruised and aching body, Julie's anger erupted. "I refuse to become someone's 'responsibility.' I will not be treated like a possession and an unwanted one at that," Julie fumed, incensed by Rod's lack of sensibility. She would be a burden to no man. "I don't need your protection. You don't love me and I certainly don't love you! Do you think your father will accept me as your wife? No! Neither will Elena. It's impossible, Rod. This whole situation is impossible," she contended. "It can't be and you know it."

"It will be, *querida*," Rod schooled sternly. "I won't hear another word about it. Our marriage will not be disputed. The strict code of honor under which I was raised demands I do this. You are my wife and nothing or no one will change that."

Julie sighed heavily, too weary to protest further. Sensing her exhaustion Rod rose to leave. "Sleep, *querida*," he advised. "When you awaken it will all seem like a bad dream. When you are fully recuperated we will leave for my *hacienda*."

Two days later Julie found herself bidding a tearful farewell to both Mae Parker and Marty Sloan. No matter how long and hard she had protested, in the end she was forced to comply with Rod's wishes. Not even her argument of continuing her search for her father served to dissuade him from his misplaced sense of duty toward her. In Julie's estimation their loveless marriage was destined for more trouble than either of them was prepared to face.

In the two days and nights prior to their departure Rod made no demands upon her, leaving her in Mae's capable hands while he prepared for their trip down El Camino Real to San Luis Obispo. Perhaps he had no intention of consummating their marriage, Julie thought dismally, suddenly recalling how her body had once come alive under his hands and lips. No doubt he now thought her not good enough for him and wanted no part of her. Well, that was all right with her, she decided evasively. She had no desire to experience a man's lust again. Brute Kelly had cured her of all her girlish romantic notions with his attempted rape, for Julie knew he had not completed his vile act.

Finally, all her goodbyes were said and Rod was loading her belongings in the bed of the wagon which also contained an assortment of supplies needed for their journey south. Because Julie could not ride, the wagon was necessary. Rod's own mount was tied behind the disreputable but sturdy vehicle.

"Are you ready, *querida*?" Rod asked in an attempt to hasten their departure. "It grows late."

"You bring her back, Don Rodrigo, you hear?" commanded Mae, swiping a roughened hand across her misting eyes. "It's not so far that you can't visit once in a while."

"I promise," laughed Rod, boosting Julie onto the springless seat.

Before long the wagon was traveling along the forty-foot planked toll road that led out of San Francisco's muddy business district and which ended abruptly at Sixteenth Street. Soon even the wheel ruts and prints of animals and men disappeared into the grassy fields. The dunes in the background were studded with chaparral. Julie gazed dispassionately at the cattle grazing for miles between peninsula foothills and the wide southern arm of San Francisco Bay.

El Camino Real, the king's road, was the name given to the old mission trail, Julie knew from what Rod told her, consisting sometimes of nothing more than rude paths connecting San Francisco with San Diego, an arduous six to eight day journey. It would take over four days and nights just to reach San Luis Obispo.

Along El Camino Real lay the missions established by the Franciscans as early as 1769. Now, the chain of

adobe buildings stretched from San Diego to San
Francisco. In 1833 the Secularization Act doling out
half the holdings of prosperous missions and settle-
ments to the state vastly reduced the missions. The other
half was divided among Indians capable of living
independently of the missions. The Franciscans were
then relegated to nothing more than curates as the
missions were turned into parishes.

Their first day along the trail was exhausting as well
as nervewracking for Julie. Rod not only kept his pistol
at the ready but a rifle placed at his feet for added
protection. He patiently explained the need for caution.

"Brigands and *banditos* frequently travel these roads
in search of easy prey, *querida*. No one knows the actual
count of the number of persons who met violent deaths
along El Camino Real. Robbery, murder, even
lynchings are common occurrences."

Julie suppressed a shudder, imagining a brigand
behind every dune and rock waiting to pounce upon
them. At noon the first day they had lunch at the
Grizzly Bear, a well known roadhouse. That night Rod
secured a room for them at the Nightingale. Julie was
relieved when he made a pallet on the floor for himself
and fell immediately asleep.

The next day, after having lunch at the Mansion
House, Rod informed Julie that civilization for them
would end at the Red House Inn. From this point on,
they would sleep in the wagon during the remainder of
their journey.

The going was sometimes rough, the paths taking
them at times along stretches of road hugging mountain
sides, through swollen streams and across miles of
parched semi-dry desert country. Julie held her breath
each time they began yet another of the steep climbs and
descents, but Rod's expert driving brought them
through safely. After all, he was no stranger to the
pitfalls of El Camino Real.

That evening Rod built a fire and Julie prepared a simple meal of beans, bacon, biscuits and coffee. While she cleaned up, Rod made their beds amid the sacks and barrels, laying down a thick pad of blankets. When it was time to retire he thoughtfully turned his back while Julie slipped off her dress and slid between the rough blankets wearing nothing but her thin chemise. She did the same for Rod until she felt him settle down beside her, squirming to make himself comfortable.

Because of their close quarters Julie could feel the heat of Rod's body scorching her along one side. She felt him shudder at the contact and flushed, mistaking his reaction for revulsion. Was he still thinking about Brute Kelly and how he had laid hands upon her, she wondered? Did he think she had enjoyed his foul touch? Finally, she felt him relax and allowed sleep to overtake her.

Sometime during the night, the wind arose and Julie instinctively moved closer to Rob, seeking his warmth. As if to hold her in place, Rob threw a leg over her slight form, his body half covering hers. Julie awoke with a start, suddenly aware of the weight pressing down upon her. She screamed, reliving in her mind that horrible moment when Brute Kelly was attacking her even though she remembered very little of it.

"No! No!" she cried out, thrashing about wildly. "Please don't hurt me!"

Abruptly, Rod awoke to find Julie in his arms, crying out and fighting off an imaginary assault. "Julie, it's Rod," he soothed gently. "No one will hurt you, *mi amor*, Kelly is dead. He won't be able to harm anyone again."

His words must have gotten through to her for she immediately calmed down. "Kelly is dead?" she repeated dully. "How do you know? Did you . . . are you the one who—"

"No, *querida*," Rod admitted ruefully, "but I wish I

had been the one to snuff out his worthless life.''

"Then, who—''

"No one knows. He was found along the trail the day after . . . after . . . he abducted you. His tongue was missing and so were his . . . genitals.''

"My God!'' gasped Julie, hiding her head against Rod's shoulder.

"He bled to death. Some think *banditos* were the culprits but I'm more inclined to think the Tong responsible for the killing.''

"The Tong?''

"A secret Chinese society that seeks their revenge by cruel, almost inhuman methods. I believe your friend, Wong Li, had a hand in it.''

"I'm not sorry he's dead,'' Julie grimaced, "but the method, it's . . . it's . . .'' She shuddered, unable to continue.

Suddenly aware of the thinly clad form burrowing into the protection of his arms, Rod's body reacted violently. For days he had fought against his rising need for this honey-haired enchantress, deliberately turning his back upon her, sleeping apart so as not to become aroused by her nearness. *Por Dios*, he wanted her! And now, here she was, pressed intimately against his growing hardness. Instinctively his arms tightened and Julie cried softly against the pressure.

Without warning Rod's lips found hers in the darkness. At first his kiss was gentle, but swiftly turned hungry, possessive, his hot tongue driving into her mouth to ravish the velvet recesses within. One kiss melted into another until it became a continuous blending of their bodies. Against her will, her lips parted to the sweet, hot thrust of his tongue. The kiss was the magic that released her response.

Their bodies touched, clung and molded together as his lips slid from her mouth, along the long column of her throat, settling finally at the hollow where a tiny pulse beat furiously. Julie sighed as Rod impatiently slid her chemise from her shoulders to her waist. When his greedy mouth found an engorged nipple she grew weak with desire as his rough tongue lapped lovingly at the tender bud.

"I want you, *mi amor*," Rod whispered hoarsely.

Julie's voice cracked but she mastered it as she replied. "I . . . I thought that . . . that you didn't want me, that I wasn't good enough for you."

"I wanted you from the first moment I saw you," admitted Rod in a burst of insight, "but knew that we had no future together. Kelly succeeded in bringing us together as no one else could. Now that I have been forced into this marriage, I feel free to take you with no regrets."

Julie froze, his words like a dash of cold water in her face. It was obvious to her that Rod held no feelings for her other than lust. He wanted her, that much was true, and felt an obligation, enforced by his strict code of ethics. He felt dutybound to protect her but other than that cared nothing for her. It was Elena he loved. At that moment her future seemed bleak and she began to struggle against Rod's passion and her own rising ardor.

"Don't fight against it, *querida*," Rod urged when he felt her stiffen in his arms. "We both want this. Relax, I won't hurt you the way Kelly did. I haven't approached you before because I thought to give you time to recuperate from your ordeal."

"You're wrong, Rod. I don't want this. Let this be a marriage in name only," pleaded Julie.

Rod laughed harshly, crudely running a hand over her breasts and hips. "Would you deny me your lovely body? I think not, *querida*. I don't intend to live like a eunuch. I also want a family. You will serve the purpose for which God made you, whether you like it or not. You'll find I'm quite expert at making love."

Julie's angry retort died in her throat as Rod's mouth

slammed down against hers, plundering the sweet, velvet depths with his stabbing tongue. Julie moaned in protest against the violence of his passion but it did no good. She was powerless against Rod's superior strength. If he chose to exercise his marital rights at this time it was his prerogative to do so and all her struggles went for naught.

Within minutes Rod had her chemise worked down over her hips and kicked to one side. His trousers soon lay beside it. What followed was a sweet assault upon her senses as Rod sought to prove his prowess as a lover. His hands teased her breasts until they blossomed into peaks of sensual awareness, his touch deliberate, yet honey-smooth as they slid down to her hips and below. Against her will Julie felt herself filling with a fever born of growing passion.

"*Querida*, your skin is like smooth alabaster, so cool, yet hot to my touch," Rod murmured, his mouth playing a tune of sweet pleasure upon her heated flesh. "How I've dreamed of burying myself deep in your body. *Bruja* . . . witch. Only a witch could entrance me as you have."

Rod's long fingers, light and teasing, moved unerringly to the honey-gold triangle nestled between her thighs, tangling in the silky mound before exploring further. Julie could not suppress a groan of pleasure. She nearly screamed aloud as his finger caressed her flesh in a circular motion that drove her wild with wanting. Each tremor that began in the pit of her stomach drove flashes of lightning along her nerves to every part of her body. When he deemed her moist and receptive, he pushed her knees apart.

Easing himself between her thighs he began to penetrate her, hesitantly at first, then more forcefully. Julie arched her back until she felt sharp stabs of pain radiating from the point of his deep thrusts. Uncontrollable gasps of pain escaped her lips and her eyes glazed over. The agony drove all thoughts of passion from her body and she was filled with confusion and resentment.

When Rod finally realized that he was in a passage where no man before before him had entered, it was too late to stop. The thin veil of her viginity was all that stood between him and the greatest pleasure he had ever known. Pulling nearly all the way out he thrust forward strongly, eliciting a muffled gasp from Julie as he sheathed himself completely in her tight flesh. Realizing that the pain of being deflowered had killed her ardor, Rod finished quickly.

Disappointment clouded Julie's face as Rod swiftly brought himself to a climax and lay quietly beside her. How could anything that started out so beautifully end in such pain, she wondered?

"You're a virgin," Rod accused irrationally, momentarily forgetting that it was he who had drawn the wrong conclusion in the first place.

"You were the one who insisted I had been raped!" shot back Julie. "I tried to tell you it wasn't so. It's my body and I would know had I been violated."

"*Por Dios*!" Rod cursed. "I would not have touched you had I thought you were still a virgin. Nor would I have been so persistent about honoring my commitment to you."

Julie fumed in impotent rage. "Take me back to San Francisco and get your damn annulment. We can forget this ever happened. It seems to me that lovemaking is vastly overrated anyway and I have no desire to partake further."

Rod smiled wickedly. "It's done, *querida*. If a child is born in nine months I will have no doubt as to its paternity."

"A child!" gasped Julie as if the idea were repugnant to her. "I . . . I hadn't thought about that."

"And as to your disappointment," Rod continued

smoothly, "it is always that way the first time. In a moment I will remedy that."

Julie was surprised when he began the ritual again, but even more astonished that her body eagerly responded while her mind fought the delightful sensations wrought by his hands and mouth. She had no wish to be used for pleasure alone, but with Rod's hands on her and his mouth searching out every crevice and curve she could only hope that he would not leave her empty and unfulfilled again.

But she need not have worried. This time when Rod entered her there was no pain, and when he began to move, her body easily learned the rhythm, matching his thrusts stroke for stroke. This time he took her all the way. A warmth radiated in her loins and spread through her body in undulating waves until, reaching her throat, she cried out her joy. Only then did Rod allow his own passion to explode in a climax more dramatic than any he had ever known. Had Rod cared to look he would have seen a sense of wonder in Julie's expression.

Julie was only half awake when she threw off the constricting blanket covering her nude body. The sun had already risen and perspiration beaded her glistening flesh. A playful breeze tickled her damp stomach and Julie sighed and rolled over in in order to seek a more comfortable spot. This placed her in a vulnerable position with her rounded rump thrust deliciously upward. A yelp of outrage rose in her throat when a heavy hand connected painfully with her exposed flesh.

"Get up," a rough voice ordered. "You've slept long enough. We have one more stop to make before I can take you home."

Julie rolled over to face a glowering Rod. There was no trace of the tender lover of the night before in either his stern countenance or cold voice. It was as if last night had never happened. Did he still feel that she had somehow trapped him into marriage? Julie wondered.

He should have believed her when she told him that Brute Kelly hadn't raped her. Besides, it was Rod's fault for making love to her in the first place. She would still be a virgin but for his uncontrollable lust.

"Did you hear, Julie?" Rod repeated. "I said get up. I want to be at the mission by noon." Though his voice was cold, his eyes kindled as he continued to stare at her, moving from her breasts to stomach, and lower still.

Only then did Julie realize that she was completely nude and she flushed hotly as she felt her breasts firm and thrust pertly upward beneath his probing gaze. Belatedly she reached for the blanket. Muttering an oath, Rod turned on his heel and left her to dress in private.

If Julie was puzzled by Rod's strange behavior, Rod was even more confused. He had awakened shortly after dawn feeling more at peace and relaxed than he had in a long, long time. Julie's nude body was nestled trustingly in his arms, her head tucked beneath his chin. In his mind he relived every moment of their lovemaking the night before, and became so aroused he nearly awakened her to enjoy again the passion that had passed between them.

But then he had remembered that he had married Julie under a misconception. That she hadn't been raped by Kelly as he first believed. In assuming a responsibility toward Julie he was knowingly disregarding a far greater obligation; one of long standing. His father would never forgive him for bringing home an Anglo bride and he certainly had earned Elena's contempt for breaking his marriage contract.

Why? he asked himself bitterly. Rod knew the answer to that question immediately. He had lusted after a honey-haired witch, married her before he had gained his good senses, then foolishly left her at the mercy of men like Brute Kelly. Even if he hadn't been the one to deflower her, responsibility for her welfare still would weigh heavily upon him. *Caramba!* he cursed beneath his breath. If Julie would have returned east none of this would have happened. As it turned out he was saddled with a wife he didn't want, an irate father and a fiancée—or ex-fiancée—who was likely to slit his throat.

5

As soon as Julie dressed and they wolfed down their meager breakfast, they continued their journey south. The weather was milder than in San Francisco and Julie enjoyed the gentle sunshine warming her back and shoulders. In New York it would be snowing, she thought idly.

Rod had hardly spoken to her all morning. Whenever she ventured a tentative smile in his direction she was met by cold indifference. Even her attempts at conversation fell upon deaf ears. Finally, she gave up, deciding she could be just as taciturn and unpleasant as Rod. How could he expect their marriage to work if he continued to blame her for something that was none of her doing, she sniffed angrily.

After Rod had made love to her and she learned she could become pregnant from their encounter, Julie decided she would do her best to make their marriage successful. She probably could have done a lot worse than marry a man like Rod Delgado. It could well have been someone like Brute Kelly. After all, she took her chances when she joined Polly in this madcap venture. If only Rod's father wasn't so dead set against an American daughter-in-law perhaps she and Rod might have a chance. And then she remembered Elena, the woman Rod was to marry.

"We're nearly there," Rod announced sullenly, breaking into her reverie.

"At your *rancho*?"

"No. At the mission of San Luis Obispo. We'll be stopping there first."

"Why? Shouldn't we go on if you intend to reach your *hacienda* by dark?"

Just then Julie caught sight of the mission rising in the distance. The crude adobe and brick building with red tile roof was founded in 1772 by Father Serra and surrounded by a small town of sorts. The town consisted of one or two *cantinas*, a few shops, and several adobe houses sporting ominous iron shutters at the windows and doors. When Julie questioned Rod he told her that outlaws and bandits frequently raided the area and residents resorted to the ironwork for protection.

As they approached the mission Julie could see that it was in need of repairs and obviously poor. Several Indian children played in the yard while their parents worked the fields nearby or cared for the animals.

The mission had solid, massive, stucco-covered adobe walls with broad undecorated wall faces built around a patio with a garden. Arcaded corridors and low-pitched red tile roofs with wide projecting eaves protected the inhabitants from rain and wind. Several smiling children ran up to Julie and Rod as they descended from their wagon, chattering in Spanish. Rod smiled, judiciously handing out coins and patting dark, shining heads.

"You spoil them, Don Rodrigo."

Julie looked up to see a small, dark man approaching through one of the arcaded corridors. His brown, cowled robe proclaimed him to be one of the Franciscans. From a rope belt around his waist hung a set of prayer beads and his sandaled feet slapped noisily against the hard-packed sand. A fringe of hair surrounded a nearly bald head but the *padre's* gentle expression gave the impression of suffering and deprival.

"*Buenas dias, Padre*, it's good to see you again,"

greeted Rod affably. "Have you been saving many souls in my absence?"

"As many as God allows," smiled the *padre*. "But you know my duties are more than just priest. To my people I am farmer, businessman, trader, doctor, teacher, builder, whatever is necessary. My children look to me for all manner of guidance."

"Ah, *Padre*," mocked Rod, laughing, "you are indeed a wonder."

"You jest, of course, Don Rodrigo, but who else is there to teach our less fortunate brothers to make blankets, tan hides, manufacture shoes, make soap and pottery, mill flour, and care for themselves, if not for the Franciscan fathers?"

"I'm sure your efforts will be rewarded by God," replied Rod seriously.

All the time Rod and the priest talked, Julie stood silently by. Their entire conversation was conducted in Spanish, of which she understood little. She shifted uncomfortably from foot to foot while they continued speaking, ignoring her completely.

If Julie thought the two men had deliberately ignored her she would have been shocked to learn they were now discussing her. "I would have a favor of you, *Padre*," Rod said, lowering his voice conspiratorially.

"Does it concern the woman with you, my son?" asked the *padre*, sparing a glance in Julie's direction.

"*Si, Padre*," admitted Rod. "I wish you to marry us."

"No! Impossible! Have you forgotten? You are already betrothed to Dona Elena."

Rod flushed guiltily at the *padre's* shocked expression. He realized that the priest could not be half as surprised as his own father when he learned what Rod had done. "Would you have my child born a bastard?" he asked quietly.

"But she is an Anglo," sputtered the good *padre*. "I have known you all your life, Don Rodrigo. Whatever possessed you to take such a woman? Grant you she is lovely, but the kind of woman who comes to California can be nothing more than a *puta* . . . a prostitute.''

"You are wrong, *Padre*," Rod countered firmly. "Julie is a young, innocent girl. I took her virginity and am bound by honor to marry her."

"But, Rodrigo, an Anglo?" the *padre* protested. "She is probably not even of our faith. Would it not better serve your honor if you found another man to wed her?"

Rod bristled indignantly. "And if there is a child of our union? Should I allow another man to claim what is mine?"

The priest shrugged helplessly. "It will anger your father greatly, not to mention Dona Elena, but I will do what I must." Then he turned to Julie, stretched out a calloused hand and said in broken English, "Welcome to the mission of San Luis Obispo, child. I am called *Padre* Juan."

Julie smiled shyly, accepting the proffered hand warmly. "Thank you, *Padre* Juan. Your mission is very impressive."

Rod relaxed visibly, sensing that his first obstacle had been met and surmounted with *Padre* Juan's acceptance of Julie. My . . . wife's name is Juliet, *Padre*," Rod said, stumbling slightly over his words.

"Appropriate," mumbled *Padre* Juan, thinking of the ill-fated Romeo and Juliet. "Come inside children and rest while I prepare for the ceremony."

Julie stopped short. "Ceremony? What ceremony?"

"I am to marry you and Don Rodrigo," informed the priest.

"But we are already married," protested Julie.

Padre Juan's dark eyes glared accusingly at Rod. "You may be wed but certainly not in the eyes of God. Don Rodrigo is well aware that his father will never accept a marriage performed by anyone but a priest according to the rites of the Holy Church. And even then his blessing will not be easily won.''

When Julie still hesitated, Rod grasped her hand and pulled her with him into the cool building. The priest led them to a small, crudely furnished room and bade Julie enter and rest until she was summoned. When the door closed, Rod had departed with the holy man and she found herself alone.

Julie paced nervously for several minutes, barely aware of her surroundings. Why was Rod marrying her again, she wondered? If he didn't consider himself truly wed before, why marry her now in his church? How less complicated things would be if he just returned her to San Francisco where they could live their separate lives as if they had never met. The chance that she would become pregnant from their one encounter seemed so remote as to not even exist. All he had to do was wait a month to find out if his seed took hold before he brought her before a priest. Julie knew enough about the Catholic religion to know that once they exchanged vows before a priest they would be irrevocably bound. She could not understand the code of honor that dictated their marriage just because Rod had taken her virginity, especially in the face of such irreconcilable differences. The least of which were Rod's disapproving father and jilted bride-to-be.

A mute Indian boy brought a large pitcher of water and Julie ceased her silent ragings to enjoy the unexpected luxury of washing all over. After her bath she tested the crude but clean bed and, finding it surprisingly comfortable, fell immediately asleep. She knew nothing more until she awoke abruptly to find a plump Indian woman shaking her. It was dark outside and a single candle sputtered feebly on the nightstand.

The woman said something in Spanish and motioned toward the chair, grinning broadly. Julie looked in the direction of her gesture and was stunned to see a

beautiful white outfit carefully laid out. She arose,
rubbed her eyes and carefully inspected the lovely
garments made almost entirely of delicate lace. The
woman, whose name Julie learned was Rosa, called the
blouse a *camisa*. It had short, puffed sleeves ending at
the elbow and a low neckline adorned with a wide ruffle.
The skirt consisted of yards of ruffled lace ending at the
ankle which Julie thought indecent. A lace mantilla to
cover her hair and low heeled white slippers completed the outfit surely meant to be her wedding
dress. Julie could not imagine where Rod had obtained
such a lovely garment on such short notice.

After Rosa helped Julie dress and comb her long hair,
she guided the bride to the chapel. Julie found the
chapel lavishly appointed, even rich, considering the
crude state of the rest of the mission. She could detect
the sparkle of gold in the tall candlesticks, chalice,
statues and huge cross that adorned the wall over the
altar.

Rod stepped out of the shadows and Julie gasped at
his imposing figure clad entirely in black and silver. He
resembled a handsome pirate in his tight black trousers,
short black jacket lavishly trimmed in silver and tall
shiny boots made of expensive leather. Though she
could not read the expression on his face, Julie thought
she detected a glimmer of approval in his dark eyes as
she approached the altar where *Padre* Juan stood
waiting to begin the ceremony.

When Julie reached Rod's side the tension between
them almost crackled. Whatever they felt for one
another certainly was not apathy. By the time *Padre*
Juan began the ceremony, Julie's legs were shaking. The
thought that this arrogant, intimidating man, often
moody, yet capable of reducing her to the consistency of
jelly, would have complete control over her life, was
truly frightening.

As if sensing her thoughts, Rod squeezed her hand

and whispered softly, "Courage, *querida*. Would you have the *padre* think you are a reluctant bride?"

Julie slanted him a quelling look but nevertheless stiffened her slim shoulders as she gave the correct responses during the blessedly brief ceremony witnessed by several of *Padre* Juan's flock. She lifted shocked eyes to Rod when he grasped her hand and slipped a heavy gold band on her finger. Suddenly it was over and Julie followed Rod from the chapel to the small dining room where *Padre* Juan joined them for a hastily prepared wedding feast.

"You look lovely, *querida*," Rod said as he gallantly seated her.

"The dress is beautiful," Julie acknowledged. "Where did you get it on such short notice? Surely it isn't the dress your . . . Elena . . . was to wear."

"Even I would not stoop to such a gesture," Rod said, somewhat hurt by her low opinion of him. "The dress you are wearing, even my own clothing, was meant for another *caballero* and his betrothed. The clothes will be cleaned and returned in time for their wedding. I would not have my bride clothed in rags for this important occasion."

Before she could answer, Rosa served their food on large platters and Julie devoted herself to the plain but savory fare. Besides *frijoles* (delicious beans mashed and fried in bacon drippings), there were *enchiladas*, *quesadillas* and *tortillas*, circles of thin flour dough rolled and filled with bits of meat, beans and cheese, some in a rich red sauce and some plain. The meal ended with a flaky custard pastry and cups of thick sweetened chocolate whipped to a froth.

Julie had barely finished her last morsel of dessert when Rod abruptly arose from the table. "*Padre* Juan has suggested we spend the night at the mission and I have accepted, Julie," he informed her, moving to help her from her chair. "It grows late. Bid the good *padre* goodnight.'' Julie felt herself grow warm beneath his hot gaze as she rose stiffly and made her exit after a hasty word to the bemused priest.

Rod was but a step behind her when she entered the small room assigned to them. Her stomach jumped convulsively when she heard the key scrape in the rusty lock. She turned to face him. His closeness had a physical impact on her and she felt herself grow giddy and weightless. Strange, exotic fantasies began to bite into her thoughts as his dark eyes visibly undressed her.

Rod made no effort to conceal his appraisal as his hot gaze traveled boldly from her face to her soft, rapidly rising and falling breasts, to the gentle swell of hips beneath the thin lace gown. ''You're beautiful, *mi alma*,'' he breathed, his words uneven and heavy with passion. ''Your enticing body is one of the benefits of this contrived marriage that I intend to enjoy fully.''

Julie bristled, her eyes shooting blue flames. ''And if I refuse you?'' she shot back caustically. ''What then?''

''You have no choice, *querida*,'' Rod grinned, amusement curving his sensual lips. ''I told you before I won't live as a eunuch. I expect children of this union. The sooner the better.'' By now he was standing before her, close enough to feel her soft breath against his cheek.

''You arrogant ba—'' The sentence died in her throat as Rod curled one arm about her tiny waist and pulled her roughly against his tough, sinuous body. His other hand moved to the center of her back, forcing her straining breasts against his chest while he smothered her lips with demanding mastery.

A lightning bolt seared her mouth and burned far down into her body. Strangely soft, yet violently demanding, an odd blending of fierceness and tenderness, his lips covered hers and she shuddered, silently cursing herself for succumbing to the forceful domination of his mouth. Her senses reeled as if short circuited when he parted her lips with his tongue to ravish the honey-sweet recesses within.

As if by magic, Julie's beautiful wedding gown lay in a lacy froth at her feet. She was aware of nothing but Rod's fiery hot palms against her feverish flesh. Gently he eased her down onto the bed and stood back a moment savoring her perfectly formed body as he quickly shed his own constricting clothing.

Julie, though fighting desperately to control the sensations surging through her veins, could not help but admire Rod's broad chest and shoulders developed to an extraordinary degree. His thighs were twin columns of power and her eyes widened when they dropped to the thatch of dark curls out of which sprang his engorged manhood, purple and throbbing. She gasped, drawing his attention.

Noticing the direction of her gaze, Rod laughed, settling himself beside her on the bed. "See what you do to me, *querida*," he teased. "This marriage won't be half so bad as I imagined."

His thoughtless words were like a splash of cold water in her face and Julie attempted to leave the bed, but Rod was too quick for her. "There's no need to play the reluctant bride, Julie," he said nastily. "Not after last night."

"I refuse to be your plaything, Rod!" Julie insisted hotly, repudiating the aura of his manly attraction. "Nor will I be your brood mare!"

"You have no choice, *querida*. Lay back and enjoy it," Rod countered crudely. One hand slid across her silken belly while the other fondled one small globe, its pink nipple marble hard beneath his palm. Exerting her will power, Julie commanded her body to shy away from his seeking hands but the message of her senses demanded she stay.

He moved almost lazily, playing with her body, his tongue tantalizing her nipples which had swollen to their fullest. Julie moaned with pleasure, reflexively pulling him closer as she ran her hands along the length of his back. Of its own accord, her mouth parted beneath his as he ran his tongue along her full lips and into her mouth. Suddenly his mouth left hers, searing a path down her stomach and onto her thigh. Julie stiffened, uncertain where his exploration would take him.

"There are many ways to make love, *querida*," Rod said, sensing her confusion. "I will teach you that pleasure can come from many sources." Before she could protest, his mouth continued its relentless torture until he found the swollen bud of her womanhood, and Julie moaned aloud with an erotic pleasure she had never before experienced.

"Rod! Please stop!" she cried, writhing beneath his passionate onslaught. "I can't stand any more!"

His answer was to tighten his hold around her waist to hold her close as he again nuzzled the blond triangle of curls that beckoned him with the promise of delights he could not resist. He felt the exquisite pleasure he gave her shudder through her body and wanted only to give her more. Julie felt the tension building in the pit of her stomach, radiating into her loins, exploding in a frenzy of sensations that caused her to cry out, gasping for breath. Only when she lay quiet did Rod inch upward and begin the whole process again, kissing her mouth, neck and breasts until she began to stir beneath him. His hands swept demandingly across her thighs, dipping between her legs, brushing into her moistness, manipulating her into a breathless desire that she would have thought impossible after her explosive climax only moments before. Once again the drugging sweetness wrapped around her and she was lost . . . lost . . .

Her body surged upward to meet his, straining closer, tighter. He groaned, pulling her mouth to his. They clung together, feeling and exciting each other. His hand dropped to her knees but she needed no urging, they parted of their own accord. He began to penetrate her with strong, forceful thrusts, the tight, hot feel of her closing around him, nearly driving him to a premature finish. Taking deep, steadying breaths to control his rampaging ardor, Rod began moving, slowly at first, until she learned the rhythm, then faster, his breath rasping painfully in his chest. She cried out and felt him ride her wave with a long deep thrust.

For the second time that night Julie couldn't disguise her body's reaction to Rod's expert lovemaking as she yielded fully to the searing need which he had painstakingly built with his hands and mouth. She gasped in sweet agony as she joined him in his race to the stars, their cries of joy mingling in a tuneless melody. Afterwards, Julie lay contentedly in Rod's arms, a deep feeling of peace soothing her tormented soul. Would sex alone be sufficient to build a life upon, she wondered in the few moments before she fell asleep? If only he could learn to care for her . . .

6

Looking back over her shoulder at the mission barely visible now in the distance, Julie felt herself grow warm as she remembered the blazing passion Rod had brought her to last night within those crumbling walls. In the privacy of their darkened room he had been like another man, tender, demanding, making certain her own desire had peaked before allowing his own release. Not only once, but many times during the night when she thought it impossible to become aroused again, she had found herself being catapulted into a maelstrum of uncontrollable desire by his all consuming hands and mouth.

Upon arising this morning, her childish dream of their marriage becoming anything more than a mockery came crashing down around her. Rod's callous disregard shattered her fragile hopes for a new beginning as he wordlessly dressed and left their cell-like room to prepare for the last leg of their journey. Was he so anxious to see his father—or Elena—Julie could not help but ask herself. Not anxious to meet either one of her faceless foes, Julie dawdled until Rod appeared, angrily berating her for the delay. As a consequence (or punishment), Rod hurried her from the mission after a hasty goodbye to *Padre* Juan without allowing her breakfast. After the strenuous exercise of the night before, if Julie ever felt the need for sustenance it was now. But rather than give Rod the satisfaction of hearing her complain she suffered hunger pangs in silence, occasionally casting murderous glances in his direction.

As they journeyed farther and farther away from the mission Julie could not help but notice Rod's tenseness, or the way his keen eyes darted about continually, alert and watchful. Finally she could no longer hold her tongue. "Is something wrong, Rod? Are we in some kind of danger?"

Rod started sharply at the sound of her voice, as if suddenly aware that he was not alone. "Perhaps," he allowed reluctantly. "*Padre* Juan told me before we left the mission that Joaquin Murieta and his *banditos* have been active in the neighborhood recently. Only last week a group of Anglos traveling to San Diego were robbed. One of them swears it was Murieta. Shortly afterwards Murieta appeared in a small village not far from here to distribute food to oppressed Mexicans."

"I . . . I don't think I've heard of Murieta," Julie said, glancing about fearfully. "Who is he?"

"If you were a romantic, you might call him Robin Hood," informed Rod, his voice holding a note she could not decipher. "He is well known for robbing from the rich to give to the poor."

"Then he can't be too dangerous," scoffed Julie, relaxing.

"Don't be fooled, *querida*. Murieta is not above murder now and then. And most of his followers are ruthless mercenaries bent on rape and plunder."

"How . . . how do you know so much about him?" questioned Julie, suddenly curious."

"At one time I knew Joaquin Murieta as well as I know my own family. He was my friend. He lived on our *rancho* in a small *casa* with his wife, Rosita, and his brother. His . . . his sister, Maria, worked at our *hacienda*." His words etched subtle lines of tension across his handsome features, puzzling Julie.

"Murieta has a wife?" she asked, amazed. "What

made him turn to a life of crime?''

Rod was quiet a long time, carefully considering whether or not to relate all the grisly details to Julie. Finally, he shrugged, and said, ''Joaquin was a *vaquero* on our *rancho*. One day my father sent him to San Diego for supplies and he took Rosita and his brother with him thinking to make a family outing of it.

''They camped along the road the first night and their fire attracted a group of Anglo miners taking the southern route to San Francisco. They . . . they took a liking to Rosita; she was young and very beautiful, and insisted that Joaquin share her. A fight ensued. Joaquin and his brother were tied to a tree, whipped, and made to watch while the five men raped Rosita. Joaquin passed out and when he came to he found Rosita dead and his brother hanging from a tree. He would have suffered the same fate had the miners not thought him already dead from their beating.''

''Oh, Rod! How horrible!'' cried Julie, tears turning her blue eyes misty. ''That poor man! No wonder he turned bandit.''

''The myth surrounding his image has spread until his name evokes a romantic aura of rescuing ladies in distress and giving to the poor.''

''Is none of it true?''

''I suppose some of it could be. He certainly is handsome enough.''

''If you were such great friends, why are you so concerned about meeting up with him?'' questioned Julie.

''It's been ten years, *querida*. A man changes with the company he keeps.''

''What ever became of his sister, Maria? Is she still on your *rancho*?''

Rod turned stony, his stern face belying his inner turmoil. Maria, he thought, the very name dredged up painful memories he thought had died long ago. But do memories ever die, he wondered bleakly? ''I don't wish to talk about Maria, Julie," he said cryptically. "I will only say that Maria is no longer employed by my father."

Julie sensed his withdrawal and immediately sought to change the subject. "When will we be on your property?"

Rod chuckled, his eyes twinkling mischievouly. "We have been on Delgado land ever since we left the mission."

Julie gasped, her eyes sweeping the endless vista. "So much?" she asked.

"Nearly 70,000 acres," replied Rod proudly. "Have you noticed the cattle grazing on those hills?" She followed the direction of his outstretched arm and nodded. "They all bear the Delgado brand."

Julie was about to reply when a loud grumble of protest from her empty stomach drew both their attention. A bright crimson stained her cheekbones and she tried to act as if nothing had happened. From the corner of her eye she caught Rod grinning at her. His amusement at her obvious discomfort caused her to bristle angrily.

"Are you hungry, *querida*?" Rod asked, feigning grave concern.

"You're damn right I am, Don Rodrigo!" exploded Julie, bringing an outburst of laughter from her husband. "You use me all night, keep me from sleeping, then expect me to go all day without nourishment! What kind of man are you?"

"Obviously a thoughtless one, *querida*," grinned Rod roguishly. "But I wonder who used whom? Your enjoyment was as great as mine."

"You're despicable, Rod," sniffed Julie, anything but amused. "I'll bet you had a big breakfast." She deliberately chose to ignore his gibe about her enjoyment of his lovemaking.

"As a matter of fact, I did," he admitted shamelessly. "But seriously, I did not mean to starve you. I was so anxious to get an early start that I was forgetful of your needs. Forgive me. I hope to remedy my thoughtlessness right now. Rosa prepared a basket of food for our lunch and I can see I'd better stop immediately or be serenaded by your growling stomach."

Pulling off the trail Rod halted the wagon beneath the shade of a large rock and sprang lightly to the ground. He helped Julie from her perch and both promptly disappeared in opposite directions to relieve themselves. It was obvious that Rod was well acquainted with every inch of ground they traveled for Julie soon stumbled upon a small stream. Uttering a cry of delight she knelt to bathe her face and neck in the clear cool water. It felt delicious, emboldening her to unbutton her bodice and splash the refreshing liquid on her chest and into the hollow between her breasts. Then, glancing surreptitiously in all directions, she gave in to an impulse and removed her bodice altogether, undoing the strings of her chemise so that it gaped open to reveal her breasts. Happily she began splashing water on her exposed flesh.

"*Caramba*! Today is my lucky day," came a harsh voice from behind.

Julie whirled, clutching frantically at the gaping edges of her chemise. "Who . . . who are you? What do you want?"

"I have been watching you, *señorita*, and if you lower your eyes you will see for yourself what I want," laughed the man coarsely.

Against her will Julie's eyes dropped to the huge bulge straining against the man's dirty trousers, leaving her no doubt as to his salacious intent. Though short in stature the man gave the impression of great strength. A wide *sombrero* shadowed his small eyes but a droopy mustache did not conceal huge yellow teeth as his lascivious grin raked Julie's exposed breasts. He had a villainous face with a scar that pulled up the corner of his mouth into a snarl. His gunbelt held a pistol on either hip and he wore a bandolier slung over one shoulder and across his barrel-like chest.

Julie gulped convulsively several times before finding her voice. "My . . . my husband is nearby. He will be here at any moment."

"Do you think Pedro is a fool, *bruja*? I do not travel alone. Your husband will be detained long enough for me to enjoy you. If he becomes quarrelsome, he will be disposed of. Then *mi amigos* can also have their fill of you."

"No!" screamed Julie, more terrified than she had ever been in her life. She willed her legs to move, knowing that her chances of escape were almost nil.

Laughing raucously, Pedro grabbed at Julie, catching her about the waist. She kicked and screamed as his dirty hands fondled and played with her breasts. His foul-smelling breath nearly gagged her as he tried unsuccessfully to capture her lips. Outraged, Julie drew blood as she bit down hard on his lip. With a cry of disgust Pedro threw her to the ground and fell heavily atop her, fumbling with the fastenings of his trousers. "Enough, *puta*!" he shouted angrily. "Save your strength, you will need it."

Julie closed her eyes and prayed. Suddenly, the answer to her prayer came in the form of six-feet four of snarling, enraged manhood as she felt Pedro's immense weight leave her body. When she opened her eyes Rod was helping her from the ground, his voice gentle. "Did he hurt you, *querida*?"

Julie looked to where Pedro sat shaking his shaggy head groggily. "N . . . no. You came in time."

Just then a movement caught her eye and she screamed. Rod turned, crouching low as Pedro's pistol barked. The first shot missed. The second never left the barrel. A tall, dark man stood to the left of them. At his command Pedro reluctantly sheathed his weapon, but not before his scathing look warned Rod that they were far from finished with one another.

Rod turned slowly to face his savior.

"*Buenas dias*, Don Rodrigo," the man said, the glimmer of a smile curving his soft, sensual lips.

Though Julie could not understand all the Spanish words she had picked up enough the last few days to follow their conversation.

"*Buenas dias*, Joaquin. It's been a long time, *amigo*," answered Rod.

From where Julie stood she could see a group of silent men flanking their leader. She hadn't expected Murieta to be so handsome. In comparison to his band of *bandoleros* he was immaculately dressed in leather pants and short jacket. Of course, the inevitible gunbelt hugged his slim waist. Though swarthy, he was extremely attractive and Julie could easily see how romantic tales were spun around his exploits. A thin mustache graced his upper lip and his smile revealed a complete set of white teeth. His graceful build reminded her of a sleek tiger, his stance proud and defiant.

"Nearly ten years, Rodrigo," Murieta countered. "Much has happened in that time."

"What do you want, Joaquin? Why are you in this area? On Delgado land? Have you come to steal our cattle?"

"If I could, *amigo*, I would ruin your father for what he did to Maria. Have you forgotten her so soon? Did she mean so little to you? Your father, the almighty *el patron*, decided his son was too good for a lowly *mestiza*, a woman of mixed Spanish and Indian blood, whose heritage rendered her unfit to become a Delgado."

Rod listened intently to Murieta's long tirade, seemingly unmoved until he mentioned Maria. "You've seen Maria?'' he asked, apparently shocked by his disclosure. ''You know where she is? You've spoken to her?''

''No,'' Murieta answered, unsmiling. ''Like yourself, I searched for her but never found her. One day, though, I'll find her, and discover for myself why she ran away. And if your father had anything to do with her disappearance.''

Rod seemed to crumble inwardly and Julie was amazed that the mention of a mere woman could wrought such change in him. Her gasp caught Murieta's attention for the first time and he turned to study her, his fathomless ebony eyes missing nothing of her disheveled appearance or expanse of exposed flesh. Reluctantly his gaze left her as Rod said, ''I only hope she has found peace where she has gone.''

''It's rather late for that, isn't it, *amigo*?'' sneered Murieta derisively.

''*Por Dios*, Joaquin! I was young, a mere boy. What did you expect of a lad barely eighteen?''

''I expected him to defy his father for the sake of the woman he loved!''

''*Madre de Dios*! I searched! You know that! Even when my father forbade it I kept right on searching for her! I wanted to marry her! I loved her!''

''Had you truly loved Maria you would still be searching for her.''

Julie could not stifle the cry that escaped her lips. Once again Murieta's appraising gaze fell upon her. ''Who is this woman, Don Rodrigo? Surely you do not bring an Anglo servant to your *hacienda*? If she is your *puta* I commend you on your excellent taste but I question your sanity. I know Doña Elena well enough to know she will not be pleased to welcome such a woman into your home. Your bride-to-be is known to all for her fiery temper.''

Rod's eyes flew to Julie, seeing for the first time the

state of her undress, the expanse of exposed flesh she could not hide with the tatters of her chemise, and he hastened to her side, placing his own jacket about her quaking shoulders. He deliberately spoke in English for Julie's benefit.

"Julie is my wife. *Padre* Juan married us yesterday."

Murieta looked as if he had been struck by lightning. "Your wife! An Anglo?!" He laughed raucously, as if at some private joke. "You have indeed grown up in ten years, *amigo*, if you are brave enough to bring home an Anglo bride. I would like to be there to see your father's face when you present her. An Anglo bride," he repeated gleefully. "Ah, Rodrigo, fate has intervened to deal a blow from which Don Diego is not likely to recover. The irony of it all."

Rod glowered angrily. But with Murieta and his men facing him with drawn weapons there was nothing he could do. "What do you intend to do with us, Joaquin?" Rod asked, his arm curving protectively about Julie's slim shoulders.

"Contrary to your beliefs I am not a monster like Pedro, here," he motioned toward his scowling lieutenant. "Neither do I harm beautiful women. But if I were you, *amigo*, I would guard my wife well. I am almost persuaded to win her from you."

On graceful catfeet, Murieta slinked forward until he stood before Julie. With one finger he tilted her chin upwards until her wide blue eyes met his. Strangely, Julie felt no fear. There was no menace in his gesture.

"Would I be able to steal you from your husband, *niña*?" he asked gently. Instinctively Rod's arm tightened around her. Murieta smiled wryly. "I think, Rodrigo, the little one means much to you. Be careful, *amigo*, your father once took someone from me I loved dearly, see that he doesn't do the same to you."

"You need have no fear for my wife, Joaquin," bristled Rod, surprised by the sudden flare of jealousy he felt toward the *bandolero*.

Reluctantly, Murieta dropped his hand and stepped aside. "You are free to go, Don Rodrigo. I will not harm you or your lovely bride," he smiled beguilingly at Julie. "*Vaya con Dios*."

Taking Julie's small hand Rod edged past the fierce Pedro toward their wagon nearby. Before he drove off, he turned to Murieta once again. "Will you tell me if you find Maria?"

"Perhaps, *amigo*." Rod had to accept the vagueness of his answer. "Take your woman and get out of here."

Without another word, Rod flicked his crop across the horse's rump and they shot forward. Julie could not help but glance over her shoulder as they drove off. Joaquin Murieta and his men had already begun to melt back from where they came but one man still stood staring intently after them, his wide *sombrero* completely shading his face. Julie had noticed him before but was so intent upon what was happening between Rod and Murieta that she hadn't the time to delve into her strange feeling when she first noticed his eyes upon her.

Though the *bandito* was dressed much like the other *bandoleros* there was something hauntingly familiar about him, his stance, the set of his shoulders, even though the striped *serape* he wore effectively concealed his form, making it difficult to tell whether the man was fat or slim. Shrugging, Julie turned her attention on the road, certain that she could not know one of Joaquin Murieta's *bandoleros*.

They rode in silence for several miles, Rod withdrawn and thoughtful, Julie intensely curious. Finally she could stand it no longer. "Tell me about Maria, Rod," she asked softly.

Rod scowled darkly, at first reluctant to reveal that which was so painful to him. At last he shrugged and began the tale Julie had gained only bits and pieces of during Rod's and Murieta's conversation in rapid Spanish.

"I was just seventeen, nearly eighteen, Maria was twenty. She was beautiful, with large doe eyes and a sweet smile," Rod began wistfully. "Joaquin's father, an impoverished Spanish *hidalgo*, was forced from his land when he couldn't prove his boundaries and sought work with my father. They were given a small *casa* on our land. Joaquin's mother was dead but his father soon took a beautiful Indian mistress, Maria's mother.

"When Maria's mother died she came to work in our *hacienda*. We were but children when we first met. Companions. The four of us; me, Joaquin, his brother, and Maria. Joaquin's father died and Joaquin took his place on the *rancho*. He met and married Rosita. When Joaquin's wife and brother were killed he left Maria in our care and became a bandit, out to revenge the death of his loved ones. I was sent to Mexico to school about that time and when I returned two years later, Maria and I renewed our friendship."

"You and Maria fell in love," Julie said softly.

"*Si*," answered Rod. "I worshipped her, set her on a pedestal. I . . . I wanted to save her for marriage." He paused several minutes, recalling those times when his passion raged but he deliberately withheld himself, wanting to keep Maria pure and unsullied until their wedding day. Sighing, he took up where he left off.

"It wasn't long before Maria began acting strangely and urged me to ask my father's permission to marry."

"And he refused," supplied Julie.

"Not only refused, but became angrier than I have ever seen him. Maria was a *mestizo*, part Indian. I come from an old Spanish family whose blood lines have remained pure through the centuries. My father coldly informed me that I was to marry Elena and nothing would change that.

"Of course I threatened to take Maria and run away but my father only laughed at me, calling my love for Maria a childish infatuation. Then suddenly Maria disappeared and I was certain my father had sent her away to keep us apart. But he vehemently denied having any part in Maria's disappearance. Even now I cannot absolve my father of guilt in this matter. Something or someone drove Maria away. Later, I found Joaquin and together we searched for Maria. After a year I gave up."

"Your father must be a cruel man, Rod," Julie said, saddened by the tragic young lovers forced to separate by a father's pride.

"You might call him that, *querida*. Stern, certainly. He is a man steeped in tradition, proud of his ancient blood lines. He did what he did out of love for me, his only son."

"Have you forgiven him? Even though he may have been behind Maria's disappearance?" asked Julie, amazed that Rod could have forgotten his first love and forgiven so easily.

"Ten yeas is a long time, *querida*," Rod smiled sadly. "One tends to forget as well as forgive with the passage of time. "I left home after that and anger at my father kept me away for five years. But in the end my home and land meant too much to me. My father and I exist now in a truce of sorts. He still maintains he had nothing to do with Maria's disappearance, yet somehow I believe him behind her flight."

"Yet you agreed to marry Elena," cut in Julie.

"Our marriage was arranged from the time we were children. I knew I must marry sometime and it was inevitable. There was no one else . . . so . . ." he rejoined lamely.

Julie was silent a long time, digesting everything Rod had told her. Suddenly she asked, "Rod, why are you taking me to your home when you know I won't be welcome."

Rod's dark brows shot sharply upward. "You are my wife." His tone of voice implied that he thought her addled for asking."

"After hearing about Maria I'm not so certain I'll be safe in your home."

"I am older now, not so easily intimidated by my father as was the naive eighteen-year old boy," Rod said dryly. "I am quite capable of protecting what belongs to me. Have no fear, *querida*, my father will have no choice but to welcome his son's wife."

But Julie did fear. Not only the proud *hidalgo*, Don Diego Delgado, but the haughty Dona Elena Rodriques y Montoya.

7

The first inkling that they were approaching the *hacienda* came with the sighting of countless head of cattle grazing in the surrounding hills and the *vaqueros* who tended them. Even from afar she recognized the cowboys clad in working clothes of goatskin chaps, broad brimmed hats and vests.

Julie soon spotted the red tile roof of the sprawling adobe building, whose weathered, mellow adobe walls glowed a soft pink-beige in the shimmering sun. Gracefully arched doorways gave the *casa* the elegant look of old Madrid with its black wrought iron grills at the windows. Beyond the spacious *casa* were corrals filled with mustangs, barns, and outbuildings used to house the servants and *vaqueros* needed to work the land and see to the family's needs. Rod informed Julie that there was also a private chapel and bullring used for bullfights and bearbaiting. Julie cringed at the thought but said nothing.

Upon closer observation, Julie saw that the *hacienda* was L-shaped, forming a patio or courtyard sheltered on two sides. Several sets of double doors opened onto it from the house. A large fountain graced the center of the courtyard and urns of hibiscus, jasmine and other flowers placed amid tall pine trees and lush bushes created a private wonderland.

Julie was also surprised that the *rancho* was so close to the ocean, for behind the one-story rambling *casa* she could glimpse sparkling water. Rod told her they had their own private dock and fleet of barges. A young boy appeared out of nowhere to take the reins from Rod as he came around to help Julie from her high perch on the wagon seat.

Her heart pounding wildly in her breast, Julie passed beneath the wide veranda that ran the length of the house and approached the sturdy door a step behind Rod. She could not help but notice the inevitable iron grillwork gracing the long windows which were open to garner the gentle breeze. Rod had no need to knock for the door swung open immediately to admit them. A small, pretty Indian girl stood aside as they entered a wide hallway. It was ten degrees cooler inside, Julie noticed immediately. Unhesitantly, Rod led her into a large, comfortable room she assumed was the parlor. Rod said a few words to the little maid in Spanish and she scooted off, darting a brief glance in Julie's direction.

Every stick of furniture, each tasteful decoration in the huge room suggested luxury, from the highly polished paneled floors, cushioned seats, double-hung windows and intricately woven tapestries decorating the white-washed walls. An enormous fireplace took up one whole wall. Julie fell in love with the place immediately.

"What do you think of it, *querida*?" Rod gestured proudly around the room. "Is it what you expected or did you think all Americanos lived in hovels?"

"It's . . . it's so grand," stammered Julie, searching for the right word. Her vibrant blue eyes sparkled and her face was flushed with pleasure and Rod, struck again by her beauty and innocence, drew her into his embrace, clearly on the verge of planting a kiss on her delectable lips.

"What is the meaning of this, Rodrigo?" demanded an authoritative voice.

Guiltily, Rod rudely shoved Julie aside even though

they certainly had nothing to be guilty about. Judging by his proud carriage and impeccable dress Julie guessed the middleaged man to be none other than Don Diego Delgado, Rod's stern father. Though not as tall as his son, Don Diego commanded immediate attention with his slim, lithe form and stern-faced arrogance. His fifty-odd years lay sedately across his handsome face and body despite the liberal sprinkling of silver in his black hair. There was nothing of the gracious mannered grandee about him now as he faced his handsome son.

Rod stood his ground, greeting his father affably while Julie shifted nervously beside him. "You will be pleased to know everything has been settled in Monterey to our satisfaction," Rod informed his father grandly. "The lawyers' fees were outrageous but well worth it. In the end, the court decided in our favor. There is no longer a question of ownership of the Delgado land grant."

A genuine smile creased the older man's handsome features, an aged replica of his son. "I had every faith in your ability, *mi hijo*. Not for a moment did I consider failure. What I do not understand is your delay in returning to the *rancho*." His wary eyes slid to Julie but he did not acknowledge her presence. "Doña Elena was frantic that you would not return in time for the wedding. Did you forget you are to be married in four weeks?"

"No, *mi Padre*," Rod explained, "but I could not help the delay. Unforeseen circumstances," here he paused and drew Julie forward, "altered my plans."

Finally Don Diego deigned to look down his patrician nose at Julie. "Who is this . . . this . . . woman, Rodrigo? If she is your *puta* you certainly have your nerve bringing her here under my roof. Send her away immediately." His voice brooked no argument and Julie quailed inwardly.

Rod remained undaunted. "I'm sorry, *Padre,* but that

is impossible."

"Nothing is impossible, *mi hijo*," Don Diego scolded sternly. "What is this woman to you?"

Drawing himself up to his full height, Rod said, "Julie is my wife. *Padre* Juan married us yesterday."

Don Diego went dead white beneath his swarthy complexion as all color drained from his face. He began to sway from side-to-side and Rod sprang forward to steady him. Angrily the older man pushed aside his son's helping hands. "*Madre de Dios*! How could you, Rodrigo? After all I've gone through to keep the Delgado lineage pure!" Don Diego was livid with rage. "Once you had gotten over Maria and returned home I was positive you had finally come to your senses and was prepared to accept your responsibility. But this! To bring this *puta* home! To foist her off as your wife! This is unforgivable!"

"Julie *is* my wife, *Padre*, and I will not have her treated so rudely, not by you or by anyone," Rod said with grim determination. "If she is not welcome here then neither am I. We will leave immediately."

Julie's eyes flew open. Never in her wildest dreams had she expected Rod to stand by her to the extent that he would leave his beloved land for her. "Rod," she began hesitantly, "perhaps it's better if I . . ."

"Be quiet and let me handle this," he interrupted coldly. Julie flushed at his proprietory tone but did as she was told, biting her tongue to keep from shouting back.

Don Diego, sensing Rod's determination, began backing down from his original stance, though he was far from happy with the prospects of an Anglo daughter-in-law. "There is no need for drastic measures, Rodrigo," he cajoled. "We will talk later, in private, about your precipitous marriage. There are things we can do. Ways to remedy your hasty action, fix your mistake. I am a man myself and am not foreign to the wiles of crafty women and the tricks they employ to snare a husband. Especially a beautiful woman like . . . like . . ."

"Julie," supplied Rod, thoroughly bemused by his father's crude attempts at reconcilliation.

"*Si*, Julie. You will see, *mi hijo*, that money has its privileges. You will soon be free of this *puta*. Free to marry the woman meant to be your wife."

"If you are finished, *Padre*, I will show my wife to her room," Rod said coolly. "There will be no need for further talk on the subject. Julie will remain my wife. If you wish us to leave, say so now and you will never have to set eyes on us again."

Rod's impassioned declaration was met with silence. Don Diego did not have the heart to utter the words that would send his only son away forever, even if it meant accepting an Anglo daughter-in-law. When Rod left before, he had suffered five long years wondering if Rodrigo was dead or alive. When his son finally returned, Don Diego swore he would do nothing to send him into exile again. Nor would he risk losing his son again by telling all he knew about Maria.

"So be it," said the older man resignedly. "You . . . and your . . . wife will stay. But you must be the one to tell Elena that you have jilted her." Then, slanting a scathing glance in Julie's direction, Don Diego turned on his heel and strode from the room, his pride and anger preventing him from uttering one word of welcome to his new daughter-in-law.

Heaving a sigh, Julie collapsed in a nearby chair. The ordeal of meeting Don Diego was more harrowing than she had imagined. She felt bruised and battered from the verbal abuse heaped upon her and was ready to turn around and return to San Francisco.

"He'll come around, *querida*," Rod told her with more assurance than he felt. "He has no choice," he added grimly.

Julie was not fooled. Don Diego would never, never, treat her as one of the family. To him, she was an interloper; a woman who used her feminine wiles to lure his precious son into marriage. Well, for all she cared . . . Suddenly Julie's dismal thoughts were cut off in mid-sentence by a high pitched shriek.

"Rodrigo, *mi novio*, you are back! How I missed you!"

Mouth agape, Julie could only stare as an absolutely stunning woman in a bright pink brocade gown that presented a striking contrast to her creamy tan skin flung herself into Rod's waiting arms. Her hair was a luscious blue-black pulled sleekly behind her ears and spilling down her back in a rich profusion. Her eyes were flashing brown, full of expression. Her mouth was wide, red, and undeniably sensual. A mouth designed for passion, Julie thought jealously. Though petite, she possessed a curvacious body, the clinging pink brocade bodice accentuating smooth shoulders, full breasts and slim waist. Though undeniably lovely, there was a hint of greed in the pouting mouth, an avaricious gleam in those dark, flashing eyes. Her lips pouted prettily as she stared up at Rod. She had not yet seen Julie sitting quietly in the chair.

"You are naughty, Rodrigo," Elena chided archly. "I expected you home weeks ago. Did you find some *puta* in San Francisco to make you forget about your *novia*?" Her words were evidently meant to tease but Julie could sense an underlying threat in them should they prove true. Warily, Julie waited for Rod's next move.

It came almost immediately as he unwound her clinging arms from around his neck and stepped back. "Elena, there is something you should know," he began, undecided exactly what he should say to the volatile Elena.

Elena was immediately wary. "But, *mi amor*," she

smiled beguilingly, "you know I was teasing. I am aware of a man's . . . needs. If you dallied with a *puta* I cannot fault you for you have returned to your intended, have you not?"

"Elena, listen to me," implored Rod, attempting once again to gain her full attention. "We cannot be married. It is no longer possible."

Elena froze, anger turning her expressive face almost ugly. "What are you saying, Rodrigo? Of course we will be married. The inviations are already delivered. My wedding dress is completed. In four weeks I will become Doña Elena Delgado."

"I am already married, Elena. *Padre* Juan performed the ceremony yesterday."

"*Bastardo*!" spat Elena, pounding her clenched fists against Rod's substantial chest. "Who is she? Who is the *puta* who stole my *novio*? Do you know how long I've waited for you to finally set the date? I am twenty-six years old, Rodrigo! Do you hear me? Twenty-six! I grew old waiting for you to come to your senses."

Julie could remain silent no longer. She arose from her chair placing herself in the distraught Spanish woman's full view. Elena's black eyes flashed menacingly as she stared at Julie, then she whirled on Rod, crying, "You jilted me for this? A yellow-haired *puta* dressed in rags?" She laughed raucously, her mirth turning into tears.

"Elena, calm yourself," soothed Rod, suddenly at a loss for words. "It's not the end of the world. You are a beautiful woman. You will have no trouble finding someone to take my place. Come, dry your eyes and meet my wife." He turned to Julie, unaware of the hatred blazing from Elena's black eyes. "Julie, this is Elena Montoya."

It was the wrong thing to say and Rod could only stand there, mouth agape while Elena flew into yet another rage. Julie felt almost sorry for the woman.

Hesitantly, in a gesture of sympathy and friendship, she put a small hand on Elena's shaking shoulder.

"Take your hand off me, *puta*!" Elena spat angrily. "You may be Rodrigo's wife but you are nothing to me, nor will you ever be. What did you do? Lure him into your bed and then scream rape? It's the only way he would ever marry you. Somehow you learned that Rodrigo is an honorable man and used that knowledge to further your own purposes."

"It wasn't like that, Elena," said Julie softly. "I understand your hurt and I would like to be your friend."

"Never! Because of you I will become nothing but a source of embarrassment to my friends and family. They will laugh at me once they learn Rodrigo has cast me aside for an Anglo."

"I'm sorry," said Julie, meaning it. "Truly I am."

"I don't want your sympathy, *bruja*. You haven't won yet. When someone has taken what belongs to Elena Montoya, beware, that person does not know the meaning of trouble," she threatened.

"That's enough, Elena," Rod said sternly, placing himself between the two women. "Somehow I will make this up to you, I swear it. Let the matter rest for now. I don't expect you and Julie to become friends, but as long as you both remain under my roof you will conduct yourself with decorum."

"Are you asking me to leave *Rancho* Delgado, Rodrigo?" Elena asked haughtily.

"Of course not, Elena. You are my father's guest. You may remain until your own father returns from Spain. Longer, if you wish."

Slanting a superior look in Julie's direction, Elena flounced off, pink skirts flying.

"I'm sorry things turned out so badly, *querida*," apologized Rod sheepishly.

"It's no more than I expected," sighed Julie tiredly.

"Come," gestured Rod, suddenly sick of the entire episode. "I'll show you to your room, you look ready to drop. I didn't allow you much sleep last night."

Julie allowed herself to be led down a corridor and around a corner, too exhausted to care where Rod was taking her. Though Rod had defended his right to marry when and to whom he pleased, inwardly guilt and betrayal rode heavily on his shoulders. Long ago when he wanted to marry Maria it was because he truly loved her. But this time he couldn't justify his marriage to Julie so easily by claiming a similar love. How could he admit to his father that honor alone dictated his marriage to an Anglo? That lust, not love, was the emotion he felt for his beautiful bride. But was that entirely true? Did he feel nothing but lust and the need to consume her sweet flesh, he wondered? suddenly recalling their tender moments of the night before. Would he have felt same with Elena? Inexplicably he became angry. Angry at himself for falling under the spell of an opportunist who came to California under false pretenses, and even angrier at Julie for disrupting his entire life.

By the time Rod opened the door to an attractive, rather masculine room decorated in vibrant earth tones, his dark visage was set in stern lines and his eyebrows drawn together in a deep scowl.

Julie looked about curiously, thinking she would be decidedly uncomfortable sharing this room with Rod. But she needn't have worried for Rod crossed the room and opened a connecting door. "I think you will find this room more to your liking. It was my mother's. These two rooms were recently redecorated and prepared for Ele . . . my bride."

"It's . . . lovely, Rod," breathed Julie, enchanted. In truth, Julie had never seen a more beautiful room with its clean, white-washed walls, sunny yellow curtains and bedspread, and tall French doors leading to a wide veranda. Beyond the veranda lay the courtyard she had glimpsed earlier, with its sparkling fountain playing in the sunlight. Walking out onto the veranda Julie could see that each room in the sprawling house led out into the carefully tended courtyard. Not only could each room be reached from the inside hallway but from the outside also, the common walkway being the veranda.

Julie turned happily to Rod, her face radiant. But the smile died on her face when she glimpsed his stony expression. Once again he had retreated behind a facade of cool indifference. "Is something wrong, Rod?" she asked, well aware of the change she had wrought in his life.

"What can be wrong, *querida*?" he answered heavily. "My father is forced to accept a daughter-in-law he obviously detests and my fiancee—my ex-fiancee—is expected to welcome the woman who has replaced her. Can there be anything right in that?"

"Never will I understand you, Rodrigo!" Julie retorted crossly. "Your moods run from hot to cold. If you recall, I didn't force you into this marriage. You can blame your own damn honor for that! You should have left me with Mae Parker, gotten your annulment and forgotten all about me."

While anger flashed across Julie's face, Rod thought he had never seen her so beautiful. Not even her tattered dress and disheveled appearance could detract from her physical allure. He felt drawn to her, like a bee to honey. Julie was right, he decided in a flash of insight. He did run hot and cold where she was concerned, his emotions constantly at war with one another. He wanted her, yet he didn't. At this moment he wanted to tear off her clothes and make violent love to her. The thought left him riddled with guilt. How could he make love to Julie with Elena, the woman who rightfully should be his bride, living under the same roof?

Julie tried to decipher Rod's expression, but failed.

At first there was no mistaking the lust-filled eyes raking her body. But it was quickly replaced by confusion. "I think we both need to rest, Julie," Rod finally said, the tiniest hint of regret in his voice. "We'll just have to work around this impossible situation."

"You could send me back to San Francisco, Rod," Julie reminded him softly.

A stubborn frown settled across his features. "You know better than that, *querida*," he informed her arrogantly. "You're mine now. I do not easily give up what is mine. Your body has known only mine and it shall remain so."

"Sure of yourself, aren't you, Rod?" Julie taunted in a fit of pique.

"Of course, *querida*. I will kill anyone who tries to take you from me, including Joaquin Murieta."

"Murieta!" Julie repeated blankly.

"I saw the way he looked at you. His thinly veiled lust was there for all to see. And if I was not mistaken, you found him not unattractive."

"You're crazy, Rod," Julie said, disgusted. "He is a bandit, an outlaw."

"Nevertheless, *querida*, I do not intend to lose what is mine ever again. Even if I must kill to prevent it."

"Even if you don't want what is yours?" asked Julie quietly.

"Not even then."

For a brief moment Julie was truly frightened by the grim-faced man facing her. She was absolutely certain he meant what he said. Did his words also contain a threat to her, she wondered, her heart hammering dangerously in her breast. If she decided to leave him, would he kill her before he let her go? Of course not, she chided herself, shaking her head to clear it of such disturbing thoughts. She was being foolish. But still, the suggestion lingered. Involuntarily she took a step backwards.

"Are you frightened of me, *querida*?" Rod asked,

sensing her confusion.

"Of course not," scoffed Julie.

He was standing close to her now, close enough to place a hand caressingly on her smooth cheek. Then it slid down to cup the back of her neck, slowly forcing her forward until their bodies touched. "I don't think I could ever hurt you, *querida*," Rod said, his voice thick with an emotion she found hard to define. "But if you made me angry enough, who knows . . ." He left the rest of the sentence hanging in the air.

Like a falcon's swoop, hungry, demanding, his mouth captured hers, punishing in its intensity. Julie's knees buckled and she would have fallen had Rod not caught her about the waist to hold her upright against his hardening body. She moaned, the hot stab of his tongue plundering, tasting, savoring. She went limp in surrender and Rod's kiss gentled, softened, his tongue withdrawing to outline the contour of her parted lips. One hand left the back of her neck to mold the underside of a taut breast, his thumb rubbing experimentally against the hardened nub.

Julie's breath quickened, her heart slamming dangerously against her ribcage. How could she allow this exasperating man to gain control over her senses to such a degree that nothing mattered but her body.

Rod was never more aware of his own growing need for the honey-haired seductress he had married, albeit reluctantly. "*Bruja*," he groaned against her mouth. "Witch. You enchant me. I gave up all for you. Now it's your turn to surrender to me."

Scooping her up in one smooth motion he carried her to the bed and began tearing frantically at her clothes, impatient to taste once again the wonders of her fragrant flesh. "Oh, excuse me," intruded a small voice. "I did not think . . . I mean . . . am I intruding?"

Rod froze, turning to face the interloper who was

denying him his heart's desire. Elena stood poised in the doorway, her cheeks pink but her eyes cold and brittle. Julie searched frantically for something with which to cover her partially exposed breasts, found the sheet and pulled it protectively in front of her. "Don't you believe in knocking, Elena?" Rod asked, clearly piqued.

Elena's dark gaze flew downward where the hard pressure of his arousal spoiled the smoothness of his tight trousers. A wry grin lifted the corner of her sensuous mouth when she realized her intervention was timed exactly right. It was obvious Rodrigo and his Anglo *puta* had been interrupted before they could complete the act that should belong to her alone. She batted her long lashes innocently.

"I did knock," Rodrigo, but no one answered. I thought Julie was taking a *siesta* and didn't wish to awaken her."

"Now that you are here, Elena, what do you want?" he asked crossly, sounding much like a deprived child.

"Your . . . wife's bag. I wished only to have it placed in her room."

"I'll see to it. Is that all?"

"No," answered Elena smugly. "Your *padre* wishes to speak with you in the study."

"*Por Dios!*" cursed Rod, smoothing back his dark locks with long, tapering fingers. After one lingering look at Julie which Elena did not miss, he turned abruptly on his heel and stormed out of the room.

Elena leaned lazily against the doorjamb, smiling triumphantly. "It will not be easy here for you, Julie. You will find that Rodrigo has little time to devote to a wife."

"And you will make damn certain what time he does have will be spent dancing attendance on you and his father," replied Julie sweetly.

"You said it, not I," retorted Elena haughtily. In a swirl of pink and frothy white she was gone, leaving

Julie to wonder at the strange relationship between herself and Rod that fate had thrust upon her. A love-hate relationship that was doomed from the very beginning.

8

Julie awoke from her *siesta* refreshed, and after a hot bath she dressed herself in her most attractive gown and prepared to face the family. Lopita, the young maid assigned to assist Julie, did wonders with her long blond tresses, and when Rod came for her she squared her small shoulders and set out bravely to face the enemy.

Though Rod's greeting was friendly enough, he made no mention of their interrupted interlude of the afternoon. Nor did he suggest they continue where they left off later, before Elena so rudely interferred. Julie felt like an interloper herself during the long evening meal. Rapid Spanish flew around her like pistol shots. When Rod attempted to explain in English he was immediately forestalled by either Don Diego or Elena. Though she was hungry and the food delicious, Julie could do no more than listlessly push her food around with her fork. She was grateful when Don Diego rose, signalling the end of the meal, so she could escape from beneath Elena's soul-piercing, ebony eyes. Between Don Diego and Elena, she sensed Rod's former fiancee to be the most threatening. The lengths she would go to vent her animosity was less clear.

After the meal, Julie chose to escape to her room immediately while Rod lingered to play chess with his father. Elena also remained to watch the outcome of the game. From her room Julie could hear their voices raised in laughter. Covering her head with her pillow to

125

drown out the happy, intimate sounds, she drifted off to sleep.

Rod chaffed impatiently, his chess moves forced. Though his need for Julie drove him wild, he had no wish to play the besotted bridegroom eager to lose himself in his wife's sweetly curved body. Elena's untimely interruption of the afternoon weighed heavily upon him. He could barely keep his mind on the chess game in his anxiety to go to Julie and bring to a pleasurable completion that which they had begun earlier. It was growing very late and still Don Diego lingered over the board, deliberately prolonging the game until Rod screamed inwardly with frustration, his body tense and unfulfilled. By now Julie would be sound asleep, he groaned beneath his breath, picturing her amber hair spread out about her sweet smelling flesh.

Sensing his distraction, Elena took matters into her own capable hands. "Can't you see that Rodrigo is bored with chess, Don Diego," she smiled archly. "I, too, grow weary of sitting inside on a beautiful night such as this. Come, Rodrigo, let us walk in the garden. Has marriage changed you so much that you cannot spare a few moments for an old friend?"

Rod shifted uncomfortably. He had no desire to wander aimlessly in the garden with Elena when Julie lay within his reach. But he was left with no alternative but to acquiesce graciously with the persuasive Elena tugging on his arm. Even Don Diego sided with Elena as he waved his arm toward the open French doors, saying, "Go on, *mi hijo*. Elena is right. The night is too fine to remain inside." Then he rose gracefully and left the room, the trace of a smile curving his lips.

The night was indeed fine as Rod drew in deep lungfuls of clean, cool air, savoring the pungent aroma of his beloved land. The only discordant note was that somehow the wrong woman was clinging possessively to his arm. He was very fond of Elena; in fact, had often imagined what it would be like to possess her voluptuous body, to be the first to awaken her to passion. But at the same time he felt certain that love was an emotion that had never touched his heart where Elena was concerned.

"This is the first chance we've had to talk alone, Rodrigo," Elena pouted prettily. "Sit here, beside me," she pointed to a bench placed beside the babbling fountain, "and tell me why you have chosen to disregard our betrothal and marry another. You owe me that much, Rodrigo."

While Elena and Rod talked quietly beside the fountain, Julie awoke suddenly from a troubled dream in which Rod was alternately making love to her and then ignoring her. She looked longingly toward the closed door that separated their rooms, fighting off the impulse to go to him. Instead, she chose to walk in the garden to ponder the predicament she had unwittingly imposed upon herself. Catlike she slipped through the French doors, slid noiselessly across the veranda, and immediately was lost in the shadows of the courtyard.

"It will do no good to talk of my reasons for marrying Julie," Rod said. "You would not understand. Only know that Julie and I have repeated our vows in accordance with the teachings of the Holy Church. Nothing will separate us but death. I'm sorry, Elena, I did not mean to hurt you."

Elena was smart enough to realize it would best serve her purposes to allow Rod to think she was resigned to his marriage. "Grant me one favor, Rodrigo," she pleaded beseechingly, her velvet eyes luminous in the moonlight.

"Of course, Elena," Rod agreed, eager to appease the willful spitfire.

"Kiss me, *mi amor*. Kiss me as you would a lover so you will know what you have given up."

"Elena!" Rod was shocked by her request. "Why torture yourself?"

"Please, Rodrigo. If you care for me at all, do as I ask."

"*Si*, Elena," Rod shrugged. "If it means so much to you."

Taking her slender form in his arms, Rod tenderly placed a kiss on Elena's ripe lips. But Elena wanted no part of tenderness. She wanted to feel Rod's passion, to experience his hard body burgeoning with desire. Pressing herself against his body until the points of her breasts stabbed into his chest, her arms curled tightly about his neck, Elena groaned softly. When her soft lips opened beneath his, Rod could not help but fill the sweet void with his tongue.

It was at that precise moment that Julie abruptly came upon the intimate scene.

Breathlessly Elena leaned back in Rod's arms, staring raptuously into his glazed eyes. The kiss had affected him more than he cared to admit.

"I love you, *mi amor*," Elena whispered softly.

"And I love you, Elena . . ." Upon hearing Rod's impassioned words, Julie spun on her heel and fled back to the safety of her room before she heard the rest of Rod's sentence, ". . . just like a sister, or a beloved friend." Neither Elena nor Rod were aware that Julie had overheard them.

No longer did Julie harbor any doubts about Rod's true feelings for her. She could not help but feel sick at heart, rejected, even though her own feelings for her husband were confused. How Rod must hate her, she agonized, trapped, so to speak, by their loveless marriage. But God knows she never meant to ensnare him, nor did she force him to marry her. Finally, exhaustion claimed her as her troubled thoughts gave way to sleep.

Rod hadn't the heart to awaken Julie when Elena

finally allowed him to escape. She was sleeping so peacefully that no matter how badly Rod wanted her he decided to forego his pleasure and allow her her rest. It had been a long, trying day for both of them.

The following day Julie saw little or nothing of Rod. Don Diego coldly informed her that it was roundup time and Rodrigo was needed on the range with the *vaqueros*. After roundup came the cattle drive to San Antonio. It was a busy time on the *rancho* and there were many nights Rod did not return at all, preferring to spend his nights in the open with the *vaqueros*.

Julie found she had much time on her hands with nothing to do. Don Diego went about his own business, Elena was barely civil to her, and the servants padded about the house in silence, uncertain how to treat her. One fine day Julie wandered out into the yard and came upon a child, a girl about eight or nine years old, sitting on the corral fence watching a *vaquero* break a horse to the saddle.

Julie was immediately struck by the child's fragile beauty and walked over to speak with her. The child turned large, luminous eyes on Julie, melting her to the core.

"*Hola, chiquita*," Julie said in halting Spanish. "Do you live here?"

"*Si, señora*," answered the child solemnly. "I live in a *casa* on the *rancho* with *mi tia and tio*. You speak very good Spanish for an Anglo."

"If you speak slowly I can understand," smiled Julie, enchanted by the elfin-faced cherub. "What is your name?"

"I am called Felicia, *señora*. Mi tia, my aunt, is Teresa, the housekeeper in Don Diego's household. *Mi tio* is a blacksmith."

"Why haven't I seen you before, Felicia?"

"On most days I have lessons with *Padre* Juan," replied the child. Then she turned raptly to the action taking place inside the corral. "Isn't he magnificent, señora?" she asked, meaning the pure white horse being broken to the saddle.

"*Si*," agreed Julie. "A truly beautiful animal.

"Do you ride, *señora*?"

"No," replied Julie wistfully. "I've never had the opportunity to learn."

"I could teach you, *señora*," piped the child brightly. "I am an excellent rider. Don Diego lets me ride his horses whenever I please. Would you like to be my friend, *señora*?"

Julie smiled eagerly. What a sweet child, she thought, thinking of the children she and Rod might have. She must remember to compliment Teresa on her enchanting niece. She wondered about the child's parents and why she was living with her aunt and uncle. Suddenly she became aware that Felicia was waiting for an answer.

"I would be honored to have you as a teacher and friend, Felicia," Julie said, meaning it. "I will ask Don Diego if I might use one of his horses and we can begin our lessons the next time you are allowed time off from your studies."

Felicia grinned, throwing her arms about Julie's neck. "We will surprise Don Rodrigo, *señora, Mi tia* told me you are Don Rodrigo's wife, that he chose you over Doña Elena. I . . . I think he made a wise choice, *señora*," she said shyly. "You are much nicer . . . and more beautiful, too."

"*Muchas gracias*, Felicia," Julie replied, touched by the child's words. This beautiful but obviously lonesome child made her feel more welcome than anyone else on the *Rancho* Delgado, including her own husband, who of late had ignored her as if she didn't exist.

Later that day Julie came upon Don Diego and Elena, heads bent together, engaged in serious discussion. At her intrusion their talk immediately ceased, both staring at her as one would an unwelcome visitor. Embarrassed, Julie blurted out her request to ride one of the horses and permission was grudgingly granted by a distracted Don Diego who immediately went back into his secretive huddle with Elena the moment Julie left the room.

Felicia proved to be an apt instructor and within a few days Julie was enjoying a brisk trot around the yard. Felicia was pleased with her pupil, telling Julie that she was a born horsewoman. Julie wished she could show Rod her new accomplishment but he had not been home for a week. Oddly enough, she missed him. The sardonic lift to his dark brows, his mocking smile, even the expression in his eyes that told her he found her desirable. Rod might not love her but there was no denying he wanted her.

Two days later Rod returned. The roundup had been completed and the cattle being fattened in preparation of their long trek to San Antonio. Julie was riding with Felicia and did not see him until later, after he had cleaned up and was sitting on the veranda with Elena, obviously waiting for her.

Rod watched avidly as Julie, accompanied by an attractive child, rode up to the *hacienda*. He admired her trim figure, her upright carriage in the saddle, the way her honey-colored hair floated free in the wind behind her. She is beautiful, he thought, watching intently as she spoke to the child then raised her head in laughter. The tinkling sound was like music to his ears.

"Your wife spends all her time with that silly child," remarked Elena disparagingly. "But then, she is little more than a child herself."

Rod turned his eyes toward the little girl riding with Julie. For a moment he was struck by an elusive memory, as if there was something hauntingly familiar about the child. But whatever it was was quickly lost as he watched the little girl and his wife part. Julie dismounted and walked to where Rod sat with Elena.

"I had no idea you could ride, *querida*," Rod drawled lazily.

"Felicia taught me," Julie replied, smiling proudly.

"An attractive child," Rod admitted thoughtfully. "Is she the daughter of one of the *vaqueros*?"

"She is Teresa's niece. I've grown very fond of her."

"If she is Teresa's niece, then she is a *mestizo*," sniffed Elena disdainfully.

Julie bristled at Elena's condescending tone but before she could retort, Don Diego made his presence known. "So, *mi hijo*, your work on the range is done. It is good. We will fatten the cattle up a few weeks before we begin the drive to San Antonio."

"*Si, mi padre*. The herd has fared well this year. The *vaqueros* worked hard and need a rest before they begin the drive. Will you accompany us to San Antonio?"

"I have other plans, Rodrigo," he said cryptically. "And now that we are all together, I will tell you about them." He glanced meaningfully at Elena then moved to stand behind her chair, laying his hands possessively upon her slim shoulders. Elena blushed prettily as Rod waited curiously for his father to continue. Julie already had an inkling of what Don Diego was about to say.

"Since your return from San Francisco, Rodrigo, I have sought a way to make up to Elena for your thoughtless disregard of family honor. It was understood from the moment of Elena's birth that she was to become a Delgado."

"*Padre*, I . . ."

"No, Rodrigo, allow me to finish," chided Don Diego sternly. "As I was saying, Rodrigo, you deliberately chose to ignore your duty when you married another against my wishes. The fact that the wedding plans had been put into motion, the invitations sent out, meant nothing to you. But I do not hold honor so lightly."

Rod scowled but said nothing.

"To cancel the wedding would heap humiliation upon Elena as well as insult an old and dear family friend. The wedding will take place as planned."

"*Padre!*" gasped Rod, jumping to his feet in alarm. "Would you have me commit adultery?"

Slanting him a scathing glance, Don Diego calmly continued. "Elena has consented to become my bride. Nothing will have changed except for the name of the bridegroom."

"*Por Dios, Padre*, have you gone *loco*?" exploded Rod. "You are no longer a young man."

"No, *mi hijo*, you are the one who is *loco*. I know the responsibilities of duty. Elena was meant to be a Delgado, and so she shall be. I am free to take a wife and certainly not too old to produce another heir," he said indignantly, drawing himself up proudly.

"What will your friends think?" Rod queried, still unable to accept his father's shocking decision. In desperation he turned to Elena. "Is this what you want? To marry an old man?" Somehow the thought was obscene.

Elena smiled a secret smile. It was obvious to her that Rod was jealous, just as she intended for him to be. "Your father has done me a great honor as well as saved me from embarrassment," she shrugged, eyes properly downcast.

Julie was deeply hurt by Rod's blatant display of jealousy. It only served to reinforce her belief that he was in love with the delectable Elena.

It was obvious to Rod that both Elena and his father were prepared to overcome all obstacles and marry despite the difference in their ages, and no matter what their friends might think. But he felt it his duty to try one more time to dissuade his father from such folly. Elena was too young, too vital, for a staid, middleaged man set in his ways. To his way of thinking, a marriage between Don Diego and Elena was a travesty.

"What will your friends think when you take my place as bridegroom? Will you not feel . . . uncomfortable, *Padre*?"

"If our friends think the arrangements strange they will keep it to themselves. They are much too polite to humiliate their host with questions. In less than two weeks Elena and I will be wed and by this time next year I may even have another heir. One who will be obedient to my wishes."

Once again Julie was made to feel like an interloper as she was completely and thoroughly ignored. Her opinion was neither asked for nor given. Unnoticed by the three people caught up in the heated conversation, Julie crept into the house, going directly to her room after asking Teresa to have a tub filled for her in her room.

As Julie relaxed in the hot bath she tried to visualize her life in this house with Elena as mistress. It was bad enough living here while Elena was merely a guest. Her life would become unbearable, Julie concluded sadly. Although Elena was marrying Don Diego it was obvious she wanted the son, not the father. How long would it take for Rod and Elena to succumb to their mutual desire and become lovers? Having Elena permanently in the same house would prove too great a temptation to a passionate man like Rod, Julie was quick to realize, especially since he held no strong feeling for his own wife.

The longer Julie thought about the deplorable triangle she found herself emerged in, the more upset she became. She knew Rod wanted children, expected them, actually. So he would continue to do his duty by her, making love to her, all the while wishing it was Elena lying beneath him. Well, she would stand proxy for no woman, she decided in a fit of determination. Let Don Diego beget the heirs. Rod could find his pleasure

elsewhere for all she cared. Julie was certain Elena
would be happy to accommodate him once she was
married.

"Aren't you afraid your skin will pucker up,
querida?" Rod asked lazily, a sardonic grin quirking
one winged brow.

Julie was so immersed in her own misery that she did
not hear Rod open the connecting door or notice him
slouching against the doorjamb watching her through
slitted eyes. "What are you doing here, Rod?" she
asked crossly.

"Is that any way to greet a bridegroom you haven't
seen in nearly two weeks?" he asked, assuming a pained
expression. "You hurt my feelings, *querida*."

"Go away, Rod."

For an answer Rod came out of his slouch and
ambled forward until he stood beside the tub. Julie
gasped with indignation as he lifted her easily from the
cooling water and set her on her feet. Scooping up a
towel placed nearby for her use, he began to dry her
with meticulous care until her body assumed a rosy glow
and her flesh tingled deliciously. Repeatedly she
attempted to twist from his grasp, remembering her
decision of only moments before in which she vowed to
remain aloof, but he was too strong for her and once
again her wayward flesh was betraying her. Sighing in
exasperation she allowed him to have his way, gritting
her teeth to keep from reacting to the pleasurable
friction caused by the rough towel against her suddenly
tender skin. Rod grinned impishly, knowing exactly
what he was doing to her.

Finally, he tossed aside the wet towel, his patience at
an end, and eased her backwards until her knees hit the
edge of the bed and she sat down heavily.

Immediately she was on her feet, but Rod gently
eased her down again, this time holding her there with
the weight of his own body.

"Do you mean to deny me, *querida*?" he asked, amused. "I told you before, our marriage would not be in name only. I've missed you, *mi alma*. I find I've acquired a taste for your silken flesh."

"Is that all I am to you, Rod? A warm body? If so, then you would do just as well with a *puta* from the village."

Rod was puzzled. What did she want from him, he wondered? "Of course that's not all you mean to me. You are my wife. Didn't I give up my intended bride for you? You are to be the mother of my children. What more do you want from me? I stood up to my father for you; hurt a lovely, unsuspecting woman in your behalf. What more can I offer?"

For the first time in her life, Julie felt truly defeated. To Rod's way of thinking he had given her all that he was capable of giving. His love was reserved for Elena and she was left with the crumbs. He would continue to make love to her because it was his duty and because he was a virile man who enjoyed women, but for no other reason.

"You're right, Rod," Julie recognized wryly. "I have no right to expect anything more from you."

"Then be quiet, *querida*, and let me make love to you," Rod said, his voice softening. "Your body is made for love. Everything about you pleases me. The silky feel of your skin against my lips and hands, the way you respond to my touch, your soft cries when I please you. *Dios*, Julie, I am burning with desire."

Julie was lost from the moment of his first caress. Rod's gentle love words told her he was not totally immune to her, that he had some feelings for her, even if they were purely physical. At least it was a start.

"Oh, Rod," Julie sighed wistfully, "if only things could have happened differently between us."

"You talk too much, *querida*, and make no sense. Let's just enjoy each other for now and forget all else.

You are so beautiful and I want you desperately. Let that suffice.''

He began gently, carefully and patiently arousing her as he lavished special attention on first one breast and then the other, tonguing both nipples into erect points of fire. Julie gasped aloud as he took each pink bud deep into his mouth and sucked greedily. When his hand insinuated itself between her damp thighs and found the tiny bud of her feminity nestled amid curling hairs, Julie could not still her restless hips from writhing beneath his searching fingers.

His mouth stilled her soft whimpers, shattering whatever sense of reality that might have lingered. His drugging kiss demanded a response, and she freely gave it, drowning in the desire he had created.

"*Dios*, Julie," Rob groaned hoarsely. "You are so sweet. You taste like honey."

As if to prove his words, his lips and tongue were everywhere, no part of her dewy flesh was sacrosanct as he teased, tasted and probed every plane and crevice of her body. Only when she pleaded for release did Rod shift slightly and hastily shed his own constricting clothing before settling again between her outstretched legs. Despite her rampaging emotions Julie could not help but admire the smoothness of his dark skin, reaching out tentatively to caress a muscular flank. Rod shivered, her touch sending hot splinters of desire racing through his veins. He grasped her hand, startling her by placing it around his huge erection. "Feel my need, *querida*?" Rod murmured huskily. "Open your legs, *mi amor*. Guide me to paradise."

Entering her slowly, their bodies were in sweet harmony with one another, moving cautiously at first, then faster, until his body began to vibrate with liquid fire. Suddenly she was hurtled beyond the point of no return, her outcry of delight mingling with Rod's harsh cries as he, too, went spiraling into a world beyond reality where only the two of them existed.

Afterwards Julie was filled with an amazing sense of completeness as she listened to Rod's even breathing. Although Rod voiced satisfaction with a marriage based on desire alone she wanted more, much more. Was love too much to hope for, Julie wondered, as she nestled deeper into the curve of Rod's body. Was gaining her husband's love an impossible goal to aim for? How could she expect him to love her when he loved Elena? On that bitter note Julie sank into sleep's waiting arms.

9

The next days passed in a whirlwind of activity as wedding preparations for Elena and Don Diego began in earnest. The ceremony was less than a week away and the house servants were cleaning and polishing with a vengeance. Cook and her helpers were preparing enough food for an army, or so it seemed to Julie. A huge *fiesta* was to be held immediately following the ceremony and all the *vqueros* and their families were invited. Teresa told Julie that the festivities would last far into the night when the house servants were allowed to join the celebration.

Though Julie and Rod were to act as witnesses to the wedding, Julie was left much to her own devices as the three other family members appeared to band together. She spent more and more time with Felicia, learning that both the child's parents were dead, killed by Indians, and she had been given to Teresa and Jose when Teresa's own baby died at birth. More than that the pretty child did not know.

Of Rod, Julie saw little until late at night when he sought her bed. And when he did, freed from the heavy weight of his father's disapproval and Elena's disappointment, he became another person, tender, loving, caring. Though he made no mention of love during their long nights of ecstasy, Julie was certain he cared for her. His ardent lovemaking told her that much. Her own feelings for the dynamic, sensuous man she married were more complex.

139

Julie was certain she could never love a man who didn't love her in return. But to her chagrin, she discovered that the heart followed no rules. Against her will she found herself falling deeply in love with her own husband. It was a source of amazement that one look from him could send her blood singing through her veins; a single touch render her weak and helpless with desire. One word of love from him and she would have bared her soul, Julie realized, aware of the hopelessness of her cause.

One day while Julie was out riding with Felicia, the child asked innocently, "What are you wearing to the *fiesta, señora*?"

"I haven't given it much thought, *chiquita*," Julie answered, frowning. She had brought little enough with her to San Francisco and had nothing new since. "One of my better dresses, I suppose." Rod rarely looked at her during the day to notice her lack of clothing and at night he preferred her naked.

"If you would permit it, *señora*," suggested Felicia shyly, "I would like to give you a dress to wear. It is a very beautiful dress."

"Where would you get a dress like that, *niña*?" asked Julie curiosly.

"*Tia* Teresa told me it belonged to a young woman who used to work here. It will be many years before I am able to wear it," Felicia informed her. "It would make me very happy if you wear it. When Don Rodrigo sees you in it he can't help but love you."

Julie was amazed at the child's perception. Was she so transparent, she wondered distractedly, that a mere child could look into her soul and see the unrequited love trapped there? Even more astounding was the fact that Felicia knew that Rod cared so little for his own wife. Was it common knowledge around the *rancho* that Don Rodrigo was in love with Elena despite the fact that he had married an Anglo? That in reality he yearned for another?

"If the dress fits, I will wear it gladly, Felicia," Julie finally said. Her words were rewarded with a bright smile and a hug.

The day of the wedding dawned bright and clear. It was warm, but not too warm. The day before, long tables had been set out in the courtyard to display all the food and a platform was built to hold the mariachi band engaged for the event. The wedding ceremony itself would take place indoors in the small chapel that served the family for many years. *Padre* Juan would perform the rites against an altar banked with hundreds of flowers and burning candles. Seven o'clock in the evening was the time set for the ceremony with the *fiesta* to follow immediately afterwards.

Julie was excited and pleased with the dress Felicia presented to her on the day of the wedding. No one, not even Rod, had seen it, so it would be a complete surprise to everyone. Somehow Julie had gotten the idea that not even Teresa knew Felicia had given her the gown so she did not call her maid in to help her dress. At the last minute she decided against putting her hair up, choosing instead to let it hang loose in a riot of waves to her waist.

The wedding guests were already seated when Julie entered the chapel on Rod's arm. Rod was stunned when he had first seen her. She looked hauntingly lovely in a dress that gave him a vague feeling of unease, as if he had seen it before on someone who meant a lot to him. But of course that was impossible. Rod allowed his eyes to roam freely over her trim figure seductively displayed in the two-piece cotton dress. The extremely low neckline of the *camisa* was embroidered with turquoise and pink flowers, the puffed sleeves pulled off the shoulders in a display of creamy white flesh that set his blood racing through his veins. The vivid turquoise skirt that billowed over several petticoats was embroidered at hem and waistband with pink and silver flowers.

Rod was so enchanted by Julie's appearance that he gave little thought to the fact that her choice of apparel was vastly unsuited for an artistocratic Spanish wedding. Or that a well bred Anglo would not appear in public dressed as a *mestiza*. Even Julie was unaware of the sensation her appearance caused. Most of the guests had come prepared to witness a marriage between Don Rodrigo Delgado and Elena Montoya, and the mumur of surprise that rippled through the chapel when it became obvious that Rod was not to be the bridegroom became a low rumble. But the collective gasp of shock when Don Diego stood before the altar ablaze with hundreds of twinkling candles, was deafening.

Elena looked like a fragile magnolia blossom in a traditional gown of creamy satin and lace fashioned with high neck and long pointed sleeves. She carried a huge bouquet of white flowers and her face and hair was completely covered with a white mantilla held in place by a high jeweled comb. Grudgingly, Julie conceded she looked virginal and extremely lovely. From the rapt expression on Rod's chiseled features it was obvious he felt the same way. But if the truth be known, Rod's thoughts were on his own wife and not on his father's bride.

Don Diego was correct in his assumption that his friends would be too polite to ask questions concerning the strange turn of events. The congratulations bestowed upon the couple following the ceremony were given freely and without reservation.

The first free moment Elena had she made directly for Julie and Rod, her black eyes shooting fire. "How dare you show up at my wedding looking like a *puta* from the village!" she spat angrily. "I expected you to dress with dignity befitting the wife of a Spanish don."

Julie gasped at the insult, red dots of rage exploding behind her brain. She wanted to scratch Elena's eyes out but refrained from embarrassing Rod with her hoydenish behavior.

"I think Julie looks charming, Elena," allowed Rod, shocking both women. "I'm sure you're placing too much importance on her choice of apparel." Julie's smile was blinding, further enchanting Rod.

Exasperated, Elena whirled on her heel and was quickly swallowed up by a throng of well wishers while Rod led Julie to another group whom she hadn't yet met. That evening Julie became acquainted with so many friends and neighbors that she felt her head swimming with tongue-twisting Spanish names.

Shortly afterwards the feasting and music began in the courtyard illuminated by hundreds of lanterns strung on lines high above the festivities. An orchestra of the best *vaquero* musicians softly serenaded the guests with guitars and marimbas. Julie found herself whirled from partner to partner as the exuberant *vaqueros* joined the celebration. From the corner of her eye she could see Rod dancing with Elena and reluctantly thought they made an attractive couple. Rod was dressed all in black and silver, his short bolero jacket and tight trousers leaving nothing to the imagination. Julie cared little for the brazen way in which Elena flirted with Rod, her dark eyes sending messages only a husband should receive.

Don Diego was oblivious to Elena's faults. It was obvious to all that he was completely infatuated with his bride. But Don Diego was far from feeling the confidant bridegroom he pretended. It had been a long time since he had bedded a woman. And even longer since he had a woman as young and beautiful as Elena. For years his desire for a woman had waned so as to be practically nonexistant. Until he decided to wed Elena, that is. Now his one burning desire was to consummate his marriage, to become the lover he was in his youth, to father another heir upon his young bride and thus prove his virility before all the world.

In order to bolster his courage, Don Diego imbibed freely of the alcoholic beverages he had thoughtfully provided for his guests so that by the time the guests began departing, the proud Spaniard had to be helped to his bridal chamber by some of his boisterous friends. Elena followed demurely, her sensuous lips curved in a secret smile.

Alone in their room Elena moved unerringly to a bottle of wine she had ordered earlier to be placed in their room. Don Diego made an ineffectual swipe at her passing figure but missed, causing him to frown with confusion.

"I wish to toast my husband privately," Elena said coyly, handing him a brimming glass of burgundy liquid.

"I don't think, Elena," began the don hesitantly, "that I need any more strong drink. The sight of my beautiful wife is heady enough without the aid of liquor."

"Just one, my husband," pleaded Elena, pouting prettily, "to please me."

"How can I resist so pretty a request?" Don Diego shrugged helplessly, accepting the glass. His hand, usually so steady, shook so badly he spilled several drops on his pure white shirt.

While he sipped his wine, Elena began undressing slowly, pausing from time to time to refill her husband's empty glass. Don Diego, so entranced by his wife's partially clad body, barely noticed as the level in the wine bottle dropped dramatically. By the time Elena had donned a filmy nightgown that revealed more than it concealed, the elderly don was literally drooling.

"Go to bed, my husband," Elena purred silkily. "I will come to you as soon as I comb out my hair."

Don Diego needed no further urging as he threw off his clothes and staggered drunkenly to the bed, sliding confidently between the sheets. He was certain he would acquit himself admirably this night with his young bride. Elena kept her eyes purposely averted from her husband's nude body, having no desire to view his aging flesh, so different from that of his virile son. By the time Elena slipped into bed beside her sleeping bridegroom, he was snoring lustily, his open mouth and sagging jaw objects of disgust to the young and beautiful woman. Don Diego was deep in his dreams, completely unaware of Elena's stiffened body lying next to him. In his dreams he was a young stallion again, vigorously claiming his wife's maidenhead, her cries of joy bringing a smile to his lips.

In another part of the sprawling house Julie retired alone. Rod was busy seeing to the comfort of their guests who would remain overnight. Julie was exhausted, for tonight she had been much sought after by *hidalgos* and *vaqueros* alike, anxious to claim her hand for one of the lively dances. Several times during the evening she caught Rod frowning at her as she whirled about the yard in the arms of a handsome man. By the time Rod crept into her room much later, she was sound asleep. He wanted badly to awaken her, to make love to her, but against his better judgment he let her sleep, returning to his room unsated and aching with desire for the amber haired enchantress he had reluctantly married.

Elena listened with annoyance to the disgusting sounds coming from her sleeping husband. The house was quiet as she arose from her virginal marriage bed and padded on bare feet through the silent hallways, pausing before a closed door, her ears attuned to the slightest sound within. Turning the knob carefully, the door opened on well oiled hinges and Elena peered inside, by now her eyes accustomed to the darkness. Perceiving no activity from the vicinity of the bed, she slipped wraith-like inside the room, closing the door noiselessly behind her. Catlike, she crept to the bed and eased herself beside the sleeping man.

Though drugged by sleep, Rod's body reacted violently to the softly curved form pressing urgently against him. Moving restlessly, in a state somewhere between wakefulness and sleep, Rod's arms closed about the warm woman's flesh, murmuring softly, "Ah, *querida*, I'm glad you have come to me. My body aches for you."

Rod's hands began a slow arousal of Elena's quivering flesh as his mouth tasted greedily, devoured hungrily. Unhesitantly he drew the thin nightgown over her silken body and flung it aside.

"You smell like roses," Rod murmured, burying his lips in the soft hollow of her throat. Elena whimpered in response.

Elena's mouth was open and eager when Rod's lips covered hers hungrily. His seeking tongue sent shivers of delight racing through her and she clung to his broad shoulders, fearful she would drown in an eddy of desire. Slowly his lips traveled downward to caress a sensitive swollen nipple. For the first time in her life Elena was experiencing true passion as her body squirmed beneath his. Taking her hand he guided it to himself while his own hands roamed freely between her outstretched legs, his fingers exploring the inner reaches of her femininity. Elena was electrified by his hardness as a moan of ecstasy slipped through her lips.

Rod took the sound as a signal to sate their mutual passion as he rose above her and thrust forward sharply, all gentleness forgotten in the heat of passion. He felt Elena stiffen, stifling a cry of pain as he brutally assaulted her maidenhead, and he froze. But Elena would have none of it, urging him on with words of encouragement as well as by wrapping her arms and legs about him so he could not escape.

Had he wanted to, Rod would have been unable to stop. He was well past the point of no return as his body took hers fiercely, pumping, grinding, burying himself to the hilt in soft, moist flesh. Elena matched his urgency with her own lusty, unsated needs. Rod's tormented groan was a heady invitation and soon both achieved the ultimate joy as they whirled and spun into a world of their own making.

"Rodrigo, *mi amor*," whispered Elena when her breath slowed enough to speak. "My true husband. I knew you wouldn't deny me the wedding night I have dreamed of."

Rod shook his head groggily, painfully aware that he had just deflowered his father's bride. But it was difficult to think clearly while eager lips were nibbling playfully at his neck and chest and tiny hands exploring his flesh. Then suddenly the words the woman in his arms had spoken became all too clear. Wedding night? True husband? The full impact of his deed this night hit him and the breath left his lungs in a mighty whoosh.

"*Por Dios!*" he cried aloud. "*Madre de Dios*, Elena, what are you doing in my bed? Where is my father?"

"Your *padre* is sleeping peacefully, Rodrigo," said Elena complacently. "We need not worry for hours. I fear Don Diego has drunk himself into a stupor."

"That doesn't give you the right to seek another bed on this of all nights," condemned Rod, horrified.

"I deserve a proper wedding night, Rodrigo," replied Elena sullenly. "For years I've dreamed of nothing but how it would feel being made love to by you. I couldn't let an old man take what is rightfully yours."

"This is impossible, Elena. I have a wife and you are married to my father. Go back to his bed. Forget this ever happened and act like a dutiful wife."

"*Bastardo!*" spat Elena, black eyes flashing dangerously.

"Please, Elena," pleaded Rod, "Julie lies sleeping just beyond that door."

Inexplicably, Julie's slender form rose up to mock

him, her beautiful face condemning him for his terrible sin.

"Bah," chided Elena scornfully, "if your wife was any kind of a woman she would be sleeping at your side instead of in another room. Do not tell me you love her because I know better."

Rod was too busy removing Elena's caressing hands from the various parts of his body to answer. At length he found his voice. "Elena, *Dios mio*, stop tormenting me before I forget you are my father's wife!"

"Make love to me again, Rodrigo, it was beautiful, just like I dreamed," breathed Elena, clutching at his shoulders frantically.

"Have you forgotten something, Elena?" ground out Rod in a hoarse voice, his self control rapidly vanishing beneath Elena's silken trap. "How will you explain your lack of virginity to your husband?"

Elena laughed, a high tinkling sound. "Simple. When he awakens in the morning I will tell him what a magnificent lover he is. There will even be drops of blood on the sheet to prove my words as well as support his own virility.

"*Perdicion*! You have it all figured out!"

"*Si, mi amor*," returned Elena's silken whisper. "Everything but how to convince you to make love to me again."

"My wife—"

"Has nothing to do with this. This moment in time was preordained long ago. Nothing and no one can alter the fact that I love you and belong only to you, Rodrigo. No other man had a right to claim what has always been yours."

Elena's impassioned words seemed to release Rod's inhibitions as he felt her silken flesh glide over his hardening body and all coherent thought fled in a rush of heat so intense he felt himself dissolve into white hot lava. Then suddenly Rod seemed to regain his wits as he rudely pushed Elena aside. How could he behave in such a despicable manner? "Go back to my father, Elena. I will try to forget this happened, if you will."

Deciding not to push Rod any further tonight, Elena obediently arose and left the room, smiling a contented smile. Silently she slid into the bed she shared with Don Diego, but not before puncturing the tip of her finger with a darning needle and smearing blood on the sheets.

Rod's guilt over what happened that night was such that it took all the courage he possessed to face Julie at the breakfast table the next morning. Their conversation was brief and stilted until Elena sailed blithely into the room, fairly sparkling with happiness. The long, loving look she bestowed on Rod was not missed by Julie.

"Marriage seems to agree with you, Elena," Julie remarked sourly.

"It does when one has a magnificent lover," purred Elena, slanting a sidelong glance at Rod that spoke volumns.

Somehow Julie couldn't imagine the aging Don Diego as a magnificent lover. But then, Elena probably had no basis for comparison. "Where is Don Diego this morning?" Julie asked curiously.

"Still abed," smirked Elena. "The poor darling is exhausted after . . . after all the activity of yesterday."

Abruptly Rod jumped up and fled, nearly upsetting his chair in his haste to be gone. Julie's puzzled frown followed him from the room while Elena suddenly became intensely interested in her food.

Don Diego entered somewhat sheepishly about then, placed a fond kiss on his wife's brow and took his seat at the head of the table. Julie thought he looked haggared and older than his years, and wondered vaguely what Elena had done to cause the change. Could it be that Don Diego was unable to satisfy the passionate Elena, Julie wondered? stifling a giggle behind her hand. Deciding to leave the newlyweds alone, Julie went off to find Felicia.

The moment they were alone, Don Diego began apologizing profusely to his bride. "Elena, *mi amor*, you must forgive me."

"Forgive you?" Elena asked innocently. "Whatever for?"

"For drinking too much. For falling asleep on such a momentous occasion. I must have been a great disappointment to you."

"On the contrary, Diego. You were all a woman could want in a husband. A tender lover, passionate, skillful. You were wonderful. A tiger among men." If Elena had any doubt that her words held a ring of truth she had only to behold Don Diego's glowing face.

"I do not remember . . . all of what happened," admitted Don Diego sheepishly, blinking his eyes rapidly. "But, this morning, the blood on the sheets. I . . . I hope I did not hurt you, *mi alma*."

"I told you, Diego, you made me very happy," Elena assured him. "You were very gentle."

Late that night, in the privacy of their bedroom, Don Diego tried unsuccessfully to bed his wife. No matter how hard he tried, his efforts were met with failure. It couldn't have made Elena happier.

"Perhaps a drink will help, my husband," Elena suggested slyly, "to relax you. After last night you are probably exhausted."

Gratefully Don Diego followed his wife's suggestion. One drink led to another until his head slumped upon his chest and he began snoring noisily. When gentle shaking failed to awaken him, Elena left the bed, generously splashed on her favorite scent, and tiptoed through the dark halls into Rod's room. Somehow she knew he would be alone.

After carefully avoiding Julie most of the day, Rod wanted desperately to go to her tonight. But he was

afraid that somehow she would discover his despicable
secret, that he had cuckholded his own father, albeit
unintentionally. So he kept to his own bed despite the
fact that he wanted to bid her a proper goodbye. In just
a few hours the *vaqueros* would begin the cattle drive
and he was to join them.

As the day passed Julie was perplexed by Rod's cool
behavior. It seemed to her that he deliberately went out
of his way to avoid her. She knew Rod was due to leave
the next day and he had not come to her bed since before
his father's wedding. Was she imagining things or was
his unwillingness to make love to her directly related to
that event? Julie couldn't help but wonder. Elena
certainly seemed happy in her marriage. She was absolutely blooming these days.

As the day wore on, Julie decided that if Rod didn't
come to her tonight she would go to him. After all, he
would be gone for weeks and she could not allow him to
go without learning the reason for his aloofness. Thus it
was that Julie opened the connecting door just as Elena
shed her nightgown and slid into Rod's bed. Neither saw
Julie lurking in the shadow of the doorway. But Rod
had left a candle burning on the nightstand and Julie
had no trouble making out their forms entwined on the
bed.

In silent rage she listened as Rod reared upon his
elbows and said, "Elena, what in the hell are you doing
here?"

"Your father was more amorous than usual tonight,
mi amor," Elena laughed, "and it took much wine to
render him senseless. At least he has the comfort of his
dreams in which he is still a vigorous lover instead of an
impotent fool."

"You're the fool, Elena, if you think to continue with
this . . . this outrageous behavior. You are married to
my father and I have no wish to betray my wife. You
fooled me once, but no more."

"No, Rodrigo, don't say that. You took my maiden-head and I belong to you. Make love to me. I burn for you."

Julie's loud gasp of outrage alerted them to her presence as both heads turned in her direction, but she was too stunned to move. Evidently this was not the first time Elena and Rod had made love. How long had this been going on? Seeing her stricken expression, Rod groaned as if in pain. Not so Elena. Her triumphant smile goaded Julie into action. Spinning about on her heel, nightgown swirling about her ankles displaying a pair of well-turned calves, she slammed the door with a loud bang that reverberated throughout the silent house.

"Go back to your room, Elena," Rod ordered curtly. "And don't come back. We've already done enough damage to my father as well as to my wife." He did not wait to see if Elena did as she was told as he bounded through the connecting door, closing it behind him with a resounding clatter.

"Julie," Rod said softly. "I swear I didn't mean for things to happen the way they did."

"Tell that to your father!" retorted Julie, unmoved.

Rod had the grace to flush. "I can't condone what I've done but I can say I'm sorry, that I never meant to hurt you. When Elena came to me the first time I was asleep and thought it was you. She tricked me and it was only that one time."

"Go away, Rod. I have nothing more to say to you. From the beginning you made it clear that I am nothing but an encumberance to you, that it is Elena you love. Well, you are welcome to her. If your father does not object to your relationship, then neither shall I."

"Julie, *querida*, Elena means nothing to me."

"Is that why you became lovers? How long has it been going on? Were you lovers from the day you brought me here?"

"No! I swear it. It was only once. After—"

"After the wedding? Well, no matter, two can play at that game," she hinted, wanting to hurt him as much as he had hurt her. "If you feel free to take a lover, so shall I."

"Never!" shouted Rod with typical male conceit. "I will see you dead before I allow that to happen! And so that you won't forget in my absence that you are a married woman, I will leave you with a reminder.

Before Julie realized Rod's intent, he grasped the front of her sheer nightgown and ripped it in two, carelessly tossing both halves across the room. Fearfully Julie began backing away, suddenly afraid of the dark, angry stranger she had married. But . . . was it fear that caused her breasts to tingle in that strange, exciting way when he touched her? Was it fear of him that sent hot color flashing to her cheeks? Is that why her nipples grew swollen and sensitive as he raked her with his arrogant glance? Or fear that caused the intense heat to flood her belly? Swooping down on her, Rod tossed her carelessly across the bed, falling heavily atop her.

His kiss was cruel, punishing, her lips flattened painfully against her teeth until she tasted blood. "You're mine, *querida*. Don't ever forget it," he ground out remorselessly. His stabbing tongue tasted of her blood and he experienced a moment of guilt, but it was short lived as he quickly remembered her threat.

"Please, Rod, don't. Not like this," begged Julie. Until now she was unaware of what he was capable of when aroused to jealousy.

"You will survive, my wife, and when I am finished you will know better than to taunt me with other men again."

"Don't the same rules apply to you, my husband?" Julie goaded angrily, beyond the point of caring how far his rage would take him.

Rod did not answer. Thoroughly aroused, he wanted

only to vent his anger upon the woman writhing beneath him, to brand her his forever.

Had he not been so incensed he would have taken time to stoke her desire to the fullest, playing her body as he would a finely tuned instrument. But Rod's anger was twofold. Not only had Julie's heated taunts riled him, but his own shortcomings goaded him; namely committing adultery with his father's bride. To his way of thinking, Julie must be made to bear the brunt of his rage because she had discovered his secret. Perversely he meant to salve his own conscience by thoroughly humiliating his wife, though she was guiltless.

He thought to take her forcefully, slamming brutally into her unprepared passage with ever deeper strokes until his conscience smote him and he gentled his strokes, deliberately stoking her own ardor until she felt herself responding against her will. His lips and hands coaxed and softened, bringing her along with him as she exploded in a blaze of glory and he reached his own zenith.

"You bastard!" Julie sobbed, pushing him aside. "I'll never forgive you for this!"

"But you will remember me," he retorted sardonically. Then he was gone, leaving her in a shattered heap upon the rumpled bed.

10

Rod was already gone when Julie awoke the following morning. She felt nothing but relief that she was not forced to face him after he had so cruelly taken her the night before. But she did have to face Elena. They met at the breakfast table and Julie would have given anything to get up and flee. But her pride was such that she would not allow the gloating Elena the satisfaction of knowing how much Rod had hurt her. Or how much he meant to her.

"Are you going to tell Don Diego?" asked Elena without preamble. Her tone indicated that she did not care one way or another whether her husband found out her brief affair with Rod.

Though Julie held little love for the proud don, for he had shown her little in the way of affection or courtesy, she could not bring herself to hurt him in such a manner, "I have no intention of telling Don Diego anything," retorted Julie hotly. "If you want him to know, you will have to tell him yourself."

"Perhaps I will," shrugged Elena smugly. "Do you care so little for your husband that he has your blessing to . . . take a lover?"

"My feelings for Rod are none of your concern," snapped Julie, hating Elena for her condescending tone.

"It is obvious that you give him little in the way of pleasure," concluded Elena snidely, "else he would have no desire to seek release with another woman.''

"How long have you been betraying Don Diego, Elena?'' Julie asked suddenly.

Elena smiled mysteriously. "Why don't you ask Rodrigo? While you're at it, ask him to tell you how wonderful it is between us.''

Julie could take no more of Elena's malicious goading. It was enough to know that Rod had taken his former fiancée to bed with his own wife in the next room, without having to stand helplessly by and hear all the intimate details of their coupling. Gathering herself to her diminutive height, squaring her small shoulders resolutely, Julie strode purposefully from the room. Elena's tinkling laughter followed her long after she was gone.

During the ensuing weeks Julie noticed a subtle change taking place in the once proud Don Diego. It was almost pathetic the way his bleak eyes hungrily followed his young wife's voluptuous form. Everyone in the household was aware that Elena had moved out of her husband's room into her old room. It was as if her action had emasculated him and Julie felt almost sorry for the man even though he had barely spoken civilly to her in all the time she had been living in his home. It was obvious to Julie that Elena meant to continue her relationship with Rod when he returned, and the Spanish woman didn't care who knew it. Suddenly Julie felt a great empathy with Don Diego.

During those weeks Julie kept much to herself, preferring to ride out with Felicia whenever the child was released from her lessons. By now Julie was an expert equistrienne and enjoyed the freedom it allowed her. She had much thinking to do and, Felicia, sensing her distraction, rode in silence beside her idol, as the precocious child came to think of Julie.

Julie had no idea what would happen once Rod returned from the cattle drive. Of one thing she was certain, she could not stand idly by while her husband carried on with his stepmother. During those long daytime rides and interminable nights in her lonely bed, Julie came to the sad realization that she loved her proud, aristocratic husband despite the fact that he loved another. His cruel taking of her the night before he left, the night she learned he had bedded Elena, was proof enough that he did not love her, that he felt trapped in a loveless marriage and had turned to Elena. After long hours of soul searching, Julie decided to ask Rod to take her back to San Francisco the moment he returned from San Antonio, leaving him free to live his own life as he pleased. She couldn't be any worse off than here on the *rancho* with Rod and Elena flaunting their passion beneath her very nose.

One day Julie was passing by Elena's room when she heard loud, angry voices coming from within. She had no intention of eavesdropping, but curiosity kept her standing outside the door.

"Elena, my wife," Don Diego's broken voice was pleading, "I can't go on like this. For you I have given up strong drink because it clouded my memory of the pleasure we shared in bed. But it wasn't enough. Why are you determined to torment me? You said I was a wonderful lover. What have I done to change your feelings? I want you in my bed."

"You repel me, Diego," Elena sniffed spitefully. "I can't stand your scaly hands upon my flesh."

Don Diego looked striken. "What is it, *mi alma*? If I have done anything . . ."

"That's just it, Diego, you have never done anything."

"I . . . I don't understand," stammered Don Diego, hurt and confused. "You led me to believe you enjoyed our coupling."

"What coupling?" laughed Elena derisively. "If it was left to you I would still be a virgin."

"*Por Dios*! What are you saying?"

"Your aging flesh sickens me!" gibed Elena hatefully. "I married you for only one reason, to be near Rodrigo."

"Rodrigo? What does he have to do with us?"

"Everything," Elena declared cruelly. "When too much wine rendered you incapable of fulfilling your husbandly duties, another Delgado was only too willing to oblige a young bride needing comfort on her wedding night."

"*Dios mio*, you mean—"

"My wedding night was spent in Rodrigo's arms. It was wonderful, Diego. Your son is a marvelous lover."

Don Diego's face went blank. "But . . . you told me . . . The blood on the sheet . . ."

"All contrived. Do you think me stupid? Your son and I are lovers. We have been since the night you and I were married," she exaggerated maliciously.

Don Diego seemed to crumble inwardly, aging at least ten years in a matter of seconds. He was completely demoralized. Sinking dejectedly into a chair he muttered distractedly, "It is no more than I deserve, I suppose. How fitting that my son should cuckold his own father."

"What nonsense are you talking, Diego?"

"Nothing that concerns you, *puta*," replied Don Diego venting his spleen on the woman he had honored with his name. "But tell me, have you no guilt over the wrong you did my daughter-in-law?"

Listening outside the door, Julie was shocked to hear Don Diego speak of her with compassion.

"I feel no sympathy for a woman who cannot keep her husband from straying," concluded Elena haughtily. "She does not deserve Rodrigo. He was always meant to be mine."

Don Diego looked at Elena with loathing, as if seeing her for the first time. It's funny how he had never noticed her vindictive nature before, or her selfishness. But was he any better, he asked himself in retrospect? Feeling nothing but disgust, he suddenly wanted nothing more to do with his wife, had nothing more to say to her. Slowly, with an air of defeat, he rose to his feet, his head bowed in resignation.

"I am finished with you, Elena," he said, his voice laced with sarcasm.

Julie did not wait around to hear Elena's answer for she had fled the moment she heard Don Diego's shuffling steps approaching the door. She went out of her way to make herself scarce for the rest of the day.

The following day she was not so lucky. Before she could leave the house, Don Diego, looking years older, intercepted her and asked her to step into his study. Julie thought she knew what was coming and steeled herself for Don Diego's words. She wished she did not have to witness the proud don's degradation. Acquiescing gracefully, Julie had no choice but to follow the aging don to his private domain.

Julie had barely settled herself into a chair when the older man spoke. "I know we have not exactly been friends, *mi hija,*" began the don. Julie thought that was a gross understatement but said nothing. "It is time to make my peace with you. I have not been kind to you, and my wife and my son have . . . have . . ." He began choking on his own words and Julie became alarmed by his coloring and rapid breathing. She sought to ease the task he set for himself. "I know, Don Diego," she admitted softly. "You don't have to say it."

"You know? How? When—?"

"I . . . walked in on them the night before Rod left to join the cattle drive."

"*Madre de Dios*!" cursed the older man, "and to think I took that *puta* for a wife!"

His face was becoming very red and Julie sought to sooth him, forgetting how he had cruelly maligned her when she first arrived at the *rancho*. "It is all right, Don Diego. I am resigned to the fact that Rod loves Elena. *I* am the intruder. If not for me, Rod and Elena would be married just as they were meant to be."

"You are wrong, *mi hija*," countered Don Diego, startling Julie by calling her his daughter. "If Rodrigo loved Elena he would have married her years ago instead of continually putting her off."

"There was Maria, and—"

"No, Julie, you are wrong. His love for Maria was a childish love, one that would have died a natural death as Rodrigo grew older. I should have told him . . . I should never have . . ." His sentence faltered and died. Then he asked abruptly. "Do you love my son?"

Julie flushed hotly, feeling her face go red. "I . . . I . . ."

"Do not be afraid to admit it, *mi hija*. I always sensed you were a fighter. If you love my son, fight for what is yours."

"Why are you telling me this?" Julie asked suspiciously.

"Because I wish my son to be happy," the don surprised her by saying. "And I sense his happiness lies with you. Try not to judge him too harshly for what he and Elena have done. It is partly my fault for marrying that woman and throwing them together when I knew she married me only for the Delgado name."

"There are times when he is not very kind to me," admitted Julie in a low voice, remembering their last night together. "And there are times when he is tender, even loving. He is arrogant, proud to a fault, and sometimes I could kill him. But I . . . I love him despite the fact that he does not love me."

For the first time Don Diego looked with compassion at his lovely daughter-in-law, commiserating with her pain. But her answer had satisfied him. Julie was no coward. He was certain she would remain on the *rancho* until Rodrigo returned no matter what Elena might say to drive her away.

Julie watched curiously as Don Diego opened his desk drawer and drew out a sealed envelope. "*Mi hija*, I would ask a favor of you. Should I . . . for any . . . reason . . . not be here when Rodrigo returns, I want you to give this envelope to him. The letter inside explains much about many things."

"Why won't you be here, Don Diego?" asked Julie, suppressing a glimpse of some dark premonition.

"That is not important," shrugged the don impatiently. "What matters is the contents of this letter. Will you do what I ask?"

"Of course, if that is your wish," nodded Julie. "But can't Elena—"

"No!" exclaimed the don, jumping to his feet. "Elena is not to know! Is that understood?"

"Yes," promised Julie, not really understanding a thing.

"Good," sighed Don Diego, obviously relieved. "I will show you where the letter is kept." Somewhat shakily he walked to the fireplace across the room. "Come here, *mi hija*." Obediently, Julie did as she was told.

Carefully the older man pried out a brick that Julie hadn't even realized was loose. He placed the letter inside. "No one but you knows of this hiding place, Julie. Not even Rodrigo. When . . . when the time comes, show this to Rodrigo. There are other things inside besides the letter. My son will understand."

Then he replaced the brick and turned to face Julie, his skin like old parchment, yellow and brittle beyond his years. By this time, bereft of speech, Julie could only nod.

"I want you to know, *mi hija*, if we could but start over, things between us would be different."

"It's not too late, Don Diego," Julie reminded him, touched.

"For you . . . perhaps not, but for me . . ." He shrugged fatalistically. "Elena has made me realize just how useless I am."

"Don Diego, I think—"

"Go now, *mi hija,*" he interrupted. "I am weary. No matter what happens, remember your promise to me," Don Diego said, smiling a sad smile that frightened Julie. "Tell . . . tell my son I love him."

Before she knew it, Julie was standing outside the closed door. Try as she might she could not dispel the deep foreboding that left her chilled. Walking slowly she passed through the house and out the door, concentrating on her father-in-law's last words. It sounded almost as if he were entreating her to carry out his dying wish, she thought irrationally, mulling over the whole disturbing interview.

Suddenly she paled, all color draining from her face. "My God!" she cried aloud. "Nooooo! Don Diego, don't do it!"

She was halfway through the house on her way back to the study when she heard the shot. Sobbing and crying out Don Diego's name, she and Elena reached the study at the same time, but it was Julie who flung open the door. Don Diego lay in the middle of the floor, a hole through the center of his forehead. The small caliber pistol was barely visible in his large hand. Julie wished desperately the screaming would stop until she discovered the noise was coming from her own mouth. Beside her Elena went limp, slowly crumbling to the floor at Julie's feet.

Two days later the remains of the proud Spanish grandee, Don Diego Delgado, were laid to rest beside his first wife, Rod's mother, Doña Alicia. *Padre* Juan read the short service witnessed only by Julie, Elena, the servants, and the few *vaqueros* who had remained behind to protect the *rancho*.

In order that Don Diego might be accorded a church burial, *Padre* Juan was told by Elena that her husband's death was accidental, that it occurred while he was cleaning his small pistol. Only the two women and Teresa, who helped lay out the don's body, knew the truth.

After Don Diego had been laid to rest, Julie felt sufficiently recovered from the shock of seeing her father-in-law dead by his own hand to confront Elena. "It's your fault Don Diego is dead," Julie accused the haughty woman.

"I did not pull the trigger," shrugged Elena carelessly.

"You might as well have," shot back Julie angrily. "I heard you telling him that you and Rod were lovers. How could you be so cruel, Elena? You above all others should be aware of Don Diego's pride. You could not be ignorant of what the knowledge of your infidelity would do to him. Why did you tell him when you knew he could not bear the shame?"

"How did I know the old fool would kill himself," Elena replied with a toss of her ebony curls.

"What are you going to tell Rod when he returns and finds his father dead of his own hand?" Julie asked curiously. "Do you think him so smitten that he will hold you blameless in all this?"

"He is not to know the truth," Elena warned, her obsidian eyes flashing dangerously. "Only three people know what really happened and Teresa will never dispute me. That leaves only you." Her implied threat was not lost on Julie.

"How can you be certain Teresa will say nothing?" Julie asked suspiciously.

Elena smiled maliciously. "She is very fond of that niece of hers," she hinted slyly. "It would be a shame if something should happen to her."

"My God, Elena! Even you wouldn't stoop so low!" Julie cried, outraged.

"You do not know me if you think that, *bruja*," Elena contended haughtily. "I know you hold that little *mestiza* in high regard. If you want to keep her healthy, you would do well to follow Teresa's example and hold your tongue. Better yet," Elena advised, "leave the *rancho*. Do it before Rodrigo returns."

"You would like that, wouldn't you, Elena?" Julie was quivering with barely suppressed rage. "Forget it. I'm staying. At least until Rod returns. As for Felicia, make one move against that innocent child and you'll live to regret it."

After that disturbing conversation with Elena, Julie went out of her way to avoid the Spanish woman. Shortly after that she noticed Elena in the stables deep in conversation with Manuel, a handsome *vaquero* who did not join the cattle drive because he had injured his leg while breaking a fractuous horse. He remained behind doing odd jobs around the *rancho*. Julie could not help but wonder what Manuel could have to say that would be of interest to a woman of Elena's background. But at the moment she had little time to wonder about the strange alliance for she had something of more importance on her mind. She had not seen Felicia for several days and she was worried about the child's safety. She decided to question Teresa about Felicia's absence.

Julie found Teresa in the kitchen and immediately asked her about her niece. Teresa's answer did not please Julie. "Doña Elena has sent Felicia to the mission. She . . . she did not want her about the *rancho*. I . . . I thought you knew."

"I was not consulted," Julie said bitterly. "But on second thought, it is probably best she remain with *Padre* Juan. She is not safe here and the good *padre* will not let anything happen to her while she is under his care."

Teresa understood perfectly. "*Muchas gracias*, Dona

Julie, for your concern. Felicia speaks of you often. She loves you very much."

"I love her, too, Teresa. That's why I want her safe. In fact," Julie said thoughtfully, "I will talk with the *padre* myself and see that she is watched closely until Rodrigo returns."

Teresa smiled broadly, her teeth large and white in her handsome brown face. "Felicia does not like to be away from the *rancho* but she will remain with the *padre* until she is permitted to return."

As the days passed Julie became increasingly aware that Rod and the *vaqueros* would be returning soon from San Antonio. How would she act when he came back, she wondered unhappily. Was she still bitter about his cruel treatment of her the night before he left? Would he continue his affair with Elena now that Don Diego no longer stood in their way? Could she ever forgive him for humiliating her, for treating her like a possession, while he freely gave his love to Elena? Her brain was awhirl with emotions and feelings that left her on the brink of despair.

Why couldn't Rod love her, Julie asked herself bleakly? If only Elena wasn't living in the same house perhaps she and Rod might have a chance at happiness. But of course, that was only conjecture. There was no guarantee that Rod would love her once Elena was no longer a contender for his affections. No guarantee at all. Julie's mind was so confused that she had no idea how she would greet Rod until that moment arrived.

Several times during the past days Julie spied Elena talking with Manuel, but she was so incensed with the proud Spaniard for banishing Felicia that she wouldn't have cared if Elena was conversing with the devil himself.

Julie was taken totally by surprise one day when Elena approached her and asked if she might join Julie on her morning ride. Julie's blue eyes narrowed

suspiciously, certain that Elena was up to no good. By
way of explanation, Elena said, "It is lonely here with
both Rodrigo and Don Diego gone. We could at least
try to be friends if we are to live here in harmony."

Julie was openly skeptical, unwilling to trust a woman
of Elena's temperament. Her better judgment cautioned
her to be wary of Elena's innocent plea for friendship.
At length, she said, "You may ride where you please,
Elena." Unfortunately Julie turned away before she
saw the crafty smile curving Elena's sensuous lips.

The day was perfect; the weather brisk, but not
unpleasantly so. The ride in and around the surrounding
hills was exhilarating, the scenery spectacular. Julie
never tired of the sight of tumbleweeds bowling past,
great balls of nothing; soapweeds, their straggly pink
heads waving like banners; and spiny clumps of cactus
called Spanish dagger.

With Elena leading the way, Julie rode farther than
was her habit, unaware of how far they had strayed
from the *rancho*. Thus, Julie was totally unprepared
when a band of men came thundering out of the hills,
swooping down on them like a horde of Mongols. It was
useless to flee, and Julie realized with a sinking heart there
was no escape. Within minutes she and Elena were
completely surrounded by a dozen or so scruffy men
brandishing every kind of weapon imaginable.

A silent scream rose in Julie's breast the moment she
recognized the man bearing a scar on his face that
turned up his lips in a permanent snarl. "Pedro!" she
cried out harshly, fear settling in her chest like a hard
lump.

"*Si, señora*, it is I, Pedro," replied the bandit. "Did
you think I had forgotten you? How could I when we
have unfinished business. His meaning did not escape
Julie and she choked back a cry as sheer black panic
swept through her.

With stricken eyes she searched frantically for a

friendly face among the brigands. Where was Murieta? Surely he would not allow Pedro to harm her, although Rod had warned her the bandit could be merciless and cruel when it suited his purposes. Glancing at Elena, Julie was shocked to see that her companion was outwardly calm, exhibiting no fright whatsoever.

Forcing her attention back to Pedro, Julie watched warily as he angled his mount to within inches of Elena, once again amazed at the Spanish woman's courage in the face of adversity. Though she was literally quaking with fear Julie listened intently to Pedro's words as he spoke to Elena.

"You have it with you, Doña Elena?" Julie heard Pedro ask.

"*Si*," nodded Elena enthusiastically. "Did Manuel not assure you all would be as I said?"

"My cousin Manuel is a good man," replied Pedro agreeably. "I took him at his word." He paused, licking his thick lips as he slanted a glance in Julie's direction. "Does she know?"

Elena smirked smugly and Julie's heart jerked painfully. Something was wrong, terribly wrong. She learned soon enough what it was.

"The *puta* has no idea what lies in store for her," Elena told Pedro. "Just take her and carry out your part of the bargain before someone comes along."

Pedro held out his hand and Elena withdrew a weighted bag from the pocket of her riding skirt, placing it in his grimy paw. Frowning, Pedro hefted it carefully in his palm, as if judging its worth. "It is not so heavy as I would like, doña," Pedro said sourly.

"Don Rodrigo feels it is sufficient payment for what is required of you," Elena informed him haughtily.

Suddenly Julie came to life. Rod! she screamed silently. Rod was behind this! "What is this all about, Elena?" she demanded to know, mustering her courage. "What has Rod to do with all this?"

"What an innocent you are, Julie," Elena mocked derisively. "Do you think your husband cares for you?" Before Julie could form an answer, Elena continued blithely. "Before Rodrigo left he asked me to find a way to get you out of his life. He left the method entirely to me but made it clear it mattered little to him if you were dead or alive."

"I don't believe you, Elena," retorted Julie furiously. "Rod may not love me but I know him well enough to realize he would not stoop to murder to rid himself of an unwanted wife. You are a liar."

"You're wrong, Julie," Elena contradicted. "Rod finally realized that we were meant to be together. He belongs to me and always has. He is too tender hearted to drive you away himself, that is why he left your disposal to me."

"Surely he didn't mean for you to hand me over to a band of cutthroats!" Julie cried out, overwhelmed by the extent of Elena's cruelty. "Had Rod asked I would have gladly left the *rancho* peaceably."

"Rodrigo did not specifically order your death," Elena admitted grudgingly, "but he did leave everything in my hands. After Diego conveniently killed himself I decided you were best gotten rid of permanently."

"No!" Julie screamed, panicstricken.

"*Si, señora,*" put in Pedro, growing impatient to be off with his prize. "You are mine, now. When I grow tired of you, and *mi amigos* have had their fill, you will be disposed of, providing you are still alive by then." His crude laughter sent shards of fear lacing through her body.

"If she escapes alive I will send every *vaquero* on *Rancho* Delgado after you," Elena warned ominously, eyes blazing at Pedro.

Elena's words galvanized Julie into action as she frantically searched for some way to escape the cruel fate that surely awaited her at the hands of Pedro.

Digging her heels hard into the flanks of her horse, Julie made a wild dash for freedom even though she knew she was doomed to failure.

Uttering a loud curse, Pedro spurred his own mount, easily capturing his prey as he plucked her from the saddle and settled her before him on his own horse.

"So, *Señora,*" he said nastily, "you do not wish to accept my hospitality."

"Let me go!" Julie demanded hotly, struggling against the two iron bands that held her in place. "Elena, don't do this to me!" she pleaded. "I'm positive Rod never meant for you to harm me. Let me go and I'll not bother either of you again."

Elena did not bother to answer. Instead she turned her mount and calmly rode off in the direction of the hacienda.

"Elena! Noooo!"

Julie might well have been calling out to the wind for all the attention Elena paid her.

As luck would have it, no one noticed the small, worried face peering at them from behind an out-cropping of rocks a short distance away.

11

"Where are you taking me?" queried Julie, risking a glance at the ugly bandit who confined her within his burly arms.

"You will find out soon enough, *señora*," Pedro grimaced, the scar lifting his upper lip in a travesty of a grin.

"Where is Murieta?" Julie asked hopefully. "Does he know what you and Elena are up to?"

"*El jefe* is gone," Pedro shrugged carelessly. "By the time he returns you will already be disposed of."

"Oh, God, no!" Julie despaired. Murieta had been her last hope. Somehow she believed he would come forward and rescue her before Pedro could harm her.

"He left me in charge," Pedro bragged, puffing out his barrel-like chest proudly. "I am *el jefe* until he returns from San Francisco where he had business." Julie's heart sank, and she deliberately turned her face away so that Pedro could not see her fear.

For the next hour Julie was so preoccupied with protecting herself from Pedro's grimy hands as they roamed freely over her body that she had little time to give into her rising terror. But her gasps of outrage served only to amuse the bandit and he laughed cruelly at her futile attempts to protect her tender breasts and thighs from his crude fondling.

Escape uppermost in Julie's fertile brain, she began to pay closer attention to the terrain, noting the position of

the sun in relation to the ridge of foothills they had been
climbing steadily, memorizing the landscape for future
use. She noted with interest that they traveled along an
arroyo, a dried stream bed, and were entering a *cajon,* a
box canyon, and she carefully stored all this within her
brain. Once she escaped, and she was certain she would,
she wanted to be able to find her way back.

But find her way back to where, Julie asked herself
despondently? After what Elena had done to her she
could never return to *Rancho* Delgado. And if Elena
could be believed, Rod was as much to blame as his
Spanish mistress for her predicament. How could he,
Julie screamed silently. How could Rod betray her in
such a vile manner?

Suddenly Julie noticed that the band of thieves were
strung out single file and disappearing one by one into a
crevice formed by two towering rocks. She watched
curiously as Pedro approached the opening, urging his
mount through the narrow passage. There was scarcely
enough space for horse and man but somehow they
scraped through and emerged into a small, narrow
valley nestled snugly at the foot of the hill. Several
dilapidated cabins seemed to sprout from the hillside and
it was toward one of them that Pedro now headed, the
rest of his motley band at his heels.

Pedro halted before a cabin much like the others, dismounted, and roughly pulled Julie to her feet beside
him. Only when he shoved her rudely toward the door
hanging loosely on one hinge did he notice that the other
men were clustered about him, shuffling their feet
nervously in the dust.

"What the hell do you want?" he asked crossly. "Go
about your business."

"What about the woman?" spoke up one man braver
than the most. "When do we get her?"

"*Bastardo*!" spat Pedro contemptuously. "Who is *el
jefe* here? You will all get your turn after I am finished.

Comprendo?'' Now *vamos* . . . go!''

Still the grumbling men seemed reluctant to leave. Each was aware of Pedro's cruel nature and realized that the girl probably would not survive his violence, thus depriving them of their own sport.

While the men bickered among themselves for the privilege of raping her first, Julie searched frantically for some means of escape. But it seemed hopeless. Pedro's brutal grip bruised Julie's arm and she felt herself growing black and blue beneath his grasp. To struggle was futile, but the alternative was even more horrendous.

With consternation Julie suddenly realized that the bandits were slowly melting away, their differences obviously settled. "Now, *puta*," Pedro grinned salaciously, "it is time to pay your debt."

Julie uttered a long piercing wail as Pedro sent her sprawling across the cabin floor, her skirts twisting about her waist as she landed heavily. Pedro's eyes gleamed wickedly and he licked his lips wetly at the sight of slim white legs and tender rounded buttocks. Reaching down he hauled her unceremoniously to her feet and flung her face down on the dingy blanket of the narrow cot that occupied one corner of the sparsely furnished room. Then he began tearing at her clothes.

Julie fought valiantly, kicking and screaming, but to no avail. Pedro's superior strength kept her pinned to the hard surface of the cot. Muttering a vile oath he flipped her on her back, stripped off her shoes and stockings, using the stockings to bind both her hands to the iron bedposts, leaving both his own hands free to bare her breasts and rip her skirt aside while at the same time exposing himself before her horrified gaze.

Fear, stark and vivid, swept through Julie at the sight of Pedro's swollen member, enormous and pulsing, standing straight out from his squat body. Just thinking of his punishing tool ravaging her shattered her into a million pieces.

"There is no escape, *puta*," Pedro sneered as Julie twisted away from his exploring hands and mouth. "Pedro knows how to please his women. It strikes me that you are one of those who like to be roughed up first. Pedro will be glad to oblige. *Si*, when I finish you will beg me for more."

Then Julie felt his thick lips slobbering wetly over her face and breasts and she gagged at the foul odor of his garlic laden breath. When he cruelly bit down on a tender nipple the sudden burst of pain caused her to cry out, which only served to inflame him further. His ham-like hands pinched and prodded ruthlessly, and when Julie felt his huge erection pushing against her, seeking entrance, panic like she'd never known before welled within her.

Then a strange thing happened. Pedro uttered a muffled cry and went limp, his thick body nearly smothering her as he collapsed heavily atop her frail form. Because her arms were bound Julie could not shove him aside and she lay still, barely able to breath beneath Pedro's considerable bulk.

Suddenly the unbearable burden was lifted and Julie breathed deeply, dragging in long, shuddering gulps of air. Turning her head she saw Pedro's inert body lying on the floor, as still as death, a pool of blood forming beneath him.

Only then did Julie become aware of the bearded, scruffy man standing over Pedro, calmly wiping his knife on his striped *serape*. Though his wide brimmed *sombrero* shadowed his face, Julie knew she had seen him before. He was the same *bandito* who stared at her so intently that day when she and Rod encountered Joaquin Murieta on their way to the *rancho*.

Julie was in a state of shock. First she had suffered near rape at the hands of the vile Pedro, and now it looked as if one of Pedro's companions meant to have her. Never would she forgive Rod for putting her through such pain and anguish, Julie vowed as she waited for the *bandito* to make his first move.

What happened next was something Julie would never forget if she lived to be one-hundred. "Did he hurt you, Julie?" the man asked in a voice completely devoid of any accent.

That voice! How many times had Julie heard that same voice speaking to her with love and tenderness? How many times had she hung onto every word, clinging to that gentle tone in her times of sorrow and need? Yet, it couldn't be, not here! Not riding with Joaquin Murieta and his *bandoleros*!

"Papa?" Julie asked, her own voice quivering with emotion. "Is . . . is it really you?"

Carl Darcy moved swiftly to his daughter's side, freed her hands with a quick slash of his knife and drew a blanket over her partially nude body. "Oh, Julie, my dear, dear, daughter," he said, flinging his arms about the terrified girl. "Did . . . did that brute hurt you? This is the last place I would expect to find you."

"No, Papa, you arrived before he . . . he . . . was able to . . . to . . . harm me," Julie stuttered bravely. "But what are you doing here? With Murieta? Why didn't you reveal yourself to me when I first saw you? I don't understand."

"It's a long, sordid tale, my dear," Carl said. "One that will have to wait. My main concern now is your safety and removing you from here before someone comes looking for Pedro."

Julie glanced down at the bleeding body, suppressing a shudder of revulsion. "Is . . . is he dead?" Carl nodded after prodding a booted toe in Pedro's midsection and getting no response.

"If he isn't he soon will be," he replied wryly.

"Oh, God, Papa, what will we do?"

"No one saw me come in here," Carl explained in a low voice. "I made certain of that. But we have little time to dawdle. Put your shoes on, Julie, and fix your clothes as best you can. It's imperative we leave this place as soon as possible."

Julie did as she was told, arranging the tatters of her dress about her as best she could. "You weren't with Pedro and his men when they took me," Julie said as she fussed with her clothing.

"I remained in camp," Carl informed her, "to keep watch. I'm older than most of Murieta's henchmen and they often leave me behind to serve as guard. I wouldn't have known you were with Pedro if I hadn't chanced to overhear the men grumbling about the beautiful woman he had in his cabin and speculating on how long it would be before they had a turn with her. When someone mentioned Don Rodrigo, I knew it had to be you."

"I'm ready, Papa," Julie said, glancing at him expectantly. "What do we do now?" There were so many things she wanted to ask her father but they would all have to wait until they were safe.

Unerringly Carl moved to the only window in the drab cabin, pulling Julie along with him. "See that line of trees above the cabin? I make it out about one-hundred yards," Carl pointed out. Julie nodded. "At this time of day most of the men who aren't on guard are taking a *siesta*. It shouldn't be difficult to slip out the window and reach those trees without being seen."

"What then, Papa?" You said there are guards posted around the camp. How will we get out of this valley?"

"Trust me, daughter," Carl smiled mysteriously. "I've done a lot of scouting around these hills. If we can reach those trees without being seen, the rest will be easy. Are you ready?" He gave her hand a squeeze for courage.

"Yes, Papa," Julie said, breathing deeply to still her fears.

Carl climbed through the window first, thankful that his naturally spare frame had never turned to fat. Because of the way the cabin tended to cling to the side of the hill, the drop to the ground was virtually non-existent. As Carl had hoped, no one was about and he motioned Julie through the narrow opening with a wave of his hand. She slipped out much easier than her father and within seconds was standing beside him.

"It's a long climb, Julie," Carl whispered, "do you think you are up to it?"

"I can do anything as long as you are with me, Papa," Julie assured him, starting forward.

"Wait," Carl cautioned, staying her with an outflung hand. "If we are discovered, keep going. Don't stop for anything. I'll hold them off for as long as I can."

"No, Papa!" Julie gasped. "I won't leave you!"

"Daughter," Carl schooled sternly, "you'll do as I say. You know what those lust crazed men will do to you if you are caught. I've ridden with them long enough to know that you'll wish for death long before they are finished with you."

Julie studied her father's beloved features, seeing in her mind's eye not the bearded bandit who stood before her begging her to abandon him, but the gentle man who loved and nurtured her for sixteen years, and she knew she would obey him. "I'll do as you say, Papa." The words caught painfully in her throat, threatening to choke her.

Satisfied, Carl took Julie's hand and tugged her after him up the grassy incline. The going was rough but not extremely so. At any moment Julie expected to hear a warning cry, or worse yet, feel a bullet slam into her body. Halfway to their goal she was gasping for breath, more of a hindrance to her father than a help. But thankfully, there was no shot and no warning shout as they darted into the welcome cover of trees.

When at length Julie sank to the ground, her chest heaving with the effort, Carl allowed her but a heaving with the effort, Carl allowed her but a moment's respite. "We can't rest yet, Julie," he warned, urging her to her feet. "There are guards about."

"Where can we go, Papa?" Julie asked worriedly, glancing down at the camp just beginning to stir after a long *siesta*.

"Follow me," Carl ordered brusquely. "Try to make as little noise as possible. I know of a place where you'll be safe."

Julie needed no further urging as she staggered to her feet and struggled upward after her father toward the crest of the hill. Though she trusted him implicitly she could not help but think what a good target they made outlined as they were against the horizon.

Abruptly Carl stopped, causing Julie to stumble against him as he pointed toward a tangle of dense brush. "You'll be safe inside," he assured her. Though he spoke with knowledge, Julie thought he had lost his mind until he began attacking the mesquite with a vengeance, and then Julie was certain he had gone mad. But against all odds a small opening, heretofore completely obscured by brush and mesquite, yawned before her.

"Oh, Papa!" she breathed, excited. "A cave! How did you find it?"

"I've done a lot of exploring in these hills, darling. I know them like I know the back of my hand. When I found this cave I decided to tell no one, thinking there might come a time I would need such a hiding place. Hurry inside. You'll have to crawl through."

Obeying instantly, Julie dropped to her hands and knees and within seconds found herself inside a dark, damp area roughly the size of a small room but with much lower ceiling. Carl was close at her heels.

"We'll rest here awhile and then I'll sneak back into camp. I don't want to be linked with Pedro's death. Later, when it's safe, I'll come back for you," Carl informed Julie when he noticed her blank look.

"Why can't we leave now? Why must you go back to camp? It's too dangerous."

"We need horses, dear," Carl explained patiently. "We are miles from nowhere. I'm certain the men will search for you once they learn of your escape. I'll arrange to remain behind again. Once they leave I'll steal two horses, ride out of the valley and come back through the tunnel for you."

"Tunnel? What tunnel?" Julie peered about but failed to notice in the darkness the tunnel of which her father spoke. "Where does it lead to?"

"The tunnel is located at the far end of the cave," Carl revealed. "It leads to the other side of the valley not far from where you entered with Pedro."

"How long must I remain here alone?" Julie asked, shuddering.

"Not long, daughter," Carl assured her, patting her shoulder comfortingly. "A night, perhaps. I'll enter through the other side and come for you. Under no circumstances are you to leave your concealment. And whatever you do, don't attempt to find your own way through the tunnel. There is more than one passage off the main tunnel, you'll never be able to find the right passage on your own. You must obey me in this, Julie."

Reluctantly Julie nodded. Now that she had found her father she regretted parting from him even for an instant. "Can . . . can we talk for awhile before you leave?" she asked in a small voice.

Carl's gaze softened as he gazed upon his lovely daughter whom he hadn't seen in nearly three years. She had emerged from childhood and developed into a great beauty, and married, besides. She was no longer the little girl he used to dawdle on his knee. So much had happened since then that he, too, felt the need for talk.

"I can stay fifteen minutes, darling, no longer."

"Just tell me how you came to be riding with Joaquin Murieta. What happened to bring you to such a pass?"

Carl flushed, undecided where to begin. It was a tale of foolish hopes, broken dreams and disillusionment. A saga of man's greed and his cruelty to his fellow man.

At length, he said, "I should have never left New York. I wasn't cut out for the life of a miner. I had my tobacco shop . . . I had you. But I chose to abandon all I held dear for the promise of riches."

"I don't care if you never struck it rich, Papa, I found you and that's all that matters."

"But that's just it, darling. I did strike it rich. I found a vein that was rich beyond my wildest dreams."

"What happened?" Julie asked, puzzled.

"The man who was working the claim next to mine found out about my strike. He told some of his friends. The day I was going to San Francisco to file my claim, they were waiting for me along the road."

"How terrible!" gasped Julie.

"Before I realized what was happening they shot me, stole my papers and left me for dead. Later they filed the claim in their own names."

"Didn't you go to the authorities?" Julie asked, aghast.

"Not until much later. Joaquin Murieta found me on the trail more dead than alive. Some of the good things they credit to the man must be true for he brought me to his camp and nursed me back to health. When I was able, I went to San Francisco to report my loss, but it was hopeless. There is no law to speak of in California. Possession is nine-tenths of the law and I had nothing to prove my claim."

"Why didn't you write to me? Or return to New York?"

"I was too ashamed," admitted the older man. "I had nothing. My pockets were empty, my claim stolen, my supplies gone."

"What did you do?"

"The only thing I could. I found Murieta and asked

to join his band of outlaws. I think he took a liking to me for he allowed me to ride with him despite the objection of Pedro and some of the younger men.''

"That explains why you were riding with Murieta that day when Rod and I were on our way to *Rancho* Delgado.''

"Ah, yes, your husband,'' acknowledged Carl quietly. "Do you want to tell me how you came to be in California, and married to a Spaniard?''

Julie sighed, painfully aware that it was now her turn to lay bare her soul. She began with Aunt Lavinia's sudden death and Hugo's salacious pursuit, progressing to the point where she met Polly.

Carl was sorry to learn of his sister's death but voiced his contempt for the despicable Hugo. "I never did like that man,'' he said angrily. "If I ever return to New York I'll make him rue the day he laid a hand on you.''

Julie hid a smile behind her hand, finding it difficult to imagine her slender father trading punches with the brawny Hugo, several years younger than himself and pounds heavier.

"So you joined Polly and came to California to find me and found a husband instead,'' mused Carl thoughtfully. "It truly surprises me that Don Rodrigo would even consider taking an Anglo wife.''

Immediately Julie launched into the tale that explained fully Rod's motives for wedding her. "He doesn't love me, Papa,'' she divulged at the end of her story. "His damn Spanish honor forced our marriage. He already had a fiancee. And . . . and his father hated me. Until just before he died and he made his peace with me. I . . . I'm convinced Rod hates me, too.''

"No one could hate you, darling,'' Carl assured her kindly. "Least of all your husband. I'm sure you are exaggerating. When I saw the two of you together I was certain it was a love match.''

"Why didn't you reveal yourself then, Papa? If only I

had known who you were then all this could have been avoided.'' Julie couldn't help but feel a certain resentment toward her father for being allowed to ride away with Rod into the hostile atmosphere of *Rancho* Delgado.

"At first I was so shocked to see you in California when I thought you safe in New York that I could neither think nor act. Then I saw how protective Don Rodrigo was of you. He seemed so loving, so caring, that I felt it best to leave you to your new life. You certainly had no need of a failure like me dragging at your heels.''

"Papa, I love you! Besides, you are mistaken. Rod doesn't care for me in the least. It's Elena he loves. He proved it by making her his mistress. Our marriage should never have taken place. But for Rod, I wouldn't be in this predicament,'' Julie explained, her face darkening with pain. "He . . . he wanted to be rid of me. When he joined the cattle drive, he told Elena to make certain I was gone before he returned. He paid Pedro to take me away.''

"Oh, daughter, if I had only known,'' said Carl regretfully. "Can you forgive me for allowing my pride to overcome my love for you? I didn't want you to see me as a bandit, a man wanted by the law.''

"There is nothing to forgive, Papa,'' Julie exclaimed. "We're together again. Rod will think I am dead and he and Elena can marry.''

"I find it hard to believe Don Rodrigo would go so far as to order your death,'' Carl said dubiously. "Are you certain of this?''

"I . . . I don't know,'' admitted Julie thoughtfully. "Elena said as much, but I'm not convinced. She is not above lying to achieve her own way. I thought I knew Rod. He is a proud man, arrogant at times, but murder? Not that I think he would have any difficulty in killing. It's the method that puzzles me. He is not one to let someone else, particularly a woman, do is dirty work."

"Do you love him, daughter?" Carl asked, quick to note the underlying hint of affection in her voice whenever she spoke of her husband.

"Oh, Papa," Julie wailed, "I can't help it. I do. I love him still. I died a little inside when . . . when he bedded Elena. I thought . . . Oh, well, it doesn't matter what I thought," she shrugged, resigned to a life without Rod's drugging kisses and caresses that sent her blood surging through her veins.

Though Carl wished to talk further with Julie, he could no longer delay his departure. "I must leave, darling," he said sadly, rising. "But I'll be back as soon as I am able. There are some bottles of water and jerky strips wrapped in oiled cloth behind you. I put them there when I first discovered this cave. Now I'm glad I had the foresight to do so. Remember, don't leave for anything. I'll return for you the moment the men leave the valley."

"I trust you, Papa," Julie smiled through a veil of tears. She longed for him to remain, to console her, to talk more of their lives since their separation. "I'll do as you say."

Julie watched with trepidation as her father carefully pulled the brush and shrubs back into place before the mouth of the cave until it looked as if it had never been disturbed. It was so dark inside now that Julie felt shut off from the world. But her exhaustion was such that she soon fell into a deep sleep. And then the dreams began.

Rod. Always Rod. Loving her. Hating her. Tender, kind, arrogant, hateful, insufferable. Proud. A man of so many contradictions that she never knew where she stood with him, until he made Elena his mistress and wished to be rid of his wife. And then she became nothing but a hindrance, an unwanted burden. He proved as much when he cruelly forced a response from her on the night before he left for San Antonio.

But, oh, how she remembered the way he made her flesh sing with desire; how his lips and hands brought her more pleasure than she had ever known in all of her eighteen years. From the very first she knew his love and passion belonged to Elena, not to her, his Anglo wife, unworthy of the Delgado name. But she had her dreams.

12

Carl picked his way cautiously down the hillside, glancing nervously at the lengthening shadows which provided welcome cover for his stealthy passage. He realized from the position of the setting sun that the men were probably up and about after their *siesta* and no doubt looking for Pedro. Carl willed himself to think of anything but what would happen to Julie if she was discovered. Whatever happened he must not allow her to fall into the clutches of the desperados whom he knew would not hesitate to rape her. Not even if it meant he had to . . . to . . . but no, he must not dwell on the alternative to capture. He was determined to bring Julie to safety no matter what the cost to him.

Carl knew that if Murieta were here things would be vastly different. In his own way, Murieta was a gentleman, despite the fact he was dedicated to a life of crime. Somehow, Carl did not believe that Murieta would be persuaded into a nefarious scheme to harm Julie as easily as Pedro had been.

Carl eased himself around the corner of a cabin, his hands busy at the opening of his trousers, as if he were just returning from relieving himself. So far, so good, he breathed gratefully. But his optimism was short lived.

"*Hola*, Carlos! Where have you been?" The speaker was a scruffy young man with deceptively mild looks who called himself Paco.

"Answering nature," grinned Carl foolishly as he gestured rudely to his trousers front.

"Have you seen Pedro?" queried Paco, eyeing Carl suspiciously.

"No, Paco, I've been taking a *siesta*. I awoke only moments ago when I felt the need to relieve myself. Pedro is probably still with the girl."

Paco laughed nastily, making an obscene gesture with his hands. "Pedro always was greedy. I say it's time he shared. If there is anything left to share, that is. Come, Carlos, perhaps we will be the first after Pedro to sample the blond *puta*. I am growing hard just thinking about climbing between those white thighs."

"You go on," Carl urged, stifling the pressure to kill the foul tongued *bandito* for his disaparaging remarks about Julie. "I'm much older than you, and not so hot blooded as I was in my youth."

"All the more reason to get to the girl while she still is reasonably fresh. Even old men need a taste of woman's flesh once in a while. To prove my good will you may go first," offered Paco expansively.

There was nothing more Carl could do or say as Paco pulled the older man along with him toward Pedro's cabin. Carl hoped he was a good enough actor to convince Paco when Pedro's body was discovered.

As luck would have it, Carl's ability to act was never put to the test. Just as they reached the cabin Pedro had taken Julie to, a man brust through the open doorway, shouting and gesturing wildly.

"*Por Dios*, he's dead! Pedro is dead!"

"How can this be?" Paco asked, obviously stunned. "Who did it, Jose?"

"The girl!" accused Jose knowingly. "She is gone! Through some devious trick she managed to kill *el jefe* and escape. She is truly a *bruja*!"

"Bah!" jeered Paco derisively. "Impossible! Pedro would never allow himself to be bested by a mere woman. Come, let us look at the body. Perhaps we will find our answer.''

Carl could feel his composure slipping away as he accompanied the two men inside Pedro's cabin. The odor of death was in the air and he paled visibly when he came face-to-face with his handiwork. Though Carl rode with Murieta, it was the first time he had actually killed a man. Cautiously he approached the stiffening body, pretending an outrage he did not feel.

What he saw caused beads of perspiration to break out on his forehead as panic seized him. Pedro lay face down on the dirty floor, his right hand stretched forward. At the tip of one finger, etched in dried blood, were the letters C-A-R-L-O-S. Pedro had lived long enough to take his revenge. He had named his killer.

''*Perdicion!*'' exclaimed Paco, eyeing Carl malevolently. ''Carlos! You killed Pedro and let the girl go! You *gringo bastardo!* Seize him!''

By that time the small room was crowded with men who had been alerted by Jose's loud cries, and Carl found himself being seized and roughly manhandled by more hands than he could count. Carl quailed, his worst fears had been realized. Once again he had proved himself a failure.

''Why, *gringo*?'' asked Paco once Carl was rendered immobile by his captors. ''Did you want the woman so badly that you killed for her? Or did you seek only to aid one of your own kind? What did you do with her, *gringo*? Where is the girl?''

''Safe!'' Carl choked out. ''Where you're not likely to find her!'' No matter how badly Carl had failed his beloved daughter, nothing Paco and the others could do to him would force him to reveal Julie's hiding place. Better she should die alone in a cave than be brutally and repeatedly raped to death. If only he could be certain Julie wouldn't venture out of her concealment when he failed to return for her.

A vicious blow to his midsection brought Carl's attention sharply back to his own desperate situation as the pain caused him to gag and retch violently.

"Talk, *bastardo*, or you'll be sorry you were ever born," Paco threatened ominously. "You have ridden with us often enough to know what a vengeful lot we are." As if to accentuate his words, Paco's massive fists beat a painful tattoo upon Carl's unprotected face.

"Julie is my daughter," gasped out the battered man, "but that's all you'll get from me." His mouth was set in a slash of grim determination.

"*Caramba*!" cursed Paco, consumed with anger.

"Kill him, Paco," Jose urged, his sentiments echoed by his *compadres*.

"Not before he talks," Paco replied. "Take him outside. The rest of you, bury Pedro." No one made a move to challenge Paco's usurped authority in the absence of a leader as the bandits carried out his orders with alacrity.

Carl knew he was a dead man; his only regret was that he was unable to return to Julie and lead her to safety. His own usefulness had ended long ago, and he did not mourn his own death. Already he was dazed and badly hurt. How much more could he take, he reflected absently, as he was dragged to an open area and staked spreadeagled to the ground. During the next hours Carl was to learn the full extent of his tenuous hold on life under more pain than he had ever known.

Paco and Jose took turns torturing Carl, using wicked looking black whips and sharp knives to torment his flesh. Many times (he lost count) he escaped into oblivion, only to be revived to begin anew the merciless torture of his lacerated body, until he wished fervently for death, begged for it.

And through it all came the cruel voice of Paco, demanding, "Where is the girl, *gringo*? The girl, tell us."

"Bah, he won't talk," decided Jose, beginning to tire of the sport. "I haven't had my supper yet and I'm tired. I say we leave him here all night. If he lives, we can take up where we left off *mañana.*"

A murmur of assent rippled through the ill assorted group of men, easily persuading Paco of the wisdom of Jose's words. "You may be right, *amigo,*" he agreed, disgusted with Carl's stubbornness. "*Mañana.*"

Immediately the men went off to cook their supper over the communal campfire where later they would gather to spin their yarns of dastardly deeds and villainous acts. For the moment, the man they knew as Carlos was all but forgotten.

Julie spent her first night in her secret cave sleeping little. The cold seemed to penetrate through her skin into her bones. Though her father had thought to provide food and water, no other comforts, such as blankets, could be found though she scrabbled around in the dark looking for something with which to cover herself. Ill clad in the tatters of her torn dress, it offered little protection against the dampness of the cave.

The next morning Julie awoke early, drank some water, ate a strip of jerky, and waited patiently for her father's return. Never once did she consider the possibility that he would not return for her.

When the sun arose Carl Darcy was still alive, barely. Instinctively, Paco knew that it would do little good to torture the man further. He seemed beyond under- standing or speech, more dead than alive. With a fatalistic shrug of his broad shoulders, Paco decided to lead the men out of the valley to search for the girl. After all, how far could one defenseless woman on foot go without food, water, or a horse? They would still have their sport, Paco vowed, once he and the men ran her down, unless she was already the victim of wild animals.

Within the hour, Murieta's camp lay deserted in the

sun dappled valley, except for one lone man staked out in the dirt awaiting an ignominious death. When a search of the immediate area failed to uncover a clue to their elusive prey, the *banditos*, led by Paco, rode out of their secluded hideaway to scour the surrounding Santa Lucia Mountains.

By mid-afternoon, Julie grew frantic with worry when her father failed to materalize. She knew Murieta's men were searching for her because she heard them pass by her concealment many times, holding her breath lest they discover the opening to the cave. But at the moment it was her father's safety that concerned her, not her own well being. In her mind's eye she could now visualize all sorts of horrible things that could have happened to him.

Crouching close to the opening Julie heard nothing but the sounds of silence. It had been like that for over an hour. Not even an occasional shout from the camp below could be heard. Her imagination ran rampant. Have the men left the valley as her father predicted, she wondered? If so, why hadn't he come for her? Was he injured? Or worse yet, dead.

Tentatively, Julie poked aside a small portion of the mesquite shielding her hiding place, remembering her father's words of warning but unwilling to remain in a safe haven when he might need her. Acting on impulse, Julie began vigorously attacking the thick shrubs and brush holding her captive within the cave. Working from the inside was much more difficult than Julie would have imagined and within minutes her hands were raw and bleeding, her nails torn. But she would not give up. By the time she tumbled through the narrow opening she had painstakingly cleared for herself, every inch of visible skin was scratched and bruised by brambles and thorns.

Carelessly shrugging aside her minor injuries, Julie looked cautiously about to get her bearings. Once she satisfied herself that no one was about, she started downhill in the direction of Murieta's camp. It didn't take long for her to reach the edge of the forest where only yesterday she and her father had stopped to catch their breath. She stared intently at the group of innocuous looking huts resting against the side of the hill. Nothing stirred. Glancing toward the corral Julie noticed that nearly all the horses were gone, and she exulted. For the time being she was safe, she supposed, and was on the verge of leaving the protection of the trees when she recalled her father's words cautioning her to beware of guards left behind to protect the camp when the others rode out. Was there another man besides her father down there now, she wondered cautiously? Suddenly the threat to herself mattered little. Nothing mattered but her father. What had happened to him to prevent his coming for her in the cave?

Careless of her own safety, Julie boldly entered the open meadow to traverse the last one-hundred yards into the heart of the camp. An ominous silence greeted her ears as she rounded the cabin where she had been held captive the day before. She breathed a ragged sigh of relief. "So far, so good," she muttered beneath her breath. But sadly, her optimism was short lived.

Not twenty-feet in front of her a corpse lay stretched out on the ground, his sun blackened face swollen grotesquely and his slight body cruelly torn and lacerated. The screaming seemed to go on forever and Julie wished it would stop, until she realized the inhuman sounds were coming from her own mouth.

"Papa!" she cried, rushing to her father's side. "Oh, Papa, what have they done to you?" Sobbing hysterically, Julie knelt down and laid her head on the still chest. Astonishment crossed her sad features when she realized a faint thread of life still clung to the inert body. Even to Julie's untrained ear the shallow breathing could be detected, and then she noted the erratic rise and fall of his chest.

"You're alive!" she screeched joyfully. "Oh Papa, Papa, don't die! Don't leave me!"

Julie's brain bolted when she realized that the bandits were gone, leaving her father to die in a horrible manner. Bolstered by the thought that at least he was still alive and she was here to help him, Julie drew his knife from his waistband and slit his bonds. Then she went in search of water. Without too much difficulty she located a lazy stream meandering along the perimeter of the camp, filled a bucket she found nearby, and hurried back to her father's side. She spent the next half-hour cleaning his face and numerous wounds as best she could with a torn-off piece of her chemise. Only then did she kneel to pray, harder than she ever prayed in her life.

The next problem Julie faced was obtaining shelter. She could not leave her father outside to the mercy of wild animals or the elements. But neither was she strong enough to carry him inside one of the cabins. She could drag him but was afraid of aggravating any one of his grievous injuries. She sat down to ponder her dilemma when Carl roused himself enough to ask for water. Julie hastened to help him drink and though his glazed eyes were focused on her, he seemed not to know her. That fact nearly defeated her.

In the end, Julie was forced to do nothing more than sit beside her father all day and all night, making him as comfortable as possible. It was obvious she could not move him until he recovered somewhat and was able to help her. She dared not dwell on the consequences should the *banditos* reappear before she was able to get her father to safety.

Though Julie's firm resolve to remain awake all night in order to protect her father was made in earnest, her stamina gave out long before midnight and she fell soundly asleep curled up into a tight ball beside Carl's limp form. At least she had the foresight to scrounge around in the cabins for blankets so they would not suffer from cold.

The first pale flashes of dawn found Julie still asleep, her exhausted face streaked with tears. Beside her, Carl remained unconscious. The lone rider that entered the secluded valley did not at first notice anything amiss. He had expected to find his men gone, no doubt off on a raid led by Pedro, his lieutenant.

Deep lines of fatigue etched the rider's handsome features for it had been a long tiring journey from San Francisco where he had learned that there was a large price on his head and the entire army was scouring the hills and Santa Lucia Mountains for him and his fellow *banditos*.

Jacquin was so immersed in his own morose thoughts that he nearly tripped over the two sleeping forms sprawled on the ground. Reining in sharply, he was stunned when he recognized Carl despite his badly bruised face. all hc could see of the second shrouded form was a blond head poking through the top of the blanket.

Just then Julie blinked awake, perhaps aware that she was not alone. Two eyes, blue as cornflowers, peered up at the astounded Murieta. "*Por Dios*!" Murieta exclaimed, his dark eyes nearly popping from his skull. "*Dona* Julie! What are you doing here!"

Wide awake now, Julie jerked upright, revealing a large expanse of badly scratched flesh beneath her tattered bodice. Joaquin's eyes narrowed, puzzled and alarmed by Julie's deplorable condition.

"*Señor* Murieta!" Julie breathed gratefully. "Thank God you are here." Then, much to Murieta's consternation, she began sobbing, at last succumbing to the hysteria that had been bubbling beneath the surface ever since she discovered her father's battered body the day before.

Instantly Murieta was at her side, sheltering her

quaking body in his strong arms. She felt so good, so right in his embrace, he thought idly as he soothed her trembling with soft Spanish words. Not since his Rosita had he felt so protective toward a woman.

"Help my father, *Señor*," Julie begged desperately. "Please don't let him die!"

"Your *padre*!" Murieta was stunned. "Carlos is your *padre*?" Julie nodded, too consumed with emotion to speak. "Perhaps you'd better start at the beginning, *chica*," he invited gently. "But first let me carry your father inside one of the cabins and make him comfortable."

Much later, with her father resting comfortably in bed, Julie sat with Murieta eating the hastily prepared breakfast he had thrown together. In a low voice she told the bandit the sad tale of her betrayal by Elena, and her horrendous experience at the hands of Pedro, and her rescue by Carlos who turned out to be her long lost father.

"Pedro deserves to die for his vile treatment of you," Murieta said bitterly. "This would never have happened had I been here. I would not have been so easily gulled by Elena. What is truly puzzling is Don Rodrigo's part in all this. I find it difficult to believe he had anything to do with your abduction. It isn't like him to act in such an underhanded manner."

"I didn't want to believe it myself, but Elena—"

"Ha, that one!" snorted Joaquin derisively.

"She . . . she became Rod's mistress after her marriage to Don Diego."

"What part did that old goat play in all this? It sounds more like his handiwork than Rodrigo's."

"None. Don Diego shot himself when he learned that Elena and Rod became lovers."

"I can't say I regret his death," Murieta said. "I am only sorry he failed to reveal all he knew about Maria before he died. I'm certain he knew more than he was telling."

Julie was quiet a long time, thinking about the tragedy of the old man's death. Suddenly Murieta asked, "When did the men ride out of camp, *chica*?"

"Yesterday morning," replied Julie, "They searched for me a long time before they left."

"They are fools," spat Murieta contemptuously. "Paco probably led them. He always did envision himself as leader. But do not fear. I will not allow them to harm you." Somehow Julie believed him.

Julie's father began to heal, albeit slowly. With Murieta's help, she lavished tender care on the gravely injured man. His knife wounds were the most serious with several of them festering despite the care he received. At one point he became delirious, speaking of Julie's mother and their early life together in New York above his little tobacco shop. During the course of his rantings, Julie became privy to the great love that existed between her parents and despaired of ever being loved in the same manner.

Murieta was intensely aware of the condition of Julie's tattered clothing which proved a continual embarrassment to her, especially when she caught him time and again gazing at her raptly, his desire barely concealed. She was not yet prepared to deal with another man's lust.

But surprisingly, Murieta was a perfect gentleman as he humbly offered Julie a pair of baggy white *calzonazos* and an equally baggy shirt. Both shapeless garments delighted her immensely and she was more than happy to discard her dirty torn dress, and with it her memories associated with the garment.

As the days passed, both Julie and Murieta were aware that Julie's time in camp was growing short. Soon the men would return and it would be too dangerous for her to remain for very long, even under Murieta's protection. The *banditos* were a dangerous lot, unpredictable and blood thirsty. And though Murieta had no difficulty controlling the dull witted cut-throats, a woman in the camp presented too much of a temptation for the men who were often deprived of sex for long periods of time.

One thing Murieta hadn't counted on was the deep feelings he harbored for Julie. Seeing her each day, not being able to touch her or make love to her, was tearing him apart. He wanted her as he never wanted another woman, including his own Rosita. But Murieta was a gentleman and he had come to care for Julie. Women came easily to him. Of course, since he had taken to a life of crime, the good ones, women like Julie, were no longer possible. He usually made do with *putas* or young widows in need of money in exchange for affection. Until now his needs had been satisfactorily met.

Julie was not unaware of Murieta's feelings. His dark, fathomless eyes upon her night and day spoke volumes about his feelings. But she remained unaffected by his masculine magnetism. No other man could take Rod's place, not even one who treated her as well as Murieta. Daily, she prayed for her father's quick recovery so that they could leave before Murieta took it into his head to openly demonstrate his affections.

One humid night, Julie found the cabin she shared with her father hot and stifling and ventured outside to catch a breath of air. The bandits had not yet returned and she knew the danger to her was slight. Instinct led her to the stream that bissected the meadow and Julie stared meditatively at the moonlit shadows dappling the silvery water. Though the stream was not wide, at places it was waist deep and Julie felt the sudden urge to immerse herself in the cooling depths.

Bowing to impulse, she recklessly shrugged out of her *calzonazos*, pulled the shirt over her head and tossed it carelessly on the ground. For a second she poised there, her nude body bathed in silver, offering herself to the gods.

From a short distance away Murieta stood watching, his breath caught painfully in his chest as he stared at the beauty so unexpectedly presented to him. She was a goddess, an ethereal creature of ivory and silver, offering herself to a moon lover.

A slight breeze blew her honey locks in wild disarray about her back, the slim curve of her buttocks a delicate silver arc, the long, lithe legs gleaming like pale ivory. His eyes traced the tantalizing thrust of full breasts, the concave stomach, the silky triangle that tempted him beyond restraint.

Desire choked him, all the hungry yearnings of the past days rising up to conquer his very reason. Like a man in a trance he started forward, discarding his clothing on the way.

Julie slid into the water, laughing delightedly at the silken feel of the cool water rushing by her heated body. Playing, she turned on her back. And then she saw him; his fully aroused naked body clearly revealed in the moonlight. Unashamedly he walked slowly toward her. Mesmerized, Julie was unable to take her eyes from the sheer masculine beauty of Murieta's male form. His sleek, poweful body was much like Rod's, moving with the same sinuous grace of a forest animal. The blue-black hair glinted with silver lights. Helplessly, Julie moved her eyes to the fine matting of silky hair that grew on his broad chest, then lower, following the thin line of dark hair trialing across his taut stomach to his formidable manhood.

Murieta stepped into the water and Julie froze, knowing exactly what would happen if he entered. "No, Joaquin, stay where you are," she pleaded, her voice quivering weakly.

"I know this is madness, *chica*, but I cannot escape it. I didn't want this to happen. I fought against it since I first saw you curled up asleep next to your father."

"I'm Rod's wife. I love him."

"Julie, don't deny me, *cara mia*. I have a feeling that I will never see you again. Let me have this one night to carry into eternity."

Slowly his hands closed around her shoulders, pulling her to him, the bouyancy of the water making the movements almost dreamlike. Their limbs met, the water lapping around their bodies. His mouth crushed down on hers as his hands curled around her naked buttocks, bringing her even closer, making her intensely aware of the full arousal of his lean body.

Exerting all the strength she possessed, Julie pulled away. She did not want this. She wanted only Rod. The thought of another man's hands exploring her body intimately sickened her. If she couldn't have Rod she wanted no one.

"No, Joaquin, don't do this," she pleaded softly. "Rod may not love me but I won't betray him. I don't want you."

"I love you, *querida*," Joaquin gasped raggedly. "We both know my days on earth are numbered. Allow me this one last taste of happiness."

Julie tried to protest but he stilled her words with a wave of the hand. "No, Julie, it's true. There is a price on my head and a bandit's life is a violent one. But if you allow me to love you, I will have no regrets," he said hopefully.

"I'm sorry, Joaquin," Julie said regretfully, walking slowly toward the shore. "I can't change my feelings."

"*Si*," Murieta nodded solemnly. "Rodrigo is a lucky man. I knew that from the beginning. But if Elena's story is true, then he doesn't deserve your love."

"I can't help it, Joaquin. Perhaps one day I will learn the truth. But even if Rod doesn't love me, I don't ever expect to love again."

"Ah, *chica*," he smiled sadly. "You are young, passionate, full of life. Do not give up so easily. One day happiness will come to you and when it does, remember Joaquin Murieta; remember that he loved you but respected your feelings." Long afterwards Julie was to recall his prophetic words.

The next day Paco, Jose, and the others returned to camp. The time had come for Julie to leave.

13

When Rod, in the company of his saddle weary *vaqueros* set foot on Delgado land, he was suffused with a happiness that surprised him. The weeks of his absence seemed more like years. Why, he wondered curiously? Why was it any different now than it had been before? Smiling ruefully, Rod answered his own question. Julie! Julie's presence on the *rancho* made all the difference in the world. There had never been a honey-haired, blue-eyed witch waiting for him before, if indeed she was waiting for him at all.

Flushing, Rod could not help but recall how cruelly he had used her the night before he left home. *Por Dios*, how she had goaded him! If only she hadn't discovered Elena in his room. Elena meant nothing to him. Though he was confused as to his actual feelings for his wife, he certainly had missed her these past weeks.

In his heart, Rod refused to acknowledge that it was love he felt for the slim wisp of a golden beauty he had married. His mind was a contradiction of emotions. Inexplicably, he recalled the silken murmur of her skin against his, the desire that swept over him whenever she was near, the sweet perfume of her flesh that was hers alone, driving him mad with yearning. Would she welcome him with open arms, he wondered eagerly? Or was she still angry at him for succumbing to Elena's subtle seduction that one time? He fervently hoped that in his absense Elena had settled down to become a proper wife to his father for he vowed never again to touch the woman carnally. Why should he when it was Julie he wanted?

A collective whoop of joy rent the air when the *hacienda* came into view. Horses were spurred and crops judiciously employed in the *vaquero's* race to their homes and families. Rod was beside them all the way, as eager as a young boy to greet his loved ones.

Elena waited on the veranda looking as serene and lovely as always. A twinge of disappointment settled between Rod's shoulders as he searched in vain for Julie. When he failed to see her the pleasure of his homecoming tasted like ashes in his mouth. Not even his father was on hand to greet him and Rod wondered if somehow Diego found out that he had been betrayed by his wife and son.

Elena was in his arms the moment he dismounted, oblivious to the layers of trail dust and a week's growth of beard on his chin. "Rodrigo, *caro*, how glad I am to see you! If only you knew what I've gone through since you left!"

For the first time Rod noticed her black garb and a stab of fear punctured his heart. His first thoughts were of Julie and her failure to greet him. "Julie! Has something happened to my wife, Elena? Tell me, damn you, tell me!"

Assuming a tragic expression even though she wanted to laugh gleefully, Elena ventured, "Oh, Rodrigo, it happened so suddenly. Neither of us knew what was happening until it was too late."

"What happened, Elena? *Por Dios*! Too late for what?" In his anxiety Rod was unaware that he had grasped Elena's slim shoulders and was shaking her relentlessly.

"*Por favor*, Rodrigo! Stop! How can I answer with my teeth rattling?"

Immediately Rod released her. "I'm sorry, Elena,"

he apologized. "Where is my wife? Is . . . is she dead?"

"Murieta has her."

"What! Murieta! *Perdicion*! I don't believe it!"

"It's true. Julie and I were out riding when Murieta's men surrounded us."

Rod eyed Elena narrowly. "How is it that you escaped and Julie did not?"

Elena shrugged her elegant shoulders, for some reason the gesture infuriating Rod. "They didn't want me. Pedro, Murieta's lieutenant, made it abundantly clear that his leader wanted only your wife."

Rod cursed roundly, suddenly recalling Murieta's threat of long ago to steal Julie. "Has there been no ransom note? No word of any kind?"

Eyes downcast, Elena shook her dark tresses. "I'm sorry, *mi amor*. I received no communication or demand for money since Julie was taken three weeks ago. In fact," she stressed, lowering her voice conspiratorially, "Julie did not seem all that reluctant about accompanying Murieta's men."

"Are you telling me that Julie went willingly?" Rod croaked in disbelief.

Elena shrugged, looking at Rod pityingly. "It did seem that way, *querido*. Why else have we heard nothing?" she hinted maliciously. "By now she is either Murieta's mistress or dead."

"No!" shouted Rod. "I refuse to believe that Julie is dead. As for the other," he said, his mouth drawn into a thin white line, "I'll only believe that when I see it. Where was my father when all this was taking place? What has he done to find Julie?"

"Oh, Rodrigo, it pains me to be the bearer of such sad tidings. Your father is dead."

Rod's brows drew together in an agonized expression as he regarded Elena uncertainly. "Dead? My father is dead?"

"*Si, querido*," Elena nodded sympathetically.

"I cannot believe it. He's never been sick a day in his life."

"He didn't die from an illness, Rodrigo," Elena informed him, feigning a sadness she did not feel. "It . . . it was an accident. A dreadful accident."

"What kind of an accident?"

"Diego was cleaning his gun. It . . . it discharged accidentally and killed him instantly."

"I find that difficult to swallow, Elena," Rod repudiated. "My father was no novice with firearms. He would never allow anything like that to happen."

"Accidents do happen, Rodrigo."

Rod allowed the *vaqueros* only one night's respite before he led them out the next morning in search of Murieta. If Elena was telling the truth, and he had no reason to doubt her, Julie had been kidnapped over three weeks ago. But had she really been abducted or did she go willingly like Elena suggested? It certainly was plausable enough, Rod considered, especially in view of his own despicable behavior toward his wife those last days before he left.

It was common knowledge that Murieta had a secret hideout somewhere in the Santa Lucia Mountains and Rod's chances of finding it were practically nil. His fruitless and often frustrating search continued for well over a month, but in the end, Rod was forced to return to the *rancho* with his exhausted *vaqueros*. Julie had to be either dead or happily ensconced in the arms of Joaquin Murieta.

Reluctantly Rod took up the reins of leadership at the *rancho*, becoming *el patron* in his father's place. Wisely Elena did not force the renewal of their relationship upon his return, preferring instead to let Rod make the first move. In his own way Rod grieved for his father, but selfishly Elena refused to believe he entertained any strong feelings for his missing wife, or that Julie's abduction affected him strongly.

In that, Elena was wrong. Rod did grieve for Julie. His strong feelings for her surprised even him, and one day Elena learned how much Julie had left her imprint upon Rod.

Their conversation at supper that night left Elena angrier than she had ever been in her life.

"Rodrigo," Elena began hesitantly, uncertain where to begin. "Your father is dead, you have grieved long enough. For all intents and purposes your wife no longer exists. Don't you think it's time we spoke to *Padre* Juan?"

A muscle throbbed in Rod's lean jaw as he cut Elena a decidedly blank look. His voice was deceptively calm when he asked, "Whatever do you mean, Elena? What is it we must discuss with the good *padre*?"

"Don't be so dense, *mi amor*," Elena teased archly. "We are both young, both lonely. At one time we were betrothed. Would it be so wrong for us to seek comfort from one another? Would it not make sense for us to marry?"

"*Por Dios*, Elena, are you *loco*? You are still in mourning. Have you forgotten so soon that my father honored you with his name? What would our friends say?"

"They would see the wisdom of our marrying," Elena shot back, exasperated by Rod's stubbornness as well as his unwillingness to accept that which was meant to be. "Do you think there isn't already much talk about us living alone here in the *hacienda*? Ask the *vaqueros* if you don't believe me."

"*Padre* Juan would never sanction our marriage," Rod informed her coldly. "Talk or no talk, what you ask is impossible. There is no indication that Julie is dead. One day I will find her. And when I do, I hope she can forgive me for the wrong I did to her. It's too late to apologize to my father but if I can make it up to Julie, I will."

Elena turned away in disgust. There was more than one way to reach Rodrigo, she gloated, and it wasn't through useless talk. She had gotten through to him once and she would again, she vowed, feline eyes glinting dangerously.

That night Rod sat up later than usual in his father's study, consuming more of his favorite brandy than was his normal habit. Elena saw to it that he was well supplied. When finally he staggered groggily to his room, his mind filled with thoughts of Julie, Elena allowed him just enough time to fall asleep before she stealthily entered his room and climbed naked into his bed. At first contact with her warm body his arms went greedily around her and Elena sighed, pleased with his response and her own ability to bring about his capitulation. Without a doubt, she knew they would become lovers again.

Rod murmured in his sleep, the warm body pressed intimately against him, penetrating his deepest dreams. Instinctively he pulled the fragrant flesh closer, breathing in her special aroma. When the cloying smell of roses trickled beneath his senses, Rod's eyes popped open, aware of the fact that Julie did not wear the scent of roses. Elena smiled beguilingly into his dark eyes.

"Elena, what in the hell are you doing here? I thought I made myself clear concerning our relationship."

"You know you don't mean that, Rodrigo," Elena pouted prettily.

"I was never more serious in my life, Elena. I have neither the inclination nor the energy to make love to you tonight . . . or ever."

"Then lay back, *mi amor*, and let me do all the work," Elena purred seductively as she reached unerringly for his flaccid manhood, manipulating his limp member with such expertise that Rod's reaction was automatic and instantaneous.

The moment her greedy mouth encompassed him,

Rod bolted upright. "*Por Dios*, Elena, where did you learn that?" Elena was too caught up in sexual desire to answer.

Following Don Diego's sudden death and during Rod's absence, Elena often spent long pleasurable hours in the stable with Manuel. It had all begun when Manuel demanded her surrender as part of the bargain to get rid of Julie. At first Elena had been reluctant, but in the end loneliness and lust drove her into Manuel's brawny arms. The *vaquero* was not particularly adept at lovemaking, but he was lusty and well versed in the many ways of sensual delights. Besides, he resembled Rod to the extent that Elena often fantasized that it was Rod who held her in his arms. Now, Elena was anxious to try all her newfound knowledge on Rodrigo.

Though Rod was shocked by Elena's blatant act of lust, he could not help but become aroused by her soft, warm mouth. Elena laughed huskily when she felt his arousal between her lips and the sound brought Rod abruptly to his senses. Thoroughly disgusted with himself as well as with Elena's attempt at seduction, he rudely shoved her aside.

"Not this time, *bruja*," Rod flung out. "I won't be beguiled by you again. If and when I decide to take a lover I will let you know, but I wouldn't wait for that day if I were you. I have no desire to bed you."

Swearing profusely, Elena left in a huff. Later, Rod did not see her sneak out to the stables where Manuel welcomed her with open arms. Thoroughly rebuffed and humiliated, Elena decided it best to retreat until Rodrigo was in a more receptive mood. Therefore, in the days to follow, the tension between them eased somewhat.

One day Rod came upon Teresa as she went about her duties. Suddenly he remembered the enchanting child Julie had become so fond of and wondered why he never saw her about the *rancho* anymore. He decided to ask.

Teresa stared dumbly at Rod for a few minutes before answering. "Doña Elena did not like Felicia. The niña was warned to keep out of her way and was sent to the mission."

"Why would Elena do such a thing?" asked Rod, thoroughly puzzled.

Teresa knew the answer but chose to hold her tongue. "Who knows, señor?" she shrugged, avoiding his piercing gaze.

"Tell the child to return immediately, *por favor*. I am *el patron* here, not Elena. I know Julie cared deeply for the child and I would not have Felicia banished for the simple reason that Elena does not like her."

"*Si, señor*," grinned Teresa, pleased. "I will send word that Felicia may return. She will be grateful to you, for this is the only home she has known since *Padre* Juan put her in my arms nine years ago."

Shortly after that conversation Rod began seeing Felicia about the *rancho*, usually perched on her favorite spot upon the fence surrounding the corral where the horses were trained. Usually Rod merely smiled and nodded whenever he saw her, but one day her sad doe eyes drew him to her like a magnet.

Though he knew little about the child, he recognized the look of quality instantly. Julie had told him Felicia was a *mestiza*, but somewhere along the line there was pure Spanish blood flowing through her veins, Rod surmised, enough to make her appear as highborn and proud as Elena. He would have to ask Teresa about the child's origins, Rod reflected thoughtfully.

"*Hola*, Felicia," Rod greeted affably as he came abreast of the child. "I am happy to see you back on the *rancho*."

"*Gracias*, Don Rodrigo," Felicia said shyly. "Are you certain Doña Elena won't become angry with *Tia* Teresa for allowing me to return?"

"I have already spoken to Elena," Rod told her,

remembering the scene with Elena the day before when she had become thoroughly incensed with Rod's decision concerning Felicia. But Rod had been adamant on the subject. As long as he was *el patron,* no one was to interfere with Felicia's right to live on *Rancho* Delgado.

Felicia's piquant features lit up like a beacon as she gazed raptly at Rod. "Oh, señor! You are so good and kind. I love living on the *rancho*. I was so happy when Doña Julie and I—" Abruptly she stopped, her face flushed.

"It's all right, *niña*," Rod assured her gently. "I know you loved her. She told me many times how much she cared for you."

Felicia beamed joyfully. "We were great friends, *señor*," she admitted shyly, "but she did not love me nearly as much as she loved you."

"Did she tell you that?" Rod questioned gently.

"There was no need, *señor*, I knew."

Rod sighed. "You are mistaken, *niña*. I gave Julie little reason to love me. But I thank you for your kind words. Now, enough of this talk. Do you still enjoy riding?"

"*Si*," replied Felicia, glancing at Rod from beneath feathery black lashes.

"Would you ride with me? I would be pleased to have you join me."

"*Si*, I would enjoy that," laughed Felicia, jumping from the rail before Rod could assist her.

That began the first of many pleasurable hours spent with an enchanting child Rod grew increasingly fond of as the days flew by. Normally their rides were necessarily short due to Rod's responsibilities on the *rancho*. But one fine morning Rod found himself with some extra time on his hands and he and Felicia rode out toward the Santa Lucia Mountains. They rode in comfortable silence for about two hours when Rod suddenly realized tht the child was no longer at his side.

Instantly he spun about and spied Felicia a short distance behind him. She had halted and was staring transfixed into the foothills surrounding them. "What is it, *niña*?" he asked anxiously. "What do you see?" Automatically he reached for the weapon he carried with him at all times.

"This is the place," whispered Felicia, gazing about with sad eyes. "This is where Doña Julie and Doña Elena were stopped by the *banditos*."

Rod felt his hackles rise. "How do you know, *niña*? It could have been anywhere along here. Even Elena could not remember the exact spot."

"No, *señor*," Felicia insisted stubbornly. "It was here. I saw it with my own eyes. I was hiding over there." She pointed confidently to a huge boulder about one-hundred yards away.

Rod was flabbergasted by Felicia's unexpected disclosure. Until now he had assumed Elena to be the only witness to what really took place that day. "What were you doing so far from the mission, *niña*?" Rod asked skeptically.

"You will not tell *mi tia*, or *Padre* Juan?" Felicia asked fearfully. Solemnly Rod gave his promise. Satisfied, Felicia revealed, "After Doña Elena told *Tia* Teresa I was no longer welcome on the *rancho*, I stayed at the mission with *Padre* Juan. *Tia* said I would be safer there. Although I did not understand, I did as I was told.

"But I missed Doña Julie and our rides together. *Padre* Juan sensed I was unhappy and loaned me a horse so that I might ride again. One day I strayed close to the *hacienda* although I knew I did wrong, and saw Doña Julie and Doña Elena ride out together. I decided to follow them, keeping far enough behind so they would not notice me."

"And then?" prodded Rod. Though his impatience was great he kept his voice deliberately gentle so as not to frighten the child.

"And then I saw the *banditos* ride out from the hills. I was frightened. They looked so fierce. I rode behind the boulder where they could not see me and waited for them to leave." Felicia hesitated, looking wide eyed at Rod through a curtain of thick black lashes. "Did I do wrong, *señor*? Was I a coward to hide?"

"You did exactly right, *niña*," Rod concurred gently. "There was nothing you could have done. Those were cruel, conscienceless men. You could have been hurt badly had they discovered you."

Felicia nodded gravely, vastly relieved by Rod's assurance. "Tell me everything you saw and heard, *niña*. Did . . . did Julie go willingly with the *bandito* as Elena would have me believe?"

"Oh, no, Don Rodrigo!" gasped Felicia, horrified. "You must never believe such a thing! Doña Elena was mistaken. Doña Julie was dragged off screaming and kicking but the huge *bandito* with the scar on his face was too strong for her. Though I did not hear their words I saw everything clearly."

Pedro! thought Rod, his heart sinking. "I believe you, Felicia," he declared, a sudden joy suffusing him. He should have known that Elena could never be relied upon to be truthful where Julie was concerned. There was no love lost between the two women, whereas Felicia had no reason to lie. "Why haven't you come forward with this information sooner, *niña*?"

"I . . . I was afraid," admitted Felicia, hanging her head. "I thought *Tia* and *Tio* might forbid me to ride again if they knew I had disobeyed them and strayed so far away. And . . . and I feared Doña Elena."

"Elena? Why would she wish to harm you?"

"I . . . I don't know. It is just something I feel in my heart. Perhaps she was afraid I would tell someone that she gave something to the *bandito* who took Doña Julie."

"What did she give the *bandito*?" asked Rod curiously.

"I'm not sure, *señor*. But it could have been a purse."

"Could have been?"

"It was difficult to tell at that distance," apologized Felicia. Rod's acute disappointment caused her to add, "I'm sorry, *señor*, but there is nothing more I can tell you except that it looked like a purse, a heavy one."

"You've done well, *niña*," Rod smiled. "You are very observant and I am grateful to you. I would ask only one more thing of you." Felicia nodded. "In which direction did the *banditos* take Julie?"

"They rode into the mountains, Don Rodrigo," pointed Felicia.

For several days after that Rod rode out alone, always to the place where Felicia had last seen Julie. From that point he fanned out in all directions, hoping to come upon Murieta's hideout. After two agonizing weeks he was forced to again abandon his search. He decided it was time to force the truth from Elena.

That very night he summoned her to his study. "Elena, a few days ago I discovered something that puzzles me about Julie's abduction," he contended coolly.

Elena drew her breath in sharply, fear spiking through her innards like a sharp blade. "What did you discover, Rodrigo?" she asked innocently, forcing a calmness she didn't feel.

"I learned by accident that Felicia followed you and Julie that day. She ran when the *banditos* came riding out of the hills and hid out of fear. But she saw everything clearly."

"Just what did she think she saw?" Elena asked disparagingly.

"From what she told me I can only assume that you lied to me. Julie was indeed taken against her will. She did not go willingly.''

"It angers me to think you would rather believe that little *mestiza* than me,'' spat Elena, rage overriding every other emotion. "I told you what I saw. Can I help it if that child chose to ignore the obvious? You must know how she worshipped Julie and hated me. It would make her happy to dispute my words and make me out a liar.''

"Felicia said she saw you give a purse to Pedro. Do you want to tell me about it?'' His voice caused Elena to shiver as icy fear formed around her heart. Her fertile mind searched frantically for a plausible answer that would somehow satisfy Rodrigo.

"Of course I handed a purse to Pedro,'' Elena announced haughtily. "Do you think they would let me go without robbing me of my valuables? Though it was Julie they wanted, they took all my jewelry and the money purse I always carry on my person. I'm surprised you should ask such a stupid question, Rodrigo.''

Rod was stunned. Naturally Murieta's band of thieves would want Elena's valuables. He was so busy trying to read deception and betrayal into Elena's actions that so simple an explanation never entered his mind. Had Felicia also misread Julie's willingness or unwillingness to accompany Murieta's men? he wondered bleakly, finding himself right back where he started from.

At length, he said, "I'm sorry, Elena. I have no right to accuse you unjustly or accept Felicia's word over yours.''

"I'm relieved you've come to your senses, *mi caro*,'' Elena smiled smugly. "We've known each other since we were children. You were once *mi novio* and I still love you. I would never lie to you. One day you will realize we were meant to be together and when you do, I will be waiting.''

"Elena, I know I wronged you, but nothing can be

decided between us until I find Julie. Or . . . or learn that she is no longer alive,'' added Rod bleakly.

"Do you care so much?" asked Elena wryly.

"I . . . don't think I ever gave our marriage a chance. But in the few months we were together I came to care for her a great deal.''

"Caring is not love, Rodrigo,'' reminded Elena, refusing to face the fact that Rod loved Julie. "Besides,'' she hinted slyly, deciding to do something she had thought about for a long time, "I haven't wanted to tell you this but there is a good chance that Julie is dead.''

"*Por Dios*, Elena! What makes you say that?"

"Manuel,'' she replied hesitantly.

"Manuel?'' The *vaquero*? What the hell does he have to do with this?''

"Manuel is Pedro's cousin. Of course he doesn't have anything to do with that vile Pedro or his activities, but on occasion the two visit relatives at the same time. Pedro told Manuel that Murieta abducted Julie in retaliation for Maria. When he tired of her, he handed her over to his men. According to Manuel she didn't survive the ordeal.''

Rod's face turned deathly white and if he hadn't been sitting he would have been unable to support his rubbery legs. *Dios*, no! The thought of his Julie mauled and cruelly raped by a band of cutthroats was too horrible to be borne. "No!'' he shouted aloud, his composure shattered by the picture of her torn and abused body lying beneath those of countless men. "I'll kill them! I swear I will avenge her if they have killed her. One by one I will hunt them down and snuff out their lives!''

Rod's outburst was so emotional that Elena immediately regretted her lie, fearing she had done more damage than good. When Rod stormed out of the room to confront Manuel, Elena was hard on his heels. But as

fate would have it, Manuel was nowhere to be found.
When earlier Elena made casual mention of what she
planned to do, the *vaqueros* became so fearful of
Rodrigo's wrath that he packed his gear and stealthily
departed the *rancho* in the dead of the night.

Thoroughly demoralized by her lie as well as by
Manuel's abrupt disappearance, Elena deemed Rod ripe
for another attempt at seduction. Faced with the
possibility of Julie's death, depressed, it seemed only
natural that Elena should take advantage of his
restlessness, his spells of nervous aggitation, the long
sleepless nights spent walking the floor.

For days Elena watched Rod carefully, thinking that
soon he would be driven to either take one of the
attractive servant girls or visit a *puta* in the village.
Aware of his strict code about using any of the servants
in such a manner, although many of them would not be
adverse to bedding the handsome don, Elena suspected
that before long he would seek out one of the village *putas.*
She knew him to be virile with strong sexual urges. But
evidently she did not know Rod as well as she thought
she did. Seeking gratification with another woman was
the farthest thing from Rod's mind.

Late one night she heard Rod's footsteps pass her
door on the way out. Instantly she was out of bed and
out of the room. "Rodrigo!" she cried, immediately
halting his stealthy progress. "Where are you going so
late at night?"

"I owe you no explanation, Elena," Rod answered
crisply, turning to resume his steps.

"Rodrigo, wait!" Taking a calculated risk, Elena
whipped her filmy nightgown over her head and flung it
at her feet. Rod's muffled groan lent her courage.

"Why go to a *puta* when I can do much more for you,
mi amor?" she purred huskily, undulating her hips in a
seductive manner.

The door to Elena's room was thrown wide and her

nude body was clearly outlined in the light from her lamp, every luscious detail etched into Rod's brain. Dusky-tipped breasts slightly swollen from desire rose up sharply to tease his senses. But the sight of full curving hips, gently rounded stomach, and a mound of ebony curls lower on her abdomen did not affect Rod like Elena had hoped. The sight of her nubile body filled him with disgust. Contrary to what Elena thought, Rod was not on his way to find a woman. He was going to the study to get a bottle in order to drink himself into a stupor. Of late, sleep would come only after rendering himself senseless.

"I don't need a *puta*, Elena," Rod snarled, shoving her aside. "And I certainly don't need you! Get out of my sight, you sicken me!"

"I didn't sicken you once," Elena retorted hotly. "You had no qualms about taking my virginity."

"That was a mistake, Elena, and you know it! You tricked me. I thought you were Julie."

"Well, that one time made me pregnant!" Elena blurted out heatedly. "You had no difficulty planting your seed in my belly!"

Rod froze, all color drained from his face. "You lie!" he spat, glowering.

Elena smiled smugly, gloating over her cleverness. He would never need to know that Manuel had fathered her child. "Do you doubt me?" Elena asked reproachfully. "Believe me, *mi amor*. A woman knows these things. Put your hand on my breast." She grasped Rod's hand and placed it on her swollen breast. "Feel the nipple." His fingers began a slow exploration of the engorged nipple and his expression told her he was convinced.

"We must marry, *querido*," Elena urged, pressing her advantage. "Would you have your son born a bastard? It has been weeks since Julie's abduction and from all indications she is long dead."

The thought of Julie's death was abhorrent to Rod.

Even if she were dead he would never marry Elena. But what if she really did carry his child, he allowed grudgingly? If she were pregnant—and he wasn't certain she told the truth—could anyone else be the father?

"Rodrigo? What are you thinking?" Elena asked worriedly. "I'm telling the truth. I am carrying your child." She clung possessively to his arm and Rod shook her off as one would a pesky insect.

"Por Dios, Elena! I have to think!" Rod cried. "Leave me! The sight of you leaves me with a bad taste in my mouth. And cover yourself, you hold no appeal for me."

Stunned, Elena grabbed her robe, holding it before her nakedness. How could Rod resist her, she wondered conceitedly? Time and again she had thrown herself at him only to be rebuffed. She could only stare after him in amazement as Rod rushed by her on his way to his study where he carefully locked the door behind him.

The following day Rod slowly made his way to the stables where he encountered Felicia sitting forlornly on a bale of hay. *"Buenas dias, niña,"* he greeted, wondering if she had been waiting for him to appear. He had much thinking to do and wanted only to be left alone so he could gather his thoughts into some semblance of order. But Felicia's appealing soft eyes made him halt suddenly. Her resemblance to someone from out of his past tugged at his memory, but once again the elusive picture was lost to him.

"Is it true, Don Rodrigo?" she asked gravely, her face a study of concern.

"Is what true, *niña*?"

"Dona Elena informed me a little while ago that you are to marry her. Is it true?"

"You must not believe everything that Dona Elena says," Rod hedged. His answer did not satisfy Felicia.

"You can't, *señor*! You just can't," sobbed Felicia,

heartbroken. "How could you do this to Dona Julie? She loves you!"

"You don't understand, *niña*," Rod explained patiently. "I don't even know if Julie is still alive."

"Dona Elena doesn't love you, *señor*!" Felicia blurted out. "Not like Dona Julie. If she did, she would not have done what she did with Manuel in the stables."

Rod froze, every instinct telling him he was on the verge of a great discovery. "What did Elena do in the stables with Manuel?" he prodded gently.

Felicia became immediately wary, and her expression showed her fear. "You will not become angry if I tell you?" she asked, suddenly as skittish as a young colt.

"Why should I be angry, *niña*?"

"What I saw . . . it is not very nice. Dona Elena would be very angry with me if she knew I was spying on her."

"Were you spying, Felicia?"

"Oh, no, *señor*," denied Felicia, horrified. "I saw Dona Elena and Manuel meet in the stables many times but I never thought to spy on them."

"Then how do you know what happened?" probed Rod.

"One day I went to the stables to take a nap in the soft straw in one of the stalls," Felicia revealed, hesitating but a moment before continuing. "I was awakened by a cry, as if someone was in pain, and moaning sounds. When I went to investigate I saw . . . I saw . . ."

"Do not be afraid, *niña*," Rod said reassuringly when her voice faltered. "No one will harm you if you are telling the truth."

"Dona Elena was lying naked in the straw in the next stall and Manuel was atop her, also naked. She cried out when he put his . . . they did what the animals do when they mate." Her eyes were as round as saucers and Rod had to bend low to hear her words. "She was crying out and rolling her head from side to side but I don't think Manuel was hurting her for she urged him to continue. I crept out of the stables where they were still . . . occupied. Are you displeased with me, Don Rodrigo?''

"You have been a big help, *niña*,'' Rod smiled gratefully, "so how could you displease me?'' Instinctively Rod knew that Felicia was telling the truth. The child was but a babe, too innocent to make up such a tale.

On his way back to the *casa* Rod's mind worked furiously, recalling all that Felicia had told him. It took but a moment to deduce that Elena's pregnancy was the result of her illicit affair with Manuel. He should have known that Elena would stoop to deceit in order to protect her name as well as gain her own end. How gullible she must have thought him to concoct such a lie. Though Rod had little liking for what he was about to do, necessity demanded it be done. Elena had prevailed long enough.

Rod found Elena still lounging in bed. Now that her pregnancy had been revealed, she felt perfectly justified in giving in to the listlessness plaguing her of late. She was startled when Rod stalked into her room without warning, his face set in granite, mouth clamped tightly shut, his eyes fixed. Surely his animosity couldn't be directed at her, could it? Elena shivered.

"What is it, Rodrigo?'' Elena asked when he stood over her, glaring malevolently. "I thought you might be on your way to see *Padre* Juan about our wedding.''

"There will be no wedding, Elena. I never considered marrying you. Did you think me a fool to foist a bastard off on me?''

Stunned, Elena shot abruptly into a sitting position, allowing the sheet to fall about her slim waist, exposing her nude breasts pointing seductively in Rod's direction. The aureoles had turned dark with pregnancy and Rod cursed beneath his breath at his own stupidity for even considering he might be the father of her child.

"I . . . I don't know what you are talking about, Rodrigo," Elena stuttered helplessly. "I've known no other man but you. Not even your father."

"*Puta*!" spat Rod derisively. "What about Manuel? What about your trysts in the stables?"

"Who . . . who told you such a thing?" Fear clamped painfully in Elena's breast.

"It doesn't matter. What does matter is that you were seen, that's all you have to know."

"Felicia!" ground out Elena, her black eyes spitting fire. "Wait until I get my hands on—"

If there was ever the slightest doubt in Rod's mind it had been dispelled by Elena's damning words. "You will do nothing, Elena," he declared, cutting her off in mid-sentence. "How long has your affair with Manuel been going on?"

"He forced me," Elena whined, playing on Rod's sympathy in a last ditch effort to convince him of her innocence. "*Si*, he raped me. I could not help myself. I was alone, with no one to protect me from his attacks. It was terrible, Rodrigo." Suddenly Elena was very pleased with her own quick thinking.

"Rape? I think not, Elena," Rod refuted, his voice deceptively calm. "You went to Manuel willingly."

Suddenly something inside Elena snapped and she leaped at Rod, fingernails bared, snarling. "*Bastardo*! Who are you to condemn me? You who jilted me for an Anglo *puta*! *Si*! I went to Manuel willingly! You taught me lust then abandoned me while my body yearned for the feel of a man deep inside me. It's all your fault, Rodrigo! This child could well have been yours. It should be yours!"

Rod turned away in disgust, preparing to leave.

"Wait!" Elena cried. "What are you going to do? What about my child?"

"In two weeks I'm heading up a cattle drive to San

Antonio. I expect you to be gone before I return."

"Gone?" Elena was dismayed. "This is my home now. I am your father's widow."

"It was your home. I am making other arrangements for you. Until your child is born you will stay at the mission. *Padre* Juan will see to your comfort. I will leave sufficient funds with the good *padre* for your support. Once your child is born you may take what is left and go wherever you please. I cannot find it in my heart to punish an innocent child for your mistakes. The money I leave will provide generously for you and your child for a long time to come. Perhaps you should join your parents in Spain," he suggested.

"You can't do this to me, Rodrigo!" Elena seethed with mounting rage.

"I am within my rights, Elena. *Rancho* Delgado belongs to me and no one will think ill of me if I choose to have you live elsewhere as long as you are well provided for."

Suddenly weary of the conversation, Rod turned on his heel. In his own mind all had been settled to his satisfaction if not to Elena's. But the fiery Spanish woman was to have the last word.

"You're not finished with me by half, Rodrigo!" she flung out at him hatefully. "Nor is your little *mestiza* friend who will live to rue the day she spied on me."

That night a mysterious visitor arrived at the *hacienda*. Carl Darcy couldn't have arrived at a more inopportune time.

TWO
HONOR'S PLEDGE

14

Julie's jumbled thoughts were a million miles away as she stared bleakly out the window of her room in Mae Parker's boarding house. From the moment she returned to San Francisco she felt strangely bereft and alone despite her father's comforting presence. Murieta's parting words had left her more shaken than she cared to admit. She knew she didn't love the handsome bandit, that no one could take Rod's place in her affection, but Murieta's premonition of his own death had thoroughly upset her.

When Murieta's men had returned, Julie and her father left the secluded valley because of ill feelings over Pedro's death. Though Joaquin felt certain he could control his men, he hesitated to place Julie in danger. He realized the noose around him was drawing tighter and it was only a matter of time before he met his end. It was inevitable that his end would be a violent one considering the life he led. So he had provided Julie and Carl, still weak from his injuries, with a wagon, supplies and a generous purse of gold which no doubt was stolen, Julie surmised wryly, and they headed north for San Francisco.

Joaquin's parting words still rang hollowly in her ears. "Think of me sometimes, *chica*, and know that my love for you stretches beyond this life." It was a poignant moment but Julie still did not regret her decision to remain true to Rod.

225

The journey to San Francisco had been blessedly uneventful, for which Julie was eternally grateful. Carl Darcy was far too weak to defend them should the need arise.

San Francisco had changed drastically in the months since Julie had left with Rod. Raw, new buildings of untreated wood stuck out like sore thumbs among their weathered neighbors. The first thing she noticed was the absence of Marty Sloan's mess tent along the main street. In its place stood a new building sporting a gaudy sign advertising food for the discerning customer. The prices quoted were so outrageous Julie's mouth gaped open with shock.

The streets were more crowded than ever. Men seemed to be hurrying about with no purpose or destination. The noise was deafening, and several languages were distinguishable in the melee. But one thing about the sprawling city had not changed. The streets. Still a sea of mud. Still rutted and deeply groved by wagons, horses' hooves and countless pairs of miners' boots trodding a path to fame and fortune . . . or obscurity and death.

Julie made directly for Mae's house, thanking God that there was one other thing besides muddy roads in San Francisco that hadn't changed. Mae welcomed Julie and her father with open arms, asking no questions though she suspected something had happened between Julie and Rod that caused her to leave *Rancho* Delgado. Of course, finding her father was an incredible stroke of luck and Mae expressed her happiness for the girl.

It was inevitable that Julie should reveal to Mae the strange circumstances that caused her to leave Rod and the *rancho*. Though Mae expressed grave doubts that Rod had been behind Elena's actions, she thought Julie had done the right thing in coming to San Francisco with her father.

From Mae, Julie learned that Marty had pulled up stakes and headed for the gold fields where her services were desperately needed. With all the new restaurants springing up in the city, her mess tent was receiving less and less patronage. So one day she packed up all her belongings and headed toward Sacramento with Wong Li. Mae missed her greatly.

Under Mae's expert ministrations, Carl healed swiftly. As he gained his strength, he began to question Julie concerning her future. Did she wish to return east? No, she decided. Did she want to obtain a divorce? She wasn't sure. In fact, Julie had no idea what she wantd to do. Her troubled mind gave her little in the way of respite. Though her father was pressing her for a decision, she had no answer for him. It seemed her life was at an impasse.

Julie watched dispassionately from the window as her father walked toward the boarding house. It was amazing how much he had changed in a few short weeks, she thought. His too slim frame had filled out noticeably, thanks to Mae, and his scruffy beard was gone, revealing once more the dear face she loved. His sandy hair was neatly combed and he was fashionably attired in a business suit. No longer was there a resemblance to "Carlos the *bandito*" who rode with Joaquin Murieta. Quick footsteps sounded on the stairs and Julie turned as her father entered the room.

Carl was struck by his daughter's lack of spirit these past weeks. It was almost as if the life had gone out of her. She seemed to wallow in a mire without aim or direction.

"Where have you been, Papa?" she asked without curiosity.

"To rent a horse," Carl replied in an effort to gain her attention.

"Are we going somewhere?"

"I am going somewhere, daughter, but you're not."

Carl finally gained her attention as Julie slanted him a puzzled glance. "You're going without me?" Julie was incredulous. The possibility that her father would leave her again never entered her mind.

"Only for a little while," Carl's voice softened affectionately. "When I return, I will know more of what we are to do."

For weeks on end Carl had sat back and watched Julie sink deeper and deeper into apathy, insulating her from life until he could no longer bear to see the withdrawn, colorless creature she had become. And all because of Don Rodrigo Delgado, the man she had married. It was obvious that Julie still loved the man no matter what he may have done. As Julie's father, Carl felt it his duty to discover for himself the source of Julie's unhappiness, even if it meant confronting the proud don himself.

After much soul searching Carl Darcy decided to pay a visit to his son-in-law and learn first-hand whether or not the man was capable of betraying the trust of a young, innocent girl in the vile manner Julie described. He had always heard Spaniards were a cruel race, but somehow he did not think his daughter could fall in love with such a man. Therefore, he was left with no alternative but to descend upon Don Rodrigo and learn the truth of the matter without Julie being the wiser. If he found out that the don was indeed the kind of man who would callously order his mistress to do away with his wife, then Julie was better off without him.

But if Julie's husband was innocent of any wrongdoing, Carl decided they deserved a chance at happiness. To Carl's way of thinking, he was duty bound to go to *Rancho* Delgado without Julie's knowledge, using an assumed identity, and learn all he could about the character of Don Rodrigo Delgado. Once he had his answers, he could either take Julie back east or see that she was reunited with her husband.

For the next few days Julie railed and ranted against

her father's surprising decision to leave, but to no avail. Carl's mind was made up. So one bright morning, leaving nearly all their resources in Julie's keeping, Carl Darcy rode out of San Francisco, his destination, *Rancho* Delgado.

Carl's departure left a terrible void in Julie's life. Although Carl assured her he would be gone only a few weeks, she couldn't help but feel depressed when his mysterious mission took him away at a time she needed him most. It just wasn't like him to be so secretive.

As they so often did these days, Julie's thoughts dwelled on Rod and the all too short moments of bliss they had shared as husband and wife. Was he happy now that he and Elena were free to express their love without hindrance or interference, she wondered glumly? Did he ever pause to wonder what had become of her? If she was dead or alive? There were times when she felt certain he cared for her. Not in the same way he cared for Elena, certainly, but the way he made love to her told her he cared. Or was he just a good actor?

There were nights when Julie ached for the feel of Rod's strong arms about her, his mouth teasing, caressing, his hands tenderly discovering all the vulnerable places on her sweetly curved flesh. Would she ever feel that way again? Certainly she would never feel love again or experience the ecstasy she had known with Rod. No other man could ever make her feel as Rod did.

"Why don't you go shopping, honey?" Mae urged when the sight of Julie moping about the house like a lost soul drove her to distraction. Her father's departure over a week ago had left her more downcast than usual. "There are several new stores that should be of interest to you. Buy something pretty, anything to perk up your spirits."

Sighing heavily, Julie made no protest when Mae literally shoved her out into the bright sunlight. The day was fine with a brisk, rather cool breeze blowing in from the sea.

For awhile she walked aimlessly through the busy thoroughfare looking idly in store windows. There were more women in San Francisco now than there were a year ago and suddenly she found herself taking an interest in the cut of their clothing, and their various hair styles. She even went so far as to exchange friendly nods and a few words with several of the ladies in passing.

Feeling far better than she had in months, Julie entered one store after another, spending hours trying on ready-made dresses. With the few coins she had brought with her, preferring to leave the bulk of her money safely at home, Julie purchased an attractive day dress in soft mauve with matching bonnet and shoes. Two new petticoats and a chemise completed her purchases as well as depleted her ready cash. Wearing her new clothes, and after arranging to have her old ones delivered to her lodging, Julie was ready to return home, tired but happy.

But fate willed otherwise. Once out on the street Julie became aware of the insistent clanging of bells. The next thing she noticed was the hordes of people rushing all in the same direction. Then the acrid smell of smoke and ashes assailed her nostrils and she no longer was in doubt as to the cause of excitement. Fire! A word so feared that just the mention of it caused panic. Once started, a fire could easily level every hastily erected structure in San Francisco with great loss of life.

Within seconds Julie was caught up in the shifting crowd and carried along with the force of their motion. She was not even aware of the direction she was being taken until she recognized the neighborhood in which she lived. A silent scream rose in her throat when she neared Mae Parker's boarding house and saw flames shooting up into the air, returning in tiny stinging embers to dust her face and head.

The entire block was ablaze. Already flames licked along the sides and roof of Mae's house, sending sooty clouds of smoke soaring upward. Dragging in deep gulps of charred air, Julie pushed frantically through the lines of men hastily forming a bucket brigade. The fire wagon had already arrived, pumping furiously and futilely into the seemingly unquenchable inferno.

Julie heaved a huge sigh of relief when she spied Mae's round form standing at the edge of the crowd staring with glazed eyes as her livelihood went up in flames. Desperately she elbowed her way to the weeping woman's side. "Mae," Julie said, touching the woman's shoulder compassionately. "I'm so glad you're safe."

Weeping, Mae turned into Julie's arms. "Oh, Julie," Mae sobbed, turning to the young girl for comfort. "It's gone. All I own is going up in smoke."

With a twinge of regret Julie realized that her own possessions, including the money her father left her, was being consumed by flames. In the face of such a disaster, commiserating with Mae was not difficult. But what could she say to a woman well past middleage whose very life depended upon her boarding house and all it contained?

"My money!" Mae moaned, growing increasingly wild eyed as she watched the flames shoot to the roof and ignite. "I must have my money!"

The noise from the pump and from the throngs of people running about, some without obvious purpose, was so deafening that at first Julie failed to read any meaning into Mae's words. Only when the stricken woman broke from Julie's grasp and darted toward the blazing house did Julie realize what Mae had said. "No, Mae!" she cried, making a futile grab at her landlady's billowing dress. "Come back!"

But shock inured Mae to danger and she turned

exceedingly fleet of foot as she dashed past Julie, past stunned on-lookers, into the leaping flames after her cashbox stashed under her bed. Caught completely unaware, Julie could only stand and stare after Mae, her bluebell eyes glazed with fright and her mouth working up and down convulsively. She had to save Mae!

Concern over someone she cared about released her feet as Julie impulsively shot forward, propelled by a force stronger than self preservation, seemingly unconcerned that she raced toward certain death. Fate intervened in the form of a tall, carelessly handsome man whose brawny arms locked like two steel bands about her tiny waist, dragging her with grim determination from the jaws of certain death.

"Let me go!" screamed Julie, struggling against the restraint placed upon her by her rescuer. "I've got to help Mae!"

Just then a loud whoosh rent the air and Julie watched helplessly as the roof of Mae's house collapsed inward, effortlessly snuffing out the kindly woman's life. Mercifully, Julie fainted.

Julie awoke to the smell of ashes and brimstone, but the Hell she found herself in was all too real. She opened her mouth to scream when a soothing voice next to her said, "Are you all right, young lady?"

Julie slewed around to look into a face with high cheekbones, strong nose, a smiling, well-shaped mouth and penetrating green eyes. Thick chestnut hair curled attractively at the nape of his neck and over his forehead, lending him a boyish air. It was a face she had seen before. At length she became increasingly aware that she was cradled protectively in the man's arms, her bright head tucked beneath his chin.

"I'm fine, thank you," Julie murmured. "You can put me down now."

"Only if you promise not to do anything foolish. You almost got yourself killed."

"Mae! Oh God, Mae!" Everything came back to her in a rush of suffocating pain. She began to sob softly, her copious tears dampening the man's lapels.

Moved by Julie's heartrending tears, the man abruptly turned and began walking away from the scene of destruction with the weeping girl still held securely in his arms.

"Where . . . where are you taking me?" choked out Julie.

"I'm going to take you home." His words brought on a fresh barrage of tears. "I'm not going to harm you, my dear. My name is Brett Casey and though my reputation isn't as pristine as I would hope, I do not hurt defenseless young women."

At first the name meant nothing to Julie. Until she risked another look at his smiling face. Brett Casey. The man who had saved her life was the same one who had gallantly carried her across the muddy street months ago, inciting Rod's anger. He was also the owner of Casey's Pleasure Palace. Julie was certain he did not remember her. There was barely a soul left in San Francisco who even recalled that she was the wife of Don Rodrigo Delgado.

"I am Julie Darcy, Mr. Casey," Julie said hesitantly.

"Please call me Brett, Julie," Casey smiled engagingly. "Now, where do you live? And what was Mac to you that would cause you to risk your life for her?" Noting that Julie appeared recovered from her faint, Brett reluctantly set her on her feet, keeping a hand about her tiny waist in order to lend assistance should she still need it.

"Mae was a very good friend," Julie said, swallowing with difficulty the hard knot of tears clogging her throat. "The only friend I had in San Francisco. She was also my landlady. I lived in her boarding house. And now she's gone."

"What about your parents? Surely they will find

another place to stay."

"My father left town a few days ago on business. I was to stay with Mae until his return." Julie's sad voice and tragic eyes struck a chord somewhere in the hardened chambers of Brett's heart. "Everything we owned was destroyed in the flames. Clothing, money, everything," she repeated, dazed by the enormity of the dilemma now facing her.

"We'll send for your father, my dear. Once he finds out what happened, I'm sure he will return immediately."

Julie's bluebell eyes blinked at Brett Casey several times, and his heart was immediately lost. "I don't know where he is," she admitted somewhat shamefacedly. "His business was of a private nature. He assured me he would not be gone overly long."

Intuitively, Brett knew that Julie's emotions were near the breaking point. He was also aware that he could not in all good conscience abandon her on the lawless streets of San Francisco. Brett realized immediately that she was not a woman in the habit of caring for herself. Abandoning her would be tantamount to tossing a babe to a pack of wolves. Besides, he had just found her and was not about to let her get away so easily. Already he was half in love with her.

"There is no one who will take you in?" Brett asked carefully. "No friends? No family?"

Swallowing convulsively, Julie shook her head. She was well aware of what would happen to her if left to her own devices. In order to survive until her father returned she would be forced to support herself, employing the only means open to her. Her expressive face conveyed her thoughts perfectly to Brett Casey, definitely a man knowledgeable in the many aspects of life in the wide open city of San Francisco. And if Brett had his way, Julie Darcy would soon be firmly ensconced in his bed.

Taking Julie's elbow in a way that brooked no argument, Brett said, "Come along, Julie."

"Where . . . where are you taking me?"

"To my place. You need to rest. You've just had a terrible shock and I would never forgive myself if I left you alone and something dreadful happened to you." His softly spoken words implied more than they said.

Brett Casey may have been a gambler, a ladies' man well known for his impeccable taste in women, a man who changed his mistresses as often as he changed his shirt, but he was generous to a fault to his lovers; a man who rarely relied on violence in his dealings. Above all, Brett was not a ravisher of young, unwilling women. There was never any need.

To Brett's way of thinking Julie had come into his life at an opportune moment. His current mistress, Rita, a fiery Mexican, was becoming far too possessive for his liking. She had become boring, too. Of late, even her considerable charms and expertise failed to arouse him. He was beginning to think he was becoming jaded and that no one would succeed in moving him to great heights again. Until he saw Julie, that is. Instinctively he felt that he had finally found a woman who would never bore him or fail to arouse him. Now that he had found her, he did not want to let her slip away.

Many things went through Julie's mind as she considered her fate should she be left to make her own way. All of them worse than going along with Brett Casey, who seemed neither threatening nor dangerous compared to her other alternatives. Clearly at the end of her tether, Julie allowed Brett to guide her to the entrance of his saloon several blocks from where the fire was finally being brought under control.

Julie surveyed the main salon of the Pleasure Palace curiously. It was the first time she had seen the inside of a gambling establishment and she was not likely to forget the experience.

The first thing Julie noticed were walls papered in gold. Vivid red velvet drapes hanging from the long front windows and upon the stage complemented the plush red carpet on the stairs and along the balcony of the upper floor. The next most prominent object in the room was the long bar, stained and polished with beeswax until it shone with a dark, burnished gleam, as did the hard wooden floor and stage. Over the bar hung a gold-veined mirror that reflected rows of bottles and glasses lined upon shelves. Elegant was the only word Julie could think of. Even the potted plants and brass spittoons were clean and shining. Julie knew that her mouth was agape and eyes wide and staring as Brett, green eyes twinkling mischievously, seated her at a small, highly polished table. At that time of day there were few customers, and except for the bartender eyeing them curiosly, there was no one to interrupt.

Once Julie was seated, Brett ambled over to the bar and brought back a delicate glass half full of an amber liquid that appeared to capture the highlights of her sherry-hued hair, causing Brett to catch his breath in admiration. "What is this?" Julie asked suspiciously as she swirled the golden liquid in her glass.

Brett chuckled goodnaturedly. "Just brandy, my dear. I thought it might soothe your nerves." Julie made no move to bring the glass to her lips, still distrustful. She had heard many rumors of the various ways to render helpless young women meek and pliable.

Exasperated, Brett took the glass in hand and sipped generously. "See, no drugs, nothing to harm you. Trust me, sweetheart, I would do nothing to hurt you. I've already told you that."

Convinced that Brett wasn't out to do her any harm, Julie sipped delicately of the soothing liquid, surprised at how good the brandy felt sliding down her parched throat. Against her will she began to relax, albeit

keeping a wary eye on the devilishly handsome Brett
Casey.

"Feeling better?" Brett asked, smiling. Julie nodded.

"Do you own all this?" Julie dared to ask, sweeping a
slim hand before her.

"The Pleasure Palace is all mine," Brett said
proudly. "The first of its kind in San Francisco."

"It's . . . very nice," Julie offered. For some reason
Julie's innocent observation appeared to amuse Brett
and he chuckled low in his throat, a not unpleasant
sound that caused crinkles to form around his fine,
green eyes.

At length Brett ordered supper for them. Julie ate
hungrily, suddenly aware that she hadn't eaten since
breakfast. While they ate, the Pleasure Palace appeared
to burst into life around them as men began to drift in
from the street now that the danger of the fire spreading
to other sections of town appeared remote. Some of the
customers were grimy and soot covered, making Julie
painfully aware of the cruel fact that Mae Parker was
dead. Her expression became so sad that Brett fought
the urge to gather her slim form in his arms and console
her.

"What is it, sweetheart?" he asked, concern
roughening his voice.

"I can't help but think of Mae. She's dead . . . and
. . . her funeral . . . I don't know what to do."

"I'll take care of it," Brett assured her, patting her
hand comfortingly.

"Why should you? You don't even know Mae?"
asked Julie warily.

"Ah, you're wrong there, my dear Julie. Everyone
knew Mae Parker. She was well liked and respected in
this community. I will consider it an honor to make all
the arrangements. Don't worry your pretty head about
it."

"You're very kind," Julie said softly.

Truly, Julie had never met a man like Brett Casey.
Not even Joaquin, who professed love for her, could be
placed in the same category as Brett. Murieta was a
hardened criminal, a man whose life was dedicated to
crime. While Brett, not exactly above reproach, was
from all that she heard a non-violent man who flitted his
time away in pleasurable pursuits. Compared to her
proud, arrogant husband, he appeared uncomplicated
and thoroughly charming.

Pleased by Julie's timid response to his initial kindness, Brett sat back contentedly and studied her profile.
Her bones were delicately carved, her mouth full and
generous, and her smooth skin glowed with pale gold
undertones despite her obvious fatigue. She sensed his
scrutiny and her thick feathery lashes swept down across
her cheekbones, completely obscuring her bluebell eyes.
Brett was so entranced by the fall of honey-colored hair
caressing firm, high perched breasts that he failed to
notice the snapping-eyed woman advancing upon them
with a murderous expression screwing up her lovely
features.

"Who is this *puta*, Brett?" the fiery woman asked
insultingly. "She does not belong here."

Brett appeared not at all perturbed by the woman's
outburst as he smiled in a friendly manner at the
intruder. "This is Julie, Rita. She has just had a terrible
shock. As you can see, we are just finishing supper.
Julie, meet Rita, one of my . . . employees."

Julie smiled amiably but Rita would have none of it.
"What else did you offer her with supper, *querido*?"
Her voice was like oiled silk, and as deadly as a viper.

"You jump to conclusions, Rita," Brett replied, the
smile fading from his voice. Rita immediately
recognized the note of warning and reluctantly desisted
from her line of query. Though Brett had never harmed
her, there were times, like now, when his tone belied his
mild mannered reputation.

"I meant . . . nothing by it, *querido*," Rita purred obsequiously.

"Jealousy does not become you, little one. Julie can take nothing from you that is not yours." His meaning was perfectly clear and Rita had the grace to flush.

Julie watched and listened to the exchange between Rita and Brett with wide eyed apprehension. The last thing she wanted was to come between a man and his mistress, which was obviously Rita's status. Thinking it was time to take her leave, she arose somewhat unsteadily to her feet. Brandy was something she could hereafter do without, she reflected as her head spun giddily.

"Where are you going?" Brett asked sharply.

"I . . . I think I should leave," Julie blurted out foolishly, as if she had someplace to go.

"Where will you go?" Brett asked laconically.

"I . . . I . . ."

"Just as I thought," he intervened curtly. "I won't allow you to leave here only to end up in some back alley sprawled on your back."

Julie gasped, shocked by his blunt language. But it seemed to spark a response in her as she abruptly resumed her seat. "You aren't responsible for me, Brett."

"I'm making you my responsibility, Julie," Brett said softly.

"Are you *loco*, Brett?" cut in Rita nastily. "She's right. Let her go. She's not your worry. She's trouble. Big trouble."

"Shut up, Rita," Brett warned sharply. "Get out of here. Julie and I need to talk."

"Harumph!" Rita said, turning on her heel in a swish of short red and black ruffled skirts swirling about her shapely knees. "Be careful, Brett, or you'll find your bed empty tonight."

"Is that a promise, Rita?" Brett smiled devilishly.

Julie blushed furiously and wished desperately to be anywhere but privy to Brett Casey's love life.

The moment Rita left, Brett devoted his full attention to Julie. "Let's talk about your immediate needs, sweetheart. What are your plans?"

"My father will return to San Francisco soon," Julie said hopefully. "I will survive until then. I'm strong, I'll find work."

"I have a proposition, Julie, that should solve all your immediate problems to both our satisfaction."

Julie bristled indignantly. "I'm not interested in your proposition, Mr. Casey. Now, if you'll excuse me—"

"Hold on, sweetheart, don't jump to conclusions. I only meant to offer you employment."

"Here?" Julie croaked. The thought was ludicrous. "What could I do?"

"Can you sing?" Julie shook her head. "Dance?" ventured Brett. Another negative shake. "Are you familiar with cards?"

"Look, Brett," contended Julie, "I appreciate this, but . . . it's hopeless."

"Not as hopeless as you think. I can teach you all you need to know about dealing blackjack in one day."

"I don't know," debated Julie skeptically.

"Well, I do, sweetheart. You can have one of the rooms upstairs and I'll pay you a small salary besides. There are plenty of clothes around here so you won't have to buy any."

"What . . . what does Rita do?" asked Julie, suddenly recalling the indecently short skirt and low necked bodice that revealed all but the girl's dusky nipples.

Brett was quiet for a long time, choosing his words carefully. "Rita entertains the customers, seeing that they buy enough drinks, helping them . . . forget their troubles, that sort of thing."

Julie was not totally innocent in the ways of the

world. She understood only too well what Rita and the other saloon girls did. "I will not entertain your customers, neither above nor below stairs," she declared emphatically. "And that includes you, Brett Casey."

Brett's cheeky grin completely disarmed Julie. "No one asked you to, sweetheart. Your job is legitimate. I have plenty of girls to take care of the men above stairs. But I have no one with your looks or manners to lure them to the gaming tables."

"It will only be until my father returns," she wavered.

"Agreed." Brett was jubilant, certain that Julie had decided in his favor.

"Then it's a deal," Julie declared, holding out her slim hand.

"Come along, I'll show you to your room," Brett smiled, enfolding her small hand in his smooth palm.

15

Carl Darcy's unexpected arrival at *Rancho* Delgado proved to him that things were not always as they seemed. He sensed the tension swirling about him the moment he was shown into Don Rodrigo's study and finally faced his son-in-law. He decided long before he left San Francisco to keep his identity secret. If he was to learn anything at all about the character of the man his daughter loved, he could only accomplish it while remaining incognito.

Rod looked up sharply, scowling fiercely the moment Carl invaded his inner sanctum. His thoughts were still on Elena and how badly he had misjudged her. He had known her all his life and it seemed improbable that she was capable of such deception. He could not help but wonder if she was in some way responsible for Julie's disappearance. He would put nothing past her. But attempting to foist off a bastard as his own flesh and blood had been more than he could stomach.

Carl could not know Rod's thoughts and he was taken aback by the unfriendly welcome he was accorded by the proud don. Then, as suddenly as it had come, the fierce look died in Rod's eyes as he realized how his greeting must look to a visitor. *Rancho* Delgado had few visitors but Spanish hospitality was legion.

"Forgive me," Rod apologized, flashing a friendly smile. "It was discourteous of me to greet you so poorly. I have much on my mind of late and meant no discourtesy. But enough, *señor*, my problems are none of your concern. I am Don Rodrigo. Teresa tells me you wish to see me."

Carl forced himself to relax beneath Rod's curious scrutiny. "Actually, I came to see your father," Carl lied smoothly, "but was informed that he is dead. I am sorry to hear that, Don Rodrigo."

Rod waved his hand gracefully in ackowledgement of Carl's condolences. "What is your business with my father?"

"Months ago Don Diego wrote and invited me to the *rancho*. You see, I am a horse breeder. *Rancho* Delgado is well known for its many fine horses. I was invited to remain for as long as it took to decide whether or not I wished to purchase some of your fine stock. But, if it's no longer feasible—" Carl deliberately let his sentence trail off.

"I will honor my father's agreement with you, *Señor . . . Señor . . .*" Suddenly Rod became aware that he did not know the stranger's name.

"Blair," Carl supplied. "Carl Blair."

"*Señor* Blair, you are welcome to remain in my *hacienda* until your decision is made concerning your purchase," Rod offered. "I am only sorry that it could not be at a happier time. My father's death was quite sudden and . . . and my wife . . . has . . . has been . . . she is not here at this time." Suddenly Rod had no wish to discuss Julie with a strange man.

"I will try not to impose myself upon your private life, Don Rodrigo," Carl contended. "I will go about my business as unobtrusively as possible."

Elena chose that moment to burst into the study, her nose flaring with barely suppressed outrage. "Did you order Teresa to pack my clothes?" she accused hotly. "You have no right!"

"Elena, we have a guest," Rod warned through gritted teeth.

Elena glanced disdainfully down her patrician nose at the man seated across from Rod and immediately dismissed him as no one of importance. "Well, did you, Rodrigo?"

"Did I what, Elena?"

"Order Teresa to pack my clothes?"

"I thought we had settled everything last night," Rod said tiredly. "*Si*, I asked Teresa to help you pack. One of the *vaqueros* will drive you to the mission. I've already dispatched a message to *Padre* Juan explaining everything."

"Rodrigo, if you would only—"

"Not in front of our guest." The tone of Rod's voice was distinctively unpleasant and Elena retreated under his implied warning. "This is *Señor* Blair. He is to stay on the *rancho* as my guest." Turning to Carl. "*Señor* Blair, this is Elena, my father's . . . widow."

"Ah, yes, I heard Don Diego had married," Carl acknowledged innocently. "You have my condolences, *Señora* Delgado."

Slanting Carl a look of pure loathing, Elena whirled abruptly and stormed out of the room. "You must forgive Elena, *Señor* Blair," Rod apologized, flushing darkly. "She is high-strung and . . . not herself. I thought it best for her to spend time at the mission and she disagrees with me."

Carl had no idea what was going on but from what he observed it did not appear as if Rod and Elena were lovers. Could Julie have been mistaken, he wondered? Or was Don Rodrigo the type of man who tired of women quickly and just as swiftly got rid of them. That question was exactly what brought him to *Rancho* Delgado in search of an answer.

Later that day, Carl watched from a distance as Rod calmly escorted a fuming Elena and a host of trunks and boxes to a wagon driven by one of the *vaqueros*. His goodbye to the fiery Spanish woman was brief and unemotional, once again giving Carl cause to wonder about his son-in-law's cold heart. From his observation it was obvious Elena had no desire to leave *Rancho* Delgado. Even from where he stood her parting words came through loud and clear.

"*Bastardo*! One day you will pay for this!"

In the days that followed Carl learned his way about the sprawling *rancho*. Often he rode out with Rod and little by little he began to understand the complex Spaniard. Proud, arrogant, unfailingly kind and generous to his men and their families, universally respected by all, Carl could appreciate his daughter's love for the man. What he failed to comprehend was Rod's failure to love Julie in return.

After the first week of living, riding and eating with Rod, day after day, Carl began to suspect that Julie was mistaken in her belief that Rod wished her out of his life. Somehow he could not associate Rod with the type of cruel deed that placed her in the hands of Pedro, Murieta's henchman. So far Rod had spoken little about his missing wife. Carl decided it was the time to probe his son-in-law's innermost feelings; time to learn the truth in his own subtle way.

They were riding at a leisurely pace, the conversation trivial, when Carl abruptly asked, "Do you expect your wife back anytime soon? I would be honored to meet her. Is she Spanish?"

The swift flash of pain that marched across Rod's face made Carl almost sorry he had brought up the subject. "I feel I know you well enough, *Señor* Blair, to tell you that my wife has been abducted, and . . . and is probably dead." Rod's voice was strained, his words stilted as Julie's lovely face came back to haunt him.

"Who would do such a thing?" asked Carl, feigning shock.

"Elena was with Julie, that was my wife's name, when it happened. She said it was Joaquin Murieta."

"Do you believe her?"

"I have no reason to doubt Elena . . . at least I didn't at that time," Rod added thoughtfully. "But now, I don't know, although Elena will admit to nothing."

"If you will pardon my curiosity, Don Rodrigo," Carl interrupted, "but what is Elena to you? Besides your father's wife?"

Rod stared at Carl a long time, wondering why he was talking so intimately with a man he hardly knew. But strangely, he felt no embarrassment speaking with this forthright, compassionate man he had come to respect in a short time.

"Elena was my *novia*, my intended. I was to marry her when I met Julie. I married Julie under rather . . . er . . . strange circumstances and brought her home with me to the *rancho*.

"I realize now it was a terrible blow to Elena's pride but I fear I misjudged the extent of her jealousy and hatred for Julie. Then my father married Elena and things went from bad to worse."

Carl had heard almost the same story from Julie. What he wanted now was the truth behind Julie's abduction, and if Rod actually put Elena up to it. "Didn't your father and Elena get along?"

"I don't really know," shrugged Rod pensively. "During that time I allowed Elena to . . . well, never mind. Suffice it to say I hurt Julie in a way I never intended. I would give anything for the chance to make up to her for treating her so vilely that last night when—" Abruptly Rod faltered, aware that he was about to divulge intimate details of his marriage that were better left unsaid.

"You sound like a man who loves his wife, Don Rodrigo," Carl hinted innocently.

"I'm afraid that emotion was too late in coming, *Señor* Blair," Rod admitted readily. "But for what it's worth, I do love my wife. That's why I refuse to believe she is dead. It is not like Murieta to kill an innocent woman. I would rather believe she went along with the bandit willingly than accept her death.''

Carl had heard all he needed to know. Somehow these two young people were unaware of the love they held for one another, thus allowing Elena to separate the star-crossed lovers despite the fact that she had benefited little from her efforts. It was up to Carl, or so he supposed, to play Cupid and reunite husband and wife now that he was convinced that Julie's fears concerning Rod were groundless. Obviously it was Elena's plot from the beginning.

Considering his daughter's pride, Carl sagely decided silence was the better part of valor. He would be wise to keep his own counsel concerning Julie's whereabouts and remain unidentified until he returned to San Francisco and informed Julie of his findings, particularly the fact that Rod loved her. Yes, that's exactly what he would do, hurry back to Julie. If all went well they could be back at the *rancho* within two weeks. Of course, Carl had no way of knowing Rod was leaving on a cattle drive the following week, for the subject had never come up.

Later that same day Carl informed Rod he would be leaving the next morning, assuring him that though the Delgado stock was among the finest he had seen hereabouts, it was not exactly what he was looking for. They parted that evening on excellent terms and Carl left *Rancho* Delgado exactly as planned.

During his nearly two week stay at the *rancho*, Carl had made a concentrated effort to meet the child whom Julie had become so fond of. Carl and Felicia spent many happy hours discussing Julie and the love that existed between them. In his own subtle way he questioned the child about the relationship between Elena and Don Rodrigo. Felicia had been of tremendous help in weighing Carl's decision in Rod's favor.

The morning Carl left the *rancho* he was completely unprepared to see a lone figure riding out after him as if chased by the devil. They were some distance from the *hacienda* and he reined in to await the child's arrival.

"What are you doing here, child?" Carl asked not unkindly when Felicia's horse stood next to his, shoulder to shoulder.

"You know where she is, don't you?" accused Felicia, frowning. "She's alive and you never told Don Rodrigo. Why?"

Carl was amazed at the child's perception despite her tender years. She was indeed an exceptional child just as Julie had described. "I don't know what you are talking about, Felicia."

Felicia glared obstinately at Carl. "Who are you really? How do you know Dona Julie? Why didn't you bring her back?"

Carl sighed heavily. Felicia left him no choice but to tell the truth. It would be cruel to do otherwise. "Yes, little one, Julie is alive. I am her father."

"Oh, *señor*!" Felicia cried, ecstatic. "Take me to her! *Por favor*!"

"I can't do that, little one," Carl smiled fondly. "Would you have your *tia* and *tio* worry?" Felicia's downcast eyes and sad little face was more than Carl could bear. "I will tell you a secret if you promise to tell no one."

"A secret, *señor*?"

"Yes, a very nice secret. Do you promise?"

"If it is a good secret, then, *si*, I promise."

"I am on my way to Julie now. To bring her back to the *rancho*."

"Oh, *señor*, that is indeed a very good secret. Does Don Rodrigo know?"

"Then it would not be a secret, would it?"

Felicia looked confused. "But it isn't right. Don Rodrigo should know."

"He will know, little one. In a short while. If all goes well I should return with Julie in a few short days." Placated for the time being, Felicia beamed.

They then parted, Felicia to go her own way hugging
the secret to her heart, Carl toward a course that would
drastically alter his well laid plans.

Carl got no further than the mission at San Luis
Obispo when his horse went lame. Though he had
neither visited the mission before nor met *Padre* Juan,
Rod had spoken often of the good father and Carl felt
certain the *padre* could be counted upon for help. If the
padre had no horse with which to trade for Carl's lame
mount, then at least he could be relied on to send word
to Rod.

But as luck would have it, *Padre* Juan was calling on
the sick among the villagers and it was left to Elena to
greet the visitor. At first Elena failed to recognize Carl
but as he began to speak, explaining his predicament,
comprehension dawned.

"You're Rodrigo's guest, aren't you?" she asked,
eyeing him narrowly.

"Yes, Dona Elena. If you remember, we met once in
Don Rodrigo's study the day I arrived."

"*Si*, I remember. Did Rodrigo tell you anything
about me?"

"Should he have?"

Elena flushed angrily. "Don't play games with me,
señor. He must have told you something."

"If he did, I don't recall."

"It's lies, all lies!" spat Elena vehemently. "The
truth is that he got me with child then abandoned me!
Sent me off to the mission when I was of no further use to
him!"

Carl was flabbergasted. Could it be true, he
wondered? Could he have misjudged Rod so badly?
Had Rod and Elena actually conspired to get rid of Julie
and when Elena became his mistress did her pregnancy
interfere with his pleasure to the point where he would
callously discard her? My God! blasphemed Carl
silently, did he now have to rethink his position, re-
evaluate his opinion of the man he thought he had come

to know? Or was Elena deliberately lying in order to discredit Rod? In a flash of insight Carl decided to keep to his original plan, to bring Julie back to *Rancho* Delgado and let Rod provide his own explanation. He had no right to condemn Rod out of hand.

When *Padre* Juan returned Carl exchanged his lame horse for a fresh mount, albeit an inferior one admitted the good father, and continued on his journey north on El Camino Real to San Francisco, unaware of the pitfalls that lay ahead.

That night, because of his delay at San Luis Obispo, Carl sought sanctuary at San Miguel Mission about eight miles from Paso Robles where *Padre* Luis made him welcome. After a simple but nourishing breakfast the next morning he started out early, the tortillas and boiled eggs sitting pleasantly on his stomach.

Carl had just left the village of Paso Robles when out of the mountains swooped Three-fingered Jack Garcia and his band of desperados who preyed on unsuspecting travelers up and down El Camino Real. Before he knew what had hit him, Carl was shot twice, one bullet grazing his head, the other lodging in his side, robbed of all his valuables and left for dead. He lay all day and all night where he had fallen before he was discovered by Ramona Sanchez, the impoverished widow of a proud *ranchero* who had lost his lands and died shortly afterwards in poverty. Luckily Ramona was on her weekly round to salvage fire wood for her hearth.

Good woman that she was, she immediately summoned help and had Carl taken to her crude hut where she unselfishly attempted to save his life. It mattered little to Ramona that Carl was an Anglo. What did matter was the fact that the man could die without her help. Employing her considerable knowledge of healing, liberally dosed with fervent prayers, her patient still lived the next morning, a good sign in itself.

Ramona carefully removed the bullet from Carl's side and waited for fever to set in. When it came she was

ready with her infusions and medicines brewed
especially to cool and soothe his heated flesh. Given his
state of health, weakened from the previous injuries he
had received from Paco and Jose, it was somewhat of a
miracle that Carl survived at all. If he owed his life to
any one thing, it was to Ramona's stubbornness and her
refusal to let him die.

Carl remained in a coma for days. And when he
recovered enough to speak, he was too weak to travel.
He could only lay back on his sick bed and worry and
fret over Julie and how fearful she must be over his
failure to return as promised. At least he had left her
well provided for under the guardianship of Mae
Parker, Carl reflected gratefully in one of his more lucid
moments.

It was several more weeks before Carl recovered to
the point where travel would no longer endanger his
health. After much soul searching he decided to return
to *Rancho* Delgado because it was closer and also
because it was now imperative that Rod go to San
Francisco after Julie, for Carl was in no condition at
this time to attempt a lengthy trip. After convincing
Ramona to accompany him should he become ill along
the way, Carl set out at long last for *Rancho* Delgado.

It seemed to Carl that his efforts to reunite Rod and
Julie were doomed to failure when he reached *Rancho*
Delgado only to learn that Rod had just recently
returned from the cattle drive and left immediately for
San Francisco. Disheartened, Carl realized he was too
weak to follow. The best he could do was to remain
where he was to recuperate and allow fate to reunite the
lovers and trust in God's judgment. As for himself, he
was content to remain at the *rancho* with Ramona at his
side, for he was becoming exceedingly fond of the
slender widow who had literally snatched him from
death's door.

16

As the weeks passed, Felicia began to despair and wish she had never promised Julie's father that she would not reveal the secret they shared. After one week passed, Felicia eagerly anticipated Julie's return, but with the passage of the second week and still Carl did not appear, she grew frantic with worry, imagining all sorts of terrible things that could have happened to Carl before he reached San Francisco. When a month elapsed, Felicia genuinely despaired of ever seeing Julie again. She moped around the *rancho* with such a tragic face that Teresa threatened to dose her for fear she was sickening.

Rod and the *vaqueros* returned to *Rancho* Delgado after another successful cattle drive. He had been gone nearly two months. After sleeping the clock around and stuffing himself with some of cook's delicious food, he set out on an inspection tour of his *rancho*, particularly the stables where he expected to find many new foals. He was not surprised, in fact, rather pleased, to find Felicia currying one of her favorite mounts. It was amazing, Rod reflected thoughtfully, how much he had missed the enchanting child.

Upon seeing Rod, Felicia flung herself joyfully into his arms, completely forgetting that he was *el patron* and she a lowly *mestiza*. "I've missed you, Don Rodrigo," she said, managing a shy little smile.

"And I've missed you, *niña*. But do I not deserve a bigger smile?"

"*Si*, Don Rodrigo," Felicia agreed, trying desperately to overcome her melancholy as she flashed an enchanting grin in his direction.

Intuitively, Rod sensed her unhappiness and sat down on a bale of hay, settling her on his knee. "Do you want to tell me what is wrong, *niña*?"

Felicia thought for a long time, then asked, "Is it wrong to tell a secret, *señor*?"

"Not if keeping it hurts someone, *niña*." Felicia was quiet for so long that Rod was prompted to add, "Does it, *niña*?"

Felicia shrugged her slim shoulders. "I think it might, *señor*."

"Then the secret is best revealed," Rod advised. "If you tell me I promise to keep it to myself. Unless there is someone else you'd rather—"

"Oh, no," Felicia quickly assured him. "If I tell anyone it should be you." Rod waited curiously, certain that he would never willingly betray the confidence of this trusting child.

Felicia drew a deep breath, then plunged on. "Do you remember *Señor* Blair?" Rod nodded, wondering what an Anglo horse breeder had to do with all this. "He is Dona Julie's father."

"What?" cried Rod, nearly upsetting Felicia when he jumped to his feet. Could it be true? "How do you know this, *niña*?" he asked, his emotions shattered into a million tiny fragments.

"I spoke with him often while he was here and Dona Julie told me so many things about her father that put me in mind of *Señor* Blair, that I became suspicious."

Rod was amazed at how much more this child knew about Julie than he knew himself. "Why didn't Julie's father reveal his identity? I understand none of this. Did he tell you anything at all, *niña*?"

"Not much, Don Rodrigo. But I think he was testing you, trying to decide if Dona Julie should return to the *rancho*."

"If she should return . . . *Por Dios*! You mean Julie is alive? And her father knows where she is?"

"*Si, señor*. Dona Julie is in San Francisco and her father promised me he would bring her back to the *rancho*. But he did not return," she wailed, her small face screwing up pathetically. "He promised, *señor*! A few days, he said. It was to be our secret. What if something terrible happened to him? What if he never reached San Francisco?"

It was difficult for Rod to think beyond the fact that Julie was alive. Surprisingly he could understand her reluctance to return to him considering how badly he had treated her. He wondered how and where she had found her father. But none of that mattered now except the fact that Julie was alive and under the protection of her long lost parent.

The reason behind Julie's failure to return as *Señor* Blair promised was another matter altogether. Had the man been attacked along El Camino Real and never reached San Francisco as Felicia feared? Or had Carl examined his character and somehow found him wanting? The longer Rod thought, the more he convinced himself that the sad truth of the matter was that Julie wanted nothing more to do with him.

"*Señor*, did you hear me?" Felicia asked, breaking into his reverie. "What if something terrible happened to Dona Julie's father?"

"I intend to find out, *niña*," Rod assured her firmly. "There is but one place Julie could be in San Francisco, and if she's there I'll find her. I . . . I only hope she hasn't already returned east with her father."

"She wouldn't do that, *señor*, I am sure of it." Rod smiled at Felicia's thinly veiled rebuke.

"Perhaps you're right, *niña*, but I promise you that if Julie is in San Francisco I will find her and bring her back to *Rancho* Delgado where she belongs."

Rod left for San Francisco the following day.

* * *

Julie had more than one reason to feel grateful to
Brett Casey. Not only had the charming gambler
offered her employment, thus saving her from
starvation, or worse, but his protection had far reaching
results. Julie's sudden appearance at Casey's Pleasure
Palace was the cause for much speculation. Some
thought she was an old girl friend of Casey's newly
arrived to resume their relationship. Other's considered
her fair game and were quickly relieved of that notion
when Casey blandly declared that Julie was his mistress
and the first man to make a move on her was dead.

At first Julie was enraged by Brett's bold, as well as
unfounded, disclosure. But she cooled down considerably when Brett explained that it was for her own
protection that he lied. She had to admit that she was
bothered little after that by the rowdy miners looking
for a woman to satisfy their urges after long months in
the mine fields without female solace.

But the truth of the matter was that Julie was not, nor
would she ever be, Brett Casey's mistress. She liked and
respected Brett for all his kindness on her behalf, for his
protection, and yes, even for the attention he showered
upon her. In the months during which she dealt blackjack at the Pleasure Palace, Brett had begged her
repeatedly to become his mistress in fact as well as in
word. And each time she had refused, Brett advised her
that he was not the type to give up so easily.

It was ironic, Julie thought, that two men should
profess love for her while the only man she could ever
love cared for another. She wondered if Rod and Elena
were happy together now that she was no longer around
to interfere with their lives. Did he think her dead by
now and had he already wed Elena?

If Julie was not happy, she was content. What kept
her from complete happiness was her father's continued
absence. She had heard nothing from him in months
and she feared that something dreadful had happened to

him. Surely he would have returned, or at least contacted her in all this time if he were well and safe. Julie fretted constantly over his strange disappearance and began to despair that she had lost him for good this time.

One evening shortly before she was due to make an appearance at the gaming table, Julie sat before the mirror, staring at her reflection. She had changed a great deal since she first arrived in San Francisco over a year ago. She had matured, grown more sure of herself, no longer the untried girl naive enough to set out on her own to find her father in an untamed land. Though much had happened to her it had not coarsened her flawless features nor dimmed her spirits. Though Rod had tossed her aside like so much unclaimed baggage, Julie had emerged unscathed and far stronger, much more aware of life around her. Even her beauty had been honed and defined in such a way as to add to her appeal.

The gentle rap on the door brought a smile to her lips. In all the weeks she had been at the Pleasure Palace Brett never failed to show up and escort her below stairs to begin her duties. "Come in, Brett," Julie called out fondly.

The door opened and Brett Casey stepped inside, as vibrantly handsome as ever. "Are you ready, Brandy?"

Brandy. Another illusion to add to the mystique surrounding her. The name had been given to her by Flossie, one of Brett's girls who coaxed the customers into buying drinks, among other things. On the first day Julie showed up downstairs to take up her duties, Flossie had remarked that her hair was the color of warm brandy. The name was immediately picked up until even Brett now called for Brandy. But Julie didn't mind. Somehow it fit in with her new lifestyle.

"I'm ready, Brett," Julie announced, patting a stray curl in place.

Brett's green eyes roved appreciatively over Julie's trim figure perfectly displayed in an emerald green gown fashioned in shimmering satin that barely concealed two rose-tipped nipples. The dress was designed purposely to delight the customers' eyes and divert their attention away from their troubles long enough to separate them from their gold. It worked exceptionally well. Though the Pleasure Palace employed many women, some more seductively attired than Julie, only the woman known as Brandy had the ability to draw in the men like bees to honey. From the moment she walked sedately down the stairs on Brett's arm until she returned at night in the same manner, she was a constant source of admiration as well as speculation.

It was obvious to all that Brandy was a lady as well as a woman who did not stray far from her protector. There was not a man around who did not envy Brett Casey or dream of what it would be like with a woman like Brandy in his bed. For the most part Julie was liked and respected by men and women alike, except for Rita.

Once Julie entered Brett Casey's life, Rita's relationship with the gambler deteriorated swiftly. Though it was already on the wane, Brett's affair with the fiery Mexican came to an abrupt halt the moment Julie walked through the door of the Pleasure Palace. Brett never again took Rita to his bed, or any other woman for that matter. Julie had firmly entrenched herself into his life and his heart and no other would do. Consequently, Rita did her utmost to make Julie's life miserable.

"You grow more lovely every day, sweetheart," Brett grinned roguishly. "Are you aware that every man in San Francisco is jealous of me?"

Julie blushed becomingly. "You have a silvery tongue, Brett Casey," she retorted archly. "And I suspect you are a rogue."

"Guilty," laughed Brett. "But you could change all that."

"Brett," began Julie, turning serious. "Please don't—"

"All right, sweetheart, you win," he gave in graciously, hiding his hurt beneath a facade of good humor. "I won't press you. But if you change your mind . . ."

"I won't."

"What if I offered marriage?"

Oh, God, Julie silently prayed, please help me out of this mess. "I'm eternally grateful for all you've done for me, Brett, truly. But marriage? It's out of the question. Shall we go?"

That evening Julie's thoughts were badly fragmented and more distraught than usual. The offer of marriage from Brett was something new. Previously he had wanted her for his mistress. Now he had brought a new dimension to his proposal. Of course there was no possibility of their marriage taking place. She was still married to Rod. But she was a woman awakened to the joy of love, how long could she go on without Rod's comforting arms? Loneliness was not a state she cared to explore for years to come. She was human; a warm, passionate woman newly awakened by an extremely virile man adept in the art of arousal. Could she be happy with a man she didn't love? Divorce was not the answer even though she knew Brett would be good to her. Somehow the thought of marriage to anyone but Rod was repellent. She fervently prayed for her father's swift return as she automatically began dealing the cards to the crush of men ringing her table.

Without a doubt Rod knew he had never made a faster trip to San Francisco. He ate and slept in the saddle, stopping once or twice to refresh himself in a bubbling stream. Had he encountered bandits they would have been hard pressed to catch him. Dusty, saddle-sore and badly in need of a shave, Rod unerringly turned toward Mae Parker's boarding house, certain that he would find Julie there if she was still in

San Francisco.

You can imagine his shock when he reined up before what should have been the boarding house only to find a newly erected structure standing in its place. At first Rod thought Mae might have built a new, larger house until he realized that Mae hardly had the resources for such a venture. Where Mae's house once stood now reposed the law offices of Murphy and Harper. In fact, now that Rod thought about it, the entire block had an unfinished look about it, certainly nothing like the weathered buildings that once stood side by side on this street.

The first person Rod encountered knew exactly what had happened, describing in great detail the terrible fire that took not only Mae Parker's life but the life of several others unlucky enough to be trapped inside their houses.

"A girl," asked Rod, not even aware that he was holding his breath. "Was a girl about eighteen among the victims? A beautiful girl with blond hair? She and her father were probably tenants of Mae's."

"Don't recollect anyone of that description," replied the man, scratching his bald pate. "Course it ain't impossible. But it seems to me most of those killed were older, less agile folks unable to escape the flames fast enough."

Rod allowed himself a few private minutes to mourn Mae Parker, a woman he respected in every way, before contemplating his next move. It was obvious he was no closer to finding Julie now than he was before he left *Rancho* Delgado. Rubbing his stubbly chin in vexation Rod decided to find himself a room, grab a few hours sleep and clean up before beginning his search.

Hours later, looking rested and extremely handsome in leather trousers hugging his powerful thighs and a short fringed jacket of the same material, emphasizing broad shoulders, Rod prowled the streets of the city. Though the hour was late the revelers in Casey's Pleasure Palace were a boisterous lot, drawing Rod inexplicitly through the swinging doors and into the smoke-filled interior.

The first sight to greet his eyes was a somewhat ragged line of scantily clad dancing girls prancing about the stage amid hoots and howls from cheering, clapping miners hungry for the sight of a woman's flesh. Rod chose a seat at a small table well out of the way and settled down to watch the proceedings. Within a few minutes a striking, dark haired Mexican girl sidled up to Rod, posed seductively for his benefit, and asked throatily, "What are you drinking, *señor*?" There was no mistaking the invitation in her flashing black eyes.

Rita had spotted Rod the moment he entered the saloon. It had been a long time since anyone of his looks and obvious breeding had come her way. Rita immediately assumed him to be a rich *hidalgo* from one of the sprawling *ranchos* nearby and quickly staked her claim. Rita decided she was just the right woman to provide entertainment for the virile stranger who was no doubt bored with horses and cattle and was on the prowl for a little fun.

"Whisky," answered Rod, raking Rita's ripe figure with disinterest. Though he hadn't had a woman in months, he had more important things on his mind than a quick tumble.

Rita sauntered off with a provocative wiggle and returned forthwith carrying a bottle and two glasses. Rod carelessly tossed her a coin which promptly disappeared between her ample breasts. "May I join you?" she asked silkily.

"Suit yourself," Rod shrugged negligently while Rita settled beside him, poured a hefty measure of whisky into two glasses and handed him one. Rod sipped slowly, allowing the amber liquid to slide smoothly down his throat while Rita quaffed hers in one gulp.

"The name's Rita, *querido*," she said, batting her long lashes seductively. "What's yours?"

"Rod suits me just fine," Rod drawled lazily. They drank in silence for a few minutes and then Rod asked, "How long have you worked here, Rita?"

"Eight, ten months," Rita shrugged carelessly, caring little for the way the conversation was going. "Why do you ask?"

"I'm looking for a woman."

Rita giggled. "That's what I'm here for, Rod. "Come, *querido*, my room is at the top of the stairs."

"*Perdicion*, Rita! That's not what I meant. I'm looking for my wife. She . . . she disappeared and I have every reason to believe she is in San Francisco."

Rita laughed lustily. "And you come to the Pleasure Palace looking for her? I have an idea your wife is hardly the type of woman to hang around saloons."

Rod flushed, realizing the truth of Rita's words. "You're right, Julie would never be seen in a place like this. I don't know what I was thinking of."

"Obviously not me," teased Rita archly. "But the offer still stands. I could make you forget your wife for a little while."

"No doubt, Rita," replied Rod dryly, rising to his full height. "But I—" Suddenly he froze, his eyes zooming in on a woman in an emerald green dress seated at a blackjack table dealing and smiling at the adoring men clustered about her.

A mass of honey-colored curls were artfully arranged around a face that had haunted Rod's dreams for months. "Julie!" His words were but a whisper but Rita heard them and stared at Rod strangely.

"Who is that woman? The one in green dealing black-jack," Rod asked in a strangled voice. He was positive it was Julie. A more mature, lovelier—if that were possible—more elegant Julie than he remembered. But Julie nevertheless.

"That's just Brandy," snorted Rita disparagingly.

"Brandy? do you know her last name?"

"If I did I don't remember," pouted Rita.

"How long has she been working here?"

Rita shrugged, disinterested. "Two, three months. Why do you ask? Do you know her?"

"I . . . I thought I did but . . ." Rod hedged.

"She affects all men that way. Can't see why myself," she sniffed. "If you have any ideas about her, forget them," Rita advised sourly. "She's Casey's private property. No one touches her but him."

"She's Casey's mistress?"

"*Si*, that's what I said, isn't it?" Rita glowered, becoming weary of the subject. "She appeared out of nowhere and Brett hasn't looked at another woman since. *Caramba*, I'd like to tear her hair out!"

What must Julie's father be thinking of? Rod wondered angrily. For that matter, where was the elusive Carl Darcy who seemed to flit in and out of Julie's life like an errant butterfly. To Rita he said, "Does this . . . er . . . Brandy have any relatives in town?"

"None that I know of. Listen, Rod, I don't want to talk about another woman. Come, *querido*," she coaxed, "I promise to make you forget about Brandy or that wife you're looking for."

Rod had no desire to make love to Rita. How could he expect a woman like Rita to take the place of a honey-haired vixen with bluebell eyes whose special brand of loving was forever imprinted upon his heart and body?

The thought that Julie had become another man's mistress was repellent to Rod. The longer he dwelt on the picture of her in another man's arms, responding passionately to another man's caresses, joined in the act of love with another man, the angrier he became. Forgotten was the fact that he had rushed pell-mell to San

Francisco expressly to find his wife and bring her back
to *Rancho* Delgado. Forgotten also was Rod's fervent
desire to tell Julie of his love once he found her.

By now Rod's emotions were a boiling cauldron of
turmoil. In light of what he had just learned from Rita,
he no longer was certain of his own feelings. From the
moment he learned about Julie and the gambler,
whatever love was in his heart seemed to wither and die
within him. All his emotions were held suspended in
that painful void betwixt love and hate. He had no idea
what he would do next nor how he would deal with Julie
when he confronted her. He could only hope that the
edge was gone from his anger before they met, else he
could not be responsible for his actions. His Spanish
pride allowed him little room for forgiveness.

"Why the scowl, *querido*?" Rita asked lazily.

Startled to find the sultry beauty still at his side, Rod
stared distastefully at her. "I'm sorry, Rita, I'm not in
the mood tonight." He began moving away.

"Do not hurry away, *querido*," Rita purred, hoping
to entice him. "I'm certain I can please you if you give
me the chance."

Rod extracted a coin from his pocket, flipped it
carelessly in her direction where it landed with a soft
thud against her chest and slipped down between her
breasts. "Another time, perhaps," he drawled
laconically.

"Suit yourself, *querido*," Rita replied, a pout turning
the corners of her mouth downward. "I'm here every
night."

Rod slipped back to his table, his thoughts
dangerously volatile. Rita watched him through
narrowed eyes, then shrugged and turned away in
pursuit of a more likely customer. Like magnets, Rod's
ebony eyes were drawn to the blackjack table where
Julie sat like a goddess upon a throne robed in
shimmering green. Looking handsome and debonnaire,

Brett Casey sauntered over to Julie and Rod's hands clenched into white-knuckled fists when he saw the gambler slide an arm possessively about Julie's slim waist and whisper intimately into her shell-like ear.

Rod thought the sultry look she gave him conspiratorial, as if only the two of them shared a secret. He scowled darkly as his imagination ran rampant, causing a grinding ache deep in Rod's bowels. Like two burning coals his eyes stared fixedly at Julie and her lover, the heat of his gaze enough to ignite the entire room.

Suddenly Julie looked up, as if sensing Rod's gaze, and she felt the brutal attack of his brilliant eyes as they found and held hers. Shock waves raised goosebumps on the surface of her skin and she swallowed convulsively. His pebble-hard, black eyes seemed to reach out over the distance that separated them, locking her in the prison of his barely concealed contempt.

A dainty hand flew to Julie's lips. She opened her mouth but could summon neither words nor breath. Their eyes still riveted, Julie surged unsteadily from her stool and felt her legs turn to rubber as she collapsed. Luckly Brett was beside her, his strong arms lending her strength.

"Brandy!" Bret exclaimed, his concern clearly evident. "Are you all right?" Julie nodded weakly. "Good God, you gave me a fright, sweetheart! What happened? You look like you've seen a ghost."

"Not a ghost, Brett, but a demon."

For months Julie lived with the fear that Rod might one day venture to San Francisco and inadvertantly run into her. And now her worst fears had been realized. Why wasn't her father here when she needed him? Was there no one to protect her from the violence she knew dwelt beneath the surface of Rod's icy veneer? No, she silently answered her own question. Not even Brett could protect her from her husband's fury.

17

Rod watched through slitted eyes while Brett saw Julie to her room, handling her slim form as if she were a fragile bloom. Rod had to admit Julie even looked fragile with her pale face and huge blue eyes eating up her delicate features. It was obvious to Rod that Julie's guilt over her behavior these last months was the cause of her sudden malaise. That and her fear of him. She had good reason to fear him, Rod reflected bitterly, for he still had no idea what would happen when he actually faced his unfaithful wife.

Rod made a mental note of the room Casey and Julie disappeared into and also of the time lapse before the gambler promptly reappeared alone, making his way to the blackjack table where he took Julie's place. A tiny bubble of joy burst somewhere inside Rod's brain at Casey's prompt exit from Julie's room.

Rod waited a short time, fretting anxiously until he was certain Casey had no intention of rejoining Julie in her room before he arose and made his way unobtrusively toward the stairs. As fate would have it, luck was on his side. Just as Rod started up the stairs the dancing girls strutted out on stage again and all eyes turned in the direction of the scantily clad hoofers, allowing him to enter Julie's room undetected.

Julie lay sprawled on her bed thinly-clad in nothing but a short shift. Misery gnawed at her, rendering her numb and tense. Knowing Rod, she realized it was only a matter of time before he showed up at her door, angry and vindictive. What would he do? She shuddered apprehensively. If Elena could be believed, Rod wanted her out of the way for good, maybe even dead. Would he be angered to find her still alive? Drawing a long, shuddering breath, Julie tried to imagine Rod's reaction to finding her at Casey's Pleasure Palace.

So intense was her concentration that Julie neither saw the slow movement of the doorknob nor heard the soft whisper of the door open under Rod's gentle pressure. Only the muted rasp of the key turning in the lock alerted her to the chilling fact that she was not alone.

Raring up into a sitting position, Julie saw Rod's long, lithe form lounging against the closed door, his sardonic gaze raking her scantily clad body insultingly. Julie felt the unleased violence of his tightly coiled muscles strike her from across the room. It was almost like a physical blow and she recoiled instinctively.

"Rod," she whispered shakily, the tremor in her voice unmistakable.

"Who were you expecting, your lover?"

Julie flushed, a look Rod instantly mistook for guilt.

"What do you want? How did you find me?"

With studied calmness, Rod walked loose limbed toward the bed, but his stance did not deceive Julie who likened him to a sleek panther about to strike. "I've come to take my 'loving' wife home where she belongs," Rod mocked nastily. "Surely your father must have told you he was at the *rancho*."

"My father!" cried Julie, becoming very excited. "You've seen him? Oh, thank God! I thought something terrible had happened to him when he failed to return to San Francisco. I had no idea where he had gone."

Rod's black eyes narrowed suspiciously. Here was a turn of events he was unprepared for. "Your father turned up at the *hacienda* shortly before I left on the last cattle drive. He stayed but a short while." A puzzled frown gathered along Julie's brow. "Your beloved parent didn't bother to reveal his identity to me. He also failed to mention that you were still alive after all these months when I thought you dead."

Julie could not tell whether Rod was happy or disappointed to find her alive and healthy. "If my father didn't tell you, how did you know I was alive and in San Francisco?"

"Felicia told me," Rod stated sourly. "She spent much time with your father and guessed the truth. When confronted with Felicia's suspicions he admitted his identity and revealed to her that you were alive and living in San Francisco. He promised Felicia he would return you to the *rancho* and Felicia was ecstatic. Of course he never showed up and Felicia was devastated. She told me the whole story when I returned from the cattle drive. Needless to say, I left immediately for San Francisco." He paused for breath but Julie was still stunned by the news that her father should have returned from the *rancho* weeks ago. Where was he?

"How did you know I was working at Casey's Pleasure Palace?"

"Purely an accident. I've been watching you all evening, you and your lover. Did you think I wouldn't learn that you are Casey's mistress when everyone in town is aware of it?"

"Rod, I'm not—"

"Julie," he interrupted sternly, "the time for lies is long past. What I want now is the truth. Start from the very beginning, from the moment you were abducted until you became Casey's mistress. Were you Murieta's mistress, too?"

The lavishly appointed room was amply lit by two tall candles resting on the nightstand as well as by firelight from the hearth across the room and Rod nearly lost control of his senses when he saw how the lamp glow played over her tawny hair, alive with gold, russet and copper. He had not forgotten the silken feel of those gleaming tresses caressing his body when they made love. Nor the sweep of her dark lashes as she unsuccessfully tried to hide the desire that flared in her blue eyes when she wanted him, or the seductive curve of her smile when sated with love. She was a beguiling creature and Rod fought desperately to corral his rampaging emotions, and in so doing his face appeared harsh and unforgiving, his eyes cold and empty.

Julie knew a moment of panic when she viewed Rod's rigid features, but in her determination not to be cowed, retorted angrily, "You know more about my abduction than I do!"

"What is that supposed to mean?"

"Take it any way you want!" Deliberately she turned her head away.

"Damn you, Julie, answer me!" Rod demanded as he grasped her small pointed chin between thumb and forefinger, forcing her to look at him.

"All right, Rod. I know you're stronger than me," Julie shrugged, momentarily defeated. "You can force me into anything. If you want me to put into words how you and Elena planned my death, so be it."

"What in the hell are you talking about?" I wasn't even at the *rancho* when you were taken by Murieta's men."

Eyes spitting blue flame, Julie ground out mercilessly, "Elena told me you wanted me gone by the time you returned from San Antonio. Just because she carried out the deed instead of you doesn't absolve you from guilt. Do you have any idea what Pedro had in mind for me before he killed me?"

"*Por Dios, querida*, you don't think . . . Surely you don't believe I had a hand in anything so despicable? What kind of monster do you take me for?" The thought of Julie in the hands of Pedro was terrifying. But the knowledge that Julie blamed him for her abduction and possible death was too horrible to contemplate.

Julie looked long and hard into Rod's horrified eyes and read the truth for herself. Whatever happened to her had been all Elena's doing, but that did not change things between them.

"Rod, perhaps you are blameless as you say," Julie acknowledged slowly. "But I can't forget what I was put through by your mistress. Or the pain you caused me when you deliberately bedded Elena."

Rod winced. "Did Pedro . . . was it so terrible, *querida*? Tell me about it. I know Murieta and I find it difficult to believe he could behave so cruelly, especially toward a beautiful woman."

"Joaquin was not there. Pedro was in charge." Julie ignored Rod's loud groan and continued, telling him all she knew. When she came to the part about her father, Rod interrupted.

"So that's where your father had disappeared to. Thank God he was there when you needed him."

"And nearly lost his life in the bargain. Joaquin arrived in time to save my father's life. I'll always be grateful to him. As soon as he recovered sufficiently, we left Murieta's camp and came directly to San Francisco."

There was a faraway look in Julie's eyes that Rod had no desire to delve into at this time. Instead, he asked, "Why did your father come to *Rancho* Delgado?"

"I don't know. He told me only that he had business to attend to. I expected him back in a couple of weeks. That was months ago."

"I suppose he wanted to learn for himself what a despicable libertine you had married," Rod couldn't help but remark. "Especially after you told him that I had engineered your abduction."

"After what Elena told me, how could I believe otherwise?"

"You could have trusted me, *querida*," Rod said with bitter emphasis. Abruptly he changed the subject. "How long have you been Casey's mistress?"

Julie fumed with impotent fury. If Rod chose to think she was Brett's mistress, she wouldn't disabuse him of the idea. It served him right. Knowing well his pride and arrogance, he probably wouldn't believe the truth anyway. "Do you know about Mae Parker?" she asked, deftly avoiding Rod's question.

"*Si*, I went there first," Rod said grimly. "It . . . it was a great tragedy."

Julie nodded sadly. "She would be alive today if she hadn't run back inside the burning building to rescue her valuables. And I might well have ended up just like her but for Brett. He stopped me when I attempted to follow Mae inside the burning house. Afterwards he found I had no place to go, the money my father left was destroyed in the fire as was everything I owned. Brett brought me here, offered me a job until my father's return and treated me with kindness. I owe him much."

"You could have come home, Julie, instead of becoming his mistress," Rod said, a thread of steel tempering his softly spoken words.

"Believe what you want, Rod, you will anyway. I can see it will do me no good to deny being intimate with Brett."

"None whatsoever."

"Hadn't you better leave? Go back to the *rancho*. No doubt Elena is anxious for your return."

"Elena is no longer at the *hacienda*."

"No longer at the *hacienda*?" Julie repeated dumbly.

"That is what I said, *querida*. I . . . I sent her away. When we return she will no longer interfere with our lives."

"Return? I have no intention of returning with you. At the rate you casually cast women aside it's no wonder that you have replaced Elena already."

"You are my wife, Julie. I married you according to the rites of the church and as long as you live I can never replace you. It is your duty to return with me and fulfill your duty."

"My duty?" Why must I repeat everything Rod says, Julie asked herself dully?

"I need an heir. As my wife you are the only woman capable of providing one. Legitimately, that is."

Red dots of rage exploded in Julie's brain. "Never!" she retorted hotly. "I will not be your brood mare! When my father returns he will take me back east where I belong." Julie had no intention of leaving California but she wasn't about to admit that to Rod.

"You belong with me. What if your father doesn't return? What then?"

"I have my job. Brett is good to me. I can stay here as long as I like." Julie had no idea how damning her words sounded. If Rod harbored any doubts before, Julie's outburst convinced him that she was Casey's mistress just as Rita claimed. Besides, not once had Julie denied his accusation.

Now it was Rod's turn to become incensed. "*Puta*! Slut! You are no better than Elena! Is Casey such a good lover that you prefer him to me?" His words smote her like tiny pebbles.

"Yes! Yes!" cried Julie vehemently, wanting to hurt, to wound, as he had hurt and wounded her. "He is a much better lover than you could ever hope to be!"

"Perhaps you have forgotten, *querida*?" Rod said with deceptive calm. "Perhaps you need to be reminded how I made you feel, how your passionate body came alive beneath my touch. Come, wife, let us recapture the bliss we once shared."

Julie was not gulled by his soft words. "Leave me

alone, Rod. Just go away and leave me in peace. You have my permission to tell everyone I'm dead.'' She wished she had more than words to fling at him, for once he touched her she knew she was lost.

Rod laughed sardonically, sensing her confusion. "Afraid you might like what I do to you, *querida*?'' One long finger traced a delicate path from brow to jaw, then lower to outline the pale skin rising above her filmy chemise. "Afraid Casey might not measure up after I finish with you?''

"You arrogant bastard!'' Julie gritted from beneath clenched teeth. Must she fight her own body's arousal as well as Rod's compelling voice and male allure, she reflected miserably?

A devilish smile curling his sensuous lips, Rod's fingers curved insultingly on the thin material covering her breasts and ripped downward. Julie gasped as she felt the chemise slide from her body and the hot rush of Rod's breath caress the tender flesh he had bared to his passion-glazed eyes.

"Don't do this, Rod,'' Julie begged, vividly recalling their last night together when he took her with a cruelty that left her bruised and disillusioned. "We were wrong from the start.''

"Ah, *querida*, do you not remember what was right about us?'' She remembered. "Can you deny the magic of our lovemaking?'' Julie could deny nothing. "I have no desire to ravish you, but I will if you resist me. Show me what makes Casey mad for you.''

Hard fingers stroked her shoulders and slid down confidently to enclose her breasts. Hungrily his mouth claimed hers, his tongue surging between her lips to possess her, reminding her that she belonged to him and he intended to possess her utterly, in all ways. His tongue withdrew, and slid along the moist contours of her lips like a searing flame, then delved suddenly between them to drink greedily of her special nectar. He stroked and caressed, fingertips trailing fire down her throat, playing over her breasts to continue across quivering stomach, settling in the shining curls covering her womanhood.

Julie groaned, fighting her rising ardor, cursing the way her body rose and swelled beneath his trailing fingertips. "Please, Rod, don't do this to me."

"Do what, *querida*?" he asked innocently. "Make you feel like a woman? I love to watch your blue eyes kindle into flame, your slender body flush with desire." He laughed nastily, breaking the spell he had cast upon her senses.

"I hate you, Rod!" Julie spat, nearly choking on the lie. "I don't want you! I don't want this!"

"Your body tells me otherwise, *querida*. See how your nipples reach for my lips?" His tongue brushed back and forth across a sensitive nub and Julie felt it spring to life beneath his touch. His lips could not resist the tender bud as he drew it into his mouth, flipping gently with his tongue and sucking with maddening thoroughness. When he began the whole process again with the other nipple, Julie groaned aloud as an ache began in her loins spiraling upward throughout her entire body.

"Will you still deny me, *mi amor*?" Rod chuckled, a mocking sound low in his throat.

"Yes! Yes!" agonized Julie, fighting desperately to hang on to her sanity.

Apparently in no hurry to sate his own desire, Rod's hands dipped downward to cup the furred mound at the junction of her thighs, massaging gently with the heel of his hand. When his two fingers found her open, her honeyed sheath ready for his entry, he murmured huskily, "You are wet with desire, *mi amor*. Do you still say you do not want me?"

Somehow, Julie found herself stretched out on the bed with Rod lying beside her. She turned to him, burying her face in his chest, need riding her like a wild stallion. "Oh God, Rod, hurry!" she sobbed, writhing against his lips and hands.

"Not yet, *querida*," Rod rasped raggedly. "I've waited too long for this. I want to touch you, to taste you, to fill you with me in my own good time."

His weight shifted away from her and Julie cried out in deprivation. Once again she heard his amused chuckle and if she wasn't in such desperate straits she would have gladly strangled him. "I'm only going to remove all of my clothing, *mi amor*," Rod laughed softly. She heard the whisper of leather and then his weight was pressing her down into the soft mattress, crushing her full breasts against the furred expanse of his chest.

His manhood thrust hard against her soft belly, smooth as satin yet stiff and demanding. Beginning with her mouth, he touched a trail of sweet fire along her body, to her painfully sensitive breasts, drawing them one at a time into his mouth, toying with their dusky aureoles until they honey-combed and their peaks filled his mouth. When his hands parted her legs and his lips descended to close over her most sensitive spot, Julie protested violently.

Rod slid his body upward to stare into her eyes. "You win this time, *querida*, but next time you won't escape so easily."

His smoldering gaze held her enthralled as he thrust strongly into her velvet moistness. Her long legs rose to imprison his flanks and draw him more deeply into her. His hunger overpowered her and Julie felt herself drawn into it as rapture consumed her and flung her skyward with a cry of release, bringing her to spasms of hot delight, matching her rhythm to his as he guided her through a continuously mounting passion to the peak of exploding desire.

Rod felt the magic of her enfold and enclose him with

her warm flesh, heard her shrill wail of release and allowed his own passion free reign. He rode the crest of his own desire; his cries of pleasure mingled with hers and filled the firelit room.

They lay side by side for some time, her head cradled on his chest, his heartbeat hammering loudly in her ear as Rod ran a hand caressingly along her spine bedewed with perspiration. Julie was so at peace that she felt herself floating in a state of euphoria, until Rod's mocking laughter quickly shot her back to earth. "Well, *querida*, do you still prefer your lover to me?"

"Yes, you devil, yes!" she shouted unthinkingly. "At least he doesn't attempt to draw the soul from my body. When you are finished with me I have nothing left. I am drained, my will destroyed."

Her hastily flung words brought an immediate chill to Rod's humor. He did not want to hear about Brett Casey. "Get dressed," he ordered curtly. "We're leaving."

"Like hell! Julie argued. "I'm staying here."

"You are coming back to *Rancho* Delgado with me."

"Over my dead body!"

"That can be arranged, *querida*." He was regarding her now with eyes that were cool and amused, dark orbs that seemed to peer right through her, while his lips twitched in a crooked grin. Though his words were spoken with calm deliberation, his implied threat was explicit.

"Rod," Julie hedged, her voice softening. "Allow me to remain at least until my father returns. After that we'll discuss it further."

"Do you think me *loco, querida?* Your father could well have met with an accident and never return. You are my responsibility."

"Rod, please," pleaded Julie. "How could you be so heartless?"

"Heartless! Is that what you call a man who wants his

wife with him despite the fact that she has warmed
another man's bed?''

Rod still wanted Julie, despite everything, but he
wanted her to come to him of her own free will. Just
thinking about life without her created an aching
emptiness deep within him, for which there was no
solace. Only his fierce pride prevented him from
admitting how much he had missed her, how badly he
needed her. He would not be foolish enough to voice his
love until he was sure Julie returned those same
emotions. And at the moment it appeared that Brett
Casey held her heart.

"I . . . I can't go with you, Rod," Julie reiterated.
"Not just yet, anyway. I can't leave Brett in a lurch. He
depends on me. I owe him that much for all he's done
for me.''

"I would say he's been well paid," Rod alluded dryly,
raking her naked body insultingly.

Julie flushed angrily. "Rod, Brett and I, we're
not . . . we haven't . . .''

"Don't, Julie, lying doesn't become you. But I'll
make you a deal. I'll allow you to remain a while longer
in the unlikely event your father should show up. In
return I expect you to withhold your delectable body
from your lover.'' Julie nodded vigorously. It was a
promise she would have no problem keeping. "Wait,
I'm not finished," added Rod dryly. Julie waited
patiently, eyes questioning. "To keep you from
becoming too lonely, passionate bitch that you are, I
will continue to visit you here in your room from time to
time . . . whenever the need . . . arises.'' He laughed
heartily at his play on words.

"Bastard!" Julie muttered darkly. "I should have
known you'd demand your pound of flesh.''

"You're wrong, *querida*, a pound would hardly do. I
want it all. Every delectable ounce of you belongs to me.
Haven't I just proved as much?''

"You proved that you are adept at lovemaking. I always knew that."

Rod's eyes blazed with annoyance and he slanted Julie a penetrating glance. "Be careful, *querida*, you go too far." Julie's lips clamped tightly together but her murderous glare spoke volumes.

Later, after Rod let himself quietly out of the room, Julie gave vent to her anguish. It was true she was still Rod's wife and he could very well force her to return with him whenever he decreed, but did he have to humiliate her, treat her like a possession. Worse yet was the knowledge that he would continue to treat her in a callous manner as long as she refused to return with him to *Rancho* Delgado.

But what kind of life would she have with Rod, Julie asked herself glumly? He hadn't said much about Elena except that she was no longer at the *rancho*. Would she come back one day to wreak havoc with their lives?

If only Rod loved her, Julie sighed unhappily, she could almost forgive him anything. If only he would tell her he cared for her a little. Did he feel any other emotion for her but lust? It was obvious to Julie that she was nothing but a possession and Rod did not relinquish his possessions lightly. Even if he did not want her, he would never allow another man to have her. Yet, Julie was strangely aware that no matter how often she screamed out her hate for her virile husband, no matter how much humiliation she suffered at his hands, she loved him.

18

During the following week Rod studiously avoided Julie's room. Though he sat nearly every night at his usual table in Casey's Pleasure Palace, remaining coldly contemptuous until Casey escorted Julie to her room and returned to the blackjack table, he made no move to speak to her. Instead he whiled way the hours drinking with Rita who fawned over him until Julie grew livid with rage. Rod seemed perfectly content to sit and sip whisky all evening while the Mexican spitfire literally seduced him before Julie's eyes.

Julie could not help but wonder if Rod was partaking of Rita's ample charms after she retired to her room late at night. Somehow the thought of Rod making love to Rita strangely unsettled her. More than likely that's exactly what was happening, Julie surmised, else Rod would have come to her before now, lusty pig that he is, she thought disparagingly. Her first emotion was one of relief. At least he would not demand she satisfy him if another woman was taking her place in his bed. Inexplicably, the next emotion to strike her was much stronger. Could it be jealousy? Pure, green-eyed, jealousy. Though she strongly berated herself for feeling such conflicting emotions, there was no help for it.

Brett Casey, ever alert where Julie was concerned, noticed Julie's distraction during that long week. At first he laid it to her father's continued absence, but

281

quickly disabused himself of that notion when he caught her eyes drifting time after time toward the handsome Spanish don who Rita considered her private property. What was Don Rodrigo Delgado to Julie, he wondered? Jealousy consumed him like a blazing brush fire. Though Julie had never given him a shred of encouragement, Brett harbored the thought that one day she would be his.

That night Brett decided the time was ripe to press his suit in a more forceful manner, do something more than stand by and wait for Julie to come to him of her own accord. Brett was determined that tonight was the night Julie would become his mistress in more than name only. He wasn't about to stand idly by while another man happened along and swept her off her feet. Julie belonged to him, the gambler firmly avowed, and to no one else. Immediately he began making preparations for an evening he hoped would set a precedent.

Rod lounged loose limbed at his usual table, sipping his usual glass of whisky, when Rita sidled up behind him, winding her slim arms about his neck. Her soft breasts pressed sensuously against his back as she leaned her slight weight against his muscular shoulders. Noting Julie's eyes upon him, Rod thought the opportunity too great to resist as he turned, grasped a squeeling Rita by the waist and flung her around into his lap. One hand cupped an unfettered breast intimately while his mouth plundered hers. He had tried everything short of telling Julie how much he really needed her to bring her to her senses, so why not try jealousy? He smiled deviously.

Julie was shocked as well as disgusted by Rod's amorous overtures toward Rita. Therefore, given her frame of mind, she was not adverse when Brett casually suggested she take a break and join him for a late supper. When she smiled her compliance, he ordered something special to be set up in her room, a sort of celebration to mark the months they had been together.

"I've arranged with Zack to take over for the entire evening," Brett informed her smoothly. "Of late you appear tired and out of sorts. You need and deserve a break." Zack was a combination bouncer and part-time jack-of-all trades whom Brett had recently hired.

Julie was prepared to do anything to keep from watching while Rod made a fool of himself with Rita. Not that she cared what he did, she tried to convince herself. "I suppose you're right, Brett," Julie agreed hesitantly. "A night off might be just what I need."

"Come along then, sweetheart," he drawled lazily as he slipped an arm about her slim waist. His grin was infectuous as Julie's answering smile lit up her beautiful features. Together they started up the stairs. Even with her back towards him Julie could still feel the intense scrutiny of Rod's dark, accusing eyes.

The moment Julie disappeared into her room with Casey, Rod rudely shoved Rita to the floor, snarling at her to leave him in peace. Picking herself off the floor with as much dignity as she could muster, Rita flounced off in search of more likely prey, spitting abuse at the arrogant Spaniard who ran alternately hot and cold.

When an hour passed and Casey did not reappear, Rod was on the verge of bursting into his wife's room and bodily dragging her from the arms of her lover. Instead he began drinking heavily, emptying one bottle and then calling for another. Rage twisted his handsome features and his gut roiled painfully as he thought of Julie responding to another man in the same maddening way she did to him. She was a wanton bitch, he decided spitefully, who couldn't go one week without falling into bed with a man.

A second hour passed and then a third, and Casey was still secluded intimately with Julie. Did he intend to spend the night, Rod wondered? His mind was reeling drunkenly.

Julie was thoroughly enjoying herself. Brett had gone

out of his way to have a special feast prepared, along
with the appropriate wine, and they lingered leisurely
over the elegant repast. He regaled her with amusing
stories until her sides hurt from laughing. Brett was at
his best, witty and charming, attentive and thoroughly
beguiling. Even Rod and their impossible impasse were
thrust to the back of her mind as she began to relax in
the seductive atmosphere, just as Brett had planned.

The wine flowed freely and soon Julie felt herself
overcome by a strange lassitude, unaccustomed as she
was to strong drink. Her limbs felt heavy, her body
drifting on a cloud of euphoria. Sensing her mood,
Brett took full advantage of her languorous state and
proceeded accordingly.

Grasping her hands, Brett led Julie to a chinz loveseat
and settled down beside her, pulling her limp body into
the curve of his own muscular form. "Are you comfortable, sweetheart?" he asked, rubbing his chin
against her sweetly scented hair.

"Ummm," murmured Julie sleepily. It did feel good
nestled protectively against Brett, not having to spar
verbally as she would with Rod. With Rod she could
never relax, she was ever afraid to let her guard down
lest she give away her true feelings in one of her weaker
moments when her body and mind were being
consumed by his passion. With Brett, passion never
became a part of their relationship. With Rod she could
think of nothing but his hands on her quivering flesh,
the taste of his hot, hard mouth, the feel of taut muscles
rippling beneath her caressing fingers. In fact, she could
almost feel his hands on her breasts now.

Brett moved cautiously as he slowly undid the tiny
buttons down Julie's back. When they were all
unfastened, he carefully slid the material down her
sloping shoulders, baring two sweet mounds of firm
flesh crested by pink-hued buds that rose against his
palms like ripe cherries the moment his hands took

possession. Without volition, a low moan rose in Julie's throat, lending Brett courage.

His mouth could not resist the urge to take those suddenly erect nipples between his lips, nipping and sucking gently. "I've dreamed of this for so long, sweetheart," Brett murmured between nibbles. "Stand up and let me undress you. I can't wait to bury myself deep in your sweet flesh. I swear you'll not regret this, Brandy. I love you."

Suddenly something inside Julie snapped and she sobered almost immediately to find herself being thoroughly seduced by Brett Casey. My God, she shuddered! Should Rod find her like this, he would kill her! He was probably aware, to the very minute, of how long Brett had been in her room. There was no doubt in Julie's mind that she could not allow Brett to make love to her. The only man she truly wanted to possess her was her own husband.

"No, Brett, don't," Julie resisted, surprising him by pushing him aside with renewed vigor. "I don't want this."

"I know better, sweetheart," grinned Brett smugly. "Do you think me inexperienced in the ways of women? Look at your breasts," he directed, touching a long finger to a ruby hued nipple. When it sprang into instant erectness, he chuckled knowingly. "Your body tells me differently."

Julie flushed, becoming angry. "A woman can't always control her body," she informed him coldly. "Especially when a man is adept in the art of arousal." Not only was she thinking of Brett, but of Rod who played her like a finely tuned instrument, using her body in such a way that her responses were never lukewarm but intense to the point of pain.

Brett was torn. Lord knows he wanted Julie, more than he ever wanted another woman. But beyond that he loved her. He would never intentionally do anything to betray that trust she held for him. He knew he could never force her, even though his yearning for her drove him to the point of no return.

"Brandy," he muttered, the anguish evident on his handsome features, "I hoped tonight would be special, that it would be a new beginning for us. But I can see you are not in a receptive mood. I won't force you, sweetheart. You mean too much to me. But neither will I give you up so easily."

"Brett, I'm sorry," Julie whispered in a small voice. "It's not meant to be between us. Please leave now, I'd like to go to bed."

Brett's green eyes turned sad, his smile melancholy, but he managed to kiss her forehead chastely before he turned to leave.

"Don't ever stop being my friend, Brett," Julie begged, suddenly moved to tears. "Someday I might need you."

"Never, sweetheart," Brett promised. "I'll always be here for you." Then he was gone, leaving Julie feeling strangely bereft.

Though Julie had sobered considerably, she was still slightly tipsy as she finished undressing, slipping nude between the sheets, too tired to don a gown. Below stairs Rod was in even worse condition. His hands were no longer steady as he lifted the bottle and attempted to pour another drink. But the container was empty. Muttering an oath he tossed it aside and started to rise somewhat unsteadily to his feet when he spied Casey making his way slowly down the stairs. The gambler's face held a peculiar expression that Rod could not decipher. He certainly did not look like a man who had just spent the last three hours making love to a desirable woman, Rod thought grimly.

Regaining his seat, Rod waited, albeit impatiently, until the dancing girls appeared on stage, capturing the attention of the entire room. Then, as he had previously, he used the confusion and noise to sneak upstairs. Not once did he consider that Julie might lock the door against him as the knob turned noiselessly beneath his gentle pressure.

In the darkened room Rod saw that Julie was sleeping soundly. Cursing the shadows that dimmed his sight, Rod carefully picked his way to the nightstand, hoping his memory served him well as to its placement, and lit the lamp he found there. Immediately the room took on a dim glow and Rod's glazed eyes fell to the bed where Julie lay entangled in the sheets, one hip and shapely leg completely exposed. Long strands of amber hair, streaked bronze by the lamplight, covered her face and one creamy shoulder. Exhausted by Casey's love-making, Rod thought bitterly as he hastily began throwing off his clothes, cursing roundly when the buttons on his shirt unaccountably became too difficult to manage. Not even the sound of ripping material awoke Julie.

Peering squint-eyed into the shadows, Rod noticed the remains of a meal congealing on a nearby table. Probably shared by the lovers, he thought wryly, as he spied an opened bottle of excellent wine and an empty glass beside each plate. Padding barefoot, he rescued the bottle and glasses, set them on the nightstand and poured, managing to spill a good deal in the process. Then he turned his attention to his sleeping wife, carefully peeling back the sheet until nothing stood between them but her long silky locks.

Rod stood there staring at her for what seemed like eons, greedily drinking in the smooth perfection of her young supple body. There wasn't a blemish anywhere that he could see and with a will of its own, his hand reached out and gently turned her on her back. Julie slept on as Rod's passion-glazed eyes feasted on fully erect nipples, tautening as if in invitation to a dream lover. Slowly his eyes fell to the honey hued forest shielding the pouting lips of her sex.

Seeing Julie exposed and vulnerable aroused Rod to a peak he had never before attained. Spasms of erotic pleasure snaked upward from his swelling loins until his entire being was a mass of raw nerve endings. When he first started up the stairs he had been angry, angry enough to do bodily harm should he be driven to it. But now, seeing Julie like this, sweet and innocently seductive, clothed in a cloak of glorious nudity, he wanted only to bring her pleasure, more pleasure than she had ever known.

Rod's eyes fell on the glass of wine he had recently poured as he eased himself beside her. Tentatively he dipped a finger in the ruby liquid and smeared it gently about the nipple of each breast using a circular motion. Then, oh so carefully, his wine bedewed thumbs slightly raised her nipples into his mouth, lapping hungrily at the tender buds.

Julie arched her back into his caress, her dreams vividly erotic, only to discover it was no dream when a voice close to her ear murmured huskily, "Wake up, *querida*, I would not have you miss the pleasure I am about to give you."

Julie's eyes snapped open and the dim light revealed her husband lying nude beside her, his generous mouth smeared with ruby stains. "Rod," she whispered dreamily. "I thought you were a dream."

"No, *querida*, no dream can compare with the real thing."

"Rod, about Brett—"

"Shhh, don't speak Julie. Let us enjoy tonight without conflict or dissension. This is not the time for confession. It is a time for love."

Ironically Julie couldn't have spoken had she tried as once more Rod dipped his fingers into the wine and began a circular motion about her breasts, lowering his mouth and sipping droplets gathered in the cleavage

between her breasts. Then his ruby stained mouth
covered her parted lips, capturing her cry of pleasure as
his wine flavored tongue tasted her own honeyed
recesses. Raising his head, he trailed a lazy path of wine
along the inner surface of her lips with a finger, folllow-
ing it with the tip of his tongue.

"Oh, God, Rod! What are you doing to me?" Julie
cried out as if in agony.

"Tonight I want to pull the soul from your body," he
whispered hoarsely.

Rod's gentle hands moved downward to caress her
breasts, once more using the wine to massage and heat
her flesh. The fluid proved extraordinarily erotic as it
dried, leaving a residue that seemed to erode her senses.
Her eyes had a liquid radiance, her passion-swollen
mouth shone wetly with ruby stains. Her body pushed
coaxingly into the warmth of his naked thighs and
stomach.

"Not yet, *querida*," Rod said, breathing heavily.
"But soon . . . soon."

In a restless delirium of pleasure, Julie felt Rod begin
a slow tantalizing descent along her stomach below her
navel to her taut inner thigh, moving in slow lazy circles
along the creamy skin. Then, Julie gasped as he dipped
his fingertips in the wine, slipping them into her, the
fluid lubricating her until his gentle manipulation nearly
brought her to rapture. Against Julie's murmured
protests, he quickly removed them before her
tumultuous explosion.

Julie's intense arousal sparking his own, Rod kissed
and caressed every part of her. She stiffened in pleasure
when he opened her gently, parting the blond curls, and
that hot, invading tongue began to explore her
thoroughly, until not a trace of wine remained. A gasp
of pure ecstasy broke from her lips as he kneaded her
breasts with his hands, his tongue creating havoc with
her again and again as he sipped at the wine tinged

sweetness between her thighs. Julie wanted him to stop but knew she would die if he did.

It was as if every nerve ending was centered in her loins as Julie writhed and twisted, her body shaking. Suddenly a sensation halfway between pain and ecstasy seemed to focus beneath Rod's relentless tongue, and Julie found herself pushing up mindlessly against his warm mouth. It was incredible, like nothing she'd ever felt before, as waves of sweet, throbbing, intense pleasure radiated from her loins thoughout her body, and she sobbed convulsively, finally going limp.

Coming back to earth slowly, Julie's eyes widened at the proof of Rod's desire which had yet to be sated. His magnificent maleness reared from the dark forest of his loins like a shaft of delicately veined marble. He whispered her name with a huskiness born of desire as he moved upward and pierced her cleanly and smoothly. Julie gasped and Rod laughed softly, withdrawing his shaft only to plunge more deeply. He wanted to explode within her but grimly hung on, digging into the soft flesh of her buttocks to relieve the pressure.

Amazingly, after the fierce climax she had experienced only moments before, Julie felt herself responding to Rod's piston-like thrusts, bringing her once more to hot spasms of delight. Rod felt her response, gloried in it, was overpowered by it, and could no longer control the explosion that threatened to tear him apart.

"Come with me, *mi amor*," he urged hoarsely into her ear, his hands cupping her into his driving body. And then his splendid violence drove them both over the brink and their ecstasy became white-hot, searing, a blaze that was too bright to look into. When he softened and slipped from her, she sighed in the drowsy aftermath of pleasurable exhaustion and was soon asleep.

When Julie awoke the next morning, Rod was gone. And to her utter confusion she did not see him again for over a month. She had no idea that he left to begin a methodic search for her father, ranging north to the gold fields near the American River and as far south as the Santa Lucia Mountains where he spent weeks roaming those lofty crests in search of Julie's elusive parent. Had he bothered to visit his own *rancho* he would have been amazed to find Carl Darcy now fully recovered and anxiously awaiting Rod's return, hopefully with his daughter in tow.

In the meantime, Julie did her best to conceal her bruised feelings from Brett. On the surface she appeared the same; friendly, bright, outwardly happy. But underneath Brett sensed a change in his lovely employee. Strangely, it seemed to coincide exactly with the disappearance of the Spanish don who had been a steady customer for weeks and then suddenly dropped from sight. He was almost persuaded to ask Julie pointblank what there was between her and Don Rodrigo but wisely kept his own counsel, berating himself for acting the jealous fool. To his knowledge, Julie had neither spoken nor acknowledged the handsome Spaniard in all the time he had spent at the Pleasure Palace.

As for Julie, she was certain she would never see Rod again and was assailed by remorse over his sudden disappearance after all they had shared. It hurt her deeply to think that it had meant so little to Rod that he hadn't even bothered to bid her goodbye. At least she was left with one memorable night, a night she could hold and cherish forever.

Julie had no inkling why Rod had chosen to leave before she awakened. He feared that after their night of indescrible ecstasy he would lose control and insist on taking her immediately to *Rancho* Delgado and away from Brett Casey. He was astute enough to realize that by so doing he would likely cause more dissension between them and further erode the thin line between love and hate that bound them together. His one chance at winning her affection from Casey, Rod concluded, was to locate her father and bring him back to San Francisco. He hoped then that Julie would return home with him. Above all, Rod wanted his loving wife back, content to remain by his side forever. He had no desire or inclination to harbor an unwilling captive in his *hacienda*.

19

One morning during Rod's long absence, Julie was having breakfast with Brett in the nearly deserted saloon when she noticed a lone woman pause in the doorway, then enter. She could not make out the woman's features because the sun was behind her, obscuring her face, but Julie noted absently she was poorly dressed and that a cloud of inky black hair floated about her thin shoulders.

The woman walked resolutely to the bar, spoke briefly with Zach who immediately pointed out Brett. As the woman drew near Julie saw that she was younger than she had first supposed, no more than a girl, really.

"Mr. Casey?" the girl said in a tremulous voice. Brett nodded curtly, annoyed by the unwelcome intrusion. "I've come to ask for a job."

Brett raked the bedraggled waif up and down distastefully for a few moments before he answered, "I'm sorry, I have nothing for you." Then he turned back to Julie, dismissing the woman as someone beneath his notice.

Julie gasped, absolutely astounded. At first she failed to recognize the poor wretch who not only appeared underfed, but sick. And then the girl spoke and Julie became absolutely certain that she knew the girl despite the fact that her face was swollen from some sort of injury.

"Polly?" Julie asked, her voice aquiver with

emotion. "It is Polly, isn't it? Don't you remember me?"

The girl turned her head slowly and stared dumbly at Julie. At that instant Julie became certain that the girl was her friend Polly. There was no mistaking those huge green eyes. But where was her husband and how did she come to such a pass? "My God, Polly, what happened to you?" Julie finally asked, appalled by her friend's pitiful appearance.

Polly stared vacantly at Julie before a glimmer of recognition lit a spark in her eyes. "Julie? Oh, Julie, is it really you?" Then she collapsed sobbing into Julie's welcoming arms.

"You know this . . . woman?" grimaced Brett, obviously mistaking Polly for a common streetwalker.

"Polly is my friend," Julie snapped, angered by Brett's callous dismissal of Polly's desperate plight. "We traveled on the same ship to California. She married and went off with her husband. I . . . I don't know what could have happened to the poor dear."

Upon learning that Polly was not what he originally assumed, Brett became immediately solicitous, insisting that she sit down. Then he ordered breakfast for the near-starving girl. His efforts were rewarded by a grateful glance from Julie.

Once Polly had eaten every bit of the delicious food set before her, Julie began probing gently for some answers to Polly's predicament. "We need to talk, dear," she said, taking Polly's thin, work-worn hand in her own smooth one. "Where is your husband, Polly? Why has he deserted you?"

Polly turned huge, tragic eyes on her friend, causing Julie's heart to contract painfully. "He is dead, Julie. Conner is dead." She began to sob softly.

"Do you want to tell me about it?"

Polly hiccupped, then nodded. "Conner discovered a small but rich vein of gold a while back," Polly began, choking back her tears. "We . . . we kept it a secret because we feared someone might steal the small hoard of gold we had accumulated and kill us before we were able to file our claim. When we had several sacks of nuggets hidden away, Conner decided it was time to take it to the assay office and file his claim."

Polly paused for breath, her eyes bright with pain. "The night before Conner was to leave for San Francisco four men burst into our cabin just as we were taking the gold from its hiding place."

"Oh no!" cried Julie, appalled.

"They were miners who worked the claim next to ours. Somehow they became suspicious and decided to find out for themselves if Conner really had found gold. They gave him no chance to defend himself once they spied it. They killed him, Julie. Then they divided the gold and . . . and . . . oh God, I can't go on!"

"It's all right, Polly," Julie soothed. "You don't have to say anymore. I understand."

"Do you, Julie? Do you know what it's like seeing your husband killed before your eyes? I . . . I was held prisoner by those four depraved monsters who took turns on me for weeks. Do you know what it's like being beaten into submission for failing to comply with their vile requests?"

"I'm so sorry, Polly," Julie murmured sympathetically. "It must have been horrible for you. How did you escape? Or did they let you go?"

"Let me go! Ha! If it was up to them, three of them at least, I'd still be tied to the bed praying for death. One of the men, younger than the others, began feeling sorry for me. I used his pity, as well as his lust for gold, to my own advantage. Not only did I appear to welcome him whenever he approached me in that manner, but I offered him a sack of gold for his own if he helped me to escape."

"You had a sack of gold?" This came from Brett who

had thus far remained silent.

"There was still one sackful hidden beneath a loose floorboard when they broke into our cabin. I offered it to Hank, that was his name, if he helped me reach San Francisco."

"Thank God he agreed," breathed Julie gratefully, "and that you found your way to the Pleasure Palace. You can stay here, share my room." Then she looked imploringly at Brett. "When Polly is well you'll give her a job, won't you, Brett?"

Brett looked doubtfully at Polly but compassion moved him to nod his head. Magnanimously, he offered, "There is no reason for Polly to share your room. There are any number of empty rooms above stairs. I'll leave it to you to settle her in one of them. Once she is recovered we will talk further about employment."

"Thank you." Polly murmured gratefully, somewhat intimidated by the handsome gambler's imposing looks and stature.

"You have my thanks, too, Brett," Julie said warmly. "You are the best friend a girl could ever want."

Brett grimaced. "I could be more, Brandy, much more." Before she could answer, he rose gracefully, excused himself, and left.

Polly stared after Brett thoughtfully, then at Julie. "What is he to you, Julie? Why does he call you Brandy? And . . . and where is your husband?"

"Not here, Polly," cautioned Julie, peering around to see if anyone had heard. "Let's go upstairs and then I'll tell you whatever you want to know."

Later, with Polly's frail form stretched out on the bed, Julie recounted all that had happened to her during the past year. Whenever she spoke Rod's name, Polly could not help but notice the wistful longing in her voice. She thought there was much about that relationship Julie was not telling.

"Do you love him, Julie?" Polly asked hesitantly.

Julie flushed, lowering her expressive blue eyes lest they give her away. "I . . . yes . . . I guess I do, for all the good it does me."

"Rod wouldn't have come to San Francisco for you if he held no strong feelings for you," insisted Polly.

"You're wrong, Polly. I'm the only woman who can give him a legitimate heir. That's all he wants from me."

"He married you, didn't he?"

"Only because his damn honor demanded it!" Suddenly aware of Polly's pinched face and total exhaustion, she added, "We'll talk about it later, dear. Rest now. The only thing I would ask of you is to keep my marriage a secret. Should Brett find out I'm married, he might insist I return to *Rancho* Delgado with Rod."

"It's obvious Brett is obsessed with you. Have you . . . are you two . . ."

Julie smiled. "No, Polly. If you're asking if Brett and I are lovers, the answer is no. We never have been, nor will we ever be lovers. Brett is a friend. A very dear friend."

It was good to have Polly around, Julie decided, as daily the girl became more like the effervescent, enthusiastic girl of old. The swelling about her face disappeared as did the bruises and welts on her body. Julie saw to it that her friend rested and ate well until Polly's slight figure began to fill out to its former curvacous proportions. When Julie deemed Polly completely recovered, she had a dress altered to fit and prepared to present her to Brett who hadn't seen her since that day she walked into the Pleasure Palace some days past.

Brett refused to believe that the lovely, raven-haired beauty dressed in shimmering gold satin was the same abused and bedraggled woman who had come to him seeking a job. Now that the swelling had receded, Brett was astounded by the girl's beauty, greatly admiring the cloud of ebony curls framing a pixie-like face, and emerald green eyes studying him most intently through a veil of dark, feathery lashes. Without a moment's hesitation, Brett heard himself offering Polly a job, which she accepted with alacrity and a burst of girlish enthusiasm that thoroughly charmed him.

One day Julie heard a bit of news that completely unsettled her. If reports could be believed, a posse of Americans fought a pitched battle just outside San Luis Obispo somewhere in the Santa Lucia Mountains with Joaquin Murieta and his audacious bandits. Though many of the notorious brigands were killed or captured, it seemed that Murieta escaped into his mysterious mountain hideout. The noose was tightening about Joaquin's neck and Julie feared for his life.

Rod returned unexpectedly to San Francisco after weeks of fruitless searching for Carl Darcy. From a distance, Julie was shocked by his appearance. He was pounds thinner than when she last saw him nearly two months ago, and exhausted, his dark eyes sunk deeply into their sockets. She wondered where he had been and why he had bothered to return at all, until she felt his smoldering gaze sweep over her with a heat born of intense desire. Oddly, his desire for her kindled her own and the look she returned pleased Rod beyond measure.

Just as he decided to go to her and forget all the animosity and pretense between them, a commotion broke out near the front of the saloon. All eyes turned toward a man in an army uniform boasting the rank of captain. He held before him a large jar containing something undefinable. Even from where he stood Rod could hear the shouting and laughter. Almost immediately a crowd gathered around the man and his grisly burden. Rod decided to investigate.

He paused at the outer ring of the crowd to listen to the captain who was holding the jar aloft and speaking to all those assembled.

"Came upon him unexpected like," the captain was saying. "Our patrol cut them off before they could escape to that secret hideout of theirs in the mountains. Killed them all, every damn one of them."

"Murieta, too?" clamored a voice from the crowd.

"I killed Murieta myself," boasted the captain. "I knew no one would believe me so I brought proof."

Rod's stunned gaze flew to the jar the captain now raised proudly above his head for all to see. It was a sight Rod would never forget as long as he lived. Inside the jar, floating grotesquely in some kind of liquid, reposed the head of the bandit Joaquin Murieta. Appropriate praise and congratulations surrounded Rod but he felt only revulsion. That his one-time friend should be displayed in such a disgusting manner was reprehensible to him. He turned away from the grisly sight and nearly collided with Julie who had just recently joined the crowd to satisfy her own curiosity.

Julie had never seen such excitement, and being the inquisitive person that she was, left the blackjack table to learn for herself the cause for all the commotion. What she saw gave her nightmares for months to come. The fist that flew to her mouth did little to suppress the scream that ripped from her throat. Then she promptly fainted at Rod's feet.

Because Rod was closer, he picked up Julie's limp body and started off toward the stairs. Almost immediately he was joined by Brett Casey and Polly. Though he acknowledged Polly's presence with a nod, he barely registered his surprise that he should find Polly in Casey's Pleasure Palace.

"I'll take her, Delgado," Brett insisted, reaching for Julie. "I know were her room is located." A silent look passed between Polly and Rod that told him Julie had confided in her friend. But rather than cause a ruckus at a time when it might be detrimental to Julie's health, Rod relucantly relinquished his precious burden into Brett's waiting arms.

Nothing would prevent him from following Brett and Polly to Julie's room, Rod decided belligerently, ready to fight anyone for that right. If anything was wrong with his wife he wanted to know, despite the proprietory air of her lover, Brett Casey. Once Julie was placed on the bed, Polly shooed them all out of the room. Both men left, albeit not without first voicing loud protests.

Fifteen minutes later Polly reappeared, a worried frown puckering her pert features. She addressed Brett. "I think you should summon a doctor, I can't seem to rouse her." Brett whirled on his heel and left immediately, taking the steps two at a time.

Rod started into Julie's room. "Where are you going?" Polly asked, blocking his entry.

"She's my wife," Rod insisted stubbornly. "I have a right to be with her." Rod's words brought a secret smile to Polly's lips and she moved aside.

When Brett returned some fifteen minute later with the rotund doctor huffing from his efforts to keep up with a worried Brett, he was shocked and angered to find Rod sitting beside Julie, pressing her limp hand to his mouth. Before he had time to protest the rather shocking occurence, the doctor, Ignacio Vega by name, brusquely requested that they all leave him to his patient.

The minute the door closed behind them Brett angrily turned to Rod, his eyes blazing dangerously. "What's the meaning of this, Delgado? What is Brandy to you?"

"The question is what is she to you, *mi amigo*?" Rod returned testily.

"Brandy is the woman I love. I hope to make her my wife," Brett replied hotly.

Rod laughed softly, a dangerous sound that made Brett's hackles rise. "Has she agreed to become your wife?"

"No, but—"

"Then I wouldn't count on it, Casey," Rod drawled, impaling him with his hard stare.

"Look here, Delgado, just what is your interest in Brandy? Why are you evading my question?"

By now their voices had become so loud that Polly sought to interfere before fisticuffs broke out. "Stop! Both of you!" she intervened. "Think of Julie. What if she should hear you arguing like this?"

"We'll continue this later, Casey," Rod growled. "I think there are certain things you should know."

"Like what?" snorted Casey, suddenly wary.

Before Rod could grind out his answer, Doctor Vega appeared and the argument was immediately forgotten as the harried man shifted his myopic gaze between Rod and Brett. "Which of you is the lady's husband?" he asked curtly.

When no answer was forthcoming, the good doctor shrugged and rephrased his question. "Who is the father of the child she is carrying?"

"Child!" both men said in unison.

"I believe that is what I said," the doctor replied testily.

Rod eyed Casey narrowly before he spoke up. After all, Julie was his wife and no matter who fathered the child it was legally his. "I, Don Rodrigo Delgado, have the distinction of being the lady's husband," he declared haughtily.

Brett was utterly astounded by Rod's bold as well as surprising declaration. Could it be true, he wondered grimly? If so, why had Julie lied to him all this time? His thoughts faltered when Doctor Vega resumed speaking.

"I've revived your wife, Don Rodrigo, and given her a thorough examination. She is in good health but you must be aware that the Pleasure Palace is not a fit atmosphere for expectant mothers." Rod nodded solemnly, in complete agreement with the doctor. "I suggest she leave here and concentrate on getting through her pregnancy with no complications.'' Then he turned abruptly, leaving three confused people in his wake.

Coming out of his shock, Rod called after the doctor's retreating back, ''Does my wife know?''

''I left it for her husband to tell her,'' he called back blithely, barely pausing in his descent down the stairs.

Brett needed answers. And the sooner the better. Holding a tight rein on his galloping emotions he looked to Polly for an explanation, knowing he could trust her to tell the truth. ''Well, Polly,'' he said in a tone brooking no argument, ''what do you know about this? Is this (he started to say 'greaser' but wisely revised his choice of words) man married to Brandy . . . Julie?''

Polly hated to hurt Brett for she had come to respect and like him in the weeks she had known him. He was unfailingly kind to her and respected her even after he learned she had been whore to four men. But Polly knew he deserved to know the truth so she drew in a deep steadying breath and faced him squarely.

''Yes,'' she admitted. ''Julie and Don Rodrigo were married over a year ago.''

Brett seemed to melt inside himself, a thoroughly defeated man. ''We need to talk, Don Rodrigo,'' he said, gathering his inner resources.

''My sentiments exactly,'' Rod echoed, following Brett down the hall and into a room Rod assumed was an office.

''I think we both need this,'' Brett offered, pouring two glasses of whisky and handing Rod one. He polished his off in one gulp and poured another while Rod sucked pensively at his first.

''The time for angry words are long past, Don Rodrigo. My God, man, don't you realize I nearly seduced your wife? Why didn't either of you bother to tell me the truth?''

"You make me laugh, Casey," sneered Rod derisively. "We both know you seduced my wife months ago. How long has she been your mistress?"

"Don't you ever talk to your wife?" scowled Brett disgustedly. "If you did you would know that we have never been lovers, though not through any fault of mine."

Rod knew a moment of intense joy as he digested Brett's words. But he was not entirely convinced. "I was under the impression that you and Julie were on intimate terms."

"I will repeat this once more, Delgado, because you apparently do not fully comprehend the situation. I have never been intimately involved with your wife. We are not nor have we ever been lovers."

"I believe you, Casey," Rod smiled, feeling more friendly toward the handsome gambler than he thought possible. "Now I need your help."

"My help?"

"To convince Julie that the best place for her is with me at *Rancho* Delgado."

"Under the circumstances I agree. A pregnant woman belongs with the father of her child even though it puzzles me how you accomplished the deed when I was under the impression that you and Julie had never met, let alone spent time together."

Rod flashed a wicked grin. "Believe me, Casey, the 'deed,' as you call it, was accomplished more than once during the time I have been in San Francisco. Often enough, in fact, to get Julie with child. Now, will you use your influence with her, convince her to leave with me?"

"I won't promise you anything, Delgado, but I'll try. You know how damn stubborn your wife can be when she sets her mind to something. Do you think she suspects she is breeding?"

"I don't know but I intend to tell her at the first

opportunity." Suddenly Rod stifled a yawn. "It's been an exhausting day, Casey. If you don't mind I'd like to retire."

Casey nodded abstractedly. There was still much he didn't know about the strange relationship between Julie and her husband.

"Casey," Rod challenged, his hand on the doorknob, "I'm going to spend the night with my wife." He was out the door before Brett, half-rising in protest, could stop him.

20

Julie blinked awake and instinctively nestled into the warm body beside her. She was so comfortable she hated to move out of the strong arms that cradled her so protectively. The realization that she was not alone came slowly, but when it did her blood pounded and her face grew red with anger.

Rod awoke almost at the same instant. He felt her softness mold itself against his hard form before he sensed her awareness and sudden withdrawal. "Easy, *querida*," he gentled softly.

"Rod!" Julie gasped, exasperated. "What are you doing here? You must leave before someone discovers you!"

"We're finished with the games, Julie," Rod said, brushing strands of amber locks from her eyes and forehead with gentle hands. "As soon as you are able to travel we are leaving."

"Leaving? Able to travel?" The fuzzy edges of her brain refused to function as she digested Rod's words.

"Do you remember anything of last night, *querida*?" Rod asked gently.

"I . . . I . . . was dealing blackjack as usual, and there was a commotion," Julie recalled, frowning in concentration. "When I went to investigate I saw . . . Oh God . . . Joaquin!" She buried her head in Rod's shoulder as her mind refused to register what she had seen.

"You fainted, Julie. Do you remember?"

Julie shook her head negatively as she yielded to the compulsive sobs that shook her. Rod petted and caressed her soothingly until the sobs wracking her slender body subsided.

"Have I been unconscious all night?" she asked suddenly. "I seem to recall a doctor, and an examination." Crimson stained her cheeks when she thought of the doctor's intimate handling of her body. At the time she seemed to think it completely uncalled for.

"No," Rod was quick to assure her, "the doctor gave you something to relax you and make you sleep."

"If I only fainted, why did you call the doctor?" questioned Julie, puzzled by Rod's evasiveness.

"You gave us quite a scare when you did not come out of your swoon immediately."

"Am . . . am I all right?" Julie asked worriedly.

Rod knew the moment had come to tell Julie about her pregnancy. He was amazed that she hadn't suspected it already, but then she had always been innocent in most things a woman should know without being told. Probably came from being deprived of a mother during her formative years.

"There is nothing seriously wrong with you, *querida*," Rod began, a humorous smile curving his sensuous lips. "We are to have a child."

"A baby! No, Rod, it's not possible," denied Julie vigorously. A child now would serve only to complicate her life. No doubt Rod would welcome an heir, but would it make him love her, she asked herself?

"The doctor confirmed it, *querida*," Rod answered, highly amused. "Had you no inkling?"

Flushing. "I . . . no . . . not really. I missed two cycles but I thought it was because . . . because your presence was so upsetting to me. It must have happened that first night," she mused thoughtfully.

"I had a long talk with Casey," Rod confided. "He told me that the two of you were never lovers. I believed him."

Julie gave him an accusing glance, wondering why he chose to believe Brett when he refused to believe her. "Brett must hate me for lying to him," she said sadly. "I tried to tell you the truth about us but you chose to believe the worst."

"I don't think Casey could ever hate you but he does agree with me that you should return to the *rancho*. I want to look after you, Julie. You have our child to think about now, *querida*."

Julie was never more aware of the fact that not once had Rod mentioned that he loved her. Not even the knowledge that she was to bear his child seemed to make any difference in his feelings for her.

"I don't want your child, Rod," Julie blurted out unthinkingly.

Rod's body went rigid and a cold, congested expression settled on his face. Never was he more aware of her contempt for him than he was at that moment, when she denied her own motherly instincts as well as scorned the child of his loins. Did Julie feel nothing for him, he wondered bleakly? Did their child mean so little to her? Rage caused his voice to come out harsher than he meant. "It makes little difference what you want, Julie. The indisputable fact remains that in seven months you will present me with an heir."

Then he sprang from the bed so abruptly, he nearly overturned the nightstand in his haste to dress. He knew that if he remained he would either be forced to make violent love to her or do her bodily harm.

"Where are you going?" Julie asked in a small voice, fully aware of his anger.

"You've made it obvious from the start just how little you care for me," Rod said scathingly. "But in this one thing I will have my say. You *will* return with me to

Rancho Delgado and you *will* present me with a child in seven months. Nothing can change that! Nothing! I'll return for you in two days. In consideration of your condition, I'll do all in my power to make your journey to the *rancho* as comfortable as possible.'' Without another word he stormed from the room.

Later, Julie felt that everyone was against her. Brett acted as if he had forgotten his vows of love as he did everything in his power to convince Julie that her place was with her husband. Even Polly lined up solidly in favor of Rod and her return to *Rancho* Delgado. Julie almost laughed aloud when her friend calmly told her that Rod loved her and that Julie should give him a chance to prove his love.

In Julie's estimation, the only emotions Rod exhibited toward her were lust and possessiveness. And those she could do well without. She was glad that she had never let slip just how much she loved him. How humiliating it would be to have him mock her love.

There were times in those two days that she actually hated the child she nurtured within her; detested Rod's seed that took root in one of her moments of weakness when her body betrayed her. Then there were times when the thought of having Rod's baby thrilled her. At least she would have a part of him to love that would love her in return, she acknowledged grudgingly.

At the end of two days, Julie was forced to bid a tearful goodbye to Polly and a subdued but nonetheless heart-wrenching farewell to Brett while Rod looked on cynically, his composure unruffled.

''You'll visit, won't you,'' Julie asked tearfully?

''We'll come for the christening,'' promised Brett gaily, although he felt anything but joy at their parting.

''We'll be there, Julie,'' echoed Polly, her adoring gaze falling often on Brett. Until that moment, Julie had no idea Polly felt strong emotions for Brett but now she wished her friend well. Polly deserved a strong, loving man to care for her, and Brett needed the love of a good woman like Polly.

The trip to *Rancho* Delgado took nearly two weeks. True to his promise, Rod was solicitous of Julie's condition and careful of her comfort. Each night they stayed at one of the several missions scattered along El Camino Real, taking the trip in easy stages. They broke their journey at the missions of San Jose in the midst of giant redwoods, and San Carlos Borromco del Carmelo de Monterey outside Carmel where the founder of the chain of missions, *Padre* Junipero Serra, lies buried. Here Julie was impressed by the snowy beach sands and gnarled cypresses as well as by its sandstone walls, Moorish towers, unique windows and its beautiful setting against the sea and the mountains.

Another stop on their sojourn south was the mission of San Antonio De Padua, located in the mountain village of Jolan, and the third oldest mission to be established in California. At Paso Robles Julie picked almonds from the famed almond orchards at Mission San Miguel. The good *padre* there offered her water from a mineral spring that wasn't much to her liking but at Rod's urging, she drank it anyway.

When they entered the Santa Lucia mountains and the Mission of San Luis Obispo loomed ahead, Julie knew that *Rancho* Delgado lay but a few miles further. Under any other circumstances Julie would have greatly enjoyed their leisurely pace, the hospitality of the *padre* at each mission they visited, and the breathtaking vista of sea and mountains coming together in unsurpassed beauty.

But Julie traveled with a stranger; a cool, withdrawn stranger who saw to her needs and little else. Not once did he attempt to touch her. Each night she slept alone in her lonely bed and each day they traveled in near silence. Deep-rooted in Julie's brain lurked the certain knowledge that Rod did not love her, while in Rod's stubborn mind dwelt the certainty that Julie did not want their child. To both stubborn people the situation between them was impossible, but owing to their fierce pride, neither made a move to remedy the intolerable impasse that had made a shambles of their lives and the great love they shared but remained ignorant of.

Julie knew the identity of the lone rider who galloped out to meet him even before she saw the tiny proud figure whose long black hair floated free in the breeze behind her. It was almost as if Felicia knew they were coming, was in fact expecting them that very day.

"Don Rodrigo, Dona Julie, you're back at last! I told them you would bring Dona Julie back, *señor*!"

"Who did you tell, *niña*?" Rod smiled indulgently, nearly as happy to see Felicia as she was him.

"*Señor* Darcy, of course," she answered calmly.

"My father is here?" Julie cried, intense astonishment turning her face pale.

"*Si, señora*," nodded Felicia. "He's been at the *hacienda* for many weeks."

Uttering a cry of joy, Julie spurred her mount and raced toward the house despite Rod's cry of warning. Carl Darcy, looking frail but fit, stood on the veranda awaiting his daughter. Ramona Sanchez hovered at his side.

"Papa!" cried Julie, throwing herself into her father's arms. "I was so worried about you! What happened?"

By this time Rod had arrived and he repeated his wife's question, a disapproving note in his voice. "That is something I, too, should like to know, *Señor* Darcy. Also why you chose to keep your true identity from me. And while you're explaining, I think I deserve to know why you deliberately withheld from me the fact that Julie was alive and living in San Francisco."

Carl sighed deeply, aware that his stern-faced son-in-law would not be satisfied until everything was laid bare before him. "Come inside," he said, "where it is more comfortable. Then I will tell all. But first," he turned and drew a blushing Ramona to his side, "I'd like you both to meet Ramona Sanchez, the woman who saved my life."

"Papa!" Julie gasped worriedly. "How did she save your life?"

Rod ushered everyone inside saying, "First we sit, then the explanations." His sharp eyes did not miss Julie's high color or her state of excitement and his main concern at the moment was safeguarding the welfare of his wife and unborn child.

"Now, Papa," Julie said impatiently, squirming in her chair, "I want to hear everything that happened to you from the moment you left me in San Francisco."

Carl Darcy launched into a story that took over an hour in telling. During the telling his gaze strayed often to the shy Ramona whose adoring eyes seemed to devour the man whose life she saved. Julie liked Ramona immediately and was effusive in her gratitude to the serenely beautiful Spanish woman.

Then Julie narrated her own sad tale, recounting Mae Parker's death and her job at Casey's Palace where Rod found her. The telling left her exhausted, which Rod noted immediately. Abruptly he arose, rudely cutting Julie off in midsentence.

"*Señor* Darcy . . . Carl, my wife needs to rest. We will continue this conversation later."

"Rod! I won't be ordered about like a naughty child," Julie raged. "I haven't seen my father in months."

"Julie," Rod schooled patiently, as if to a recalcitrant child, "you must think of our child. I know what's best for you and right now a *siesta* is called for."

"You and Julie are to have a child?" rejoiced Carl. "Daughter, you don't know how happy that makes me. When I set out for San Francisco I was convinced that you had misjudged Don Rodrigo; that he had nothing to do with your abduction. I'm truly pleased that you came to the same conclusion and have reconciled."

Julie cut Rod a scathing glance. "We are not altogether reconciled, Papa," she admitted ruefully.

"But . . . if you are to have a child . . . I thought . . . well . . . do as your husband says, dear. I'm sure Rodrigo has your best interests at heart." It was apparent that Carl was embarrassed and confused by Julie's vague remark. "We'll talk later. And Julie, I'd like you to become friends with Ramona. She's a wonderful woman."

"Come with me now, Ramona," Julie invited eagerly. "We can become better acquainted while I prepare for the *siesta* my husband insists I take." She shot Rod a lethal smile and he flashed a mocking grin in return.

Once the women left the room, Carl was quick to ask, "What did my daugher mean? Surely you two have settled your differences. She is carrying your child, isn't she?"

"I wish I had a simple answer for you, Carl, but it's rather complicated," Rod admitted frankly. "Julie is carrying my child, there is no doubt of that. But it is a child I . . . er . . . forced on her. She doesn't love me nor does she want our child. She has made her feelings perfectly clear to me many times over."

How had Julie changed so dramatically in such a short time, Carl wondered, perplexed? He could distinctly remember his daughter voicing her love for her husband on more than one occasion. "I'm sure you're mistaken, Rod," was all Carl said, preferring to speak with Julie privately before he gave any secrets away.

"I wish I were mistaken," Rod sighed regretfully. "Julie has come to mean a great deal to me; more than I ever thought possible. But enough of my problems, what are your plans? It appears that you and the lovely Ramona have become more than just casual friends.''

Carl's pleasant features lit up at the mention of the gentle widow. ''Were we so obvious?'' grinned Carl engagingly. ''Why do you think I was so anxious for Julie and Ramona to become friends? If she will have me, I plan to make Ramona my wife. These past few years have not been easy for her.''

''You are welcome to make your home with us for as long as you like,'' offered Rod generously.

''I thank you sincerely, Rod. I have to admit I had no idea where I might settle with my bride. What resources I had were lost in the fire. My claim was stolen from me long ago and I had little liking for a bandit's life. But I don't want to become a burden to you. I intend to pay my way in some manner beneficial to you.''

Rod stared intently at Carl, liking him better by the minute. ''If the truth be known, Carl, I am in need of someone I can trust. Since my father's death, there is too much to do at the *rancho* for one person to accomplish. It would mean a great deal to me if I could shift some of that burden to you.''

Carl exhaled a long sigh of intense pleasure. ''You've found your man,'' he exclaimed happily.

''If you and your Ramona would like to be on your own, there is a comfortable *casa* not far from the *hacienda* that might suit your purposes admirably. It's the same one Murieta and his family occupied and has been empty for some time. Take Ramona to see it and if it suits you both, it should take no time at all to fix up to her liking.''

''If it means anything to you, Rod,'' Carl smiled effusively, ''I think Julie made the right choice when she married you.''

The following days passed by in a flurry of activity. Carl proposed to Ramona, who promptly accepted, and *Padre* Juan was asked to perform the simple ceremony in the chapel the moment their *casa* was habitable. Julie took an immediate liking to Ramona. She was certain the beautiful and gentle widow would be a good wife to her father. She was more than a little grateful to Rod for allowing her father to stay on at the *rancho*. Rod assured her that her father would be doing him a great service by remaining to help out.

A month after Julie and Rod returned to the *rancho*, Carl and Ramona were married by *Padre* Juan before a gathering of family and servants. After a *fiesta* following the ceremony, the beaming newlyweds retired to their own newly decorated house, leaving Julie and Rod alone for the first time since their return.

Rod had not touched Julie since their return to the *rancho* though he yearned to feel her softness melting into his hard body once again. There were times when he thought he would die from wanting, so great was his need. Each day he watched her grow lovelier, if that were possible, as the bloom of pregnancy colored her cheeks and lent a particular sparkle to her bluebell eyes.

Rod remembered exactly how quick she was to take fire beneath his caresses, reluctant though she might be at first; how her slender form gave him more pleasure than any other woman he had known. But during the past weeks he had alienated her further by forbidding her to ride with Felicia, insisting she rest daily, and even going so far as to dictate the type and quantity of food she should eat.

Given Julie's independence and volatile temper she rebelled at every turn, unwilling to believe that any danger existed in riding, accusing Rod of deliberately denying her the least bit of pleasure. She ranted and railed at his solicitous manner and overbearing protectiveness until Rod felt like locking her in her room like a naughty child. It was obvious to all but Julie that Rod cared for her deeply and was doing all in his power to keep her and their child safe and healthy.

Julie looked exceptionally beautiful the day of her father's wedding. She wore the same white embroidered skirt and *camisa* that she wore at the wedding of Don Diego and Elena. Though she had carefully let out the waist to accommodate her expanding girth so that the slight bulge of her stomach was camouflaged beneath the full skirt. Rod could not take his eyes off her all evening, consumed with the desire to taste again her special brand of ardor.

By the time Carl and Ramona departed for their own *casa*, Rod knew the ache in his loins could no longer be denied. As he told Julie once before, he was certainly no eunuch and had no intention of living like one. He was a virile man with a wife perfectly capable of assuaging his ferocious hunger. Therefore, being a man of lusty appetites, a man who had been put off far too long by the cool facade of Julie's indifference, Rod decided to put an end to the coldness separating them once and for all.

Julie was too keyed up to sleep that night. She could still feel the intimate brush of Rod's dark eyes on her flushed skin as his heated gaze stabbed at her repeatedly during the evening. Her flesh burned everywhere his eyes touched, and he touched everywhere. Or so it seemed to Julie. For weeks Rod had made no move to make love to her, smothering her instead with mock concern until his pompous manner drove her mad with frustration. Even dear Felicia had been unable to draw her out of her vile temper tantrums. How could she be expected to live in such close proximity to Rod, Julie agonized, and keep from wanting him? From loving him?

Perhaps once her child was born it would provide an outlet for the love trapped within her heart, Julie hoped, and ease the terrible emptiness in her life. Sometime in the past weeks, Julie had come to the joyful conclusion that she wanted Rod's baby. Wanted it with every fiber of her being, though she was determined Rod should never learn the truth from her.

Once Julie retired for the night, Rod allowed her just enough time to prepare for bed before he quietly entered her room through the connecting door that hadn't been used since their return, and lounged in the doorway watching her brush the luxurious honey-colored waves that gently caressed her rounded hips.

The room was dark except for the soft glow of a lamp that turned her into a sculpture of silver and gold. Only the ruby tips of her breasts pushing against a wisp of silken cloth lent a touch of color to her pale alabaster flesh. Pregnancy had enlarged her perfectly formed breasts, Rod noticed, but just enough to make them even more enticing. He longed to caress the slight bulge below her waist where his child lay, and his deep sigh of longing finally alerted her to his presence.

"Don't move, *querida*," Rod whispered, wooing her with his eyes. "I have never seen a lovelier picture."

From across the room their eyes met, held, each emotionally charged moment clicking away in her heart. Rod wore nothing but a silken robe loosely belted at the waist and against every instinct Julie wanted to remove the belt until he was naked, resplendent in his maleness. A wry smile lurked at the corner of Rod's mouth, as if he could read her thoughts and was in perfect agreement.

Forcing herself to remain calm, Julie asked, "What do you want, Rod?"

"Isn't it obvious, *querida*? I want to make love to you. I want to feel your petal-soft body writhe with pleasure beneath mine. I want to hear you cry out your joy." Like a lithe animal stalking his prey, Rod uncoiled his long length and seemed to glide loose-hipped across the room until he stood before her.

Julie swallowed convulsively, his tantalizing nearness driving coherent thought from her mind. Without invitation, Rod eased down beside her on the bed where she sat brushing her hair. Taking the brush from her nerveless fingers he tossed it to the floor. Then his mouth covered hers hungrily. The pressure on her mouth deepened as he deliberately and expertly teased her lips apart and entered her, dragging her unwillingly into his kiss. Her lips, burning, aching, demanded to be soothed, and he soothed them with his own brand of fire.

With leisurely precision, his hands began to mold her writhing body. She went suddenly rigid as he lightly brushed the rounded curve of her sensitive breasts, traced along the narrow line of her ribs to her expanding waist and the flare below of rounded hips and smooth thighs. A honey-sweet warmth swept through her as Rod swiftly loosened the ties of her gown and drew the wispy cloth over her head. Within seconds his own robe lay beside it on the floor. A swirling maelstrom of emotions tormented Julie but she was powerless to resist his strong aura that enveloped her in a cloud of sensual pleasure.

21

Julie was lost. His kiss was the magic that released her heart from its frozen void and her own love directed her response. Impatience seized her as Rod gently eased her down onto the smooth surface of the bed and her soft arms entwined about his neck as she pressed herself into his hard maleness, feeling her overly sensitive nipples brush against his furred chest.

Rod's expression was tender as he gazed into her eyes and his voice a husky purr. "Love, me, *querida*, love me."

"I do. I love you. I do," she repeated over and over. If only she meant it, Rod thought when he heard her words. If only he could hold her in this one perfect moment, suspended from time, at the brink of forever.

Crushing her to him he reclaimed her lips, and she returned his kiss with reckless abandon while his hand seared a path down her abdomen and onto her thigh. She felt his heat and hardness as she surged against him. When his lips took possession of her sensitive, swollen nipple, Julie could not repress her gasp of hot delight.

While teasing one rounded globe with tongue and lips, his hand fondled the other, its rosy tip marble hard. His gentle massage sent currents of desire through her and she whimpered impatiently.

"Patience, *mi amor*, patience," Rod whispered, "it's been so long and we are in no hurry."

His hands maddeningly explored the soft lines of her

back, her waist, her hips, cupping the rounded globes of her buttocks as his mouth and lips nibbled a trail of fire along her rib cage, pausing to kiss and caress the bulge of her stomach before he moved downward to the downy forest that covered the treasure that was his alone. Parting curling hair, his stabbing tongue slid into and manipulated the tiny, rigid bud below. Julie uttered a stifled cry as her body arched into the moist warmth of his mouth and tongue, winding her hands into his crisp black hair in an effort to pull him even closer.

Passion pounded the blood through her heart as she writhed beneath his relentless tongue and mouth. She felt herself go hot, then cold, half ice, half flame as his expert touch sent her to even higher levels of ecstasy. Somehow Julie did not believe the hoarse voice crying out for release was hers, but it was. Then suddenly her body began to vibrate with liquid fire as he freed her in a bursting of sensations that sent her hurtling into space.

Rod allowed her but a moment's respite as he knelt before her parted legs and came into her fast, his body so hard he ached. At first Julie could barely muster a response, but as his strenghtening thrusts repeated with increasing urgency, she felt herself rising to meet him. She could feel his attempts to restrain his ardor because of her condition and surprisingly it touched a spark someplace in the compartments of her heart.

Bodily Rod lifted her and reversed her position until Julie lay on top. Instantly her legs surrounded his sleek hips; her back arched, slim neck thrust backwards as she set the pace. From a single place in her soft depths, liquid fire ignited and flared until she felt herself consumed once more by white-hot flames.

When Rod felt her release, long ripples began to pass down his flexed and glistening body, unrestrained thrusts caught them both in a clash of thunder and lightning that seemed to go on forever. But after a while it did end, only to begin again and again, their greed for one another seemingly unappeasable, taking each other with love-starved greed until the night had turned into dawn.

Julie awoke first, astonished at the sense of fulfillment she felt. She glanced shyly at Rod, his body naked and still moist from their recent lovemaking. During the long night her own driving need had shocked and thrilled her. The admission that she could no longer deny herself Rod's lovemaking was dredged from a place beyond logic and reason. The harder she tried to ignore the truth, the longer it persisted. She loved Rod. With her whole heart and soul. If given no other choice she would remain with him always, accepting the crumbs of his affection, living for the nights his lust drove him to her bed.

She allowed her subconscious thoughts to surface and without realizing it spoke them aloud. "Oh, Rod, my love, why can't you love me like I love you?"

Unbeknownst to Julie, Rod had awakened nearly at the same instant she had but for some unexplained reason feigned sleep. He felt himself on the brink of a great discovery and lay waiting, slowing his breathing to an even cadence while Julie moved restlessly beside him.

Her impassioned words sent a jolt of unbridled joy surging through his veins. He wanted to dance, to sing, but did neither. Very quietly he said, "I do, *mi amor*. I've loved you from the moment I first set eyes on you, from the day I made you mine even though the odds were against our union from the beginning."

Julie stiffened in disbelief. Could it be possible? Did Rod really love her? Or was this some sort of cruel game he was playing. Shock rendered her nearly speechless but somehow she managed to choke out one word. "Truly?"

"Truly, *querida*," Rod echoed, eyes shining with love. So long had he dreamed of Julie openly declaring her love for him that the actual moment somehow seemed anti-climactic. How terribly sad that they should love each other all these many months and yet remain at cross-purposes, their emotions reined in tightly, Rod sighed.

"Oh, Rod, why didn't you tell me?" Julie asked, finally finding her tongue.

"Why didn't you tell me?" challenged Rod, teasing an amber curl around his fingers.

She was momentarily lost in her own reverie as she called to mind all the reasons Rod had given her as proof that he did not love her. "At first there was Elena to remind me who held your affections. I couldn't hope to compete with someone as beautiful and refined as she appeared to be."

"I never loved Elena, Julie. You'll never know just how sorry I am for briefly falling under her spell. I know I hurt you, but I can only tell you it will never happen again.

"Julie," Rod probed, "you do forgive me, don't you?" She was silent for so long Rod feared she still withheld her forgiveness. "I know now what kind of woman Elena is. There is nothing she isn't capable of to gain her own ends."

"I forgive you, Rod," Julie turned to him smiling. "I won't let anything stand in the way of our happiness. Elena is gone and we have our child growing within me as proof of our love."

Rod cleared his throat nervously. "Uh, *querida*, about the child. You're not sorry, are you? I couldn't bear it if—"

Rising on one elbow Julie leaned over him, bright strands of hair brushing his chest as she healed his lingering doubt with a kiss. "Of course I want your child. When our son—"

"Or daughter," he teased lightly, interrupting.

"Or daughter," she acknowledged with a shrug, "is placed in my arms my joy will be complete."

"*Madre de Dios*, Julie, I love you. If anything should happen to you I would die." His arms closed about her so fiercely, she cried out in protest.

"Nothing will happen to me, my love, nothing," Julie assured him.

At that moment Rod felt invincible, so infused with love that he felt himself capable of making love to Julie all day long despite the fact that he had done just that all night. But prudence won out and he reluctantly released her and arose from bed in one graceful motion. Careful of her condition, Rod was well aware that he had surely exhausted Julie during their long hours of passion and her well being was too important to jeopardize.

"Don't get up, *mi amor*," he advised, lavishing her with a loving glance. "Go back to sleep. I'm sure I wore you out last night. I'll be in my office later. If you'd like, I'll take you for a ride."

Julie's eyes sparkled mischievously but she managed a decorous nod. Within minutes she was sleeping soundly, feeling more at peace than she had in months.

It was well past noon when Julie dressed, downed a light meal and went in search of Rod for her promised outing. Just as he had predicted earlier, Julie found him in his office, dark head bent over a sheath of papers. When he looked up he bestowed her with a radiant smile that sent her pulses racing. Her own answering smile was as intimate as a kiss.

"If you continue looking at me like that, *querida*, we never will have that outing I promised you." There was a slight tinge of wonder in his voice as if he found it difficult to believe all that had happened between them the night before and the love they shared.

Julie laughed in sheer joy, thoroughly enchanting Rod with the tinkling sound of happiness. "I think I'd prefer the outing, if you don't mind."

"I'll only be a minute longer, *mi amor*," grinned Rod in response.

Julie walked absently about the comfortable room while Rod busied himself with his ledgers. Inexplicably, her eyes flew to the bricks surrounding the fireplace and something clicked in her mind. The letter! How could she have forgotten the letter whose hiding place Don Diego entrusted into her keeping months ago? After all that had happened, she had completely forgotten the missive that was so important to Don Diego that his last words were instructions concerning its disposal.

Rod watched curiously as Julie walked trance-like to the fireplace and began what seemed to him a mindless search of its rough exterior. "What is it, *querida*?" he asked, perturbed by her strange behavior.

"I know it's here, Rod, but I can't find it," she wailed, clearly distressed. "It's been so long that I've forgotten."

"What have you forgotten? Please, Julie, you musn't excite yourself, it's not good for the baby."

"The letter, Rod! I don't remember which brick to remove."

"*Por Dios*, Julie, what are you talking about?" By now Rod was by her side trying without success to lead his resisting wife away from the hearth.

"Rod, please, you don't understand. Your father showed me a letter shortly before he died and made me promise to give it to you. He . . . he said it was very important. In order to insure its safekeeping he hid it in a compartment behind one of these bricks, but I can't find it."

Amazement marched across Rod's handsome features. "A letter! An important letter!" he repeated as he stared dumbly at the scores of bricks lining the wall. "*Caramba*! If there is a secret compartment behind one of these bricks, I shall find it."

It took nearly an hour of careful probing before Rod discovered one brick protruding perhaps a quarter-of-an-inch beyond the others. Using his knife he painstakingly pried it out, uttering a cry of triumph when he extracted a sealed envelope from inside a hidden compartment.

Julie stood by breathlessly as Rod broke the seal and silently read his father's words. His sharp gasp and sudden pallor alarmed Julie and his hand flew to his throat as if he was having difficulty breathing.

"*Madre de Dios*! This letter, Julie, it explains much!" He had gone white under his tan and the hand holding the letter shook uncontrollably.

"Rod, my love, what is it? What did your father say to upset you so?"

"It's about Felicia . . . and Maria."

"What has Felicia got to do with Maria?" Suddenly her brow cleared and her hand flew up to clutch at her throat. "Oh, no! Felicia is Maria's daughter!"

"*Si*," Rod nodded slowly. "Felicia is my—"

"Your daughter!" breathed Julie, choking on the words.

"No," contradicted Rod, an anguished look mottling his features. "I never touched Maria. Felicia is my father's child! She is my sister!"

"Oh, Rod, no! How could he when he knew how much you loved Maria!"

"According to his letter, Maria became his mistress while I was away at school." Intense pain filled his eyes. "All the time I was saving her for marriage, *mi padre* was . . . *Dios*! I loved her!"

"Is that why your father refused your request to marry her?" Julie asked.

"That plus the fact she was a *mestiza*. It's all too clear to me now. When Maria found out she was pregnant by my father, she ran away rather than tell me the truth. She went to the nuns in Sonora."

"She didn't know she would fall in love with you, Rod," Julie reminded him gently.

"Perhaps not," Rod acknowledged. "But then again,

she may have been using me.''

''Did your father know that Maria was carrying his child when she left?''

''Not according to his letter,'' Rod revealed. ''He learned it only after Felicia was born and he received a letter from the nuns telling him that Maria had died in childbirth and they could not keep her daughter. It seems that Maria had named her child's father before she died. *Mi padre* did the only thing he could think of, he brought the infant back to *Rancho* Delgado and through *Padre* Juan put her into Teresa's keeping. He wanted her about the *rancho* without having to acknowledge her. He saw to the child's welfare but little else. I think he came to regret it but by then too many years had passed and his pride got in the way of his duty.''

''At least Felicia has been well cared for and loved these many years,'' Julie mused, thinking of Teresa's selfless care of her adopted daughter.

''Thank God for that,'' Rod added his heartfelt sentiments. ''But I can't understasnd why he kept this secret for ten years.''

''He was a proud man, Rod. Too proud to admit to taking a young girl like Maria. Her being a *mestiza* didn't help, either. And then, when you fell in love with her, it was far easier to withhold permission to marry than to confess he had corrupted a young, innocent girl. If he had known about the child perhaps he would have married Maria himself.''

''I doubt it,'' laughed Rod harshly. ''And Maria knew it! *Mi padre* would provide for his child but he would never marry a woman of low birth. Bloodlines meant everything to him. If only Maria had told me she was *mi padre's* mistress I might have understood.''

''I'm sorry, Rod,'' Julie said softly. ''I know how disillusioned you must be.''

''Just thinking of Maria and my father together, even

after all these years, makes my blood boil. How could he!'' His head fell to his hands and for a few minutes he gave in to the despair and remorse he had suffered all these years because of Maria.

Silence reigned as Julie allowed him time to grieve and to come to terms with what had really happened all those years ago. Suddenly Julie's eyes were drawn back to the secret opening and she saw that though narrow in front the compartment gave way to a larger space further back. Her sharp eyes noted several other items still resting within. Calling Rod's attention to her discovery, he drew out a packet of documents that upon inspection proved to be the original land grant to the *rancho*.

''I wondered where *mi padre* had hidden these. I assumed they were in the safe but did not find them.''

''Look, Rod! There are several small sacks at the very back!'' Julie cried, excited. Carefully she extracted one surprisingly heavy bag, undid the drawstring and watched wide-eyed as a golden stream flowed into her open palm.

''Gold dust,'' Rod shrugged without interest. At that moment he was thinking about Felicia and the fact that she was his sister. ''Put everything back, Julie. They'll be safe there. I . . . I must find Felicia without delay. Will you come with me, *querida*?''

''Oh course, my love, we'll tell her together. But hadn't you better speak to Teresa first? Felicia is like a daughter to her.''

''You're right, *mi amor*. Your wisdom far surpasses mine. You go for Teresa while I replace the brick and put things in order.''

A short time later Rod told Teresa as gently as possible that Felicia was his sister and how he came by that knowledge. At first the housekeeper could only stare at Rod, mouth agape, until Julie assured her it was true; that Don Diego had kept the truth from them all these years but had confessed all in a letter he had written shortly before his death.

"Don Rodrigo," Teresa asked fearfully, "you don't think that I . . . I mean . . . I knew nothing! Felicia was given to me by *Padre* Juan. I don't believe even he knew the truth. He was told Felicia's parents were killed by Indians and that's what I've told Felicia. Of course Teresa knew all about Maria but not the reason behind her sudden disappearance. Like everyone else, she supposed Don Diego had taken Maria away to keep her from marrying his son.

"Rod was quick to put the woman's fears at rest. "I hold you blameless, Teresa, just as I do *Padre* Juan. I am grateful to you for taking such good care of my sister all these years."

"I . . . I suppose you'll want her with you now. In the *hacienda*, I mean."

"*Si*, Teresa. Felicia belongs here with me and Julie. But do not despair. You are the only *madre* Felicia has ever known. Her feelings for you will never change."

Teresa offered a shy smile. "Will you tell her, *señor*, or do you wish me to?"

"I will tell her myself. Where is she?"

"I believe one of the mares has foaled and she is in the stables inspecting the new addition."

"*Gracias*, Teresa." Teresa turned to leave but Rod stayed her with a gentle touch. "I would like you and your husband to remain close to Felicia. The two of you are her beloved *tia* and *tio*."

"We will be grateful, *señor*," smiled Teresa gently.

After Teresa left, Rod took Julie by the hand and started out the door, but Julie hung back. "Rod I've been thinking. Perhaps you should see Felicia alone. This is between the two of you. When you've had your talk bring her back to the house so I can welcome her home."

Rod found Felicia in the stables entranced by a black colt wobbling on floppy legs inside one of the stalls.

With a faraway look he watched his sister reach out tentatively to pat the colt's sleek head while his proud mother looked on. It was still difficult for Rod to believe that this enchanting child was related to him. She was so like Maria he was surprised he hadn't noticed the resemblance before. As if sensing his presence, Felicia swiveled to face him.

"Don Rodrigo! Look at Carmencita's foal. Isn't he beautiful? So regal. Like a duke . . . or a prince."

"Would you like to name him, *niña*?"

"May I?"

"*Si.*"

"Then I should like to think about it a day or two." She was so serious that Rod was hard put to keep a straight face.

"Felicia, I have something important to tell you, that is why I came looking for you."

Felicia turned her quiet, delicate features in Rod's direction. Her skin glowed with pale gold undertones and Rod was amazed by her resemblance to her mother. She even had much of Don Diego's bone structure as well as his own.

"Do you like stories, *niña*?"

"Oh, *si, señor*!" Felicia exclaimed exuberantly. "Especially if they have a happy ending."

"After I tell you the story, you can judge for yourself." Felicia moved to Rod's side, resting comfortably against his knee as she waited for him to begin.

"This is a true story, *niña*, about a beautiful girl named Maria and a proud Spanish don. The don fell in love with Maria and together they had a child, only Maria never told the don she was to have his child and Maria ran away before the don could marry her."

"Would he have? Married Maria, I mean." Felicia asked, her astute question momentarily stunning him. God forgive him for lying but he hadn't the heart to disillusion her with the sordid truth. "I . . . I like to think they would have married."

Temporarily appeased, Felicia waited for him to continue, her dark eyes showing intelligence beyond her meager years.

"Do you know what I'm trying to tell you, *niña*?" Rod asked, holding his breath.

"Maria was my mother and Don Diego was my father," Felicia whispered in a burst of complete understanding, "and . . . and I am your sister."

Rod searched her small, expressive face for signs of rejection but saw nothing but wonder. "*Si*, Felicia, you are my sister. When you were born, Don Diego took you from the convent where your mother had fled and brought you to the *rancho* for Teresa to raise. You see, *niña*, he wanted you near him. Your mother died when you were born. In his own way he loved you."

"I always felt I was different from the *vaquero's* children," Felicia mused thoughtfully. "And . . . and Don Diego was very kind to me. Do you think he would have told me one day, Don Rodrigo?"

"Had he lived I'm certain of it, Felicia. I'm sure he felt you were too young to understand, else he would have informed you before now. As it was he died before he could tell you the truth."

"As much as I love *Tia* Teresa I knew from the beginning she was not *mi madre*." Suddenly she grew thoughtful. "How long have you known that I am your sister?"

"I didn't find out until today. It was in a letter that *mi padre* left for me. In it he explained everything."

Being the well-adjusted child she was, Felicia accepted all that Rod had told her with her usual exurberance and strength of character that was inherent in all the Delgados. "The ending is a happy one," she smiled shyly.

Never had Julie been so happy. The addition of Felicia to the family was celebrated with a *fiesta*

attended by all the *vaqueros* and their families, the
servants, *Padre* Juan and Carl and Ramona, followed
by a bullfight in their own bullring. Julie had never seen
a bullfight before and decided she never wanted to
attend another. Rod was one of the matadors and
though she was extremely proud of his carriage and
ability in the ring she was frightened for him the entire
time. But she need not have worried. Rod had learned
the art as a young boy and had he chosen, could have
made a living in Mexico or Spain fighting bulls.

So immersed was Julie in Rod and Felicia that the
months of her pregnancy literally flew by. Having her
father involved in her life again was another cause for
her tranquility and happiness. She saw him nearly every
day and Ramona just as often. It pleased Julie no end
that her father found such joy in his marriage to the
comely widow.

As Julie's pregnancy advanced, Rod rarely left the
hacienda. Nor did he leave her bed. He chose to spend
every night with his wife, sleeping in her arms, making
love to her most of them. It was with a sense of shock
that Rod realized Julie was within four weeks of
delivering their child and he was still making love to her,
albeit carefully.

Both Ramona and Teresa assured Rod that either of
them were capable of delivering the child when Julie's
time came, but Rod still could not help but worry.
Taking Teresa aside one day he discretely began asking
questions.

Teresa was appalled to learn that Rod and Julie were
still engaging in marital relations and in no uncertain
terms told him he must desist immediately or risk the
health of his unborn child. As Rod had no intention of
harming either his wife or child he made plans at once to
move back into his own room. He knew he could not
trust himself to remain in the same bed and not make
love to his desireable wife, still beautiful to him despite

her increasing girth. Thinking Julie more knowledge-able in the ways of women and childbirth than she really was, he did not think to inform her why he had so abruptly deserted her bed.

But Julie had her own theories. Examining herself in the mirror, she knew the reason for Rod's sudden desire to sleep elsewhere. She was grotesque. Her stomach so huge and her body so ungainly that she felt certain Rod was repulsed by her. Else why would he desert her when she needed him most? She needed, no, craved, the closeness and protection of his presence in her bed, especially now when she looked her worst. She knew he could no longer desire her because of the way she looked but that did not mean he had to withdraw himself completely, did it?

Rod sensed Julie's confusion but never once considered it due to his being insensitive to her needs. Advanced as she was in pregnancy he knew she must be uncomfortable, and being unable to completely understand, left it to the women to offer comfort. Never having been around a woman about to give birth, unaware of the moods, their insecurities, their needs, he spent endless hours at hard labor instead of reassuring his wife who felt suddenly neglected and unloved. He threw himself whole-heartedly into roundup, spending long hours in the saddle until he was ready to drop from exhaustion.

He saw Julie but little, and when he did he was un-failingly tender and solicitous, which made Julie all the more miserable. Knowing well his lusty appetites, she convinced herself that Rod was seeing a woman in the village, which to her troubled mind accounted for his late nights and obvious state of exhaustion. She thought about questioning him outright but her pride would not allow it. If Rod was easing himself with another woman, she told herself irrationally, she did not want to know about it. This inexplicable lack of communication between two people deeply in love was the major cause of what transpired next.

22

Julie was not the only one aware of Rod's late hours nearly every night, or that on some nights he slept with the *vaqueros* under the stars rather than ride back home from the branding site when he was too tired to stir himself to further effort. Unbeknownst to Rod, his late night comings and goings had been under surveillance for some time.

Manuel Rojas had remained in San Luis Obispo after fear forced him to leave *Rancho* Delgado, for he was convinced that Rod would one day learn that he had been the go-between in Elena's and Pedro's plot to get rid of Dona Julie and punish him.

Then, by accident, he learned that Elena had been turned out of the *hacienda* and was staying at the mission. He contrived to visit her there and was shocked to learn that she was pregnant. And judging from the size of her, Manuel realized the child could only be his, for Don Rodrigo was not even on the *rancho* during the time Elena must have conceived.

Essentially Manuel was not a bad person. In fact, nothing at all like his cousin Pedro. Nearly as tall as Rod, broadshouldered and rugged, his resemblance to Rod, if one did not look too closely, was uncanny. That resemblance is what attracted Elena to Manuel in the beginning. Manuel did not really want to harm Julie but he had let himself be beguiled by Elena who used her sexual wiles to lure him into her devious plot.

Thus, when Manuel saw Elena and learned he was to become a father, he begged the haughty Spanish woman to marry him for the sake of their child.

Elena's harsh laughter brought a flush of anger to Manuel's dark features. "Marry you!" she spat disparagingly. "I am a Montoya and you are a Mexican," she said, as if that explained everything.

"I was good enough to bed," contended Manuel angrily. "Who will take care of you and the child? Your parents are still in Spain. Do you think they will welcome you or your bastard?" Manuel knew nothing of the money Rod had generously given Elena and as far as Elena was concerned he never would.

As the weeks passed, Manuel worked ceaselessly to persuade Elena that it would be to her advantage to marry him. Only when Elena was informed by *Padre* Juan that Rod had returned to *Rancho* Delgado with his pregnant wife did Elena finally give her consent. Two days after her hasty marriage to Manuel, Elena gave birth to a healthy son. After a two week recuperation period at the mission she and the baby moved with Manuel to a small *casa* in the village.

Elena despised her new life. The loss of status from *el patrona* to the wife of a laborer was demeaning and degrading. All her hatred was focused on Julie, whom Elena blamed. If Julie hadn't stolen Rodrigo from her, Elena contended, she would be the pampered wife of a wealthy don instead of the mate of a landless peon. It seemed unjust that an Anglo *puta* should hold a place in life that rightfully belonged to Elena. Soon her hatred and spite transferred itself from Julie to Manuel, and even to her innocent son. She began to plot for revenge and plan for the day she could wreak her vengeance on Julie and leave Manuel, taking her carefully hoarded money with her.

One day, Elena hit upon an idea that was calculated to shock and hurt Julie in a cruel manner. But in order to carry out the hoax she had concocted, she needed

Manuel's help. Accordingly, after a particularly rewarding night of intense sexual pleasure, Elena broached the subject to her sated husband.

"I think it is time we left here, Manuel," she said, running her hands sensuously over his shoulders and chest.

"I thought you wanted to remain in San Luis Obispo." replied Manuel lazily.

"Not any longer."

"Where would we go?"

Elena shrugged carelessly. "Sonora, perhaps. Someplace where no one knows me and my . . . circumstances. I can no longer bear the snide looks and cruel remarks of these . . . these peasants in the village."

Manuel sighed wearily. "Perhaps you are right, Elena. If we left his cursed place perhaps we would not fight so much and you would become a more loving wife and mother."

What a stupid fool, Elena thought smugly, curling her lips in derision. Manuel was crazy to think she would ever be a real wife to him. And his child! The brat was nothing but a hindrance. One day she would be well rid of them both.

"Of course I will become more loving," Elena lied, smiling deceptively, "but you must do something for me in return. You must prove your love for me."

Manuel's eyes narrowed suspiciously. "What do you have in mind?"

"I cannot, will not, leave here to begin our new life together until justice is served. Don Rodrigo's wife must be punished. She must be made to feel the same kind of pain she caused me."

"*Por Dios*, Elena! Haven't we caused her enough harm already? Surely you are aware of what she must have suffered as Pedro's prisoner. Can't you be satisfied with that?"

"No!" screamed Elena, consumed with rage. "You heard *Padre* Juan. Rodrigo told him Julie's father saved her before she had been harmed. Once! Just once I want her to feel the same kind of pain I suffered because of her. And I need your help.''

"The woman is breeding, Elena. Have you no mercy?"

"If you help me, Manuel, I promise not to touch her physically or cause her bodily harm. Her unborn child will not suffer at my hands."

Elena was very persuasive but Manuel was not so easily convinced. He did not hate Julie, nor wish her ill. He only wanted to make a good life for his wife who never seemed satisfied no matter what he offered her, and for his son who was more precious to him than life. Then Elena suddenly realized the only way to sway Manuel was through his son, and she threatened to take the boy where Manuel would never find him. The poor man, whose intelligence was never on the same level as his wife's, finally acquiesced. Jubilant, Elena outlined her simple plan and the part Manuel was to play. Afterwards she rewarded him with a stunning display of lust the likes of which left them both gasping for breath.

Manuel began keeping his bargain by closely following Rod's movements. At first he was disappointed to learn that Rod rarely left the confines of the *hacienda*. But then roundup began and the situation changed drastically overnight. His former *patron* began spending long hours on the range taking an active part in the roundup which Manuel knew from experience would last for weeks. When Elena was informed Rod sometimes did not return to the *hacienda* until the small hours of the morning, and oftentimes not at all, she rejoiced, for she knew her moment for revenge had finally arrived.

Given Julie's mood and condition that morning, she would have believed anything. She hadn't seen Rod for more than twenty minutes at a time in days, Felicia's time was taken up in lessons, and even her father seemed to have little time to devote to a pregnant woman so maudlin of late that she broke into tears at the slightest provocation. Her best moments during her endlessly boring days arrived at mid-morning when she took her exercise in the courtyard before the sun became too bright and chased her inside.

This morning was no exception. Alone in the courtyard with nothing or no one for company but her memories, Julie vividly recalled these happy months when she and Rod became friends as well as lovers. Until the last few days, she thought ruefully, when he acted as if they were nothing but polite strangers. Had he met someone else, she wondered jealously? Had his love for her cooled as her figure grew to monstrous proportions until she was no longer capable of satisfying his passion? Her deep sighs were echoed by the breeze ruffling the leaves above her head. The baby stirred restlessly and Julie moved awkwardly toward a far corner as if in answer to her child's silent command.

Unnoticed by Julie, a small, veiled figure detached itself from the shadows and waited until she was nearly abreast before stepping boldly in her path.

"*Buenas dias*, Julie."

Julie froze. There was no mistaking the husky, breathless voice. What was Elena doing here, she wondered, at tremor of apprehension tightening her muscles until she felt her rigid body cry out in protest? Curtailing her rampaging emotions, she asked, "What do you want, Elena?"

"To talk, Julie, nothing more." Elena could not help but eye Julie's protruding stomach distastefully, thinking that the spawn of an Anglo *puta* should not be the Delgado heir.

"Then talk quickly and leave," Julie insisted, unable to control the tell-tale quiver in her voice. She could neither forget nor forgive the woman who had nearly cost her her life.

Elena smiled inwardly, immediately recognizing Julie's fear and reveling in her mastery over her rival.

"It won't take long to say what is on my mind. It concerns Rodrigo and myself."

"You and Rod?" repeated Julie stupidly. "Whatever could you mean?"

"You may be a lot of things, Julie, but stupid isn't one of them." chided Elena derisively. "Rodrigo and I have been . . . seeing each other for weeks."

"I don't believe you!" exclaimed Julie, suddenly very frightened.

"It's true. After I left the *hacienda* I took a small *casa* in town. Shortly after your return here Rodrigo realized he could not live without me and he came to me. We became lovers."

"No!" gasped Julie, her swollen stomach lurching in revulsion.

"*Si!*" smiled Elena cunningly. "Did you know I carried Rodrigo's child when I left the *hacienda*?" At Julie's horrified look, she added, "Ask Teresa if you don't believe me."

Julie was too shocked by Elena's malicious revelations to reply as she stared gape-mouthed at Rod's lover, or so she assumed. Suddenly her wits returned and she said, "Am I expected to calmly accept your word? Where is this phantom child of Rod's?"

Without a word Elena whirled and strode purposefully to a secluded spot surrounded by shrubs, bent down and lifted from a bed of soft grass a child who couldn't have been but a few months old. "I knew you wouldn't believe me so I brought my son with me. His name is Rodrigo, the same as his father's. Is he not a handsome child?"

Julie began perspiring profusely, staggering toward a bench when she felt her legs give way. Relentlessly Elena followed, flaunting the baby before Julie as proof of Rod's love.

Against her will Julie's eyes were drawn to the child. Rod's son, if Elena could be believed. Judging from his

size he could have been fathered by Rod during Julie's
long absence. He looked much like Elena, but what
really convinced her was the boy's crisp, curing hair and
sturdy body so like Rod's that her heart constricted
painfully in her breast at the sight of him.

Elena felt Julie's uncertainty and moved in to deliver
the final insult. "If you do not believe me, come to my
casa tonight and you will see with your own eyes what
your mind refuses to believe."

"What . . . what do you mean?"

"Rodrigo is coming to me tonight. I can give him
what you cannot. When he makes love to me, nothing
exists but the two of us and our love for each other. He
has told me many times that he wishes you would leave
so he might acknowledge his son and bring me back to
the *hacienda*."

If Julie hadn't been so emotionally distraught she
would have realized just how irrational Elena's words
were. But all she could think of was Rod's sudden
coldness toward her and the baby Elena held in her
arms. Were all these months of happiness a delusion,
she wondered dismally? Was there something lacking in
her to make Rod turn to Elena?

"Will you come tonight, Julie?" she heard Elena
asking. "Are you brave enough to learn the truth? It
must hurt to realize that you are unwanted, that in fact
you are nothing but an encumbrance to Rodrigo who
should have never married an Anglo in the beginning."

"Where?" Julie whispered. "Where do you live?"
An evil smile lurking at the corner of her mouth, Elena
gave explicit instructions on how to reach her *casa*.

"Be there promptly at ten o'clock," she hastened to
add, "if you want to discover exactly what your
husband does each night. Walk along the veranda until
you come to the bedroom." The inflection in her voice
left Julie little doubt as to what went on in Elena's bedroom.

After Elena left as mysteriously as she appeared, Julie could not force her legs into motion so she sat, far longer than was her custom. So long, in fact, that a distressed Teresa came looking for her. "Dona Julie," she chided gently when she found her mistress in a far corner of the courtyard, "I became worried when you did not return in time for lunch. Felicia is waiting in the dining room for you."

Julie looked at Teresa dumbly, as if recognition was slow in coming, her vagueness alarming the housekeeper greatly. "*Señora*, are you ill?" the older woman asked. "Is it the baby? I will send for Don Rodrigo."

"No!" cried out Julie, the mention of her husband's name bringing her to her senses. "I'm all right, really," she added more gently.

"Then come along, *señora*, your lunch is getting cold."

With the help of a concerned Teresa Julie rose somewhat unsteadily to her feet, suddenly recalling Elena's words. "Teresa," she asked abruptly, "was Elena with child when she left here?"

Teresa thought nothing of Julie's question. It was common knowledge to all but Julie that Elena was now living with her husband Manuel in San Luis Obispo. Quite a comedown for the haughty Spanish woman, sniffed Teresa.

"*Si*, Dona Julie. When she left here, only Don Rodrigo and myself were aware of her condition. He took her to the mission and put her in *Padre* Juan's care until her child was born. It wasn't long before everyone knew that she had a child. Especially after she left the mission and went to live in the village with—"

"Stop!" came Julie's anguished cry. "I don't want to hear anything more! I never want to hear her name again."

Teresa was puzzled by Julie's apparent aversion to Elena, being unaware of all that Elena had done to harm Julie, as well as what had transpired in the courtyard earlier. But she was astute enough to realize that speaking of Elena was doing her mistress no good.

"You don't seem yourself today, *señora*," she soothed. "Why don't you go to your room and let me send up a tray for you. Felicia is a wise child. She knows you are near your time and will understand if you don't join her."

Numbly Julie allowed Teresa to lead her through the courtyard to the French doors opening into her bedroom. She made no protest when the kindly woman helped her undress and tucked her into bed. A short time later Felicia carried a tray to Julie. Julie's listless replies to her questions soon convinced Felicia that her sister-in-law was best left alone to her rest, and went off to find her own amusement.

Julie was in a turmoil of indecision. Did she really want to know if Elena and Rod were lovers? Would it not be far better to think Elena a liar than to face the hurt of Rod's betrayal? Did she truly wish to view his infidelity with her own eyes? Yes, she decided painfully, she could not trust Elena's word. She owed it to Rod to give him the benefit of the doubt until she proved otherwise. Julie was well aware of Elena's deceit, well-versed in the many ways Elena chose to demonstrate her hatred and cunning. This was something she had to do, Julie resolved. Somehow, someway, she would be at Elena's house at ten o'clock tonight.

Julie knew exactly how long it would take her to reach San Luis Obispo and planned accordingly. She joined Felicia, her father and Ramona for the evening meal. Rod, who hadn't eaten with them in many days, was occupied elsewhere. Following the meal she promptly excused herself and went to her room, presumedly to go to bed. Not long afterward she heard her father and Ramona leave. Shortly Felicia came in to say goodnight. If Felicia thought Julie's goodnight was rather strained, she said nothing. It seemed like forever until the house was quiet. Only then did Julie leave her room and stealthily let herself out through the courtyard door.

Julie thanked God the moon was high and the terrain clearly illuminated as she made her way quickly to the stables. Nearly all the horses were put to use during the roundup but Julie was gratified to see that Rod had thoughtfully left the horse that was normally hitched to the small carriage he had purchased for her when she could no longer comfortably sit a horse.

Moving awkwardly, Julie managed to ready the carriage and pull herself into the seat with great difficulty. Taking the reins in her hands and clicking her tongue softly, the carriage started forward slowly. At any other time Julie would not have left the premises without being discovered and probably stopped. But every available hand had been pressed into service for the roundup, leaving the *hacienda* deserted but for Carl Darcy whose own *casa* was some distance from the main house.

Thus it was that Julie moved undetected and unhampered through the countless Delgado acres without encountering any of the *vaqueros* who were camped in the surrounding hills.

It was nearly ten o'clock when Julie reached the outskirts of San Luis Obispo. Following Elena's explicit directions, she soon found the small *casa* that had been described to her. The streets were deserted even though there was considerable din coming from the several *cantinas* lining both sides of the narrow dirt street. At that moment Julie had never felt so alone in her life.

Elena's *casa* was at the end of a quiet street. Julie drove the carriage past the darkened house and into the tall brush a short distance away. Hauling her ungainly body out of the carriage, she tethered the horse to a bush and cautiously approached. The sound of her footfall was like thunder in her ears but in truth was barely discernable as she stepped lightly onto the veranda and made her way around the side just as Elena had instructed.

Keeping to the shadows, Julie stopped abruptly when she reached a pair of French doors thrown open to garner the soft night breezes. Her heart was hammering painfully in her chest, her legs shaking so badly she was certain she could move no further. She seriously considered returning to the *hacienda* without ever learning the truth, thinking that she really did not care to learn whether or not Rod had been bedding Elena. She had already seen the child, wasn't that proof enough? No, she decided stubbornly, she would never be satisfied until her own eyes beheld her unfaithful husband in Elena's bed. Elena had been the cause of too much heartache for Julie to accept her word as proof alone.

The scene inside the bedroom had been carefully set. A lamp burned brightly, leaving Julie no doubt as to the identity of the two people intimately entwined on the bed. Elena's passion-glazed features were clearly defined, her face turned toward the French doors. She and her lover had been engaged in intense foreplay for some time and needed only the appearance of Julie for final consummation.

Julie sidled from the shadows until the bed and its occupants came into her full line of view. So caught up was she in the scene unfolding before her that she was unaware of the strangled gasp that escaped her throat. But not so Elena who had been anxiously awaiting some sign of Julie's expected arrival. The moment it came in the form of a choked cry, Elena reacted instantly.

Julie could not turn her eyes from the smoldering scene erupting before her eyes like an act in an erotic play. Though she could not make out the man's face clearly, only the broad, muscled back and shoulders, Julie instinctively knew the man was her husband.

Elena's passion-drugged voice soon removed any doubt she might have had.

"Rodrigo *mi amor*, I burn for you. Take me now."

Julie could not understand Rod's low, hoarse reply but his actions spoke eloquently of his desire as he kissed Elena passionately. Their nude bodies were beautiful, as graceful as dancers caught in a pagan ceremony dedicated to the God of love.

Rod's lips and hands played a trail of fire along Elena's flushed body while she moaned loudly and called out his name over and over again. Before Julie's shocked eyes, Elena's breasts grew tumescent with her pleasure, the coral nipples taut pleasure points that thrust out like ripe cherries. Julie commanded herself to move but the message from her brain willed otherwise.

When the man's dark curly head—Rod's head—was lost between Elena's outstretched thighs, a black, suffocating pain pierced her heart. Then Elena's cries released her from limbo.

"Oh, *si*, Rodrigo, *mi amor, si*! Come to me now! Come to me!"

Raising himself above Elena's slight form, the man Julie assumed to be Rod, his face still carefully averted, plunged deeply into the warm, moist recess opening greedily beneath him.

Julie did not wait for the climax as abruptly she turned, moving as swiftly as her heavy body and protruding stomach would allow, her hasty retreat hindered by the storm of tears blinding her eyes. Her whole world had erupted beneath her, her entire life lay shattered at her feet, not to mention her broken heart. Nothing meant anything to her anymore. All she had left of her all-consuming love for Rod was his child resting beneath her heart.

As much as she hated to admit it, it was increasingly obvious that all Rod wanted from her was his heir. If memory served her, Rod began treating her like a true wife only after he learned she carried his child. She knew now he was only humoring her for his child's sake. Knowing what she did she could no longer remain at *Rancho* Delgado, Julie decided recklessly. She wanted to hurt Rod, to wound him as he had hurt her, twisting her heart in shreds. And then it struck her that the one way caluculated to hurt him most was to take his child from him. Pride riding her mercilessly, Julie decided to do exactly that.

The carriage moved slowly through the darkness, but with any luck Julie hoped her disappearance would not be discovered until late morning. By the time Rod was sent for and a search of the *rancho* conducted, she could hope for a day or two grace with which to make good her escape. But escape to where? she wondered, heedless of the harm her rash actions might cause.

Julie had no intention of involving her father in her difficulties. He had his Ramona and a life of his own. That left only Brett Casey to turn to. Did he still care for her enough to give her shelter? Or would he insist she return to her husband? No matter, Brett was her only refuge. Determined to return to the *hacienda* for nothing, Julie turned her carriage onto El Camino Real, her state of mind such that she gave no thought whatever to the dangers involved. She was penniless, without food and water, and likely to give birth at any time.

The sun was high in the sky when Julie gave her first thought of food. All through the long night as torturous images assailed her mind, Julie dozed fitfully while her horse, pulling the small carriage unfit for such hazardous travel, made its own way over the trail. From past experience she knew that any one of the string of missions along El Camino Real would be more than happy to offer her food and lodging. All she had to do was ask. Unfortunately, the good *padres* from most of the missions would remember her as the wife of Don Rodrigo Delgado.

Troubled by the dilemma facing her, Julie did not hear the wagons approaching from the rear until they were nearly upon her. Exhausted, her body cramped from sitting all night, Julie was never happier to see another human being in her life. Just knowing she was not alone on the trail was a vast relief.

There were six wagons in all. Prospectors, Julie supposed, taking the southern route to the gold fields. She pulled over when she reached a broad spot in the road and waited until they came abreast. The lead wagon stopped when Julie signaled she wished to speak with them.

A middleaged man, his features lined and weathered beyond his years, drove the rig, his thin, bird-like wife perched tall and straight beside him. Both were confused and startled to find a lone woman, well advanced in pregnancy, traveling a trail where banditry and murder were regular occurences.

"My God, girl, what are you doing out here by yourself?" greeted the man reprovingly. "My name is Micah Davis and this is my wife, Martha. Where is your husband? Is he crazy to let you wander on your own in your condition?"

"My husband is dead," Julie lied, quickly making up a story to satisfy the Davis couple. "I was left on my own in a small village when my husband died of snakebite. I must get to San Francisco. I have friends there who will take care of me."

"You won't get far in that buggy," hooted Micah derisively.

"It's all I have." Julie's woebegone expression and sad story touched a responsive chord somewhere in Martha's heart. She had left a daughter about Julie's age back in Illinois.

"What's your name, child?" Martha asked kindly.

"Juliet. My friends call me Julie." The Davises waited politely until Julie added, "Julie Darcy."

"Would you like to travel with us, Julie?" Martha asked hesitantly. "We are going right through San Francisco."

"Now, Martha," interrupted Micah sternly, "don't speak hastily. I don't rightly know if we should take on the added responsibility of a woman so far gone with child. We'd have to consult the others first to see how they feel about it."

"Micah," scolded Martha reproachfully, "it is our Christian duty to take in this poor child. I'm sure the others will agree. At least the women will."

"Perhaps, wife, but I still think—"

"Please," Julie interjected, "I don't wish to be the cause of dissension between you. Besides, I can travel much faster in my horse and buggy and I am quite familiar with the trail."

"Then what do you want from us?" asked Micah bluntly.

"I need supplies. Food, water, and . . . and a blanket or two. Enough to see me through to San Francisco. I have no money but this ring should more than compensate for what you give me." Julie slipped the heavy gold band that Rod had given her after they were married by *Padre* Juan from her finger and placed it almost regretfully in Micah's outstretched palm.

Shrewdly Micah weighted the object in his hand, glanced at his wife, then back at Julie. "Do we have enough supplies to share?" he asked.

Martha nodded with a sad tilt of her head. She hated the thought of leaving a young woman without protection on so dangerous a journey. She told Julie as much.

"I insist, Mrs. Davis," Julie smiled gratefully. "All I ask is that you sell me what I need. I'll be fine. My baby isn't due for weeks and I'll be safely in San Francisco with my friends long before then."

Reluctantly Martha was persuaded and soon Julie's

buggy was loaded with enough supplies to last several days. After sharing a meal with the Davises and their group, Julie thanked her newfound friends profusely and went on her way.

Thankfully, Julie was miles away when the wagon train was attacked by Three-Fingered Jack and his *guerrilleros*. Three-Fingered Jack was of a different sort than Joaquin Murieta and another romantic hero of the times called Pico. Whereas Murieta and Pico were much beloved by the people, Three-Fingered Jack was hated and feared. And with good reason. He attacked and pillaged indiscriminately, taking human life without thought or conscience.

When the bandits had stolen all the valuables from the hapless travelers on the wagon train and cruelly and methodically raped all the women regardless of age, they calmly killed everyone who had not already been slain in their initial attack. Then they set fire to the wagons. Had Julie chosen to join the group, her fate would have been the same.

Ignorant of the fate of her friends on the wagon train, Julie continued her journey northward. She camped the night curled up in a blanket in the buggy, her child violently protesting being cramped and abused by kicking unmercifully until Julie was forced to abandon the buggy and stretch out on the damp ground.

The following day Julie was nearing the town of Carmel when disaster struck. She lost a wheel on the buggy and received such a jolt that many long minutes passed before she could bestir herself to inspect the damage, which she discovered to her sorrow was beyond her realm of knowledge or ability. From her last trip with Rod a few months earlier, Julie knew that the Mission San Carlos Borromeo del Carmelo de Monterey lay just a short distance away. Thank God *Padre* Serra saw fit to place all twenty-one missions along El Camino Real within a day's journey of one another, she sighed wearily.

Unhitching the horse in order to lead him, Julie started forward. Before she had taken half a dozen steps the first pains struck and something she dreaded from the moment she left the *rancho* occurred. Julie was going into premature labor! Fear seized her. A fear so great she was overwhelmed by the thought of what might happen to her and her child alone in the wilderness. She could not lose Rod's child. Not now. Not ever, she vowed stubbornly. It was all she had left of him.

Breathing deeply, which seemed to ease the pain, Julie fought to conquer her terror. Spying a large rock nearby she led the horse to it and carefully positioned him so that she could mount him if she used the rock as a mounting block. Timing the contractions, Julie waited for the last one to subside, then began slowly pulling herself onto the horse's back. Once, twice, three times she failed, and tears of frustration and pain blurred her vision. But she refused to panic for she knew failure was tantamount to a death sentence for her baby.

On the fourth attempt she managed to drag her burdensome body atop her patient mount and head him in the direction of the mission and help. To Julie's befuddled and pain-wracked mind, it seemed like hours before she reached the gate. With the last of her dwindling strength, she managed to pull the bell cord before she passed out.

23

The morning after Julie crept undetected out into the night, Rod, tired, saddle-sore and dirty entered the *hacienda* in a jovial mood. The roundup was nearly completed and the branding could be accomplished without his supervision. The *vaqueros* were perfectly able to carry out that chore without him, which was just fine with Rod. He hadn't seen Julie to really talk to her in days, and guilt over his unintentional neglect was bothering him mercilessly.

Most women appeared ungainly and awkward during late pregnancy but not Julie, Rod thought fondly, picturing her dainty form swollen with child yet no less graceful and lovely in his eyes. He deeply regretted the fact that he had little spare time of late to pamper and cosset his wife as she so richly deserved, but he fully intended to make up for his lack of attention during the next weeks. Julie would have his undivided attention, Rod vowed, for he had already informed his *vaqueros* that he would not accompany the trail drive this time but would remain with his wife to see her through the birth of their child.

All was quiet when Rod entered the *hacienda*. He found Teresa in the kitchen and she informed him that Felicia was at her lessons and Julie had not made an appearance yet this morning.

"Is she ill?" Rod asked worriedly. It was not like Julie to lay abed.

"No, Don Rodrigo," Teresa assured him. "Dona Julie is not ill, although she seemed rather tired and distraught yesterday. That's why I let her sleep later than usual this morning."

"Then I'll not disturb her, Teresa. I need to clean up anyway before I'll be fit company. See that a bath is prepared for me."

Much later, after Rod had bathed, shaved and rested, he entered Julie's room through the connecting door intending to have lunch with her, but found her already gone. At first he thought it strange that he had heard no movement or any sign of activity from within his wife's room but soon forgot his anxiety as he went in search of Julie.

He found Felicia had returned from her lessons but no sign of Julie. At the sight of Rod, Felicia flew into his outstretched arms. "I have missed you greatly, Rodrigo," she said shyly. Some time ago Rod had asked her to call him by his first name.

"I have missed you also, *niña*, but now I am home to look after you and Julie. Where is she?" Rod asked, his dark eyes searching for and not finding his wife's rotund figure.

"She is still sleeping. *Tia* Teresa told me not to disturb her."

A tremor of premonition twisted Rod's guts and stone-like lumps blocking his throat made swallowing difficult. "She is not in her room, *niña*."

"You must be mistaken. She has to be in her room." Threads of panic were spun about Felicia's heart as she looked at Rod with stricken eyes.

Abruptly, Rod spun on his heel and raced to Julie's room, Felicia close behind. As he knew it would be, the room was deserted, the bed neatly made as if it had not been slept in. Slowly and methodically Rod and Felicia made a thorough search of the *hacienda*, with no success.

"Perhaps she is with her father?" suggested Felicia hopefully.

"Of course," Rod agreed with alacrity. "Why didn't I think of that?" Though his sense of relief was enormous he could not quell the prickle of fear snaking along his spine.

Julie was not with Carl and Ramona. Nor was she anywhere in the immediate vicinity of the *hacienda*. When his search took him to the stables, Rod was shocked to find the horse and buggy Julie sometimes used missing. Upon questioning the servants, he learned that no one had seen Julie after she had retired for the night the previous evening. Only Teresa was able to shed a single clue as to Julie's sudden disappearance.

"Dona Julie was upset yesterday, *señor*," she told Rod. "She was not herself at all."

"How so, Teresa. Please tell me everything you know."

"When I found her in the garden at lunch time yesterday, she seemed distraught and began asking strange questions."

A strangled look settled on Rod's handsome features. "What kind of questions?"

"About Dona Elena and . . . and . . . her child."

"*Por Dios*! Not Elena again! If she had a hand in this I will kill her. Go on, Teresa, what else did Julie say."

"Not much, *señor*. She wanted to know if Dona Elena was expecting a child when she left the *rancho*."

"What did you tell her?" Rod asked, comprehension dawning.

"The truth," shrugged Teresa uneasily. "Dona Elena was with child when she left here, what else could I say?"

"Did you explain that Manuel was the child's father?"

"She gave me no opportunity. Dona Julie told me she wished to hear nothing more of Dona Elena.

Did . . . did I do wrong, *señor*?''

Rod sighed heavily. "You are not to blame, Teresa. I fear my wife has been lied to again by Elena. After I speak with *Señor* Darcy, I will leave immediately for San Luis Obispo. If either Elena or Manuel has been here, I will find out one way or another."

Felicia began to sob softly and Rod went immediately to his little sister. "Don't cry, *niña*. I will find her. She can't have gotten too far, not in her condition."

"But why would she leave, Rodrigo? Didn't she love us?"

"I don't have the answers, Felicia, but I soon will. Julie would never leave us without provocation. You must remember, a woman with child is very vulnerable, oftentimes fanciful. I have been too busy of late to pay the kind of attention to her she deserves. I'm afraid Elena has once again plotted vengeance against me in a way guaranteed to hurt me the most."

Carl Darcy begged to accompany Rod but Rod insisted his father-in-law remain behind to protect the women and see to the running of the *rancho* in the event he should meet with difficulty and be unable to return immediately. Reluctantly, Carl agreed, but only after Rod promised to let him know the moment Julie was found or he had any idea of what happened to her. By the time Rod gave orders to the *vaqueros* concerning the branding and packed a saddlebag for any emergency, it was sundown before he rode out for the village. Julie already had several hours headstart.

Rod's first stop was the mission where he questioned *Padre* Juan and satisfied himself that Julie hadn't sought sanctuary with the good *padre*. *Padre* Juan told Rod exactly where to find the Roja's *casa* and he set off immediately to confront Elena. If Elena had been to see Julie . . . but no, he didn't even want to think about that.

The small *casa* Rod stood before was a far cry from

either the Delgado or the Montoya *hacienda*. He could hear a child crying from within. Rod hardened his heart against the pitiful sound and began pounding on the door. When no one answered after several minutes of knocking, Rod took matters into his own hands and flung the door open, surprised to find it unlatched. No one was in the main room and Rod resolutely followed the sound of a baby's frantic cries into the bedroom.

Rod was ready to do battle but was completely unprepared to find Manuel Rojas sitting numbly on the bed holding a wailing child in his arms. When Rod unexpectedly burst in, Manuel's features failed to register the least surprise.

"Where is she, Manuel?" Rod questioned angrily. "I'll find her no matter where she is hiding."

"She is gone, Don Rodrigo," Manuel replied, his shoulders drooping in defeat.

"Gone! Gone where?"

"Who knows."

"Are you telling me she left her child behind?" Rod would have believed anything of Elena but somehow the thought that she had gone away and left her child was repugnant to him.

"*Si, patron*," Manuel nodded sadly. "Elena promised we would leave here, all three of us. She said she would devote herself to me and our child. But I should have known Elena could not live the life I was able to provide."

"Surely you didn't squander all the money I gave to her?"

"Money? I don't understand, *señor*. I know nothing of money."

"When Elena left the *rancho* I gave her enough money to keep her in comfort for years to come."

"Ah, that explains much. I should never have agreed to help her. I never wanted to harm Dona Julie. But . . . Elena can be very persuasive."

"I know," flushed Rod, recalling vividly his own experiences with Elena. "You had better start from the beginning. If either of you laid a hand on my wife, your life is forefeit."

"We did not harm Dona Julie, not physically, that is. The plan was all Elena's but that does not absolve me from guilt in the matter."

Rod burned with impatience but steeled himself to listen until Manuel finished speaking. At the end his self control was nearly shattered when he learned the full extent of Elena's perfidity.

"How could you stand by and allow Elena to hurt my wife in such a vile manner?" he shouted, clenching his fists in barely suppressed rage. "My wife is eight months pregnant! How despicable of you to use your own child to bring her harm! She left me thinking I neither loved nor wanted her. Only God knows where she has gone and what condition she is in. Are you certain she came here last night as Elena arranged?"

"*Si*. Elena saw Dona Julie at the French doors looking in. We did not proceed with Elena's plan until we knew for certain she was watching."

Rod fought the urge to kill Manuel outright. Only the child in Manuel's arms prevented him. Did he have the right to make an orphan of an innocent child? "I ought to kill you, Rojas. Thank your son that you still live."

"I did wrong, Don Rodrigo. It is no more than right that you should punish me. Especially for my part in arranging with Pedro to take Dona Julie, knowing what might happen to her."

"I suspected Elena engineered Julie's abduction from what Julie told me, but I had no idea how it was done," Rod said grimly.

"Pedro is my cousin," Manuel confided. "Elena promised him gold if he would get rid of Dona Julie for her. Murieta was gone, leaving Pedro free to accept Elena's offer. Elena wanted Dona Julie out of the way permanently.

"*Dios*! exploded Rod. "I should have killed Elena instead of turning her out of the *rancho*. Had she not been expecting a child—" His words drifted off.

"I wish to make amends for my mistake, *señor*. Let me help you find her."

"What makes you think I would believe you, Rojas?" Rod blasted wrathfully. Learning the truth concerning Julie's abduction from one of the perpetrators only served to further enrage him.

"I swear on the head of my son," Manuel vowed solemnly.

Rod exhibited surprise at Manuel's obvious love for his son. "I may be *loco* but I believe you, Manuel, and will accept your help. My own *vaqueros* are ready to take to the trail. But don't expect me to forget and forgive so easily. What will you do with your son in our absence?"

"Elena left without a thought to his welfare," Manuel spat scornfully. "When I awoke this morning, my wife was gone and my son crying from hunger."

"The child must have a wet nurse," Rod said. "Take him to *Padre* Juan. He will find someone to care for him until he is old enough to be weaned."

"*Si*," agreed Manuel gratefully. "I will take him immediately. Then we will find Dona Julie."

Rod wished it was that simple. While Manuel was gone he considered his options. Where would a pregnant woman who had just suffered an emotional shock go? If only Julie had come to me, Rod thought in retrospect, all her doubts and fears could have been laid to rest.

Carefully, Rod pieced together all the facts and came to the conclusion that Julie would have only one place to go . . . to her friends in San Francisco. Brett and Polly would offer shelter should either think Rod mistreated his wife. As far as he knew, Julie took nothing with her, neither money nor food. Distraught as she was, she probably gave little thought to the danger she faced. If he left immediately he could probably overtake her before she got too far. He could travel much faster on horseback than Julie could in a horse and buggy. By the time Manuel rejoined him and they rode back to the *rancho* to inform Carl of all that had happened, night had descended. As much as he ached to be on his way, Rod decided it best to wait until first light to leave. By that time Julie had a day and a half head-start.

The farther north Rod rode without finding any trace of Julie, the greater his fear became. When he unexpectedly came upon the remains of the still smoldering wagon train, icy panic twisted his gut into knots. It was obviously the work of bandits, Rod surmised, as he surveyed the dead bodies scattered about the wreckage. Just thinking that Julie might have met the same fate shattered him. Many of the bodies lying amidst the smoking ruins were charred beyond recognition, and with sinking heart Rod realized he could not leave the scene of such brutal carnage without burying the dead.

Immediately he and Manuel began their grisly task. The most difficult chore facing them was finding a spot level enough to dig a common grave. Once the site was selected, Rod found a shovel in the rubble and began digging, leaving it to Manuel to gather up the mutilated bodies. Hours later it was done but the two men were too exhausted to ride on so they built a fire and camped beside the road for the night.

After their meager meal had been consumed, Rod curled up in a blanket and prepared to bed down next to the fire. Rod was never certain what made him glance over at Manuel. The Mexican was bending over the fire intently examining several objects in his open palm.

"What have you there, Manuel?" quizzed Rod curiously.

Manuel stuttered guiltily. "I . . . I thought it a sin to

bury the dead with their valuables, Don Rodrigo. There is enough gold in these rings to provide a good living for me and my son. Are you angry, *señor*?''

Rod was prepared to berate Manuel roundly for robbing the dead but thought better of it. The bandits had stolen nearly everything of value and if they had missed a few baubles there seemed no reason why Manuel shouldn't have them for his trouble. "No, Manuel, I am not angry. Keep your treasure."

Manuel smiled broadly, his large square teeth showing white in the firelight. "Look, *señor*," he gestured, holding up one ring in particular for Rod to admire. "I don't know how the bandits missed this one. It is delicately wrought and very heavy. There are even initials inside."

Rod choked back a gasp of terror as sheer black fright swept through him. With shaking fingers he picked up the gold band and recognized immediately the initials he had ordered inscribed months ago when he bought the gold band for Julie in San Francisco.

"*Madre de Dios*!" cried out Rod as if in pain. "Where did you get this?" He became so pale that Manuel feared he was ill.

"It's strange, *señor*," Manuel revealed, scratching his thatch of thick hair, "but when I picked up one of the women, this ring fell from her mouth. I think she hid it there when the *banditos* attacked."

"This ring belongs to my wife! I gave it to her myself. Was . . . was the woman who had the ring with child?" Rod had no idea he was holding his breath until Manuel answered his question, and then it came out in a painful whoosh. "No, *señor*," Manuel quickly assured him. "There were no pregnant women among the dead. Or children under the age of five."

Great shudders shook Rod's powerful form. "Thank God! But . . . but how did the dead woman come by Julie's wedding band?" Rod puzzled, "unless . . ." His next thought was even more terrifying than finding her among the dead. "*Por Dios*! Do you think the *banditos* took her with them?"

"It is unlikely, *patron*. What use would they have for a heavily pregnant woman? She would only prove a hindrance. It is more likely that she would have met the same fate as those poor wretches on the wagon train, had she been with them."

It sounded logical, Rod deduced with a sigh of relief. And if by chance they did take Julie, how is it that the ring was in the posesion of a dead woman? The answer came quickly. She had evidently traded it for supplies! He voiced his deduction aloud.

"*Si*," agreed Manuel with alacrity. "I am certain we will find the *señora* somewhere ahead."

Rod was not so easily convinced but he held his fears tightly in check. He placed the ring in his pocket with the intention of slipping it on Julie's finger the moment he found her. Fate willed it to be longer than Rod would have liked.

The next day they came upon Julie's abandoned buggy and once more a cold knot formed in Rod's gut. Upon examination he saw that a wheel was missing from the vehicle and so was the horse, leading him to believe that determined to reach San Francisco, Julie had somehow mounted the horse and continued her journey on horseback. Convinced he was right, Rod sent Manuel back to the *rancho* to inform Carl. Resolutely he pressed on, never dreaming that at that very moment Julie lay but a few miles away giving birth.

The city lay directly before him and Rod felt certain he was but a few hours behind Julie's entrance into San Francisco. By now she was probably being pampered by Brett and Polly and put to bed to recuperate from her arduous trip, Rod tried to assure himself. If the truth be known, Rod was never so glad to see San Francisco as he was at that moment. Not only for the obvious reason but because something strange was happening to him that he did not like.

Since he had sent Manuel back to the *rancho* he was experiencing bouts of chills and lightheadedness and he was certain he had a fever. It took tremendous effort on his part to remain upright in the saddle and even more of a chore to hang on to consciousness. He could not become ill now, Rod thought groggily. Not when he was so near to finding Julie. There was so much he wanted to say to her, so much to make up for. But what fate wills, man fulfills.

Rod dismounted in front of Casey's Pleasure Palace, staggering slightly before righting himself and lurching through the swinging doors. The casino was already filled and the din that assaulted Rod's ears nearly bowled him over. Narrowing his overbright eyes against the glare, he searched frantically for a familiar face. Polly spotted him almost immediately, her face registering shock and dismay.

"Rod! My God!" she cried out, rushing to Rod's side. "What happened to you? You look terrible!"

Hollow-eyed, disheveled, a blue stubble shadowing his jaw, Rod felt every bit as bad as Polly indicated. Not only was he exhausted beyond belief but he felt strangely vague and disoriented. He opened his mouth to speak but nothing came out.

"What is it, Rod?" Polly asked, frightened as well as concerned by Rod's unexpected appearance. "Where is Julie? Oh my God! Has something happened to Julie?" she cried frantically, assuming the worst. "Is that it?"

Once again Rod's mouth flopped wide but this time his eyes rolled upward until only the whites showed and his huge body spiraled downward as the floor came up to meet him.

Polly's scream brought Brett Casey on the run and his shock at finding Rod decorating his floor was no less greater than Polly's. "Jesus!" exploded Brett. "What's he doing here? What's wrong with him?''

"He's burning with fever, Brett," Polly replied as she bent over Rod's prone form and put a slim hand to his forehead. "Hurry! Get him up to bed while I send someone for a doctor."

"Did he say anything?" Brett asked hopefully. "Did he give you any reason at all for being in town? Did . . . did he mention Julie?"

Polly's features softened. She was well aware of Brett's love for Julie and had hoped that during these past months his feelings might have changed. She had done all in her power to make him forget Julie and in the process had fallen deeply in love with him herself. There were times when she felt her feelings were reciprocated but until he spoke of them to her, she must assume it was still Julie who held his affections.

"He said nothing, Brett," answered Polly gently. Then she hurried away to summon help.

Rod's fever was not unlike the illness that was so prevalent in this part of the country, the doctor informed an anxious Polly and Brett. There was nothing to do but keep him comfortable, sedate him with laudenum and let the fever run its natural course. For a week Rod alternately burned with fever and shook with chills. During the whole time nothing he said made sense. Though he often called out Julie's name, his words were disjointed and incoherent, further frustrating Brett and Polly's effort to discover Rod's reason for being in San Francisco at a time when his wife was due to deliver his child.

The day Rod's fever broke marked a milestone in his rapid recovery. He was young, strong and possessed of an iron constitution. From the moment he opened his eyes into full awareness and learned from a distraught Polly that Julie had not reached San Francisco, he was like a man possessed. Brett had to physically restrain him to keep him from dashing off then and there.

Brett had been devastated when he learned what had happened. He wanted to blame Rod, yet could not hold him responsible for the vile act of a jealous woman bent on vengeance.

"Was there somewhere else she could have gone?" Brett asked hopefully. "A woman so far gone with child doesn't just up and leave on a long journey by herself without a destination in mind."

"You don't know Julie if you think that," replied Rod ruefully. "Manuel told me Elena convinced her I neither loved her nor wanted her. The little act Elena and Manuel put on for her benefit was the final humiliation that sent her running from the *rancho* without a thought to her own safety."

"Rod," Polly said suddenly, "I have an idea that might bear looking into."

Both men turned their rapt attention to the beautiful brunette with green eyes and pixie-like features whose face began to glow with excitement.

"*Por Dios*, Polly!" Rod exclaimed, "if you know anything, anything at all that might help, tell me, *por favor*."

"Well," Polly began eagerly. "If I were a woman about to give birth, and I needed help, I would go to one of the missions and seek refuge."

Both men looked at each other, astounded by the simple logic of Polly's words.

"Of course!" rejoiced Rod. "Why didn't I think of that? My one consuming thought was that Julie would want to be with her friends. It never occurred to me that she might seek help at one of the missions."

"Sometimes the simplest explanations often escape us," Brett said wryly. "Do you feel able to travel? If so, I will go with you."

"Able and ready," nodded Rod impatiently. "There are three missions in the vicinity where Julie left the carriage. San Miguel, La Soledad and San Carlos

Borromeo del Carmelo de Monterey.''

"That's a start," replied Brett.

"You're not going without me," asserted Polly
forcefully. "When you do find Julie, she might need
another woman."

Brett smiled fondly at Polly. In a short time the
exuberant, affectionate woman had come to mean a
great deal to him. Though Julie would always occupy a
special place in his heart, he was wise enough to realize
her future lay with her husband, as did her love. In the
past weeks he had viewed Polly through new eyes and
liked what he saw. It was time he settled down and took
a wife. He could do a hell of a lot worse than little
bright-eyed Polly whose faithfulness he would have no
cause to doubt in the years to come.

"I see no reason to leave you behind, sweetheart,"
Brett smiled. "If Rodrigo has no objections, then
neither do I."

"As long as you can keep up, Polly, you are welcome
to join us," Rod agreed curtly, his thoughts already on
his happy reunion with Julie. He soon would have her
home to await the brith of their child, he thought with
joyful anticipation.

The next morning the trio left the raw, sprawling city
behind to begin their search of the missions for Julie.
Exactly ten days had elapsed from the time Rod
collapsed in Brett Casey's Pleasure Palace until they set
out, their hopes high.

24

Slowly Julie surfaced into consciousness, surprised to find herself lying on a cot in one of the cell-like rooms in the mission now known as Carmel, being cared for by a competent Indian woman. The soft Spanish words and soothing hands brought immediate relief to Julie's tortured mind and body. Thank God she had reached help in time and her child was safe. That's all that mattered, she thought, as another pain ripped through her abdomen forcing a moan from her lips that could not be repressed.

Though the baby was a few weeks early it was not excessively so, and Julie was confident it would live. Many times during the long, pain-filled hours, Rod's name slipped from her lips as she labored to bring forth their child.

Padre Enrico knew immediately the identity of the lovely lady who had shown up so mysteriously at the mission gate. He recognized her as the wife of Don Rodrigo Delgado from their overnight sojourn several months ago. But the good *padre* couldn't even hazard a guess as to what brought her to the mission, alone and about to give birth. Because Julie was in no condition for lengthy explanations, the *padre* did what he thought best. He sent one of his flock on a swift horse to *Rancho* Delgado to summon Don Rodrigo to his wife's side.

Julie's son was born at exactly midnight. Though the birth was not difficult and the baby small, her labor was long and painful, leaving her weak and exhausted. The moment her squalling son was placed in her arms she was relieved to see that he appeared healthy, his lusty cries falling like music to her ears. Satisfied that all was well, Julie finally allowed herself the reward of a well earned sleep.

From that moment on, Julie's recovery was rapid. Within three days she was able to get out of bed and take her meals with the *padre*. It was the first time he had seen her alone since she gave birth.

"What have you named your son, *señora*?" he asked pleasantly.

Julie had been giving a name for her baby much thought. "I'd like to name him Carl after my father," she replied, smiling, when she considered her father's reaction to his namesake.

"Carlos is a fine name," beamed *Padre* Enrico, "but shouldn't you name him after your husband?"

Julie flushed. So far the *padre* had asked no questions of her concerning her unorthodox appearance at the mission and she wished to keep it that way.

"I had thought to name him Carl Rodrigo," she added hastily.

The *padre* shrugged, then said, "Your husband should be here shortly. I sent for him when you arrived so unexpectedly. He will be happy to learn of his son's birth."

Julie went pale, her face drained of all color. "You . . . you've sent for my husband?" she stammered helplessly.

"*Si, mi hija.* I have asked nothing of the circumstances that brought you here, nor shall I. What happened is between you and your husband. If either of you wish my counsel, you have only to ask. In the meantime you and your son are safe here with me until your husband arrives."

Later, alone in her small cubical nursing little Carl,

Julie's emotions warred with one another. In the days since she had left the *hacienda* she had been given sufficient opportunity to think about what Elena had told her and reflect on everything she had seen with her own eyes. In the end, she came to regret the haste in which she had left the *rancho* without allowing Rod the opportunity to explain. Like a willful child she had fled without a thought for her own safety or that of her child. Rod's child. She could have at least consulted her father instead of impulsively running away and placing herself in all kinds of danger. Would Rod ever forgive her, she wondered bleakly? She would soon find out.

There was absolutely no doubt in Julie's mind that Rod wanted his child despite the fact that he already had a son by Elena. During her long hours spent pondering her dilemma, Julie was certain of one thing: she would never willingly give up her son to Rod or to anyone else. He was the most important thing in her life. She could not bear to be separated from him. She knew that Rod had the right to take Carl away from her should she choose to leave him, and that she couldn't live with. She would not have her son raised by Elena who was sure to take Julie's place in Rod's life the moment she left.

And what of her own feelings, Julie reflected painfully? She loved Rod. She would always love him. Could she be satisfied with the crumbs of his affection while Elena feasted in the limelight of his love? There was also Felicia to consider. Elena would make Felicia's life a living hell. The woman's jealousy knew no bounds, respected no age limits, Julie told herself bitterly. After days of wrestling with her emotions, Julie came to the painful conclusion that for the sake of her son and Felicia she would return to *Rancho* Delgado and resume her role as Rod's wife, living on the edge of his affections to the best of her ability. But she'd be damned if she'd allow Elena to defeat her. As long as she remained Rod's wife, Julie pledged with grim determination, she would fight to make him love her.

Julie was shocked when her father arrived accompanied by a *vaquero*, her mind registering the fact that Rod did not care enough about her and their son to come himself. Sobbing happily, she rushed into Carl Darcy's open arms.

"Julie, Julie," Carl scolded gently, "whatever made you leave like that? Rodrigo was sick with worry when he found you missing."

"If Rod was so worried," choked Julie angrily, "he would have come himself."

"Rodrigo has been out searching for you since he discovered you were missing. The last I heard he was in San Francisco." Julie was deeply hurt by the note of censure in Carl's voice. How could he condone what Rod did to her while condemning her for retaliating in the only way open to her? Perhaps he did not know about Elena. If not, it was time someone told him, Julie decided perversely.

"Papa, you haven't seen your namesake yet," Julie said proudly. "Come to my room and I'll try to explain everything to you."

Carl was duly impressed with his first grandson. He thought the child looked much like Rod with his dark coloring and crisp black hair and he told Julie as much.

"I'm sure Rod will be pleased with Carlos," she said tersely, using the Spanish form of the name. Somehow it seemed natural. "But were you aware that Elena has also given Rod a son? That they are lovers?" She waited for shock to register on her father's face and when none came she was puzzled. "Papa, did you hear me? Elena is Rod's mistress!"

Carl sighed heavily. It should be up to Rod to clear up this matter with his wife, he thought wearily, but he knew he could not let Julie live under the misconception that her husband had been unfaithful when it was within Carl's power to tell her the truth.

"Daughter, did you know Manuel, the *vaquero* who often worked with the horses on the *rancho*?"

"Yes, Papa, but what does Manuel have to do with this?"

"Everything. Manuel fathered Elena's child while he still worked on the *rancho*."

"Oh, no, Papa, I'm sure you are wrong! Elena would never . . . not with a *vaquero*. She is too proud. Did . . . did Rod tell you this?"

"No, Julie. Manuel told me. He and Elena were married by *Padre* Juan shortly before his son was born. She coerced him into helping her perpetrate the foul deception you witnessed."

"What . . . what kind of deception?" Julie asked, already certain of the answer.

Carl proceeded to tell Julie all that Manuel had revealed when he returned to the *rancho*, including the information that Elena had left him and their child.

"It's difficult to believe she would do such a thing," Julie said, shaking her head sadly. "Are . . . are you certain he didn't make it all up?"

"For what purpose? No, Julie, it is the truth. I even brought Manuel with me for the express purpose of telling you himself, should you refuse to believe me."

When Julie heard Manuel's words she was surprised that Rod had allowed him to live, let alone return to the *rancho*, until she remembered Elena's child would be both motherless and fatherless without Manuel. Even though Rod now knew why she had left so suddenly, Julie couldn't help but wonder what his feelings would be when she finally faced him. Would he be angry with her, blame her for putting his child in danger? Knowing well his temper, she almost feared his reaction.

Carl wished to start back to the *rancho* the moment Julie felt strong enough to travel. For Julie it couldn't be soon enough. Though she was still weak and tired easily, she was anxious to face Rod and learn what his feelings were for her. But mostly, she wanted to present his son to him.

Carl and Manuel had driven a wagon from the *rancho* in order that Julie and the baby might ride in relative comfort on their trip homeward. The moment Julie insisted she was recovered sufficiently to travel, Carl agreed they should leave immediately. So as not to tire the new mother, Carl decided to break their trip into easy stages, staying each night at one of the missions. Their first stop, according to Carl's planning, would be La Soledad Mission, an easy few hours' journey.

When Julie, cradling Carlos in her arms, Manuel and Carl left the next morning, it couldn't have been a more perfect day. Though the sun had not yet risen, glorious streaks of mauve and scarlet colored the eastern sky. There was no wind, nothing to give the slightest hint of the disaster that nature was about to unleash upon them.

The small party of travelers were made welcome by the wizened *padre* at La Soledad who fed them the best he had to offer and provided each with a bed. After feeding Carlos, Julie removed her dress and lay down on the narrow cot thinking she was one day closer to Rod and *Rancho* Delgado, the only real home she had known in years.

The first tremors caused little concern to the occupants of La Soledad. Earthquakes were common along the St. Andreas fault and at most were minor irritations. Seldom did a tremor of major proportions cause an upheaval in their placid lives at the mission.

But when the rumbling did not cease, in fact grew louder and more ominous, it became apparent that this was not a minor earthquake that could be so easily ignored. Carl awoke to find his cot sliding across the stone floor. He knew immediately what was happening for he had experienced many earthquakes when he rode with Murieta. Fortunately, none of them proved serious. But one thing he did learn. It was unsafe to emain inside the brick and adobe building for they could be hopelessly buried beneath the walls that gave hem shelter.

Carl's main concern was for Julie and his grandson. He ran into the dark hallway just as Manuel, the same dea crossing his mind, careened around the corner. Together they burst into Julie's room. Dazed and confused, Julie barely heeded her father's words as he urged her up and out of bed.

"Hurry, Julie, we must get out of here! There is great danger."

"What . . . what is it, Papa?"

"An earthquake. Hurry! We could be buried alive at any moment."

"Oh, God! Carlos! My baby!"

"Manuel has him. Come," he said, dragging her by he hand. "Follow me."

Julie held back to look for her dress but Carl rudely pulled her forward, grabbing a blanket from the cot in passing. "Leave your clothes. We've no time." Barefoot, clothed in nothing but her thin shift, Julie and Carl ran headlong through the deserted mission only steps behind Manuel carrying baby Carlos who was loudly protesting his rude awakening.

Only when they reached a gully that lay beyond the mission walls did they stop. The ground beneath their feet heaved and rolled until Julie felt herself reeling. All around them fissures opened up swallowing whole portions of landscape, shrubs, trees, and before Julie's startled eyes a whole hillside seemed to disappear. It was the closest to hell she had ever been.

Throwing the blanket around Julie's shaking shoulders, Carl settled her in the gully and quickly sized up the situation. If they were lucky enough to survive the earthquake, Julie would need transportation. She had been forced to flee shoeless and barely clothed into the night and was not yet fully recovered from childbirth. Her survival, and that of his grandson, lay squarely on his shoulders, but Carl calmly accepted his responsibility and acted immediately.

It became increasingly evident to Carl that he and Manuel must return to the mission for the horse and wagon they had brought from the *rancho*. The stables were only a short distance from the mission itself and it should take them no time at all to harness the horses and lead the wagon to safety beyond the crumbling walls. Perhaps the worst was over.

Julie begged her father not to leave her when he explained what he must do. "Don't go back there, Papa. I'm afraid. I don't need the wagon, truly."

"I'll be fine, darling," Carl assured her. "Ten minutes and I'll be back here with you." He took the baby from Manuel's arms and gave him to Julie, saying, "You've made me very proud, daughter. Carlos is a fine boy." Then he placed a tender kiss on both their foreheads and retraced his steps back toward the mission.

As they entered the gates, the insistent rumbling took on a different tone and Carl hurried their steps, realizing that the worst was yet to come. They reached the stables without mishap and between them managed to quiet the frightened horses and harness them to the wagon in order to lead them out of the stables. Just as they drew abreast of the doors of the church, they heard the *padre* calling out weakly to them. Halting, Carl peered inside and saw the frail priest attempting to lift an injured Indian woman to carry her out into the open. Without a thought for his own safety, Carl motioned Manuel to remain with the horses while he bounded off to help the *padre* rescue one of his flock.

Carl succeeded in getting both the *padre* and the injured woman out of the church and into the wagon, but suddenly the whole world seemed to explode beneath his feet as a shock wave rose up out of the bowels of the earth. Before his eyes the already weakened walls of the church crumbled down around him. They might still have escaped injury if they had been able to control the horses and lead the wagon away from danger. But it all happened so swiftly that no one had a chance to react to the danger.

The walls began to crumble as the small group watched in horrified fascination, mesmerized by the impending doom as the huge belltower atop the church began its inexorable descent downward. The hapless victims were trapped by their leaden feet as tons upon tons of adobe and brick descended upon them. Only Carl had the presence of mind to turn at the last minute and run. His quick action saved his life.

Terror-stricken, Julie watched helplessly as the walls of the mission crumbled to the ground as if they were made of sand. "Papa! Papa!" she cried out mindlessly, clutching Carlos to her breast until his startled cries brought her back to sanity.

Anxiously she watched for her father's trim figure to appear but the longer she waited, the more evident it became that he wasn't coming. The last tremor that destroyed the mission proved to be the final indignity in a series of shock waves, making Julie suddenly aware of the ominous silence surrounding her. Not even the sounds of small animals or birds could be heard in the gloom.

Cautiously, Julie left the relative safety of the gully her father had placed her in and gazed with shocked eyes at the changes wrought by the forces of nature. In some places wide gaps appeared as yawning gashes in the earth. The devastation to the mission itself was beyond repair for nothing remained of the sturdy adobe and brick walls.

Driven by the desire to learn her father's fate, Julie gingerly picked her way over the rough terrain and approached the pile of rubble, her heart beating raggedly in her breast. God, don't let anything happen to my father, she cried in silent supplication. She needed him! Ramona needed him! The few short months with his new wife were hardly enough to make up for all his years of loneliness. It wasn't fair!

By the time Julie reached the church her feet were cut and bleeding, somewhere she had lost the blanket her father had tenderly draped about her shoulders and she knew a moment of despair. She spied the remains of the wagon first, and then saw the dead horses still harnessed to the rig. She came upon Manuel's inert body half-buried in the debris. She was hysterical with grief and fear. Only baby Carlos, held tightly to her breasts, prevented her from losing her tenuous hold on sanity when further investigation revealed her father's still form lying a short distance from the mass of rubble.

Carefully placing the baby out of harm's way, Julie began clawing at the pieces of adobe and brick in an effort to drag her father to safety. Pulling him away from the debris she knelt by his side and was relieved to see the steady rise and fall of his chest. There was a nasty gash on his head and his left arm was bent at an unnatural angle, but at least he was alive. The sound of Carl's moaning was like music to her ears.

"Papa! Speak to me!" Julie begged. "How badly are you hurt?"

Slowly Carl opened his eyes, his right hand going to his head as he groaned, "My head, it hurts."

"Don't move, Papa," Julie advised. "I think your left arm is broken. I don't know what to do."

"What about Manuel and the others?"

"Manuel is dead. I . . . I see no others." What Julie couldn't know was that the *padre* and an unidentified Indian woman lay beneath tons of debris.

"Leave me, Julie, go for help," Carl gritted out from between clenched teeth. "Take the baby and go on to the next mission. I'll be fine until help arrives."

"I can't leave you, Papa," Julie shook her head stubbornly.

"You have to, honey, think of the baby. I'm in no immediate danger."

Though reluctant to leave him alone and unprotected, Julie saw the wisdom of her father's words. His life depended on her. So did her child's. Locating the blanket she had dropped earlier, she tenderly covered him, then kissed his forehead.

"I'll be back, Papa," she promised fervently. "I'll bring help back."

"Be careful, Julie," Carl called after her. "God go with you."

Determined to bring her son safely to his father as well as seek help for her own parent, Julie gathered up the baby and hobbled off, unconcerned about the pitiful condition of her bare feet which were bruised and bleeding from walking over the sharp rocks strewn about the ground in the aftermath of the earthquake.

Though the going was slow and painful, Julie walked steadily, unaware of the drops of blood staining the ground behind her. She stopped only long enough to nurse Carlos, thankful that her milk supply was still plentiful enough to safistfy her son's voracious appetite. For herself, there was nothing but water taken from a muddy stream where she paused to cool and soothe her aching feet.

When night approached Julie began searching for shelter, wise enough to realize the necessity of putting herself and her child out of reach of wild animals. If her luck held, she should reach the next mission sometime tomorrow.

Just as dusk crept away on silent feet of darkness, and Julie began to despair of finding a safe haven in which to pass the night, she spied a narrow cleft between two rocks that appeared just large enough to squeeze through. Her hasty investigation proved it to be a narrow cave with no signs of its former occupants. Heaving a sigh of relief she slid easily into the crevice, thinking it would provide a measure of warmth as well as protection from wild animals. Shifting her ill-clad body into a comfortable position in the small space, it took no time at all for Julie to realize how cold she really was as shivers shook her small form. She spared a moment thinking about the blanket she had left with her father, but knew he needed it more than she did. Sighing regretfully, she curled into a ball and prepared to feed her son who by now was wailing for his supper, his tiny face screwed up until he resembled an old, toothless man.

After nursing Carlos, Julie carefully examined her feet. With a twinge she realized she would not be able to walk on them for several days, perhaps never if they became infected. But for the sake of her father and son she would crawl on hands and knees for help, Julie vowed, tears of frustration and pain marking grooves down her grimy cheeks. Cold, exhausted, so hungry her stomach rebelled violently, Julie fell into a fitful sleep. Her dreams were terrifying. In them Rod's stern visage appeared before her, angry, accusing, unforgiving. Sometime during the long night her sleep became deeper, her weakness and exhaustion taking her beyond the bounds of sleep, past reality where pain did not exist. Julie slipped easily into unconsciousness.

25

Dusk had just given way to darkness when Rod, Brett and Polly reached Carmel where they were greeted effusively by *Padre* Enrico who immediately launched into a long dissertation depicting Julie's mysterious arrival and the subsequent birth of her son.

Rod's expressive face broke out into a grin as he listened to *Padre* Enrico's words. He had found Julie and she was safe! He rejoiced at the welcome news that Julie had borne a healthy son and both survived the ordeal. "Where is she, *Padre*?" he asked anxiously when his eyes failed to find his wife's diminutive form. "I can't wait to see her. There is much I need to explain to her."

Padre Enrico looked stricken and Rod's mind reeled, his heart thumping dangerously against his ribcage. Had something happened to Julie and the baby? "*Por Dios, Padre*! What is it? You told me yourself my wife and son are well."

"Easy, *amigo*," cautioned Brett, sensing his friend's distress. If the truth be known, his own distress was nearly as great.

"I . . . I wished only to do the right thing, Don Rodrigo," *Padre* Enrico explained guardedly. "The moment your wife appeared at the mission gate unconscious and about to give birth, I sent a messenger immediately to your *hacienda*. Several days later Don Carlos and a *vaquero* named Manuel came for the *señora*."

"Julie's father!" Rod's relief was instantaneous as great gulps of air eased his lungs. "Julie went with Carlos and Manuel? Are you certain, *Padre*?"

"*Si*, Don Rodrigo. Dona Julie seemed anxious to return home and they left only this morning. You missed them by hours."

"Did you hear that Brett, Polly?" exalted Rod. Suddenly he became serious as he asked, "*Padre*, was my wife well enough to ride so soon after childbirth? Will the trip harm her?"

"Don Carlos came well prepared," *Padre* Enrico was quick to assure Rod. "He brought a wagon so that your wife and son might ride in comfort. The trip will be taken in easy stages with their first stop at La Soledad where they will pass the night."

Rod was visibly relieved and ready to start out immediately for La Soledad but Polly suggested they all have a meal and spend the night. Julie was safe with her father, she counseled, and no doubt in need of a good night's rest after her first day's journey.

"We could easily catch up with them tomorrow," Brett agreed in an effort to convince a reluctant Rod. Against his will, Rod allowed himself to be persuaded to pass the night at Carmel after extracting *Padre* Enrico's promise to awaken them at first light. Little did Rod know that he would be up long before dawn.

The first inkling of trouble intruded into Rod's subconscious when the floor beneath him began to shift and he awoke abruptly to ominous sounds like thunder. Instantly Rod recognized the beginnings of an earthquake and grabbing up his clothes and boots, raced to warn his traveling companions. He found Brett already leading a half-dressed Polly from her room. They were soon joined by *Padre* Enrico and they all managed to reach safety just as the tremendous shock that reduced La Soledad, situated further south, to rubble shook the more solid San Carlos Borremeo de Carmelo to its very foundations.

Larger and much sturdier structurally than La Soledad, Carmel survived the earthquake nearly intact, except for several large cracks in the adobe foundation and some minor damage to the chapel walls which could easily be repaired. After helping *Padre* Enrico inspect for structural damage and see to the safety of his flock, Rod, Brett and Polly left for La Soledad much later than anticipated. Rod was greatly heartened by the splendid way in which Carmel withstood the earthquake, and though his grave concern over the safety of Julie and his son sleeping within the walls of La Soledad lurked at the back of his mind, he had every confidence in Carl's ability to look after his loved ones.

The miles between Carmel and La Soledad sped by much swifter on horseback than by the slower conveyence Julie rode in the previous day. Rod knew a moment of panic when he turned into the narrow road leading to the mission and viewed the destruction of landscape, immediately sensing that La Soledad did not survive the earthquake as well as Carmel. All around him were signs of the devastation. Great rents torn in the earth made travel difficult and Rod experienced fear greater than he had ever known before when they suddenly came upon the rubble that was once La Soledad Mission.

"My God!" cried Brett irreverently as he peered around him, his eyes wide in awe and shock. Never had he viewed such devastation!

"*Madre de Dios, Madre de Dios*!" repeated Rod in a litany of despair.

Polly was the first to discover Carl's blanket-shrouded body lying on the ground. Though unconscious he was still alive, and a sip of water from Rod's canteen revived him sufficiently to speak.

"Carl, what happened to Julie and the baby?" Rod asked anxiously. "Did she get out safely?"

"She's . . . fine, Rod," Carl assured him, attempting a weak smile. "She went for help." Then coherent speech seemed beyond him as he lapsed again into unconsciousness.

"How is he?" asked Brett. "Is he injured seriously?"

"He has a nasty head wound," Rod said after a swift appraisal. Then he lifted the blanket to begin a more thorough examination. When he touched Carl's left arm, an involuntary moan slipped through his lips. "Looks like his arm is broken, too. There might also be some internal injuries. I don't think it wise to move him until we find another wagon. He'll never be able to sit on a horse in his condition."

"I'll stay with him," Brett volunteered. "You go after Julie and your son. She might even have reached safety by now."

"I'll help bury Manuel and then I'll leave," Rod said as he bent to make certain Manuel was dead. "If there are others beneath that pile of rubble, they'll have to wait until help arrives."

"Wouldn't it make better sense to leave in the morning?" Polly suggested practically. "If Julie is on the trail somewhere, you might miss her in the darkness."

Grudgingly, Rod consented to wait until dawn to leave and they curled up in their saddle blankets to snatch a few hours respite. Engrossed as he was in his thoughts of Julie, Rod failed to notice that Brett and Polly moved some distance away before settling down in each other's arms.

Polly decided to accompany Rod and they set out at first light without breakfast, traveling slowly in order to fan out on both sides of the trail so as not to miss a single clue that might lead them to Julie. Periodically they came upon traces of blood which Rod knew were no more than twenty-four hours old. Whether or not they were human was difficult to tell.

As the day waned, so did Rod's spirits. If Julie was out there somewhere they should have encountered her by now. How far could one woman, weak and burdened by an infant, travel on foot, he agonized? Soon they came upon the small stream where Julie had paused the day before to rest and soothe her tortured foot. They pushed on, hoping to find Julie at the Mission San Antonio de Padua at Jolan. It was just possible some kindly soul had come upon her and offered to take her to that place of sanctuary.

At mid-morning the searchers rested and ate some of the dried meat and handtack they had stashed in their saddlebags in San Francisco against just such an emergency. They were about to remount when abruptly Polly froze, her ears trained toward the hills. "Wait! I hear something!"

From that day until his death, Rod blessed Polly's sharp ears, for it was several minutes before he heard the same soft mewling sounds that came to them on the wings of the soft breezes. At first Rod assumed they came from an animal, but Polly's persistence won out and he listened more carefully.

"It's a baby! Oh, Rod, I'm sure that's a baby I hear crying!" cried Polly, shaking from excitement.

Moving with alacrity they followed the thin wailing sounds to a nearby hillside where two large rocks came together to form a shallow cave. Instantly Rod dropped to his knees and peered inside, his mouth suddenly gone dry at the thought of what he might find.

"What do you see, Rod?" Polly asked tremulously, unable to disguise her anxiety.

Reaching inside, Rod grasped a tiny blanketed form and pulled it gently through the narrow opening. "Is he all right?" Polly asked when she saw the bundle in Rod's arms. "Is . . . is Julie inside?"

"The baby looks fine," Rod answered shakily after he had given his son a cursory inspection. "But Julie appears to be unconscious. I hope I can get her out of there without hurting her." His voice trembled with emotion as he tenderly cradled his tiny son in his muscular arms.

"I'm small enough to squeeze through," Polly said, shoving Rod rudely aside. "Let me help you."

While Rod cuddled his son, Polly slipped into the narrow cave and lifted Julie's shoulders. Rod then grasped her legs and together they eased her through the small aperture. Passing the baby to Polly, Rod examined Julie for injuries and uttered a loud curse when he saw the pitiful condition of her feet which were bloodied and covered with abrasions.

"She must have been in terrible pain," Polly winced, quickly ripping up her petticoat to use as bandages. "No wonder she passed out. I'm amazed she got this far in the condition she is in. Do you have any water in your canteen, Rod?"

"Julie has more courage than any woman I know," Rod acknowledged lovingly, handing Polly his canteen.

Polly used the water to bathe Julie's face and moisten her lips and within a few minutes she appeared to be emerging from her swoon. The moment she stirred, Rod dropped to his knees and gently cradled her in his arms so his would be the first face she saw upon awakening.

"Carlos," were Julie's first words. Rod was quick to assure her their son was well.

"You are safe now, *mi amor*," he crooned softly, "I am here to care for you."

"Rod?" Julie croaked, finally aware of whose arms she rested in. "My father, you must help him."

"We found him, *querida*," Rod said. "Brett is with him. When we reach the next mission, we will send a wagon back for him."

"Brett came with you?"

"*Si*, Polly, too."

Polly stepped forward and smiled at Julie. "Brett and I were worried about you, Julie. We insisted on accompanying Rod."

"I'm sorry, so sorry to cause you all. so much trouble," Julie said contritely.

"Don't think about it now, Julie," Rod admonished gently. "We'll have all the time in the world to talk when we get home. Do you think you can ride if I take you on my horse?"

Julie nodded. With Rod beside her, holding her, she would be capable of anything. Tenderly, Rod lifted Julie, placing her before him on his horse, then thoughtfully placed his blanket around her bare shoulders. Polly took charge of the baby. They were about to proceed when the child's furious cries alerted Julie to the fact that her son hadn't eaten in hours and was probably starved.

"He's hungry, Rod," she smiled apologetically at her worried husband. "I should feed him."

Immediately, Rod's brow cleared and he took Carlos from Polly's arms and gave him to Julie. "You can feed him while we travel," he told her, his voice tender. "It will give me great pleasure to watch. I'm only sorry I wasn't there to offer comfort when he was born."

When Julie put the baby to her breast she could feel Rod's eyes burning into her bare flesh, and she flushed becomingly. Rod thoroughly enjoyed the sight of his son feasting eagerly at Julie's engorged nipple while the tiny hands clenched and unclenched on the white flesh that previously had been his alone to savor. How he longed to caress and explore that tender flesh, but he knew it would be weeks before Julie was fit for his lovemaking. Would she still want him, he wondered? Or had Elena finally succeeded in altering Julie's feelings for him?

They reached San Antonio de Padua at dusk and Julie was put to bed immediately after she was cleaned up, fed, and a healing salve applied to her feet by the concerned *padre* who clacked his tongue at their deplorable condition. A wagon was dispatched

384th to fetch Carl and Julie was finally able to relax knowing her father would soon arrive and be treated for his injuries.

Rod was careful not to disturb Julie when he quietly entered the small room assigned to them. So thankful was he for her safe return that he could not tear his eyes from her sleeping form, staring at her for several long minutes, marveling at her still vibrant beauty after all she had endured. What other woman could display such bravery and fortitude in the face of adversity as had this sensuous woman he had the rare good fortune to marry, he asked himself? The soft curve of her cheek, so youthful, so innocent, caused his heart to contract with love and longing. It seemed like a miracle to have her back again safe and sound and he vowed never to allow her out of his sight.

Reluctantly abandoning Julie to her well-deserved slumber, Rod moved cautiously to the small cradle produced by the *padre*. Pride and love welled up in him as he feasted his eyes upon the smooth, downy cheeks, crisp black head, and tiny bow lips of this small bundle of humanity that had sprung from his loins. Upon reflection he decided that he was happier than he had any right to be. The miracle of his son's birth and survival against overwhelming odds would change his life irrevocably.

The weary travelers spent two days resting and recuperating before continuing on to *Rancho* Delgado. Carl's arm had been set by the *padre* and his head wound treated. Though still tender, Julie's feet had begun to heal and the baby thrived despite all he had been through since his birth. Polly and Brett were persuaded to continue on to the *rancho* for a visit and they all began the journey in great spirits. The day they left Julie was adequately, albeit unfashionably dressed in a peasant outfit and sandals thoughtfully provided by the *padre*. Rod thought she looked adorable and told her so, enjoying the bright flush to her pale cheeks that his flattery had wrought.

"I hope you don't mind my naming the baby after my father," Julie said shyly as she rode comfortably in front of Rod. She could have traveled in the wagon with her father but chose instead to ride within the circle of Rod's arms.

"It's a name he can be proud of," Rod replied sincerely.

"I feel responsible for all that has happened," Julie confided sadly. "Even though I had little liking for Manuel and what he did to me, I am saddened by his death. I feel even greater sorrow for the innocent child he left behind."

"Don't, *querida*, don't blame yourself. Whatever you did was forced upon you by a greedy, vindictive woman. I share that blame though I was also a recipient of Elena's vengeance. Your father is recovering nicely and you must concentrate on only pleasant things from now on. Like me and our child."

Julie wanted to say more, but the words stuck in her throat like dry straw. Perhaps later, she thought, when she felt more confident of his love for her. Was he truly not angry at her for running off and endangering the life of their son? Only time would tell. He could be treating her gently now because he was thrilled with Carlos, Julie reluctantly admitted.

Julie's homecoming was joyous and all she could hope for. Felicia was ecstatic when she saw the baby and from the moment Julie placed him in the child's arms, Felicia became very protective of her small nephew, declaring that no one but herself should care for him.

"May I sleep in his room, Rodrigo?" Felicia begged prettily. "Julie needs her rest and will be unable to care for him properly for some time."

"No, *niña*," Rod smiled indulgently. "You are but a child yourself. Carlos will have a nurse but you may see him as often as you like."

Though somewhat disappointed, Felicia's high spirits could not be quelled as she asked endless questions which Rod did his best to answer. Finally he sent her scurrying off to summon Nola, the young wife of one of the *vaqueros* whom he and Julie had chosen months before to be their baby's nursemaid. She had just recently given birth herself and was quite capable of taking over feedings for Julie, should the need arise.

Ramona fussed endlessly around Carl until he felt smothered by her loving concern. Shortly afterwards, Carl and Ramona went to their own little *casa*, Brett and Polly were shown to their rooms, and Rod and Julie found themselves alone at long last.

Rod would allow no one but himself to bathe Julie and settle her in bed that first night. Against her protests, declaring herself perfectly capable of bathing herself, Rod stripped off her clothes and carried her to the tub of steaming water he had ordered prepared. Julie's feet, though healing nicely, were still too tender to walk on and she had to be carried about like a child; a chore Rod minded not at all.

"You are much too thin, *querida*," Rod admonished with a twinkle. "I prefer my women with a little more meat on their bones."

"Am I still your woman, Rod?" Julie asked tremulously, her blue eyes wide and searching.

Rod was obviously shaken by Julie's question. "There has never been any other woman for me, *querida*," he replied patiently, putting into words that which Julie was longing to hear.

But there was still much left to be said. "Rod, about Elena . . ." Julie began hesitantly, "I—"

"We will talk of it later, Julie, when you are fully recovered. For now, forget Elena, she no longer can harm you. Just concentrate on our son and regaining your strength."

Rod was not satisfied until he carefully and painstakingly washed every inch of Julie's slim form. Then he washed and rinsed her long honey-blond tresses until they were clean and shiny. By that time he was becoming so aroused that he knew he must get Julie out of the tub and into bed or he would be tempted to make love to her even though it was far too soon after childbirth.

Julie could feel his arousal straining and throbbing against her as Rod lifted her from the tub and carried her to the bed where he thoroughly dried her with a large, soft towel. Then he slipped a nightgown over her head, tucked her beneath the covers, and settled down beside her.

"Are you comfortable, *querida*?" he asked solicitously.

"I'm fine, Rod, really. You don't have to fuss over me like this."

"Let me be the judge of that. You are to stay in bed until your feet are completely healed," he ordered sternly. "Nola will look after Carlos and Felicia can help. Polly and Brett will amuse you while you are confined to bed. Will you obey me in this, Julie?" Though his face was uncompromising, a smile lurked at the corners of his mouth when he thought of all the times she had deliberately flaunted her strong will and independence.

"Yes, Rod," Julie answered meekly. "I've had enough of roaming about, for the time being."

Chuckling, Rod slanted Julie an assessing look. Did he detect a double meaning in her words. "It's a good thing," he teased, "or I'd be forced to tie you to the bed." Lightly he fingered a loose tendril of hair lying carelessly against her cheek before touching her trembling lips with a calloused finger.

Julie reacted violently to the soft brushing of his fingers against her flesh as a pulsing knot within her began to grow. Something flickered in Julie's eyes that made Rod plant a tantalizing kiss in the hollow of her neck. But soon that was not enough as his mouth swooped down to capture hers, his tongue gently parting her lips, tasting, exploring, drawing from it a measure of her unique taste.

His voice was a husky purr. "Julie, Julie, I want you so desperately, but I know it's too soon. I must leave, *mi amor*, or I won't be responsible for my actions. I mean to protect you always, even from myself." Then he was gone, leaving Julie aching with need to be possessed by the only man she could ever love.

Julie recuperated swiftly, her youthful stamina returning her to full health within a fortnight. Rod quickly slipped back into the role of *patron* as he once again took up the reins at *Rancho* Delgado. The cattle drive was about to begin but this year he would remain behind. His spare time was taken up with entertaining his guests and lavishing special attention on his wife and son. He was greatly heartened by Julie's rapid recovery and happily planned a huge *fiesta* to celebrate the christening of little Carlos. Brett and Polly agreed with alacrity to act as godparents to the boy and were already spoiling him dreadfully. The date was set a week hence, after which Brett and Polly would return to San Francisco to take up their duties at the Pleasure Palace.

The first day Julie walked to dinner on her own two feet was a joyous occasion. Rod could scarcely keep his gaze from straying to her trim form enhanced by childbirth and her luminous face shining with happiness and health. She had dressed carefully for the event and knew she looked her best. Under Teresa's tender care she had regained her lost weight and glowed with vibrant vitality. She had chosen to wear a bright blue gown of heavy silk fashioned with huge puffed sleeves and wide, scooped neckline that dipped low to expose the tops of rounded breasts. The skirt was pulled back over slim

hips and caught in a bustle. Adrenalin surged through
Rod's aching loins at the sight of her.

The meal progressed pleasantly, the talk spirited,
when Polly casually remarked, "Brett has asked me to
marry him." The look she lavished on Brett was starry-
eyed and filled with love, leaving little doubt as to what
her answer had been. The look, Julie gleefully noticed,
was reciprocated. She couldn't have been more pleased.

"Oh, Polly!" she enthused happily. "This is just
what I hoped for all along! It's about time Brett found a
good woman to spend his life with."

After much congratulations, Rod made a suggestion
that seemed to please everyone. "Why not make it a
double celebration? *Padre* Juan might just as well marry
you when he comes to christen Carlos. I know it would
make Julie happy to attend the wedding of her two good
friends."

After a brief consultation the couple agreed. Later,
when Polly and Julie were alone, Polly said shyly, "I
love him so much, Julie. I know I can never take your
place in his heart but I'll be a good wife to him."

"Polly," Julie chided gently. "Brett may have loved
me at one time but the moment you came into his life all
that changed. Any fool can see he is besotted with you.
My future is with Rod and always has been."

"How . . . how are things between you and Rod?"

Julie hesitated. "I'm not sure. We have not spoken
about Elena yet. Or my reason for leaving the *rancho*
like I did. But he treats me very well, almost too well,"
she mused thoughtfully. "He has not attempted to
make love to me since our return although I'm certain
he wants to."

"You know how concerned he is over your health,
Julie," Polly offered. "I'm sure he is waiting for the
right moment. If you could have seen him when he was
searching for you, you would not doubt his love."

"I'd feel better about it if he told me," Julie retorted,

openly skeptical. "I'm not a mindreader."

"Neither is Rod, Julie," Polly reminded her. "Have you told him how much you care for him?" Julie flushed, realizing she had been as close-mouthed as Rod on the subject.

After her conversation with Polly, Julie decided the time was ripe for meaningful communication between her and Rod. Instinctively, she knew the first overtures must come from her. With that thought in mind, Julie took extra pains preparing for bed that night. The nightgown she slipped over her head fell like cobwebs over her body, revealing the full splendor of upthrust breasts and curving hips. The dark blond thatch between her thighs became a tantalizing shadow beneath a veil of gauze. Her long amber locks fell in silken strands about her tiny waist, the result of an hour of vigorous brushing, and Julie glanced in the mirror, satisfied that she looked her best. Being completely devoid of any kind of vanity, she could not know just what a tantalizing picture she made or how dramatically her appearance would affect Rod. Drawing in a deep, steadying breath, Julie gathered her courage and silently entered Rod's darkened room through the connecting door.

Rod was not sleeping. The painful ache in his loins and his desire for his lovely wife was keeping him awake. With longing he glanced toward the connecting door and blinked rapidly, certain his burning desire for Julie had conjured up her delightful image to goad and torment him. The moon was full and bright as errant moonbeams drifted in the open window to paint her in hues of shimmering silver, her pale gold body clearly visible beneath the gossamer material of her nightgown, causing Rod to groan as a surge of heat swelled his loins. He moaned in frustration as the ghostly figure of his love poised provocatively in the doorway.

"*Por Dios*, Julie, if you are real don't torment me

like this!'' he cried aloud, his anguish causing his voice to crack dangerously. "But if you are a figment of my imagination, I hope never to awaken from this dream.''

With tantalizing slowness Julie undulated into the room, the movement of her shapely hips driving Rod mad with desire. "I'm real, Rod,'' she murmured when she reached his side. "Feel me, I am flesh and blood.''

Rod needed no further urging as his hands sought the soft mounds of her breasts, molding them to fit his palms, rubbing her nipples gently with the heel of his thumbs as they surged into erectness at his first touch. Julie felt herself tauten with excitement as a warm pleasurable lassitude pervaded her flesh. It had been so long since she had felt Rod's hands on her body that her knees threatened to give way beneath her. She flushed with pleasure as she felt Rod's dark eyes rake her from head to toe. As his ardent gaze rippled over her it was as if tongues of flame seared the thin material from her body and left her bare in the wake of their wildfire.

"Come to me, *querida*,'' Rod urged, his face alive with anticipation. "If I don't make love to you this very minute, I will surely die.'' Effortlessly he lifted her into bed and deftly stripped the filmy gown from her body.

"We must talk first, Rod,'' Julie forced herself to say, the inflection in her voice telling him the last thing in the world she wanted was to talk.

"And we will, *mi amor*,'' Rod moaned with barely suppressed desire. "Later. Much later.''

Julie gasped when he drew the tender flesh of her nipple between his teeth to nibble maddeningly until she felt the pressure filling her loins and becoming unbearable. For long minutes the only sound in the room was the muffled breathing of two bodies passionately engaged, punctuated by deep groans of pleasure.

Rod's lips slid upward to capture her mouth and Julie felt the soft warmth of his tongue invade the honeyed caverns within, the moist tip sliding leisurely along the contours of her lips. Soft kisses fell like rain against the corners of her mouth, along her smooth jawline before pausing at the tender spot where throat joined shoulder.

"*Mi amor*, my life would be worthless without you beside me," he whispered, much to Julie's delight. "I love you."

When the words Julie longed to hear fell effortlessly from Rod's lips, all her doubts disappeared like ashes in the wind, serving to unleash all her pent up ardor. Rod groaned with pleasure as her hands freely roamed the hard ridges of his shoulders and back, molding his firm buttocks, finally sliding along his flanks to grasp his engorged manhood. Experimentally, she glided her hand back and forth until Rod moaned and stayed her hand.

"The night is young, *querida*. If you keep that up it will come to an abrupt conclusion. I have been too many months without you for patience." Julie giggled but obediently removed her hand from his member. "Lie back," Rod said, "and let me love you."

Julie swallowed convulsively as Rod's eager lips scalded a path downward along her body, teasing first one nipple with his teeth and then the other, molding the mounds against his palms until the coral buds grew rigid against his tongue. He suckled gently for several minutes until her milk began to flow copiously, then slid downward, murmuring hoarsely, "Food for the Gods. I hope my son realizes how lucky he is."

Julie tensed as his tongue flicked across her ribs, pausing briefly at her navel, running his tongue maddeningly around the rim in a circular motion while his hands slid between her legs and his fingers slipped inside her moistness. Julie arched her back against the intoxication of his sensual massage and when he tightened his hands around her waist to hold her close as he began to nuzzle the blond triangle of curls that beckoned him with promise of delights, she cried aloud. He growled in satisfaction as he felt the exquisite pleasure he gave her shudder through her slender body and he wanted only to give more. When his lips and tongue possessed the tender bud nestled in the golden forest she begged for him to desist, certain she would die if he did not, already contemplating death if he did.

But Julie had nothing to fear. Rod did not desist, increasing his gentle torment until she grew rigid, the tension building as his tongue darted fire against the very source of the bittersweet longing flooding through her. Then the splendid violence of his mouth drove her over the brink of reality into a maelstrom of bursting stars and erupting planets.

Uttering a cry that seemed barely human, Rod surged upward, plunging again and again into her throbbing warmth, taking her fiercely, ardently, driving between her thighs with ever deeper strokes. A burst of sensation came with penetration and Julie felt herself responding to his ardor despite the intense pleasure she had experienced only moments before. Too long denied, wanting, craving, Rod thrust and thrust, grinding his body into hers, his breath rasping in his chest, his blood pounding against his temples. Once again Julie found herself crying out for release as waves of ecstasy throbbed through her. And then he freed her in a bursting of sensations that raced like lightning between them as Rod's climax eclipsed her own violent response.

Julie felt Rod soften and slip from her body and she sighed in pleasant exhaustion. "Did I make you happy, *mi amor*?" he asked lazily.

"Extremely," blushed Julie, aware of the peace and contentment flowing between them. "Will it always be this way, Rod?"

"Always," Rod pledged solemnly, kissing the tip of her nose playfully. "But only if you don't tax me too greatly with your demands."

She answered his teasing smile with a smile of her own. "My demands!" she taunted with mock indignity. "Would you rather I lay back like some meek miss while you take your pleasure and deny me mine?"

"I want you just as you are, *mi bruja*. Long ago your saucy manner bewitched me and I'm afraid I've come to enjoy your spirit and wild nature, especially in bed."

Suddenly Julie grew serious. "Did you mean it? What you said, I mean, about loving me."

"You need never doubt me again, *querida*. I love you passionately, with my whole heart and soul. You made me the happiest man alive when you gave me my son. But even if you had not given me Carlos I would still love you, despite your willful ways."

"I have always loved you, Rod. Even . . . even when I had reason to hate you. Even when you bedded Elena and she told me you wanted me out of your life."

"I will never cause you grief again, Julie," Rod vowed, tightening his grip on her slim shoulders. "Do you believe me?"

"Yes, Rod. I believe you. Can you forgive me for leaving without giving you a chance to explain? I never meant to place your son in danger."

"There is nothing to forgive, *mi amor*. I know how persuasive Elena can be when she wants something. Manuel told me everything. I'll admit I was hurt to think you did not trust me enough to tell me what was troubling you. But afterwards, I was too worried to think of anything but your safe return."

"Rod, I—"

"No," Rod murmured, planting a finger on her lips. "Let me continue. Too late I realized that I had become so caught up in the roundup that it must have appeared to you as if I was deliberately neglecting you. But just the opposite was true. I wanted you so desperately I could not trust myself with you. Teresa warned me that to continue marital relations with you so far advanced in pregnancy would endanger our child. Under the circumstances, aware of my intense desire for you no matter what, I thought it best to safeguard your health by placing myself out of temptation's way. I removed myself from your bed deliberately, and worked long hours until I fell asleep at night exhausted. I realize now my judgment was faulty, leaving you hurt and vulnerable to Elena's false tales. I should have told you the truth and not taken it for granted that you understood."

"If you thought to explain, I would have given birth to Carlos safely in my own bed," Julie reflected wistfully. "Never again will I allow Elena or anyone else to drive a wedge between us. And you, husband, had better never look at another woman again," she warned saucily.

"How could I with an enchantress like you fulfilling my wildest fantasies? I called you *bruja* once and witch you are for you've held me enthralled since first we met, even though I knew it was folly to want you so." Then his lips created a song of love against hers as he whispered, "My need for you is so great I want you again. Come to me, *querida*."

Much later, after they had loved again and were temporarily sated, Rod broached a subject that Julie could tell he had given much thought. "I spoke with *Padre* Juan today. He told me he could no longer keep the small son of Elena and Manuel. He asked me to find a home for him."

"And did you?" Julie asked quietly.

"Julie, I feel a certain responsibility for the boy. Elena's family and mine have been friends for a long time. Montoya blood flows through the boy's veins. But I do not do this for Elena. Manuel sought to undo the wrong done to you and died attempting to bring you to safety. For honor's sake, I am obligated to find a proper home for the child."

Julie remained thoughtful for a long time and finally came to the conclusion that the sins of the mother could not be held against an innocent child.

"I have spoken to Teresa and she agreed to take the boy," Rod continued. "But first I wanted to make certain you wouldn't be upset by his presence here on the *rancho*."

"No, Rod," Julie said firmly, her words stunning him. "I don't want Teresa raising the boy."

"Julie!" Rod exclaimed, "I know Elena meant you nothing but harm but the babe is innocent of any wrong doing."

"You misunderstand, Rod," Julie contradicted softly, entwining her arms about his neck. "I want to raise him myself. I will treat him as I would my own son. We can adopt him if you like. I am a Delgado and your honor is mine."

"I love you, *mi amor*," Rod whispered, her generous offer swelling his heart to bursting.

She turned in his arms as his soft breath fanned her cheeks and his lips sealed their love forever.

EPILOGUE

Baby Carlos behaved like an angel during the christening but raised such a ruckus during the marriage of his Godparents that Nola was forced to remove him from the room so that *Padre* Juan could perform the wedding without further interruption.

Ramona and Carl moved temporarily to the *hacienda* so that Brett and Polly could spend a week alone in their small *casa* before returning to San Francisco.

Following the ceremony, *Padre* Juan imparted a piece of disturbing news to Rod. It seemed that Elena had been captured by Pico, a fierce bandit and Mexican hero. He preyed mostly on Anglos traveling El Camino Real. Though his hideout was never found, it was assumed he found refuge in the hills surrounding San Luis Obispo. It was a simple matter to identify his victims for he always left his grisly mark. He hacked off their ears.

As rumor had it, and Rod found no reason to doubt them, Pico was so entranced by Elena that he kept her with him. Several days ago, *banditos* led by Pico and an aide, Manuel Vergara, rode into San Luis Obispo to pawn valuables taken from a party of *gringos*. Elena was with them, whether by choice or not was not clear. They were surprised by a posse and Pico, using Elena and his men as decoys, somehow managed to escape. Before *Padre* Juan could be summoned, the posse, in a fit of anger over losing Pico, forthwith hung Elena, Manuel Vergara, and the half-dozen or so men in the party.

Rod was shocked. Though Elena had done much to deserve his hatred he would not wish her such a violent death. But Elena was the past. Nothing or no one mattered now but Julie, their family, and his honor.

"Each new Connie Mason book is a prize!"
—Heather Graham, bestselling author of
A Magical Christmas

Love Me With Fury. When her stagecoach is ambushed on the Texas frontier, Ariel Leland fears for her life. But even more frightening is Jess Wilder, a virile bounty hunter who has devoted his life to finding the hellcat responsible for his brother's murder—and now he has her. But Ariel's proud spirit and naive beauty erupt a firestorm of need in him— transforming his lust for vengeance into a love that must be fulfilled at any cost.
___52215-2 $5.50 US/$6.50 CAN

Pure Temptation. Fresh off the boat from Ireland, Moira O'Toole isn't fool enough to believe in legends or naive enough to trust a rake. Yet after an accident lands her in Graystoke Manor, she finds herself haunted, harried, and hopelessly charmed by Black Jack Graystoke and his exquisite promise of pure temptation.
___4041-7 $5.99 US/$6.99 CAN